MURDER YOUR DARLINGS

ALSO BY JENNA BLUM

Woodrow on the Bench: Life Lessons from a Wise Old Dog

The Lost Family

Those Who Save Us

The Stormchasers

Grand Central: Original Stories of Postwar Love and Reunion

MURDER YOUR DARLINGS

A NOVEL

JENNA BLUM

HARPER

An Imprint of HarperCollins*Publishers*

Without limiting the exclusive rights of any author, contributor or the publisher of this publication, any unauthorized use of this publication to train generative artificial intelligence (AI) technologies is expressly prohibited. HarperCollins also exercise their rights under Article 4(3) of the Digital Single Market Directive 2019/790 and expressly reserve this publication from the text and data mining exception.

MURDER YOUR DARLINGS. Copyright © 2026 by Jenna Blum. All rights reserved. No part of this book may be used or reproduced in any manner whatsoever without written permission except in the case of brief quotations embodied in critical articles and reviews. For information, address HarperCollins Publishers, 195 Broadway, New York, NY 10007. In Europe, HarperCollins Publishers, Macken House, 39/40 Mayor Street Upper, Dublin 1, D01 C9W8, Ireland.

HarperCollins books may be purchased for educational, business, or sales promotional use. For information, please email the Special Markets Department at SPsales@harpercollins.com.

hc.com

FIRST EDITION

Library of Congress Cataloging-in-Publication Data
Names: Blum, Jenna author
Title: Murder your darlings : a novel / Jenna Blum.
Description: First edition. | New York, NY : Harper, 2026.
Identifiers: LCCN 2025025996 | ISBN 9780063448087 hardcover | ISBN 9780063448100 trade paperback | ISBN 9780063448117 ebook
Subjects: LCGFT: Thrillers (Fiction) | Romance fiction | Novels | Fiction
Classification: LCC PS3602.L863 M87 2026
LC record available at https://lccn.loc.gov/2025025996

25 26 27 28 29 LBC 5 4 3 2 1

FOR MY SUPERAGENT, STÉPHANIE ABOU, WHO HAS MADE THIS WRITER'S LIFE POSSIBLE. YOU'RE THE BEST, MADAME.

Whenever you feel an impulse to perpetuate a piece of exceptionally fine writing, obey it—whole-heartedly—and delete it before sending your manuscript to press. *Murder your darlings.*

—Sir Arthur Quiller-Couch, "On Style," 1914

The process of ruthlessly editing by removing parts that are beloved but don't serve the story . . . requires stoicism and the suppression of a natural affection.

—*Harper's* magazine

The Rabbit

The problem with his house is, it's in a very remote area, so it's hard to get to. Especially now, in winter. I don't do very well on snowshoes, and I never learned to cross-country ski. It's challenging enough to keep on top of the weather and to make sure my tracks are covered. I could go when he's not home—but what would be the point of that?

The house is on an island in rural Maine, the only one there. He built it after his first monster bestseller, *You Never Said Goodbye* (which is really his second book, but the first to hit the list)—craving more solitude to write, according to the *New York Magazine* profile "The Virtuoso Retreats." The real reason is, one day he stepped out of the shower in his Martha's Vineyard mansion to find a reader standing on his bath mat with a pen and a suitcase full of his books. He's been off the grid ever since.

William's island is accessible only by causeway, blocked at the end by a gate twelve feet tall with iron spikes like the kind you'd put a head on, although the only things that've ever been impaled there are gifts really dedicated superfans leave if they somehow figure out where he is. Over the years I've seen stuffed animals (why? There are none in his books), letters with porny selfies, bras and thongs that flap in the wind like forlorn flags. The gate is basically a bulletin board of unrequited William Corwyn love. He takes everything down and tosses it, and nobody ever gets in. Except me.

The house is an A-frame, like a ski chalet, with 360-degree views of the lake. It has a hot tub and a two-story fieldstone fireplace and skylights and specially built bookshelves, all full. Of course they are. It's a beautiful house. Of course it is. He has good taste, and he has to spend all those royalties on something. Plus foreign rights—*William Corwyn is published in 47 countries!*, his website proclaims—and the film money for *Medusa*. A thread on his Goodreads page says there's also an option on his second bestseller, *The Space Between Worlds*. That movie—or series; it would have been a TV miniseries back then—never came out, though, so maybe that was just a rumor. Or maybe it just never got made. I don't know how these things work, I'm not a Hollywood type of person, but the authors I follow online complain a lot about how most options never materialize, they're only fantasies. Brainf*cks.

It seems like an awful lot of griping about getting money for nothing, like being mad about a Christmas bonus you didn't expect but still is not big enough. But what do I know. I'm just a bookseller. Author-adjacent. And probably it is disappointing to have your hopes raised and have nothing come of it.

I do know a lot about that.

Another thing I know: I know there's more than a brainf*ck going on in that house right now. Because I can hear it. I can hear her. You'd have to be dead not to hear her. I hear him, too, if I listen closely. It's harder, because mostly he just talks. He talks while he's stripping their clothes off, while he's stroking and pinching them, while he's teasing them, while he's pounding them as hard as he can. And because his talking is much lower-volume than the girls' moaning, yelling, screaming, and hollering, I have to get right up next to the house to hear it.

Like I am now. Hunkered down between his hedge and the wall beneath the bedroom window, the branches scratching one side of my face, the glass cold against the other. The ground is freezing too. My feet are numb even in my good lined boots. There's more snow forecast for tonight, and they will nap when they're done, giving me time to either sneak inside to my observation post or steal away. During the day William is a big napper, conking out, whether he's alone or with someone else, and he falls asleep within three breaths. I've never seen anything like it. One second he's awake, the next he's snoring—which he does like a cartoon character, with a whistling sound like he's blowing a feather that rises and falls with the air from his lips. It's the cutest thing I've ever seen, to tell the truth, unexpected in such a big man. Adorable, actually. It might have been the first thing I fell in love with.

Right now they are not sleeping. Nowhere close to it. "You're an angel, honey," I hear him say, his voice even deeper than usual with concentration. "Do you know how beautiful you are right now? You're incandescent."

"Oh! Oh! Oh!" the woman says, which is probably all she's capable of saying at this moment. Like most of his women, she's shouting it loud enough that when he started banging into her, she drove all the birds from the trees.

"Luminous," he says. "Radiant. And so close. I can feel it. Do you want me to finish you off?"

"Oh!" the woman says. "Oh! Oh! Oh! Yes!" She is practically sobbing. I know what's coming next.

His patented move: the f*cking narrative. Literally. For William Corwyn, the climax of the story isn't just for fiction

"Buckle up," he says, and now his own voice is a little more breathy, probably because he is thrusting deeper. I remember what this feels like, how he said to me, smiling and swiveling his hips, *I knew how avid you'd be. I could tell just looking at you.*

"You're going to come for me," he says, practically growling. "It's right there. You feel it building. It's inevitable. It's exquisite. You're trembling on the edge . . ."

I don't know how, whether it's the timbre of his voice or the power of storytelling, but the f*cking narrative always works. It did on me, in ways I can still feel in my body sometimes. Before he reaches the end of his monologue, they come. This one does it more than once, by the sound of it. Between *You're doing it, do it for me* and *You're coming now!*, she makes a coyote wail and then a *yip yip yip* noise that startles the crows, who have resettled into the branches and start cawing in rusty cacophony. A whole murder of them.

Then it's over, and I can't hear what they're saying, only murmurs. Next will come nap time. It'll be dark soon, and I have a choice to make about whether to drive home or slip inside. Through the basement window he's forgotten about, which leads to a root cellar William has never used, not being a store-onions kind of guy, and that I can ease open and just, if I hold my breath like a motherf*cker, squeeze through.

This is how I know what the women look like, what their faces look like when they climax, screwed up as if in pain, the expression he tells them he finds so beautiful. I know what their breasts and buttocks look like, jiggling as he thrusts. I know what his haunches look like, clenching and flexing, and the muscles in his back. I know what books he has on the bedside table in which he also keeps the gun, and what paths the sun and moonlight make from his bedroom skylight over his south wall, which is bare except for that one oil painting of himself and his sister, Pen, as kids. I know that he has been with this woman, his latest, before, but this is her first time here.

I know all this because he has a big walk-in closet, bigger than my whole sh*thole studio, and from behind the bag that contains his tuxedo, because of course he owns his own tuxedo, I have watched many a non-brainf*ck-fest commence.

I have made some noise or shifted my feet in the crunching dead leaves to bring the blood back into them, because I hear the woman say, "What was that?" She must be standing by the window because her voice is much closer now.

"I thought I heard something outside," she says.

"Probably a deer," he says, coming to stand beside or behind her. I know he is naked, looking out. A fine figure of a man, is how the nineteenth-century novelists would describe him, and they would not be wrong. Tall, dark, and handsome as a cliché, with those show-off silver streaks at his temples I suspect he dyes, though I've never caught him doing it or even found the coloring kit. Lumberjack-thick, more than he used to be since he shredded his meniscus on something called a double black diamond trail, according to his Reddit readers on r/WilliamCorwynAthlete. He's not an

Ironman anymore, much to his displeasure, and if he's not careful, he gets chunky fast.

But he is always careful. And he's not even losing his hair. Yet. Much.

"You probably scared away all the animals," he adds. "With your climactic aria."

She laughs. "Which you made me make. You're the best I've ever had."

They all say this. I roll my eyes.

"Seriously. You're like . . . a magnificent stag or something."

And this woman calls herself a writer? I pantomime barfing into the bushes.

"How are you feeling?" she asks.

There's a pause, then he says, "You're dear to ask, but I'm fine."

"Your heart, though. You're a little—red. Do you need to take something?"

I smile. Some men don't mind women fussing over their vulnerabilities. William Corwyn is not one of them. Sure enough, though his tone is mild, I can hear the irritation when he says, "Dear, don't manage me, please."

"Sure, sorry," she says, swiftly backtracking. "I didn't mean to overstep. Bad old habit."

"A spanking for every backslide," he says, playful again. "Or backside." There's a light slap, then: "Feel how fine I am."

"Jesus. You could hang a dozen coats on that thing. Heavy winter ones."

"That's what you do to me," he says, his voice gruff.

"But in front of the window?"

"There's nobody here for miles. I could f*ck you on the lawn and only the eagles would see. In case you haven't noticed, I live in the equivalent of a castle with a moat."

"Let's maybe save lawn-f*cking for summer," she suggests, and I hear the tentative hope in her voice. Testing their potential future.

"That and my lake dock," he says. "Meanwhile . . . put your hands on the sill."

As they start up again—this woman *is* different, no nap for him today—I contemplate slipping into the basement and up the stairs. Past his study, the hallowed space so many of his fans would give their left tit to see, as one said on Instagram. They'd be disappointed if they were expecting a squirrel's cave of creativity, a mess of papers and books and pens, evidence of genius in progress. Because it's just a bare empty room with a lamp and a desk. And one very password-protected laptop.

But I decide I've heard enough for one day. I'm cold, and I'm sad, and I have to figure out what to do about this one. This woman. What I did with the others obviously wasn't enough.

Her cries follow me back through the trees of his property, out past the gate and rocks onto the causeway, which I'll follow down to the logging road where I hide my car. They sound like someone in pain.

PART I:

SAM (and the Rabbit)

CHAPTER 1

IF THEY ONLY KNEW

S am Vetiver was lost.

Not metaphorically. Literally. Well, perhaps a little bit of both. But for now, it was actually having lost her way that counted. She was on the final event of her fourth book tour, and if the GPS of her rental car didn't come back online, Sam would be late. She had a recurring nightmare about this very thing, showing up forty minutes after the start time, so two-thirds of her audience had left and the remaining one-third were disgruntled, then opening the reading copy of her novel to find her familiar prose had been replaced with woodcuts.

She hunched over the steering wheel like a jockey urging on a horse, as if by doing so she could coax the little blue arrow back onto the road from the body of water into which it had floated. The actual lake, invisible from the road, was unfamiliar to Sam, as was everything in this wealthy exurb of a midsize midwestern city she had never visited before. "Return to the route!" the stern Australian lady who lived in the car's dashboard scolded.

"I'm trying!" Sam said.

Mercifully the GPS decided to reactivate. Sam gave thanks and cranked up the AC so perspiration wouldn't destroy her makeup. With her first novel, she had visited three book clubs a day in person, back in the dark times when she had to rely on printed-out instructions from the hostess: *Look for the driveway with the balloons! If you see a barn next to a pond, you've gone too far!* She'd thought everything would get easier with technology, and it had, but there were just so many ways to lose your path.

Sam drove as fast as she dared along a winding road bordered by very high rhododendrons, like something in a fairy tale, from which anything might pop—a centaur or a child—and shot out into an area of palatial stone homes set far back on velvet lawns. She wondered, as she did everywhere: What would it be like to live here? What did people *do*? No doubt there were patios behind those houses, on which families would gather after days of . . . golf? Tennis? Did anyone still play croquet? There would be grilling, maybe barbecue. If she lived here, Sam could be sitting with her feet in her husband's lap, drinking a gin and tonic, watching the kids cannonball in the pool, and smelling the fresh-cut grass the landscapers had tended that morning.

She felt the usual wistfulness and reminded herself, that wasn't the life she had chosen. And there were specific reasons why. And maybe it didn't exist at all, maybe Sam was telling herself a story: The husbands or wives here were having affairs or traveling on business, the kids avoiding their parents or on drugs or glued to their phones. Who knew what people did behind their castle doors, really?

A few more miles, and Sam entered a Rockwellian hamlet whose town green surrounded a limestone mansion like something in a Shirley Jackson story. That had to be—Sam checked the address—yes! The library. She turned into the drive. There it was, the marquee sign saying AUTHOR READING HERE TONIGHT! NEW YORK TIMES BESTSELLER SAM VETIVER READS THE SODBUSTER'S WIFE 7 PM. They had ringed it with the big light bulbs usually seen on hipster restaurant patios, a nice touch. Sam would post a photo of it later on social.

She checked her lipstick in the rearview—one of her top ten tour hacks was never apply a red lip in haste, lest you end up with that unfortunate cannibal look, but sometimes you had no choice—and grabbed her bag with her reading copy, book cover postcards, and pens.

"Showtime," she said, as she always did, for good luck.

She got out of the car, hitching up the bodice of her strapless red jumpsuit. All of Sam's tour outfits were red, to match her book jackets, on which heroines of whatever century Sam was writing about gazed soulfully across historical vistas with their backs to the reader, garbed in era-accurate crimson costumes. Sam's red clothes were branding—she loved it when she showed up at an event and a reader commented, *Wow, your dress matches your cover!*, and Sam said, *Oh, does it?*, and winked. This jumpsuit was a pain because Sam had to undress completely every time she used the ladies' room. But it was the last clean outfit Sam had, the rest stuffed into the laundry section of her suitcase. The end of tour. Almost.

Sam headed up the library walk, pausing to snap a selfie blowing a kiss to the promotional sign. Most authors said they hated tour. Sam was not among them. She often thought she wrote books *to* go on tour. She loved everything about it: the airport breakfasts consisting of hummus; the room service cheeseburgers she wolfed down after events. She loved the thing every other human was phobic about: public speaking. She loved being hustled through country club and community center kitchens like some sort of superstar—when else did *writers* ever get to do this? She even loved flying, marveling that she was traveling because people cared what she had to say about, amazingly, her own books.

Most of all, Sam loved the readers. The readers, the readers, the readers. The people who gave up hours of their lives they could have used to indulge in many other pleasant activities, like shopping or sex or watching TV, to read Sam's novels and then, curiouser and curiouser, come hear her talk about them. Sam spent much of her life in a room by herself, inventing characters and trying to squeeze their stories out of her head; when it turned out, years later, that her words had made a sort of magic bridge, allowing Sam to slide down into strangers' minds and making them all friends—that was an actual miracle.

Most authors also said they resented tour because it took them away from their real job, writing. Sam was not one of them, either. Once upon a time, she had loved it. When she was a kid and writing had all the mystery and magic of getting up early, when nobody else was awake and the world belonged to you alone, a time when anything could happen. When she was in college and grad school, burning with ambition so fierce it felt like, as Orwell said, an illness. When she was writing her first book, before commerce and sales entered the picture. When she'd been living with her ex-husband, Hank, so she knew when the day's work was done she could open her study door and there'd be somebody to have dinner with.

She did not love it now. She feared it. Most specifically, Sam feared her fifth book, *The Gold Digger's Mistress*, for which she was under contract and which was due in five months and of which she had yet to write a single sentence. For which she felt not only apathy but antipathy. She quailed at going home and facing the demonically blinking cursor, the empty screen. She dreaded the deep plunge of being, except for imaginary people, completely and cataclysmically alone. As she hustled up the library walk, she had the strangest, most aberrant thought:

I would give this all up if I had someone to share my life with.

Sam shook her head as if bothered by a horsefly. What the actual? She had been writing since she was four years old. It was all she'd ever done. It was all she'd ever wanted. It was who she was and who she wanted to be.

She saw the librarian waiting for her in the vestibule and waved.

"You found us!" said the librarian, whose name Sam could not remember—she was terrible with names, assigning people the ones she thought they should have as characters instead of using the ones they actually had. Pamela? Erica?

"Here I am," Sam agreed. "It was touch and go there—my GPS went offline."

"I should have warned you about that," said the librarian, whose name, it came to Sam now, was Monica. "But you made it. Do you need the ladies' room?"

"Perpetually," said Sam. "This is a beautiful library."

"Thanks," said Monica. "We're proud of it. It used to be a Rockefeller mansion, you know . . . Here you go. I'll wait here."

In the bathroom, which had Band-Aid-colored stalls and a vase of plastic flowers Sam found inordinately touching, she struggled out of her jumpsuit, used the facilities, and checked her reflection in the mirror. Her lipstick had not migrated to her teeth, and her strawberry-blond French braid was intact, but she looked tired. Another facet of life on the road. Once Sam had hit forty, flight dehydration and hotel beds created dark circles no concealer could erase. She crossed her eyes at herself and emerged.

"Ready!" she said.

"How's your tour been?" Monica asked, hustling Sam back through the library, past a fireplace, a grandfather clock, and oil paintings of, incongruously, ships.

"Great," said Sam. "I love meeting readers."

"That's refreshing," said Monica. "And we're glad to have you. We've had trouble finding authors this year—not that I'm surprised."

"What do you mean?" said Sam.

"Oh, *you* know," said Monica. "Shifts in the industry. Fewer publishers, fewer books, slashed budgets . . . it all means fewer authors on tour. It's a terrible time to be a writer. I'm surprised anyone keeps at it. Grateful, too, of course," she added hastily.

Sam smiled. She'd heard this all her life. When she was in college, waiting tables to put herself through: *Are you crazy? Choose an actual career.* When she was in grad school: *Get a job to fall back on.* When she'd graduated: *Nobody wants debut fiction; you can't get an agent, an editor, a publisher.* It was all impossible, and somehow, she had managed it.

"It's always a terrible time to be a writer," she said mildly.

"I suppose that's true," said Monica. She stopped in front of an oak door that was studded like the entrance to a dungeon and threw it open. "Ladies and gentlemen, our author!"

Heads turned as Sam followed Monica down the aisle to the podium; she did the Queen's wave, and they laughed. Not as many people as Sam had anticipated when she'd set up this event: The library had promised two hundred, and there was half that, if even. Still, despite some empty chairs, this was a decent turnout for a summer evening, and there was no place Sam would rather be.

"Where are you from, honey?" said a woman in the front row—the whole audience was female, per usual, except one husband who had obviously been dragged there and sat patiently with his arms folded.

"I flew in from Boston," said Sam, and some of the women clucked their tongues as if she'd said *I came from prison*.

"You're so young to be an author," said another woman.

"Thank you, I love you," said Sam, and they laughed. Even the husband smirked.

Monica checked the clock. "Let's go ahead and get started. Hi, everyone, thanks for joining us for our Summer Author Series. Our special guest tonight is Sam Vetiver . . ."

Sam stood with her head lowered modestly as Monica read her bio, although she could feel the readers observing her curiously, trying to sync Sam's career accomplishments with Sam herself. Bestselling author of four novels, one selected for a TV book club by a popular host. National Book Award finalist. Teacher. Speaker. It was always strange for Sam to hear herself introduced; although she was proud of and grateful for everything she'd spent her life hustling to do, there was such a gap between the accolades and what she actually did. What would these nice people with their curious smiles think if they knew what Sam's life was usually like? At the thought of where she'd be this time tomorrow—home in her empty study—Sam felt fear wash over her again.

I'd give all this up if I had someone to share my life with.

Totally untrue. Wasn't it?

And what would these lovely readers with their inquisitive, anticipatory faces think if they only knew about some of the situations Sam had left to hop onto a stage, sometimes only hours before? For a second Sam saw her fist knocking on a plywood door, *Are you in there?*, turning the knob, surprised it was unlocked, the beige carpet. The dark Rorschach on it. How it was soaked in blood. How Sam hadn't known until then how overpowering blood could smell.

"And now, all the way from Boston," Monica was saying, "please help me welcome Sam Vetiver!" and Sam stepped up to the mic.

CHAPTER 2:

A WASTE OF A BED

After the event Sam drove back to her hotel and ordered a room service cheeseburger, then stripped off the red jumpsuit and sat on the bed in her Spanx. It was such a nice big bed, a California King with crisp sheets smelling of bleach and all those extra pillows, and it was such a waste. Sam thought this whenever she stepped into a hotel room with her rollaway. Back in the day, she and her ex-husband, Hank, had despoiled many a hotel bed, but that was before Hank went to rehab. Once that happened, they pretty much had not gone anywhere at all.

As she waited for her dinner, Sam embarked upon her second job of the evening: social media. She posted her selfie with the illuminated library sign across all platforms, adding: THE *SODBUSTER* TOUR HAS REACHED THE END OF THE TRAIL! THANK YOU TO EVERYONE WHO CAME OUT TO HEAR ME READ. NEXT NOVEL UNDERWAY . . . STAY TUNED! She added book and heart emojis, tagged the library, her literary agency, and her publisher, and signed out.

She checked her texts: a couple from unknown numbers that were political or dating app candidates; one from her best friend and codependency sponsor Drishti.

u done????

Hey D! Yep, the tour is officially over.

The three dots rippled, and Drishti wrote:

congratz kid!!!! How do u feel????
Okay. Not **100%** looking forward to going home and getting back in the chair.
well but thats ur job!!!!! dont u have a contract????

CAN'T HEAR YOU, GOING INTO THE TUNNEL, Sam wrote.
Drishti sent three rolling-on-the-floor-laughing emojis.

how r u celebrating?????
Doing some coke and going clubbing, by which I mean having a cheeseburger and faceplanting.
u wilding

UNLESS YOU WANT TO SAY HI? Sam suggested hopefully.

Cant, kiddo, on shift. But c u manana at group????
Wouldn't miss it.
kk text me when u get home!!!!!! & congratz again!!!!

Sam tried her mom, Jill, next. This was probably a fruitless endeavor, since Jill was on a cruise with her brand-new sixth husband. Jill was pretty much permanently on a cruise. But she was the only mother Sam had.

Hi Mom! I don't know where in the world you are, but I just wanted to let you know, the *Sodbuster* tour is done. Flying home tomorrow to start Novel 5. Wish me luck!

Sam waited, scrolling her email in the meantime. Three blurb requests; a workshop student submitting his novel pages; an email from her agent with a command in the header: CALL ME WHEN YOU GET HOME,

ROAD WARRIOR!; a promotion promising to increase Sam's book sales *by up to 400%!*—the literary equivalent of a penis extender. Finally the three dots rippled, and Sam's mom sent her usual string of nonsensical yet sinister emojis: a penguin head, the ladder, and a hole. Jill had never quite gotten the hang of texting.

"Who knew there even was a hole emoji," Sam muttered.

Her cheeseburger arrived and she ate it with gusto, swiping through her dating apps with considerably less enthusiasm. She did this twice a day, a necessary evil like brushing her teeth. Sam had been married for fifteen years, divorced for one, and in that time it had apparently become all but impossible to meet somebody in a human, organic, rom-com way like a blind date, or bumping heads when you both reached for an apple rolling down the street. Sam worked from home, and her publishing colleagues were, like her readers, 98 percent women and 2 percent men who tended to play for the other team. Unless Sam wanted to wait for a sexy, hyperliterate window-washer to come crashing into her living room, she had to swipe.

Hi cutie nice Smile!!!!!! Wanna chat?

I see your a writer thats cool! What do you write?

Greetings! I, like yourself, am a Laborer in the Trench of Words. You may have heard of my bestselling sci-fi series *The Wormhole Galactica*, a Top 1000 Amazon Seller in self-published books! Would you like to quaff a libation?

hey princess i can write on your tits with my special pen lololol call me at . . .

As Sam closed the apps, she felt as she usually did after a swiping session: mildly beslimed and utterly despairing. Was there *anyone* out there like her? She weighed her phone in her hand. Drishti would scold her for the person Sam was considering calling. Her codependency group likewise. Even her therapist, if he hadn't retired. But Sam was tired and lonely, and she had nobody to celebrate nor commiserate with, and only one person would get how Sam felt in this moment. She hit the video-chat icon for her ex, Hank.

The phone rang and rang, and Sam was about to hang up when the screen suddenly burst into violent tumbling life. "HANG ON," Hank bellowed.

"OKAY," Sam yelled back.

She watched the ceiling and floor switch places as though Hank were on the sinking *Titanic*. Eventually the image steadied to show Hank sitting in a recliner on the halfway house porch, beneath a bare light bulb, wearing his GUGGENHEIM T-shirt and a porkpie hat.

"Heyyyy!" he said happily. "Look at you! You look fantastic."

"So do you," said Sam, relieved to see it was true: Hank was shaved, showered, and sober. At least, he seemed to be.

He took out a cigar and lighter. "Where you coming from, all dolled up?"

"I just had the final event for my *Sodbuster* tour."

Hank stuck his cigar between his teeth to clap. "Bravo, Ms. Vetiver! How do you feel?"

"Freaked out," Sam admitted. "You know how it is after tour."

Hank nodded. Like Sam, he had the rare public speaking gene, and before rehab he had traveled nationally to showcase his work. Hank was, or had been, a renowned portrait photographer. It was how they'd met, Sam's publisher hiring Hank to take her new author photo when Sam was nominated for the National Book Award.

"You have tour postpartum," Hank said now.

"Exactly! I knew you'd get it. It's so hard to go from the road back to the chair."

"At least you have the new book to dive into," Hank pointed out.

"I wish," said Sam glumly. "But that's the thing, I don't. I have five months left until delivery, and I have yet to write a word."

Hank's brows rose over his glasses. "That's not good. What's going on?"

"I don't care about the book," Sam admitted. "I can't plug in emotionally at all," and as soon as she heard herself say it, she knew it was true. Many writers Sam knew based books on an idea, a story *ripped from the headlines!* or overheard by chance. Sam's novels came from an emotional place—her bestselling debut, *The Sharecropper's Daughter*, was ostensibly about an itinerant girl and her mother doing seasonal farm labor, but in fact it was about Sam's childhood with Jill after Sam's dad died, being dragged from home to home whenever Jill moved on to a new minion, as she called her husbands. Sam's subsequent novels had been less successful, and Sam secretly suspected it was because each was more emotionally removed from her. The one she was meant to write now, *The Gold Digger's Mistress*, was loosely based on her great-great-grandfather Ole Nielsen emigrating from Norway, navigating the deadly Drake Passage to the Gold Rush, finding a fortune, losing it all at poker, and making a reverse trip across the Rockies until he reached Minnesota, whereupon he married and had eleven children. It was a terrific story, and Sam could not connect to it at all.

"I feel like I'm just reheating my leftovers," said Sam. "What happens if I don't hit a home run with this next book? Things are tough right now. Hercules could cancel my contract." This was Sam's publisher.

"Oh, come on," said Hank. "That sounds like catastrophizing."

"Because it would be an actual catastrophe," said Sam.

"Let's try some evidence-based logic," Hank suggested. Sam tried not to roll her eyes; Hank had picked up many behavioral strategies in rehab that were as annoying as they were useful. "How is this recent book doing? Have you asked Mireille?"

"I would," said Sam, "if I weren't avoiding her."

"*That* sounds healthy. Why are you avoiding your agent?"

"Because I already know what she would say." Sam adopted a French accent. "*Chère* Sam, I *complétement* understand. Making art is not like making vacuum cleaners. But you have a contract, and you must honor it, or Hercules might revoke it. So get your *derrière* in the chair!"

Hank laughed. "*Trés bien.*"

"*Merci*," said Sam. She'd been with Mireille for twenty years, longer than her marriage to Hank. She'd earned the accent.

"Can they actually revoke your contract?"

"Yes sir. And make me give back my advance."

Hank paused mid-puff. "I thought that was an urban legend to keep writers in line."

"Oh hell no, it's true. They can sue me for it. Or they could, if I hadn't spent it."

"Good Lord, girl, on what? Botox?"

"It is called a *mortgage*," said Sam, more acidly than she'd intended. Hank had been flush when they first met, but for much of their marriage she'd carried their Little House in the Berkshires and their other expenses too. The halfway house where Hank lived now was so filthy Sam peed in the bushes when she last visited, but it was state-subsidized, as were Hank's groceries. He had no overhead.

"You best get to writing, girl," said Hank.

"I know. But how? I've never been blocked like this before."

Hank blew a smoke ring and followed its progress toward the light bulb. "You'll figure it out. You always do."

Ding! Sam could practically hear the timer that signaled the end of Hank's interest. She felt a familiar irritation, more at herself than at him. It was true that she'd spent years of their married life proofreading Hank's agency contracts, analyzing gallery owner communications, and peering at contact sheets to select the images for Hank's exhibits. Not to mention all the time in emergency rooms, police stations, counselors' offices, and Family Day at rehab. But Hank had been kind to her this evening. They were no longer married. He was under no obligation to Sam. And extended attention span was not a recovering alcoholic's greatest strength. *What'd you expect, kid*, Sam could hear Drishti saying, *you went to a hardware store for bread!*

"I'll tell you one thing, you might have writer's block, but you look like a million bucks," said Hank. He made a horny Frenchman *hon hon hon* noise, but his voice was wistful when he asked, "Any chance of a visit?" He meant could Sam come to the halfway house, which he couldn't leave with his ankle bracelet on.

"I'll check my schedule when I get home," Sam promised.

Hank sculpted the end of his cigar against his ashtray. "I sure wish I could be there when you land, Ms. Vetiver," he said to it. "I still love you, you know."

Sam smiled sadly in the middle of the big empty bed.

"I know," she said. "I love you too."

The Rabbit

It's August 2 and I'm parked in my usual stakeout spot in a thicket across from William's causeway. From here, with the powerful binoculars I liberated from my bookstore—we carry them for readers who love their feathered friends, bundling them with the *Guide to North American Birds*—I can just make out the front of William's house through the trees. But he can't see me. That's one of the most important things. The other is that he can't come or go without my knowing it. Even if I'm asleep, the sound of his tires as he exits the causeway onto the road always wakes me. I know. It's happened many times.

Yesterday afternoon, for instance, I watched him depart for Portland, where he launched his latest novel, *All the Lambent Souls*. New books always come out on Tuesdays, I don't know why, it's just always been that way. But if you're a big shot like William, the publisher sometimes allows you to get the jump on your competitors and launch on Monday. That's what happened with William last night. He drove to Portland's biggest indie bookseller, introduced his fifth novel to 250 of his closest friends in the church the store uses for large events, ate cake frosted with his book cover—that's a lot of green icing—and drove home.

My job was to make sure he was alone.

Or take note of who he was with, if he was not.

I was a little surprised he drove all the way back instead of setting off on his tour from Portland. After all, it's two and a half hours from here. But maybe William wanted to sleep in his own bed one last time before all those hotel rooms. He's pushing sixty, after all. Well, he will be in three years. Although age doesn't seem to have slowed him down much, at least in one crucial respect.

Or maybe a bit. Because he came home alone last night.

I was so relieved. I did stay up a few hours longer, just in case. Sometimes women arrive after he gets home. God knows how he summons them. Via the internet. Or apps. Or it's somebody he met IRL who prefers to drive herself.

Which is what William likes too. He doesn't want to have to chauffeur anyone home, especially not from this remote locale.

He doesn't want them to stay.

These are the throwaways, the ho-aways, women he meets at readings or art galleries and invites back for what he calls a saucy time. I'm always worried he'll find one of them worthy of more than a night.

But for a while now, they've all been discards.

Thank God.

Last night nobody came, and William is waking up this morning alone. I guess he's conserving his energy for tour. Wise choice. Gotta be fresh-faced and ultra-charming for the readers. William takes his author responsibilities very seriously, I'll say that for him. The writing life is his priority. It always was.

I hear the distant rumble of his garage door rising and see light flash off his windshield as he drives out and parks. I raise the binoculars and watch him wheel his rollaway to his trunk and lift it in, along with a cardboard carton I know contains packs of breakfast bars—do you think William Corwyn would leave his health to chance on the road by eating vending-machine chips and snacks? No sir! No way. He brings his tour suits out next, two of them, both seersucker. One in case the other gets dirty. These he hangs from the hooks in his car's back seat. Do you know how many male authors I've welcomed to my store for readings who are in jeans and T-shirts? All of them. Do you know how many have had food stains or ball caps or sneakers without laces? Most. Who wears a seersucker suit on tour? Who even owns one north of the Mason-Dixon line?

William Corwyn, that's who.

He locks his house and performs his final household chore, urinating into the bushes near his front door. Like a wolf keeping other animals away. Then he goes to his car, sits in the driver's seat, and puts on his sneakers. He's been barefoot up till now, I know without looking. He never wears shoes here until it snows. How well I remember his feet, pale and flexible and spatulate as flippers. How he said, grinning, *Here you go, you might want these*, as he picked my panties up from the floor with his toes.

And here he comes down the causeway. Even though I'm camouflaged, I slide down in my seat out of habit. It's more prudent that way. Also painful. I slept in this car last night, and there's a monster crick in my neck. I'm only in my early forties, which is not *that* old. But I'm getting too old for this sh*t.

I see William's profile as he pauses at the end of the drive, then turns onto the logging track and passes me. He's in his prescription sunglasses and travel clothes, khakis and a light blue button-down. I still remember how those shirts smelled, how even in our program, when everyone else reeked of CK Obsession and cigarettes, William always smelled like a dry cleaner. Like starch.

It has been a dry summer, and the dust plume his car raises hangs in the air after he disappears from view. I watch my watch, counting the seconds, the minutes. I'll wait till he's a mile away before I get out, drag the branches back off to the side, and follow. I know where he's going, of course. His appearances are listed on his website. Still, I want to be on his tail all the way. You never know who he might meet on the road. I have to be vigilant always.

Especially when he's doing book events.

And the tour for *All the Lambent Souls* officially kicks off now.

Let the games begin.

CHAPTER 3

LITERARY CINDERELLA

The next afternoon Sam was back in her apartment in her yoga pants and T-shirt, her suitcase unpacked, her dry-cleaning bag so stuffed with red clothes that it bulged as if it contained a body. She sat at her desk in her study, face scrubbed and hair in its usual side braid, her favorite *WRITE LIKE A MOTHERFUCKER* mug full of dark roast. Literary Cinderella back from the ball, ready to do what any career writer would: Try try again.

Sam opened her laptop. She said the usual prayer—*God, grant me the serenity to accept the things I cannot change, the courage to change the things I can, the wisdom to know the difference*—and set her hands on the keyboard. She typed:

CHAPTER ONE: PANNING FOR GOLD

There. She was done. Could she be done? If only. Unlike many writers, who loved the Pollock splatter of first drafts, Sam hated beginnings. She much preferred having written and cleaning it up. She glanced at the wall above her desk, which was coated with magnetic chalkboard paint. Stuck to it were two things—her favorite quotation, from Winston Churchill: *Never give in, never give in, never give in.* And a photo of her adventurous, energetic, lucky/unlucky, and extremely virile ancestor Ole Nielsen. A man like a blade, thin and stern with the white-blond Norwegian hair Sam had had as a child. Sitting on his farmhouse porch in Minnesota, surrounded by his multitudinous progeny.

"Hey, Ole," Sam said. "If you have any inspiration to send me, this would be the time."

Ole's gray gaze remained remote. Sam returned to the keyboard.

Ole Nielsen sat up on his haunches in Dead Man's Creek and rubbed a weary hand over his eyes. His hand shook, and when he held it in front of his face he saw the missing nails, the dirt ingrained in the fortune teller's lines. Protruding as it was from a wrist scrawny with starvation, his hand which for the last several months had held a panning pan

Sam backed up and tried again:

It was early morning in the California hills above Dead Man's Creek, and when Ole Nielsen emerged from his __tent?__ the sun had just cracked like an egg yolk over the mountaintops

Well, this was terrible. Sam got up and went into the kitchen to warm her coffee in the microwave. It was fine. Everything was fine. Sam was just out of shape. She never wrote when she was on tour. She'd been at conferences with other authors who did, including one super-successful historical fiction writer Sam had affectionately nicknamed The General because she got up at 5:00 a.m. daily to run sprints in their hotel staircases, then banged out a thousand words before they went onstage. When Sam was on tour, she conserved her energy for her audiences.

The big Nordic man standing askance in the frigid waters of Dead Man's Creek had ceased days ago to even feel his gangrenous feet

Ole Nielsen hadn't come all the way from Norway to Ellis Island to ___another ship___ down the __Mississippi?___ via steamer? Paddle boat? Canoe? JETSKI

"Jesus," Sam muttered. But this, too, was part of the problem. Sam was not a *Mad Libs* writer, getting the story down first and filling in historical details later. She usually did at least six months of research before she wrote a word, so she could climb into her characters' skins as if they were virtual reality suits and replicate their lives for her readers. Her tour had not allowed her much time to do this.

Sam opened her browser to look up *Norwegians in Gold Rush* and got tractor-beamed in by her email, which she had been deliberately ignoring, in particular a message from her agent Mireille with the header: I HAVE BEEN CALLING YOU! PLEASE READ THIS!

From: Mireille Levenge
To: Sam Vetiver
Date: August 1
Time: 9:30 p.m.

Chère Sam,

Félicitations on the *Sodbuster* tour! You are a road warrior *par excellence*.

I have tried to call you several times and it went straight to voicemail, so I am sure you are writing. 😉 *Bien*. I hope this is true! Once you have taken a breath, I would like to hop on the phone to discuss where you are with *Gold Digger's Mistress*.

I was calling to tell you I reached out to your editor Patricia yesterday to see if I could get your first-month numbers for *Sodbuster*. Sam, there is not an easy way to say this, so I will tell it to you straight: they are not as we had hoped. (See attachment.) *Bien sur*, this is not your or the book's fault. Sales are soft industry-wide, and it is never easy to launch in summer. Add to this recent consolidations at every publishing house, and you have *un peu* a perfect storm.

I do not think this will necessarily affect you, given your track record.

After all, you are "The Little Author Who Could." Still, we must be prepared that Hercules House may tighten its belt, and toward that end, I want us to put all our energy on this next book. *Vraiment*, let us make *Gold Digger* a blockbuster!

Do you have pages I might show Patricia? She asked for them. It would help convince her and the Hercules team that you are producing and will hit your deadline, and that will help your standing in the house.

Call *moi* if you want to discuss. *Bisous*, my favorite author,

Mireille. XOXO

"Oh holy hell," Sam said, and slammed her laptop closed.

She did what any self-respecting writer would do: took her coffee to the bar in her living room and poured in a hefty slug of bourbon. Then she paced her apartment with it. Sam's beautiful first-floor condo in a historic Back Bay brownstone, a place she never should have been able to afford even with book sales and the occasional royalty—and honestly, she barely could. The only reason Sam had this place was that when she left Hank and returned to Boston, she'd wandered past this building and seen the OPEN HOUSE sign, and when she told the previous owner, a no-nagenarian frowning at the hedge fund bros swarming the rooms, what she did for a living, the woman had thumped her walker and declared, "This property is now sold to the writer. She needs the bookshelves." That had been that. Therefore Sam was in possession of eighteen-foot bookshelves, a marble fireplace she could stand up in—and, even with the special writers' discount, a very hefty mortgage.

She'd heard the rumors, of course. All summer, like thunder over the horizon, distant but getting closer. Of editors being fired, authors let go, contracts canceled. *Shifts in the industry.* This was hardly anything new: Sam had seen several such reorganizations in her twenty-five years as a professional author, the publishing mobile spinning and flinging people off into the abyss before settling uneasily into a new position. In the early 2000s Sam's own editor, who'd bravely taken a chance on Sam's blockbuster debut, had been let go. Sam had hustled all the harder, earning the *New York Times* moniker Mireille had cited, The Little Author

Who Could: Visiting eight hundred book clubs with her first novel had apparently catapulted her onto the bestseller list and changed literary marketing ever after.

Yet Sam was in no way immune now to being cut loose. If she missed her deadline for *Gold Digger,* if the novel was bad, if its sales were soft, she could easily become a literary footnote. Only the biggest-name authors, the ones who could sneeze into a napkin and publish it and make the list every single time, could afford not to worry.

Sam carried her laced coffee back into her study, past the hallway gallery of her framed book covers. On her desk were three things: an unlined notebook, a mason jar of disposable fountain pens, and a photo of her dad, Ethan. It was one of the few Sam had; a sad thing about parents who'd died was you could never get new images of them. In this 1970s Polaroid, Ethan was in the studio where he'd been a children's television writer. He was so young he didn't have a beard yet, although his sideburns were impressive. He was sitting at his typewriter, the Corona Sam still had in its mustard-colored tweed case, and smiling, a fuzzy puppet peering over his shoulder. His turtleneck had horizontal stripes. Sam had often wondered whether someone had just said something to make him laugh or if he was just happy.

Sam had never wanted to be anything but a writer like her dad. Her earliest memory was jumping up and down in a bouncy chair to the sound of Ethan's typewriter. She remembered the Sunday morning she'd left Hank snoring in their musty, vodka-smelling bedroom and driven to the market in her pajamas. How she got the *New York Times* and took it to the park, then sat on a bench with it and opened it to see her name and her book's title on that all-hallowed list. She was by herself, but she was not alone. She'd looked up at the sun filtering through the little green leaves and said, *Dad, this one's for you.*

Sam reopened her laptop, closed Mireille's email, and typed:

Ole Nielsen hadn't come all the way from Norway to Ellis Island to ___another ship___ that sailed south around Cape Horn, through the world's most perilous seas in the Drake Passage, up to San Francisco—

where he found himself coughed up on shore like___a thing coughed up on shore__, only to stand in this creek for months on end and come up with NOTHING OF WORTH AT ALL KIND OF LIKE WRITING THIS FUCKING BOOK

Ole Nielsen was finishing the last of his whiskey for breakfast when he first saw the one-legged prostitute crutching swiftly along the board sidewalk in front of the saloon

Young Norseman Ole Nielsen had never known a woman could have hair under her arms until he first made the acquaintance of Dead Man Creek's one-legged prostitute

Ole Nielsen was drinking postcoital corn whiskey with the one-legged prostitute when he saw the GIANT FUCKING TIDAL WAVE COME OVER THE MOUNTAIN AND WASH EVERYTHING AWAY MY LIFE IS OVER JUST KILL ME NOW THE END

Sam put her head in her hands. "What the actual," she said. One-legged prostitute? It was time to step away from the desk. It was counterintuitive, but experience had taught Sam it was useless to keep pushing at this point. She needed oxygen, a shower, food.

She responded to Mireille, asking for a call later. Then, as she was closing out of her email, *click!*, a new one slid into the queue. It was from a sender named William Corwyn—why did that name sound familiar?—and the header said, ADMIRATIONS! The first lines read:

> My dear, we don't know each other, but I know of you, and in case nobody has ever told you: You write like a ninja.

Whaaa? thought Sam. Whoever William Corwyn was, she felt fairly certain he should not be using the term *ninja*. Then she remembered: He was an author, published by her own house, and ridiculously successful. If he wasn't one of the .001 percent who didn't need to worry about being canceled, then he was on the next rung.

She googled William Corwyn, and sure enough, he was who she thought he was. His author photo showed a white man of silver-foxy age, with dark hair and little glasses, speaking into a mic. "You definitely should not say 'ninja,' buddy," muttered Sam, "in case nobody told you." She knew she should get up and leave. She needed self-care and focus.

Instead, she clicked on William Corwyn's message and read the whole thing.

CHAPTER 4

A LETTER FROM WILLIAM CORWYN

From: William Corwyn

To: Sam Vetiver

Date: August 2

Time: 7:30 a.m.

My dear, we don't know each other, but I know of you, and in case nobody has ever told you: You write like a ninja.

I suspect that, as a white male of a certain age, I'm out of line using that term. I hope I haven't offended you. If I have, I hope you'll forgive me and read on. If there's one thing we might agree on, it's that there's a delicious pleasure in deploying exactly the right word, isn't there? A pleasure so sharp, so exquisite, it's almost sexual. *Le mot juste.* Therefore I feel justified in taking the risk of using the term *ninja* to describe the way you write.

You might be wondering, Who the hell *is* this man? How does he have the audacity to write to me? And why *is* he writing to me? You would, of course, be smart to ask these questions. Any writer would, and a female author, I imagine, might have extra suspicions. (Note I did not call you an authoress, a word I despise for its smarm—do you as well? But I digress.)

If you'll indulge me, I'll explain by spinning a yarn. Professional hazard.

A few years ago, when a personal tragedy befell me, my physician advised me to take up martial arts. It would improve my flexibility, my physical and emotional balance. Initially, I rejected this suggestion. At the time, I was considered an athlete—not Olympian, but I could run a six-minute mile, throw a

TKO in any boxing ring, outrace the whippersnappers on the black diamond slopes. I'd still be doing all of those things if a tree hadn't rudely shredded my knee on an off-trail ski course near Breckenridge—but again, I digress.

When I took my doctor's advice, it was because of the sudden dawn not of wisdom but of vanity. Middle age and a convalescent lifestyle had expanded my waistline, and one morning while shaving I saw more than the suggestion of a double chin. I will spare you the description of the contortions I went through trying to see whether I'd developed the corresponding rearview condition, Old Man Butt. (If my ass ever looks lapped by wrinkles like the riverbed of time, take me out behind the barn and shoot me. But a third time, I digress.)

Off to tae kwon do I went. To my pleasant surprise, I wasn't the oldest person there. To my chagrin, I was easily the most graceless. For several classes, I was a miserable, dangerous failure, toppling over unexpectedly (I'm well over six feet tall, so TIMMMBEERRRRR!). I was shocked that I was unable to balance. Every minute in that studio was an exercise in humility.

From the first moment, I loved it. That is how I feel about your writing.

Samantha, I hope that in addition to forgiving my writing out of the blue, you'll give me a pass for being a latecomer to your work. I'd heard of you, of course. Your first novel, *The Sharecropper's Daughter*, is a household name, and we share a publisher. My editor's office is next door to yours at Hercules. (And is there anything more exhilarating than entering that building, that four-story lobby with its backlit glass-shelved rows of first editions? The temple of books. What *is* it about you that makes me digress . . . and digress and digress?)

For years I told myself I wasn't reading your novels because I'm a cultural Luddite. I never owned a Beatles album in the '60s nor a Saab in the '80s. The laptop I use for writing is an ancient beast I purchased in the last century. Therefore when everyone else was exulting, "Sam Vetiver—have you read her? You HAVE to!" I smiled and said, Thanks, I will. Someday. With zero intention of doing it.

I'll now admit the real reason I didn't. Sheer pig envy. And so well merited.

Because from the moment my editor thrust your latest book *The Sodbuster's Wife* at me in her office and said, "You MUST read this," and I forgot my book in my hotel room and found myself on a train north without reading material, and I cracked your spine—I was enraptured.

MURDER YOUR DARLINGS

This passage from page 173:

Once it grew light again in the shed, Anja lifted her face from the straw to find the chickens had tucked their heads under their wings; thinking it was night, they had gone to sleep. They stirred and clucked as she passed among them, and she thought everything might come right after all, of the bread and goat's milk she might set out for supper. She opened the door and smelled green destruction, the grass scoured from the earth by the twister and trees snapped so their sap bled, the land ravaged to the horizon, the goat dangling tangled from the branches.

Willa Cather, step aside. This is but one of a Whitmanian multitude of passages I could cite, but then this letter would be even more frighteningly long than it is. To select a few: I loved your bravery in depicting the pioneers' slaughter of the Sioux. I wept. The white man's subsequent vengeful hanging. I raged. And the lovemaking by the wagon, the farmer mounting his wife from behind as she clung to the wheel to keep from falling in the mud. Unforgettable.

Your meticulously crafted syntax, your ability to time travel: every paragraph lulls us into a stealthy, hypnotic pleasure—and then those last sentences, BAM! They deliver an emotional roundhouse kick to the throat. Hence I call you a ninja.

As I venture out on the road with my own latest novel, *All the Lambent Souls* (and is there any greater pleasure in the world than connecting with readers? OK, I will stop apologizing for digressing, since I am helpless before you), I'll bring your book with me as a reminder of what's possible. I know you're in Boston, and I wonder if there's any way you might consider dinner with me while I'm there? Or at least grace one of my New England readings?

Regardless, I thank you for your book. It's so rare that a novel has changed me forever in some invisible but indelible way. And you've done that. Isn't that what we all hope for?

Ever your admirer,

~ William.

CHAPTER 5

THE VIRTUOSO

A week later, Sam found herself driving across Boston in a nor'easter to one of her favorite indie booksellers. This wasn't something she'd normally do so soon after finishing her tour; Sam loved bookstores, naturally, but having been in so many the past month, she needed a break. However, she also needed a respite from Ole Nielsen. Sam had tried that damned opening chapter every way she could think of: first-person, third, omniscient, even from the one-legged prostitute's POV. She'd started with Ole's steerage experience on the emigrant ship. She'd chosen a scene from the novel's middle. Nothing. It was like taking a run at a mountain of ice, getting a few feet up, sliding back down every time.

And Sam might have had an ulterior motive for going to the bookstore: curiosity. William Corwyn was in town, reading his latest instant *New York Times* #1 bestseller *All the Lambent Souls*, and Sam needed to know, as William himself had predicted she might ask: Who *was* this guy? Nobody wrote missives like the one he'd written to her, nobody. Most writers received fan mail; Sam was the grateful recipient of reader praise about once a week. These messages were a paragraph or two tops. Nothing like the epistle William had fired across the bow, complete with page-referenced quotations. No writer took valuable time and energy from his own work for that.

So what did William *want*? Did he have some ulterior writer motive? Unlikely, since he was in a more powerful publishing position than Sam, but possible. Was he nuts? Or did he aspire to get into Sam's pants? Having done some cursory research on William, Sam had to admit she wasn't entirely averse to that prospect. William was older than Sam by ten years. He was also unmarried with no kids, a red flag; if a man was a lifelong bachelor, there was usually a reason. But it certainly was not that William was gay, according to the *Writer's Digest* cover story proclaiming him "The Most Lit Bachelor" and his borderline flirtatious responses to his raving female fans online. He seemed to be that rarest of all things: a straight, solvent, creative professional man.

Sam was a little worried about how much she wanted him to be real.

She arrived at the bookstore late and dashed through the rain to the vestibule, where she was greeted by William Corwyn—a life-size cardboard cutout of him, anyway. He was propped in the vestibule, arms crossed, glowering soulfully. Around his neck he wore a sign that read MEGA # 1 *NEW YORK TIMES* BESTSELLING AUTHOR WILLIAM CORWYN HERE TONIGHT, 7 PM!!! and was decorated with lipstick kisses. "Well," said Sam. Their publisher had never made her into a cardboard avatar, though Sam had once, for a brief and glittering week, been a subway ad.

She went into the bookstore, which was empty—everyone was in the reading room in the back, where Sam's *Sodbuster* event had been a month before. Late as she was, Sam detoured to the New Releases table, seeking her novel among its bright and glossy brethren, shining beneath artfully placed track lighting. She found it with sad placement on a corner. Sam waited until the bookseller on register was scrolling her phone, then moved *Sodbuster* to prime position: propped up facing the store entrance, replacing a summer romance whose author, Sam felt, would not miss a few sales. Sam patted her book and headed into the back room.

Where she ran smack into a human wall. "Okay," Sam muttered. Unlike her own recent tour with its half-empty seats, William Corwyn's attendance was not soft. There had to be a hundred readers here, squeezed into a space meant for forty. There was standing room only. Sam pushed her way through as gently as possible, murmuring, " 'Scuse me, sorry . . . ," to a spot against the rear shelves, next to a woman with coils of gray hair who was clutching William Corwyn's latest novel to her breast as though it were an infant.

Thanks, Sam mouthed. The woman gave her the most cursory of smiles, then returned her attention to the podium. The man of the hour was speaking.

As she got her bearings, Sam tried to collate her online William Corwyn knowledge with the actual man. There were just so many ways these days to get to know a person. He was a big guy, tall and solid, like he'd grown up eating only hamburgers—Sam's type. She loved men big enough to flip her like a flapjack or toss her up on a countertop. He also still had the hair featured in his author photo, dark and only slightly receding, with the showy silver streaks at the temples Sam always thought looked dyed. He also, sadly, had a goatee, which Sam disdained as the facial hair of indecision—either grow a beard or don't—but maybe he thought it made him look Shakespearean? His voice was low and sonorous, reminding Sam of an article she'd read about how women love men with deep voices because it indicated the presence of testosterone. And he had horn-rimmed glasses, over which he was now glancing meaningfully this way and that as he read. Sam recognized this move, targeting friendly faces in every quadrant of the audience so no reader felt left out. William Corwyn was the real deal.

Or was he, though? Unlike most male authors Sam knew, who showed up for readings in garage-band wear, William Corwyn was wearing a seersucker suit. Who wore a seersucker suit on tour? Then there was what William actually wrote. *The New Yorker* had dubbed him The Virtuoso because every one of William's novels was different. His debut, *The Girl on the Mountain*, published when he was still in grad school, had been a Gothic coming-of-age story about a young woman trapped in a family hell, like *Flowers in the Attic* set in the New Hampshire Whites. Some trades had slammed it as melodramatic and derivative, but it had been a Book of the Month selection, and William's sophomore effort, a contemporary romance called *You Never Said Goodbye*, stayed on the *New York Times* Bestsellers list for over a year—in hardcover. His third novel, *The Space Between Worlds*, was a sci-fi fantasy about a lost tribe of fierce intergalactic women fighting for a planet to call home, and his fourth, *Medusa*, a retelling of the classic myth, was so successful that it inspired a whole line of au naturel hair-care products that Sam remembered seeing at Target, and that was clearly responsible for all the wild manes in the room. Now he was on tour with his fifth, *All the Lambent Souls*, a poetic family saga set in the land of Joyce and narrated by the dead matriarch. There was already talk of the Booker Prize.

"Oh, *that* guy," Mireille had snorted, when Sam called to debrief and mentioned William's name. Mireille sounded like a sexy villainess from a Judith Krantz novel at the best of times, and now she spoke in almost a growl. "He is a virtuoso like I am a trapeze artist. You know what he really is? A dilettante. He cannot choose one lane and stick to it. And you know what really gets under my skin," Mireille continued. "It is this whole *woman* thing. This privileged white male, this . . . *man*, he has to write *every* book from the female point of view? Come on. He is perceived as so sensitive, so *evolved*, whereas you know what I think it is? I think it is pure commercialism. He knows, this fucking *guy*, that ninety-nine percent of fiction readers in this country are women. So what does he do? It is not *appropriation*, exactly, more like . . . faux sycophancy, this *ingratiation*, as if he is telling us, I *understand* you. But really he is just printing money. And another thing," Mireille added, really on a roll now. "Whenever I read his books, and okay, so I have read only one of his books, that ridiculous what was it, *Aphrodite*, no, *Medusa*, I get the feeling that he does not actually *like* women. Not that he's gay, it is more like the writing is . . . how do you say, ersatz, like he has a bouquet in one hand and a hammer behind his back. Do you know what I really think?" Mireille was winding up for the finale. "I think this Monsieur Corwyn does not like women at all, that *Maman* Corwyn was very mean to *bébé*

William, and he now spends his entire adult life trying to win positive female attention. Voilà!"

Mireille laughed merrily.

"Now," she purred, "enough of my half-ass psychology. Let's get back to YOU. And your new bestseller *Gold Digger*. When can I see pages?"

As she watched William now, Sam thought it was entirely possible that Mireille was correct, agents being the savvy scholars of human nature they were. They had to be, not only to negotiate deals but to manage their writers' significant neuroses. It *was* curious that William was so versatile. Most writers, Sam included, wrote variations on a theme. Sam's books would always be about love and trauma, no matter what the context. It was a sort of writer DNA forged by personality and circumstance, as particular as a thumbprint and as impervious to change.

But this was not true, apparently, of William Corwyn.

Sam wondered if perhaps she was a bit jealous. If she could write something entirely different, would she be as successful as he was? Would her books feel less stale? Would her readership revitalize? And how did one even *do* this, changing genres with every novel? Again Sam thought: Who *was* this guy?

As if he'd caught the question, William glanced at Sam. His brows rose over his horn-rims; his face split in a sunshiny grin. He mouthed something that looked like *It's you!* Heads turned. William inclined toward Sam in a way that was not quite a bow, more a sunflower bend toward the light. Then he resumed reading.

"Thank you," he said to room-shaking applause when he wrapped up. "You are so kind."

Laura, the bookstore owner, stepped over with a mic. "That was absolutely riveting, William. Will you take a few questions?"

William inclined his dark head. "My favorite part."

"ARE YOU SINGLE?" yelled a woman knitting in a middle row—of course there was a knitter. Everyone laughed.

"To the best of my knowledge, yes," said William, and a happy noise ran through the crowd—which, like Sam's audiences, was primarily female. Strike that, Sam realized, looking around: This one was all women. Nary a long-suffering husband in sight.

Laura delivered the mic to another reader. "Mr. Corwyn," she said, "your books are PART of me. I carry them right here." She tapped her chest. "My question is, how do you write women so well?"

"First, thank you," William said, "and second, dozens of female readers on Goodreads and Amazon disagree with you." More laughter. "Seriously, I get this question at every reading, and it perplexes me as much as honors me. Why *wouldn't* I be able to write women well? We're all just people, with hopes, dreams, loves, and fears—we're all lambent souls," he said, gesturing to his book poster on an easel next to the podium, the title embossed in gold over green Irish hills. "Or maybe I'm fibbing. Maybe I write female protagonists because what straight male writer would *not* want to spend all his hours in contemplation of the fairer sex?"

Oh my God, Sam thought. Did he really just say that? It sounded like something from *Pygmalion*. This roomful of feminist women would tear him apart. Instead, they laughed some more. Only one woman didn't join the jollity: She was standing a few feet away from Sam, wearing a librarian's flowered dress and a baseball cap pulled low, so all Sam could see was an overbite, a waterfall of blond curls, and a posture of concentration so rapt, she didn't seem to be breathing. Yeesh, thought Sam, and I thought I had superfans.

Laura ferried the mic to another woman, who said, "William, your books have been so influential for me—I'm a writer, too, though nowhere on your level. But what I wanted to ask about isn't your novels, it's the Darlings. Can you talk about them, please?"

"*Yes*," William said, with emphasis. "Thank you. If you'll indulge me, I'll tell you about the Darlings by spinning a yarn, trick of the trade." Sam squinted. Why did this sound familiar? Then she remembered William's letter: *If you'll indulge me, I'll explain by spinning a yarn. Professional hazard.* She did this, too, running lines in writing and then verbalizing them, in a sort of unconscious rehearsal.

William came out from behind the podium and sat on the edge of the signing table with the mic. He shrugged off his suit jacket and rolled up his sleeves to show his forearms. "Oh my GOD," the knitter said.

"Once upon a time," said William, "there was a young man who wanted to be a writer. He wasn't very good, but he was determined. And he worked hard. He wrote and wrote and wrote, and by some grace of God, after college, he got into a graduate program for creative writing. The young man was in heaven. He was learning from some of the best literary minds in the country. Every day he got to talk craft, debate, exchange shop talk with other writers. And just when he thought his life couldn't get any better, he fell in love with a woman in his program."

He drank from the bottle of water Laura had set out. The room had grown so quiet, Sam could hear the hiss of car tires on the wet road outside the store, birds chittering in the bushes. Even the knitter's needles had paused.

"They did everything together," William continued, "eat, sleep, write, critique. They spent whole weekends in the bathtub reading to each other, wrinkling like raisins."

He took out a handkerchief and blotted his forehead, sweating visibly now.

"In the early spring of their second year, the young man proposed. Which he did in workshop, by way of a terrible poem. The young woman said yes, and they began planning their wedding.

"Because they were in love, because he believed he knew her better than anyone on earth, because of their dreams . . . it came as a great shock to the young man when, that summer, he came home to find that she—forgive me, this is sensitive—she had . . . taken her own life."

A woman in the front row gasped. Sam flinched. For a second she saw her own hand reaching for a doorknob, the beige carpet soaked in blood.

William gulped his water and continued.

"The young man was devastated. Everything he'd loved had vanished, in the most sudden and shocking way. He couldn't eat. Couldn't sleep. Couldn't read or write. Everything lost all meaning. All he could think was: Why. Why?"

Sam shuddered. She rubbed her arms, which had seized in goose bumps.

"After a few weeks, the young man realized he was in danger of following his darling into the darkness, and part of him wanted that. So he did the only thing he could think of. He invited everyone in their program to his apartment. All the writers came, and it turned into an impromptu memorial that lasted three days. The writers comforted the young man, talked about his darling, tried to understand what happened. There was plenty of beer, and there might have been . . ."

William pantomimed smoking a joint. There was some uncertain laughter, though there was more sniffling. Some audience members took advantage of the moment to wipe their eyes.

"And something extraordinary happened, even more so than the generosity. The writers started to share. First one, then another, then they all confessed their struggles. Some, perhaps like the young man's fiancée, had depression, what Billy Styron called *Darkness Visible*. They all had doubt. Impostor syndrome. Worry how they'd earn a living. Fear of what they'd do if they didn't make it—they were all career writers; they'd never wanted to be anything else."

Yes, Sam thought. She was unaware she'd breathed it aloud until her coil-haired neighbor glanced her way.

"It was such a helpful jam session," said William, "that we—because of course I was the young man—decided to keep it going. We met every week until graduation, and I maintained the group after that, wherever I happened to be. Because talking to one another about the problems was so helpful in siphoning off the darkness.

"So that is the Darlings," said William. "A support group for writers. A sort of moveable feast of camaraderie that takes place around New England. Because I failed my darling—I failed to see she was in distress, to reach her—I help others as they helped me. It's the least I can do."

He stopped and drained his water. After a moment of stunned

silence, the room burst into applause so explosive Sam felt it in her throat. The women gave William a standing ovation, Sam included. The only one who seemed unimpressed was the librarian in the baseball cap, who was doing a golf clap.

Laura came to William, and they hugged, rocking back and forth.

"Oh, I got mascara on your suit!" she said, laughing and wiping her eyes. "Thank you, William. We'll check out the Darlings for sure . . . William will be signing here at the table, folks, and you can buy more of his books at the register."

"William thanks you too," called William, his voice almost lost in the scrape of chairs and stampede of feet. "Oh, and the Darlings meetings are *free!*"

Sam stayed put, waiting for the room to clear. She felt stun-gunned, limbs weighted in a familiar way. Part of her wanted to go home and crawl onto the couch. But she still wanted to meet William, now more than ever. Laura spotted her and waved Sam over.

"Two Sam sightings in a month," she said, "how lucky am I! Do you know William? You guys are both published by Hercules."

"Only by reputation," said Sam. "And he wrote me a lovely letter about *Sodbuster.*"

"C'mon, let's cut the line," said Laura. "Author perk."

At the signing table, William was scrawling his signature in a hardcover with a Montblanc fountain pen that put the disposable in Sam's braid to shame. He smiled up at the reader he was signing for. "Is that Barbra like Streisand or Barbara old-school?" he asked, and then he saw Sam. His face went still for a second, then lit again in that delighted grin.

"Excuse me a moment," he told the reader. He stood and walked around the table.

"It *is* you," he said to Sam.

Then he was hugging her. Sam stood inhaling his woodsy-musky cologne and a sharp note of sweat. He was roasting hot and damp, as she always was after she performed. His heart thudded against her cheek.

"You came," William said, when he released her. "Hi. Hi."

"You're so tall," Sam said idiotically.

"Comparatively," he agreed, smiling. He turned the mic back on. "Ladies and . . . ladies! You're in for a treat. Tonight you get two writers for the price of one: Sam Vetiver is here! Author of the classic *The Sharecropper's Daughter*. Her new book is just out, you can buy it up front, and she's agreed to sign with me."

He put down the mic. "Okay?" he said.

"Okay!" said Sam. "If you're sure. I don't want to intrude—"

"You can't intrude if you're invited," said William. He smiled and lifted one of the folding chairs over the table as easily as if it were a marshmallow. "Come," he said, and patted it. "Please. Sit here by me."

The Rabbit

One of the great things about tailing William on tour is I get to go to a lot of different bookstores, and it's always interesting to be in a store that's not mine. This one is an indie in the Boston suburbs, a precious little place with a green-striped awning, big picture windows, lots of front-table real estate—*New Releases! Fiction! Nonfiction! YA! Graphic Novels! Staff Picks!*—and impulse items like life-size literary stuffed animals and spinning racks of Sassy Socks. *F*ck off, I'm reading*, they say on the bottoms, and *100% Lit B*tch*, over cartoon women reclining in beanbags with books. This is a far cry from my store, which is a small branch of a big chain in a strip mall off the interstate near Augusta. We're between a dry cleaner and a Chinese food joint, and we sell more scented candles, tea towels, and picture frames than books. Corporate's decision. Once you walk past all those items to the back, we do have actual books, a couple of shelves featuring perennial book club favorites, classics, and bestsellers—which means we stock, now and forever, plenty of William Corwyn.

Not that I'm knocking my store. I'm not. I love it. It's a huge advancement from the one I started at, in Aegina, New York, where I grew up. Barbara's Book Nook, which wasn't actually a store but a hole in the wall on Main Street with stacks and stacks of used books, all of them reeking of cigarette smoke and mildew. The owner of that store, Barbara, called herself a bookseller, but really she just wanted to sit around smoking menthol Virginia Slims and reading romance novels. The paperbacks sold for 25 cents, the hardcovers a dollar, and would you believe people haggled over the price? If they found a suspicious stain in a book, or if it was missing half its cover, or if they were buying a bundle of them. It was one of the happiest days of my life when I quit that sh*thole to go to Upper Great Lakes Community, and when I graduated from there and left my Harrington writing program and got my job at my current strip-mall situation, I just about fell on my knees on the industrial carpet and cried.

That's another thing that's interesting, the different customers in these stores. They're always women, of course—women read. The occasional man might wander in, but usually to accompany his wife, or buy a gift for her, some title he's written on a Post-it all creased and hot and damp from being in his pocket next to his butt. Otherwise it's all women, and in my store they are soft and squishy grandmas who wear pastels and eye shadow, or women with raspy smoker's voices and lined faces that speak of hard lives they want to forget. Those ladies would not have been out of place in my original store, Barbara's Book Nook, which is where I learned that booksellers provide escape. That's what stories are for.

Here and at most of William's readings, the women are different. They have disposable income, they've been in college and graduate school, they work full-time, and they want books for the same reason they eat organic food for their bodies: to nourish their brains. They wear gym clothes, but don't let that fool you: Just one of these zip-up hoodies with the little thumb slits costs more than my weekly paycheck. And those running shoes? Two months' rent. They don't wear a lot of makeup, and thanks to *Medusa*, more than most readers here have crazy gray hair. William might have unleashed women's inner goddesses with that novel, but he also sure as sh*t f*cked up a hair-care industry.

I'm glad my baseball cap covers my wig, because I miscalculated a little bit today, I admit. It's blond and curly, and I got up at 4:00 a.m. to make those beachy ringlets with the weird iron I got at TJ Maxx. I was afraid the high heat setting would damage the synthetic hair, but it proved surprisingly resilient, so I should be able to wash it after this and bring it back to the store with the iron. Which maybe means I can get a pair of those Sassy Socks by the register here. I kind of like the ones that say *Ringmaster of the Sh*tshow*.

All of the women here are William's ideal readers.

None of them are his type.

I relax a little into the rear bookshelf I'm standing against.

The place is packed, as it always is for William. He comes in from the staff room laughing with the bookstore owner, a cute girl with tatts and purple hair. William has a goatee today, and I roll my eyes beneath my cap brim. This isn't a good look for anyone except a frat boy with a Frisbee in one hand and red Solo cup in the other. The crowd doesn't seem to mind, however. When William waves and smiles, they all go Ahhhhhh, as if they're having a collective climax. And they fall silent the instant he starts to read, like he's thrown some magic powder over them.

All except one woman who pushes her way in late.

She's small and panting, and her mascara's running like *A Clockwork Orange*. Her white tank is plastered to her body. It wasn't raining when I left Maine this morning, but it must be now. Otherwise this little chickie just walked through a car wash or something.

An alarm bell goes off in my head.

I look at William. His head has popped up like an animal scenting another at a watering hole. He's beaming right at her. But I could be imagining it. Because he always does this thing, panning his smile across the crowd.

He recommences reading, and I tune out. I've heard him so many times now, I have practically memorized this new novel along with the others. I heard this passage in Portland, and every day since then, and for a week before his launch, when I watched him pace his living room performing for nobody, making notations in his reading edition with the No. 2 pencil he had stuck behind his ear, recording himself on his phone so he could watch the videos back.

But nobody here has heard him read before, at least not this book. They angle toward him, they hold their breath. They close their eyes to let the master's words wash over them. It's so quiet I can hear the frantic *clickity clicky click* of the knitter's needles.

All except the little latecomer, who is watching William with a skeptical expression. She's wearing her red-blond hair in a side braid like a Disney princess—who does this over age 12?—and whether she knows it or not, she's twirling the end of it round and round one finger.

She has a pen in her braid. Looks like one of those disposable fountain numbers.

Another alarm bell goes off.

William finishes, everyone applauds, they ask the usual questions, how does he write women so well, what about the Darlings, blah de blah. Which is annoying, because I have to listen to William tell the story behind the story of the Darlings *again*. Not that I have anything against the Darlings. I get writer problems. They're real. And that poor girl William was engaged to—that *is* a tragic story. But the group, come on. I know why William really started it.

Finally the show is over and the signing line begins. I don't see the little braid-twirler anywhere, which is a relief. Maybe she thought Meh and went home. And I want to get out of here myself, before the crowd thins out, not only because it would not do to have William spot me but because, unlike our author, I can't afford a fancy hotel for the night, so I'll be driving back to Maine, to my sh*thole studio. And to New Hampshire tomorrow. Another day, another William Corwyn event.

But then I hear him call to those of us remaining, "You're in for a treat!" and more alarm bells go off, because I see him standing with his arm around the little braid-twirler, who's looking proud and embarrassed at the same time, an expression that looks a bit like constipation. Still, and despite the fact that half her makeup is streaking down her face from the rain, I can see that her eyes make jellybean shapes when she smiles.

Sh*t.

And she's a writer. Apparently.

F*ck.

Which I learn when William trumpets her name:

Sam Vetiver.

Who?

It sounds familiar, which irritates me all the more because I can't place it. That does it. I'll have to buy one of her books now. So much for the Sassy

Socks. And there goes my evening, my drive back to Augusta and a burrito and a beer and checking William's social before a decent night's sleep. Because looking at William and Sam Vetiver together, all my alarm bells are going off at once, it's like a f*cking five-alarm fire in there, she is exactly his type, and it's going to be a long night after all.

CHAPTER 6

AT THE CAFÉ

After the event was over, after William had signed dozens of *Lambent Souls* and Sam three *Sodbuster*s and a *Sharecropper's Daughter* for a woman who said, "My book club read this years ago!"; after William had inscribed stock and schmoozed the booksellers and hugged Laura again and Sam had done the same; after all this, they stood together on the sidewalk beneath the bookstore's awning. Sam was aware of the graphite smell of wet pavement after rain, of the heat rising from William's arm, next to but not quite touching hers. It was almost nine and nearly dark, but because it was August there was still a pink stripe in the western sky.

"Woof," said William.

"Indeed," said Sam.

They glanced at each other and smiled.

"I'm ravenous," William said. "Is there a place we could grab a bite? Will you dine with me?"

"I will," said Sam. "And there is."

William shifted his battered brown briefcase to his other hand to offer Sam his arm, and she led him toward a French café she knew would be open late. Halfway there the heavens split and it started to pour again, so they ran the final block laughing, Sam shrieking, and arrived soaking wet.

"I'm a hot mess," said Sam as they dripped in the doorway. Her white tank was transparent, and she didn't want to think what was happening with her face.

"Half of that statement is accurate," said William.

Sam laughed. "Thanks," she said, and then thought, Wait.

Their server seated them at the table in the window, lighting the candle between them. They ordered quickly, dinner as well as drinks, mindful of the late hour. William took off his horn-rims to polish them dry and beamed at Sam. In the way of most people with glasses, without them he looked completely different: less austerely impressive, more vulnerable and sweet.

"Thank you," he said, "for coming to my reading. And signing with me."

"Thanks for inviting me. And for your amazing letter. It was so generous I just slammed my laptop shut and backed away, and I'm embarrassed about that. I'm sorry I didn't respond."

William slid his glasses on and smiled at the server bringing their beer. "I suspected I might have overstepped."

"I did wonder . . ." said Sam.

"Whether I wanted to get into your pants?" They laughed, and Sam shrugged, feeling her face heat. "It might have been a motive, had I checked your author photo first. But no, my intention was pure. I was so moved by your magnificent book."

"I'm grateful," said Sam. "To *Lambent Souls*."

"To *Sodbuster*." They clinked glasses.

"That crowd back there was bananas!" said Sam. "Has your whole tour been like that?"

"Pretty much," said William. "How was yours?"

"It was—fine," said Sam. "I love tour. I know most authors hate it, but I honestly would drive over an old lady in the street to get to a mic."

William laughed. "Same. I relish it."

"I can tell," said Sam. "You're very good." She thought of how William had charmed the audience with humor, then taken the emotional deep dive into the Darlings story. You couldn't capture a crowd like that unless you loved speaking—a rare trait they shared, apparently.

"If I am any good, it's because I love the readers," William said. "I spend most of my life in sweatpants, in my basement, cranking out pages. And on the other side of that process are angels who read my books and come hear what I have to say. Some filament of me I threw out into the void landed on somebody and connected us. If that's not a miracle, what is?"

Sam realized she was staring. If she'd ever written these thoughts down, she might have accused William of plagiarizing.

"Exactly," she said.

"Do you know, Samantha, how rare it is we make our living writing books? We're in the top point-oh-five percent, not just of the general population but the *writer* population. We're so lucky."

Sam was horrified to feel her eyes fill with tears. She pressed her wrist to them, making an embarrassed face at William, who was smiling kindly at her.

"I see I've drawn blood," he said, "but I don't know how. What's wrong?"

To her astonishment, Sam found herself confessing her fears to another writer—a potential competitor at that: her half-empty tour and flat sales; her feeling of writing the same book over and over; the pressure to get *Gold Digger's Mistress* on track. Damn. William was good. Maybe she should join his Darlings support group.

"Samantha," William said when she was done. "May I call you that?"

"You may, but it's not my name."

"Then I've been a perfect fool. What *is* your name?"

"It's Simone," said Sam.

"Simone Vetiver . . . ? But that's enchanting. Why don't you use it?"

"Because it sounds like an eighteenth-century French prostitute dying of syphilis," said Sam.

William laughed. "I think it sounds like its owner, utterly beguiling. Simone, is there anything I can do?"

"I don't think so," said Sam.

"Maybe kicking ideas around? Verbal brainstorming can help."

"Oh, I never do that," said Sam. "I'm sorry, that sounded rude. I just don't talk about what I'm working on. I guess I'm superstitious."

"Not even with your editor or agent? Or friends? Or curious male writers prowling outside your castle?"

Sam laughed. "Not even them."

William raised his glass. "Let's play a game. Will you humor me, my dear?"

"I . . . think so?"

"Let's do Writer Lightning Round. I'll start. Plotter or pantser?"

He meant did Sam use an outline or wing it. "Plotter," she said.

"Same. Scrivener or Word?"

"Word," she said, "and longhand."

William's brows rose. He looked delighted. "Longhand! Old-school."

"Yep. I write outlines and notes by hand, then type the actual chapters on my laptop. And I have to use fountain pens. I can't read my handwriting otherwise. You?"

"Type it right into my laptop from my brain, baby," William said. He pantomimed inserting a syringe into his forearm. "I inject that heroin straight into Word."

"Well!" said Sam. "I guess that makes our publisher a pimp."

"People have called them that," William said, grinning.

"My turn," said Sam. "Do you write every day? Or when inspiration strikes?"

"Up every day before 5:00 a.m. One thousand words no matter what. No revising. Straight through the draft. Rinse. Repeat. And when I'm done with one book, I start another that afternoon."

"Oh, you're one of *those*," said Sam. "I thought you guys were apocryphal. Or that when you said you finished a new book and started another, you meant reading."

"Nope!" said William. "Waiting for inspiration is for amateurs, sweetheart."

Sam sighed. "Yeah," she said.

William tapped the back of her hand. "Let me guess. You're inspiration."

"Yup," said Sam. "If I'm going to spend a year, three years, five, writing a book, I won't do it unless I love it. Which means I have to feel connected. Emotionally inspired."

William sat back and gazed at her for a long moment. "Simone, I'm about to drop something incredibly paternalistic and pedantic on you. May I?"

"How could I resist?"

He leaned forward and gripped her hand, encircling it in his.

"However you do it," he said, "you *must* get inspired. I don't care if you go to a retreat in Italy or bonk the pizza delivery guy or stand on your head. You've got to channel that next beautiful book. Because the world needs another Simone Vetiver novel. I do."

Was it Sam's imagination, or did his thumb press gently into her palm? He let go of her hand. "If there is any way I can help," he said, "I would be honored."

"Thank you," said Sam, thinking: Wow. "I might take you up on that."

"I hope you do." William reached over and tucked a loop that had escaped Sam's braid behind her ear. "Forgive me. I've been wanting to do that all evening."

Sam touched her hair. "Obviously I need to go clean up," she said. "Excuse me," and she slid out of the booth, William standing as she did.

In the bathroom, with its Toulouse-Lautrec prints and hammered copper sink, Sam confronted herself in the mirror. Her eyes were shining in circles of mascara and her cheeks flushed, her damp tank clinging to her nipples. The overall effect was fetching in a louche, heroin-addict kind of way. Sam used the facilities and redid her braid, tucking her fountain pen back into it, then texted Drishti.

Hey D, you there? I'm at dinner with that writer I told you about, the one who wrote me the insane praise letter.

The three dots, then:

hallefuckinglujah! its about time you get laid.

DRISHTI.

dont worry i'm sure youll remember how. they say its just like riding a . . .

man!!!!!

DRISHTI. FOCUS.

kk sorry. so ur finally gonna get some????

I'm not 100% sure it's like that.

what else could it be like????

It could be professional.

nope. not if he asked u to dinner. whats he like

He seems great. Charming, kind. A straight, solvent creative professional.
Do you know how rare this is?

mmmhmmmm. so whats the problem?

That IS the problem, I can't tell. What's wrong with this picture?

does he have all his hair?

Mostly but with those weird showy silver streaks—and a GOATEE

he can shave. teeth?

WTH, Drish, we're not that old!

married?

I didn't see a ring.

which means literally nothing

I know.

did u ask?

We haven't even gotten our food yet!

girl have i taught u nothing? trust but verify

I will. Oh, he did tuck my hair behind my ear.

the man is a MONSTER

Also he runs a support group for writers. Over-giver? Virtue signaling?

**ok listen to me. u r SPINNING. props for reaching out but srsly . . .
overthinking is just as much a symptom of what u have been thru as
anything else. stay grounded but be open.**

Good advice, thank you, D.

just have fun FFS!!!!!! & text the code if you see anything hinky

I WILL, LOL, Sam typed. Drishti was referring to Sam's hatred of the ac-
ronym, so much so that they'd long agreed if Sam texted LOL to Drishti,
it meant she was in some serial killer's trunk and Drishti should call 911
immediately.

make sure u dont have anything in ur teeth. & use a condom

DRISHTI

text me when u get home w the deets!!!!!!!

Drishti helpfully sent an eggplant emoji. Sam texted back a bike and
left the bathroom.

But instead of returning to the table she stood near the bar, half concealed by a red velvet curtain, observing William in the booth. Their
food had arrived, but he was waiting for her like a gentleman and con-
sulting his phone, his face ghostly in the cold white glow. There was
something in his posture at that moment that spoke of vulnerability:
the slight curve of his back, or the way his hair curled over his collar.
Looking at William now, Sam thought she could spot the little boy he
had once been, the profound loneliness that had led him to seek solace
in a world of words in the first place. Or maybe it was just that he didn't
know she was watching.

What *was* William's deal? Everyone had one, some Achilles' heel of
the psyche. But not all of them were catastrophic. Maybe Sam was over-

correcting. Her first date with Hank, he'd told her outright that he struggled with alcohol but was really trying to make healthier choices, and if Sam got up and left, he'd understand. Instead of doing that, Sam had thought: *Great! At least he admits it, so we can fix it!* There were nights she'd drunk all Hank's vodka so he wouldn't and then thrown up; when he started recovery, she hadn't kept alcohol in their home. For years she hadn't had a glass of wine or gone out to dinner because of the temptations Hank was trying to avoid. This evening with William felt like a refugee's first feast after fleeing a war. Maybe Drishti was right; maybe Sam was looking for red flags because in the past she'd set her bar so goddamned low.

Sam headed back to the table. William rose at her approach. "I tested your *frites*," he said. "Just to make sure they weren't poisoned."

"So thoughtful of you," said Sam.

"I'm a giver," agreed William.

They ate then, or rather William devoured his salmon in four bites and Sam nibbled a mussel. She had never been able to eat in front of a man she found attractive.

"Do you ever," William said abruptly, "get as lonely as I do? With the writing life?"

Sam put her tiny fork down. Again, he'd read her mind. "Yes."

"Let's play round two." William dinged his fork on his glass. "Have you been married?"

"I was," said Sam. "I'm divorced now."

"Amicable?"

"Yes. He's an addict in recovery, starting his life over, and I'm very proud of him."

William made prayer hands. "More power to him. That's a hard road. Kids?"

"No. We tried, but the IVF didn't catch. And given Hank's drinking . . . maybe it was better." Sam clinked her glass. "My turn. You?"

"No kids. To my regret."

"Married?"

"Nope."

"Have you ever been married?"

"Not to the best of my knowledge," said William.

Ping! Red flag. Commitment-phobe. Although there'd be no annoying ex to contend with.

"I was engaged once," said William. "But . . ."

"Oh," said Sam, remembering. She felt abashed for judging him. "I'm sorry. Your Darling."

"Yes," said William, his grin fading. He regarded her for a long moment. "I'd like to sit over there, okay?"

Sam's stomach flipped. "Okay."

William slid into her side of the booth, close, and Sam inhaled his woodsy-sweet cologne, his warm skin. "There's a pen in your braid," he said in her ear, sending electric ripples down her neck.

"I always keep one there. You never know when you might need it."

"Fair." William tugged experimentally on the braid, and Sam gave a tiny gasp. He looked at her consideringly.

Then they were kissing, gentle at first and then not, Sam nipping William's lower lip, William growling with recognition and holding Sam's head so she couldn't move it. Sam didn't even care at this point if there was anything wrong with him. How long had it been since she'd been kissed like this? How long since a man's mouth was the whole world?

Finally she pulled away. "We should stop—we're middle-aged. And I think they want us to go." The restaurant was empty, their bill on the table. Sam and William stared at each other, and then William slapped his credit card on the check and carried it over to the kitchen.

"I must away, my dear," he said, returning to the side of the booth. He held out his hand to Sam and enfolded her in a hug, resting his chin on her head the way he'd done at the bookstore. Again she heard his heart beating.

"Godspeed, Simone Vetiver," he said, and released her. "More anon, okay?"

Then he was gone, nipping through the door like the White Rabbit, so quickly she didn't see him go. Sam stood feeling abruptly cold in the air-conditioning, her skin still damp from their passionate grappling. Had this whole evening actually happened? Sam touched her swollen lips, her cheeks abraded from William's goatee. William was, like Anne Frank, a little bundle of contradictions. His out-of-the-blue email to her, the Darlings, his genre switching, the Virtuoso versus the vulnerable little boy in the booth. And that delicious alpha kissing. Who *was* William Corwyn? It might be a dangerous distraction at a time when she could least afford one, but Sam knew one thing: She sure as hell intended to find out.

The Rabbit

The café she takes him to after the reading is French, and on the way there it starts to rain, so by the time they get there they're drenched and laughing and she's squealing like a piglet and her white tank top is see-through. I mean, come on. Could Sam Vetiver BE more of a cliché? I thought writers were supposed to avoid clichés. I bet I won't like her books, either.

Initially I'm worried I'll have to follow them inside and get a table myself to learn anything, and from the menu I pull up online, the place is dear. Does anybody really need to pay $18 for a hamburger? These are definitely not Augusta prices. I'm resigning myself to spending my week's food budget on a Caesar salad and glass of water, but then I get lucky: The hostess seats William and Sam Vetiver in front of the picture window. They're on either side of a booth beneath a copper pendant light, their faces also lit from below by a candle, and from my vantage point in the bus shelter across the sidewalk, they look like a couple in a TV show.

I watch as they order and talk. He laughs a lot, which he does only when he really likes one of them, and at one point he reaches over and fixes a piece of hair that's gotten loose from her stupid braid. He also does the long gaze thing. This is trouble. At least from his end. But I can't quite tell how she feels about him. She plays with the tail of that braid, which I can't help but think would make a good noose in a thriller—if the heroine were strangled by her own hair, who would ever suspect that as the murder weapon? She smiles at him and laughs herself, sometimes. She pays total attention to him when he speaks. At one point she gets up to go to the ladies' room—he stands, too, ever the gentleman—and returns with her mascara not quite so deranged-looking. But there is something about Sam Vetiver that indicates reserve; she's not stroking her neck or licking her lips or stirring her drink with her straw before encircling it with her mouth or any of the things I've seen the others do that signify flirtation and sexual attraction. Sam Vetiver is a little withheld.

As at the bookstore, I start to relax a bit. Maybe he's just taking the car for a test spin but won't drive it off the lot.

I use the time while I'm waiting to peruse Sam Vetiver's website. She's legit; her publisher, Hercules House, is an imprint of the Big Five and the same as William's—what are the odds of that? I don't like it. It gives them more commonality. She writes historical fiction, a library of titles that are all *this man's wife, that man's daughter*, as if women can't have a story of their own. I pull up a gallery of search engine images to compare her online presence with the woman sitting in the window. Unlike some authors, she's not too airbrushed. Her official photographer definitely scrubbed circles from beneath her eyes and evened her skin tone, and although even in her headshot she's wearing her dumb Rapunzel braid, it somehow looks more artiste than princess. The power of black and white. But she's smart, this Sam Vetiver, she's not an author who's had her photo touched up so much that when she shows up at readings, people say Who the hell is that ol' lady? She looks like herself. And she looks pretty good, unfortunately, for a woman who, I learn from Wikipedia, is almost fifty. (Well, forty-seven.)

I'm just sending her friend requests from my alt-profiles on social media when I catch movement from within the window. William is sliding into Sam Vetiver's side of the booth. Uh-oh. This is not good. She turns toward him, and he picks up the dumb braid—for a second I think he's read my mind and is going to cinch it around her throat, but instead he uses it to pull her closer to him, and then they're kissing. F*ck. This is definitely not good. This is not good at all. I realize I've half stood from my bus stop bench and make myself sit back down; I'm not directly beneath a streetlight, and I'm still wearing my baseball cap and wig, but if William looked out, if anyone did, I'd be visible. I pull back into the shadows.

William, however, is not looking. William is still kissing Sam Vetiver. Other customers leave the restaurant, the servers are clearing the tables, and they're still making out like they're going for the Guinness Book of World Records Longest Liplock. It's embarrassing, really. Doesn't he know how old he is? I wish I could look away.

Finally she's the one who seems to stop it, Sam Vetiver. They separate. William picks up the bill. About time—everyone else is gone, and I bet the staff wants to kill them. Still, the damage is done, the die is cast. I can tell by the way she looks at him, by the way Sam Vetiver turns up her face to follow William as he stands from the booth, like a flower tracking the sun. She's definitely hooked.

He hugs her and leaves alone, which is kind of a d*ck move, in my opinion—wouldn't an actual gentleman walk her to her car, make sure she got there safe? Not our boy. He heads into the night, taking out his phone the instant he leaves the café, striding right past me in the dark without the slightest awareness there's another human being a few feet away.

But even if he were inclined to think of Sam Vetiver, to wonder if she'd be all right getting to the parking lot, even if his surface chivalry were real, he wouldn't have to worry. Sam won't be going home by herself. I'll be behind her, every step of the way.

CHAPTER 7

WHAT IF

From: William Corwyn

To: Sam Vetiver

Date: August 11

Time: 4:35 p.m.

Simone,

Salutations! Hello. Hello, lip-nipper. Hello, dining companion. Hello, genius. Hello.

Tour stats: 326 miles, seven events, one convenience store sandwich gobbled behind a bookstore dumpster and countless breakfast bars from the carton in my back seat.

I greet you now from my hotel room in—where am I? A quick look at hotel stationery says: Connecticut!, where in an hour I'll be speaking at a swanky country club.

I should be doing what I always do before I speak: eat. Nap. Shower. Instead, may I confess to you what I've been doing since I checked in? Watching videos of your events. Not to sound like a total creeper.

You do the same thing I do, Simone: You give your readers a good show. I have to say, if I met you as your audience member, I'd be too bashful to approach you. I might just be able to hand you a book to be signed and stammer my thanks. Because as gorgeous as you were the other night in your casual wear, and you must know you are beautiful, in these videos you are an absolute goddess. The heels. The makeup. The red clothes. Jesus.

And you are good. You're charming and funny and so, so smart. I knew this the other night from dinner. But at the mic you turn it up to eleven.

I have been wondering many things, playing the writer's favorite game: What If.

What if your bravura performance is a kind of wall? Do you ever feel as I do, that our public personae keep us safe but also lock us in? What if you let me into your blockade—as you did a bit the other night—and I do the same?

What if you are as tired as I am of wasting hotel rooms? What if you were here with me now, putting this one to use as God intended? (By which I mean I would feed you expensive snacks from the minibar, what did you think I meant?)

What if I look up from a podium at an event, see you, and think, as I did before: *It's you.*

What if I find you when my tour is over and take you for a walk, and if your book is still being stubborn, we brainstorm together? I know you said you were reluctant to share. But what if I can persuade you to accept my assistance? What if I can give you that?

Because what if I can help bring another Simone Vetiver novel into the world? What if I could make that kind of lasting contribution, not only to the literary pantheon, but to you?

I'm so far out on a limb here. But I have so rarely felt the connection I experienced with you. What if we are the keys to each other's prisons of solitude?

There's also this: What if you're reading this with horror or dismay? If that's the case, I'll step into the wings, after bowing in your direction and giving thanks. Thank you for your company the other night, for coming to my reading. For your books and for being you.

Take that pen from your braid, my dear, chase down that Muse of yours, and *write*.

X William

From: Sam Vetiver

To: William Corwyn

Date: August 11

Time: 10:49 p.m.

Dear William,

Thank you for your lovely email. I too was wondering some things. How your tour was going. Whether I'd imagined dinner the other night. Are you actually real. Things like that.

How was your reading? You don't need to answer. I know you wowed them. So please answer this question: What is in your minibar? And what is the one thing you could do for me in a hotel room that would completely hypnotize me? (Hint: It's probably not what you think.)

I feel shy about some of the other things you said, not because I don't agree with them but because I want so badly to. I've been divorced about a year, and the only men available to date have been guys who have weirdly shaped heads, are carrying large fish, have an overly robust attachment to golf, and are completely unable to spell or use grammar. The fact that you exist gives me both pause and hope. You do exist, don't you?

My turn. What if I came to one of your events this week? NOT that I am procrastinating in any way, willing to undertake ANY evasive maneuver that would allow me to escape this hellish Gold Rush novelscape I find myself trapped in, of course not, why would you say that? (And thank you for your offer to help . . . It's really kind of you. I will think about it!)

What if half the things you said in your email are true? What happens then? Hypothetical questions. What if: The fiction writer's favorite. But it's the game we play to find the right story.

XO Sam

From: William Corwyn

To: Sam Vetiver

Date: August 12

Time: 12:13 a.m.

MURDER YOUR DARLINGS

Simone,

Tonight's audience was pure sugar. Retired librarians in purple hats and red dresses, more cozy mystery gals than William Corwyn readers, but good sports and full of wit and vim. Also wine. They plied me. I'm pretty lit. It's lucky I made it back to the hotel.

If you were here with me . . . but it is a good thing you're not. To build something real takes time, and care. Tonight I have neither.

I know precisely what would hypnotize you in a hotel room. I'd read to you. In bed. Any story of your choosing.

What if you come to another of my events? Well then our story will unfold. In ways I can only imagine. In ways I love to imagine.

I look forward to it. If you are not just teasing.

More from the road when a roomful of septuagenarians have not gotten me drunk.

XOXO! I see your XO's and raise you two and some exclamation points, XO!!!
William

PS, not one of those women could slay a red dress like you.

To: William Corwyn

From: Sam Vetiver

Date: August 12

Time: 10:08 a.m.

Dear William,

I won't keep you while you're in event mode, which I know is all-consuming. Break a leg. I hope you're not too hungover from the frisky librarians. But I have your tour schedule from your website, and what if that What If is not a plot device after all? I'd love to come to another of your readings. So keep glancing up from that podium.

XOXO and then some,
Sam.

PS, that was not my answer for how to hypnotize me in a hotel room, it was you could braid my hair, but it might work. We could test the theory.

The Rabbit

It's so welcome when William has a down morning in his events schedule, a rare one-evening-event day, because it means I get a little break too. I've saved up a lot of vacation time from work, four years' worth, and deployed it for William's tour. But I know my boss, Tim, was P.O.'ed that I asked to use it all at once, and the store doesn't run as smoothly when I'm not there. So even though technically I could do today what William was doing this morning at his Connecticut hotel, which is to put his feet up and catch up on correspondence, I go in to work.

I have some correspondence of my own to attend to.

I'm in the staff room when Tim comes in. He's the GM, but you'd never know it; he looks like a retired Marine, with a beefy build and a crew cut and biceps that strain the sleeves of his gray T-shirts. I wouldn't be surprised if he showed up one day with a whistle around his neck and made us run laps. He used to play football before he blew out his ACL, and that's how he came to books: reading Stephen King while he was recuperating. Tim is the only straight man I know in publishing besides William, though he lacks William's elegance.

"Hey," he says, sticking his square head into the room. "Somebody's sitting in my chair."

"It fits me just right," I say, pushing the rolling chair back from the desk. I heard him coming, of course, and clicked out of the screen I was working on. Now the desktop shows only his screensaver, his two adorable twin girls smashing rainbow Popsicles into their mouths.

He leans against the doorway. "Seems to me I remember somebody pestering me for the whole month off. You miss us that much?"

"Just couldn't stay away," I say.

He shakes his head. "I can't figure you out, Sparky." He calls everyone Sparky, and sometimes I wonder if he can't remember our names. "If I were you, I'd be on the beach."

"I burn," I say.

He takes a box cutter from his pocket and tosses it to me. "Since you're here, how do you feel about unloading and shelving a shipment?"

"I feel fine about that," I say.

He gives me another long, level look, then finger-guns me and leaves, whistling.

The UPS driver has left the Ingram boxes by the back door. When I was working at a much larger division of this same chain, in Portland, the books were delivered to a loading dock by an eighteen-wheeler, there were so many of them. I could get high on the smell of all that new paper. But that store was too far from William's house. Two and a half hours in good weather. Longer in bad. Just about impossible in snow. And an indie bookstore in a town nearer where he lives, even a library, would have been a much better commute but a bad idea. There's a saying, *Everyone's famous in a small town*, and I don't know about that, but I do know the more rural the community, the more visible you are. I need a situation that's as anonymous and disposable as a Dixie cup. Completely unmemorable. Hence Augusta, this strip mall, my sh*thole studio in an apartment complex on the frontage road. I was surprised to find it suits me rather well.

I slice open the boxes, mindful not to cut too deep and slit a cover. Of course, William's face stares up at me. The invoice shows we've ordered another thirty copies of *All the Lambent Souls*. Even though it's a bluebird day and nobody'll come into the store, and although everyone complains about the high price of hardcovers, I guarantee we'll sell out of these by the end of the week.

I load William onto the shelving cart, but before I wheel him out onto the floor I detour back into the staff room, bringing a *Lambent Souls* with me. From my tote bag, which I got free at the Boston Book Festival when William was on tour with *Medusa*, I take Sam Vetiver's latest book, *The Sodbuster's Wife*—we had two copies in stock. I at least love the setting, because who didn't grow up reading and watching *Little House on the Prairie*? I used to secretly side with Mary, the goody-two-shoes older sister who went blind, because most readers favor the younger, feistier Laura who became the famous author. You shouldn't ever dismiss the good girls, is my feeling. You never know what they might have up their sleeve.

Sam Vetiver is no Laura Ingalls Wilder. She's got chops. But. I looked up her numbers on Tim's computer, and that thing is happening to Sam Vetiver I've seen happen to lots of authors over the years. She had one success, so her publisher's making her write the same book over and over, faster and faster. It's like the tigers in the fairy tale who chase each other until they turn into butter. The books get thinner until they have no substance at all, and readers get bored and go away. They find different authors. There are always more.

I think this is what's happening to Sam Vetiver.

Not that I feel sorry for her.

I set Sam Vetiver's and William's books on Tim's desk face down, side by side. They look up at me from their author photos, Sam Vetiver smiling with her jellybean eyes, William leaning with his arms crossed against his living room fireplace.

They do look good together.

F*ck.

But maybe Sam Vetiver is a nonstarter. Maybe William decided not to drive her off the lot after all.

Because I know what Sam Vetiver's Jeep looks like now from when I accompanied her to it after the café, a very decrepit yellow Wrangler with a row of rubber ducks on the windshield, which makes it easy to spot. Very considerate of her.

And I did not see it in the parking lot of William's hotel this morning.

Nor last night.

Nor in the hotel or bookstore lots for the past few nights.

Nor was she at his events.

So maybe the email I'm about to send isn't strictly necessary. But it's always good to have insurance.

I reopen Tim's computer, using his twins' birthday as his password—really, a GM should be a little more circumspect—and compose an email for Sam Vetiver care of her website.

Or rather, bibliogirl081569@gmail.com writes it, from an account I just created for her. Poor bibliogirl, not very original. There are about five hundred thousand bibliogirls in the world.

STAY THE F*CK AWAY FROM WILLIAM CORWYN. IF YOU KNOW WHAT'S GOOD FOR YOU.

My usual opening shot.

I hit Send.

Then I delete the bibliogirl081569 account, erase Tim's browser history—sorry, boss—and say a little prayer.

Sometimes this is all it takes. It scares off the weak ones.

I can't tell if Sam Vetiver is in that group or not. I have an uneasy feeling she might be scrappier than she looks. A few days' time will tell.

I hope not. I don't want to have to ratchet up.

Unless I'm really really forced to.

CHAPTER 8

THE DARLINGS

Although Sam's fears were real, she had not fibbed to William: She had never shared her writer problems with anyone; she was a literary island of one. Hank had understood creativity, of course, but because Hank as a photographer wrote with light and Sam with words, their artistic empathy had been limited. There were the guys from Sam's graduate program, but although Sam had found great camaraderie there, she'd been the only woman in a workshop with eight men who wanted to be Raymond Carver or Faulkner, and she would have died before admitting any insecurity. That left Mireille and Patricia, and although Sam turned in rough-draft pages to them, of course, she preferred to get them as right as possible first. Sam thought of herself as Charlotte in the web: What good would it have done if the spider's promotion of her endangered pig friend had said HUM instead of HUMBLE? Before her dinner with William, Sam had not confessed her troubles to . . . anyone. Ever.

Therefore it was a first that Sam was now navigating the corridors of the Portsmouth, NH, Marriott, seeking the Emerson Ballroom, which she knew she'd found when she came to this sign:

THE DARLINGS
MEETING HERE TONIGHT, 6 P.M.!

Sam checked her phone. It was 6:45; she'd planned for rush-hour traffic leaving the city but not the tremendous pile-up on I-95. Was it even worth going in? It was, she decided. She hadn't told William she was coming to this meeting, wanting to surprise him—and just maybe to make sure he wasn't working the crowd for donations in a rhinestone-spangled evangelist suit—but she also had to admit she could use some assistance on her novel, if even by osmosis. She eased open the door and slipped in.

The ballroom was almost full, the chairs at the round tables occupied. It looked more like a popular event at a literary conference than a support group. Everyone was listening to a dude with a beard bun at the podium, confessing that his agent had ghosted him. There was a lot of nodding. Sam saw William at a front table, head cocked in an attitude of attention. He was in khakis and a light blue button-down shirt today, and something else was different—he had shaved his goatee! He looked handsome and a bit hammy, the exposed pink expanse of his face featuring a strong jaw and the hint of a double chin. Sam loved it. She imagined rubbing her cheek against his now smooth one and had a full-body convulsion of desire.

"So yeah, man, I don't know what to do," said the beard-bun guy at the mic. "It took me, like, seven *years* to write this novel, and now my agent said she can't sell it because *appropriation*. Just because there's a gay female POV character? I mean, she's based on my *moms*! If we can only write about ourselves now, what are we supposed to do? Just write nonfiction? Whatever happened to making shit up? It's a shit time to be a male author, I can tell you that."

This statement was a super-easy sell among most of the men in the room, who were nodding, and not so much among the women or non-binary writers, who leaned toward each other to murmur comments, smirked, or just sat. Sam felt for the beard-bun guy; everything he was saying was true, and also it was high time the men didn't have the head of the table.

"Anyway, if anyone out there has any *male* agent intel or could pass on my name, I'd be grateful. Thanks." He flashed a peace sign. William stood and gave him a bro-hug, two seconds and a back clap. Sam wondered if William would speak in response, since he was an obvious and mighty exception to both the prohibition on writing from another gender's POV and being a threatened species as a white male writer. Instead, he checked his watch.

"I think we have time for one more share," he said, and to Sam's shock she recognized the woman who waved her arms like a potential game-show contestant, calling: "Me! Me!" It was one of Sam's own workshop novelists, Tabitha.

"I cede the floor to our enthusiastic friend from table nine," said William. Sam tried to catch Tabby's eye as she made her way to the front of the room, but Tabby didn't see her. *Was* it Tabby? Yes: barely taller than the podium, late fifties, naturally red cheeks, black hair with distinctive white streaks. Dressed in a pretty flowered skirt and pink blouse. Sam hadn't even known Tabby was struggling.

Tabby adjusted the mic to her mouth level. "Damn thing," she said, to chuckles. "It's hard to be short. Hi, I'm Tabitha, and I'm a novelist—I guess. *Am* I still a novelist? That's the question. You all listen and decide. All I know is, I've wanted to write fantasy ever since I was a little girl— anyone else? Okay, thank God. All you fantasy geeks, meet me up front after.

"It took me a long time to get started. My parents wanted me to be anything but a writer. A doctor. A teacher. Mostly a wife and mother. That's what I did—got married and had kids. I was a journalist before that—kind of a strange job for someone who loves fantasy, but I figured it was a way to write and make a living. I was a reporter for the *Boston Sun*, and once the kiddos were born, I wrote for women's mags, *Good Housekeeping* and *Real Simple*. It paid the bills and I could be home with my munchkins. I bet some of you ladies know what I'm talking about.

"But I never stopped wanting to write fantasy, and after my youngest was in high school, I joined this workshop. The teacher was a best-selling author, Sam Vetiver, and you had to submit pages to get in. Boy, was I scared. I thought she might be too fancy-pants for somebody like me who hadn't written fiction since college. But she must have been on drugs or something, because she let me in."

Sam wanted to leap to her feet and give Tabitha the boxing salute, or at least cup her hands around her mouth and yell *YO TABBY!* She kept quiet. She wanted to hear how her workshop had failed Tabitha so much that she was here. Sam was at least gratified to see William smile at the mention of her name.

"The workshop has been a real lifeline," Tabby continued, and Sam deflated in relief. "I've been in it for twelve years. Some of the writers have been in it even longer. We stay in until we finish books, then send them out, then come back in to start new ones. I wrote all my books in that class. I published my first book when I was forty-one, and now I have four of them, a trilogy and a spinoff. If you're lucky, you know how it feels to have a *crew*."

Sam told herself, DO NOT CRY. She pressed her knuckles to her mouth.

"So what am I doing here?" Tabby said. "First of all, I read about the Darlings in the *Sun* and I thought: What a great idea. Writers need all the support they can get. Thanks to our famous friend here." She smiled at William, who dipped his head. "But also, there's something my workshop can't help with. I'm not sure anyone can. It's this: All my books were published by the Big Five. Well, when I started it was the Big Twelve. Not anymore. Anyway, they stopped selling my backlist. I went out of print. Then my editor got fired. My agent left to become a yoga instructor. I *have* a track record. I was a regional bestseller. Once I walked into Costco and there was a *wall* of my books. And now? I can't get a single agent or small press to even answer my queries. I just get those bounce-backs, *Thanks for reaching out, we'll be in touch soon*."

"Preach, sister," somebody called. Tabby pushed her glasses up on her nose.

"Langston Hughes asked what happens to a dream deferred," she said. "What I want to know is, what happens when you get your dream and it dies? . . . I guess you just have to find joy in what you started out with: the writing. Because that's all we can do." She punched a fist in the air as she left the podium. "Good luck, everyone! Go Sox."

She stood on tiptoe to hug William as he came to the podium. "Joy in the writing," he said. "May that be true for all of us. See you next time, friends."

Sam watched Tabby grinning for a photo with William. She felt gutted. It wasn't just that Tabby had been enduring this heartache, and Sam hadn't known, or that Tabby's career decline was familiar, or that Sam was worried about suffering the same fate—though all of those things were true. Although Sam's track record insulated her somewhat, she was suspended, like most writers, over the same chute. But what really struck Sam was that Tabby was right. Joy in the writing! When was the last time Sam had felt that? She honestly could not remember.

Tabby spotted her then and came over. "Look who's here! Did you hear my shout-out to you? What are you doing here? You don't need this group!"

"You'd be surprised," said Sam. They hugged. "I feel so bad, Tabby. I didn't know you were going through all this. Why didn't you tell me?"

Tabby shrugged. "You're so busy and important, I didn't want to bother you."

Sam laughed, although she felt awful. "First of all, I'm not important. Stop believing everything you read on social media. Second, I'm never too busy. I'm doing the same thing you are. I'm just like you!"

"Okay," said Tabby, though she didn't seem convinced. "So how was your tour?"

"Good. Over now."

"And you're working on the new book? How's that going?"

"Why do you think I'm here?"

Tabby looked around at the writers, the women in dresses or casual wear, the guys in T-shirts and beards, jockeying for position around William. They would be asking him for introductions to his agent or editor, Sam knew, or handing him their manuscripts to pass on. "You were gonna talk about your problems in this crowd? I can't imagine that."

Me neither, thought Sam, but she hoped that was because she was unaccustomed to writerly confession, not pride. Drishti would say, *Get humble, kid. Ask for help. You're no different from anyone else, no worse but no better, either.* "I'm more here to procrastinate."

Tabby laughed. "I hear that. Do you want to get some dinner?"

"I would," said Sam, glancing in William's direction, "but . . ."

"Ohhhhh!" said Tabby. Her face lit up. "*Now* I get it. Teacher's got a new beau!"

Sam rolled her eyes. "Not really. We're just getting to know each other."

Tabby nudged Sam with her elbow. "You better hop to it, missy. Looks like you've got competition." She meant the women clustered around William, including the one taking a selfie with him now: a brunette in skinny jeans and a tank top that said MS. WRITE.

Tabby squinted assessingly at William. "I can see it. He's cute. Just check his . . . you-know." She crooked her forefinger and made it wilt toward the floor with a corresponding sound: *wah, wah, wah.* "At our age, you never know. But you can always slip some Viagra in his drink." She yelled, "Hey, William! Look who's here!"

"Tabby!" Sam hissed. The remaining writers turned. William's face split in that delighted grin. *It's you!* he mouthed. Sam gave an embarrassed tiny wave.

"You're welcome," said Tabby. "I expect a full report."

They hugged again, and Tabby left. William, moving within a small amoeba of lingering acolytes, came toward Sam. "Simone!" he said. "What an excellent surprise."

He bent to kiss Sam on the lips—just as delicious as before, except better without the scratchy goatee. Sam could feel his admirers watching, and sure enough, although two of the women drifted off toward the door, MS. WRITE was still there giving Sam the stink eye.

"Melody," said William, one arm around Sam, "this is Sam Vetiver.

I'm sure you've heard of her." Melody shrugged, compressing her cleavage. "*The Sharecropper's Daughter, The Sodbuster's Wife*—no? Among the best novels of our generation."

"I didn't even pay him to say that," said Sam, extending her hand. "Nice to meet you."

Melody looked at Sam's hand. "Anyway," she said to William, "I'll email you my query, okay?" She sashayed away.

Sam and William both watched her go, hips swinging in the tight jeans like a pendulum in a clock. "Wow," said Sam. "You are one popular piece of writer man meat."

William laughed. "Ground chuck at best. Thank you for saving me from the frying pan."

"You owe me," said Sam. She was lifting her hand to touch his smooth face when somebody fell over a chair a few feet away, grunting in pain. They both looked up, and William thrust Sam away from him so quickly that she stumbled.

"You!" William shouted at the woman, who had picked herself up and was bolting for the exit. "I know you! Come back here. Don't you dare run off again!"

The woman dove for the door as William zigzagged through the maze of tables. She was short and round with a pink bob and a camouflage trucker's cap, and something about her looked familiar to Sam. As William chased her into the hall, Sam realized why: It was the woman from William's Boston reading, the unimpressed one with the cascading blond curls. There was no mistaking her overbite.

"I told you what would happen if I caught you again," William was yelling as he sprinted after her. Sam heard him bellowing in the hallway. "I see you! I know you can hear me! I'm taking photos, I'm calling the police!"

The Rabbit

Holy f*ck, that was close. That was so close. That was way too f*cking close.

I lie under the bushes lining the exterior of the Marriott, my eyeball an inch away from a bunch of squashed cigarette butts, breathing sour dirt. I'm exhaling through my mouth, trying to do it soundlessly, because William is still a few feet away, looking for me. He almost caught me, he's in so much better shape than I am, his legs about ten times longer. But first I hooked down a side corridor—I think William expected me to head for the lobby, and it took him a second to figure out where I'd gone, and then his bad knee gave out. I was just out the side door when I heard a *pop!* and a yowl and he slowed way down. Now he's gimping around the parking lot looking for me, pulling hard to the right. His feet limp back and forth not far from my nose. This is so bad.

Of course, this is his fault. He's never caught me before at an event, either a reading or a Darlings meeting, and it would not have happened today except I'm exhausted by his ridiculous schedule. I'm so tired, I'm clumsy. I fell over that stupid chair while I was trying to inch closer to him and Sam Vetiver.

Gosh damn that woman. I so did not want Sam Vetiver to show up today. I was so hoping the email scared her off. I was so happy when I did not see her decrepit yellow Jeep in the parking lot. Then there she was, smiling up at William like a little Bambi in a forest with her stupid braid and her jelly-bean eyes. She went dark after I sent the email, I didn't see her at William's

Connecticut or Rhode Island events, her car was not at his hotels. Then here she is today. Bad surprise. Very bad surprise.

Now she has visual on me too. She knows what I look like, or she would if not for the pink wig. Gosh damn it. None of this would have happened if I weren't so tired I was graying out, tailing William all the way up I-95 and sleeping only a few hours at a travel oasis. Why can't William put the rest of his life on hold like every other author on tour? But noooo, he has to keep holding Darlings meetings and book events too. Then again, he was always like this. Even back in our program at Harrington he was like the f*cking Energizer bunny, while everyone else was drinking and smoking and staying out all night and banging out pages hungover an hour before workshop, William was up at 4:00 a.m. writing for hours, then taking one of his epic naps, then writing more, then playing Ultimate or hacky sack, then attending workshop, then going to hear music or to bonfires or to the Castle. And of course f*cking f*cking f*cking any girl who moved. That man could never stay still to save his life.

You'd think he'd slow down at least a little now, though. He has a bad knee and a faulty ticker. He's going to be sixty in three years, for f*ck's sake.

He's been on the phone while looking for me, and now the 911 operator must have patched him through to the local police, because I hear him say, "Yes, hello, officer, my name is William Corwyn, I'm at the Portsmouth Marriott, and I want to report an assault."

An assault! I would scoff if my face weren't smashed into the dirt. Please. As if. Ever the fiction writer. Nobody's going to corroborate that.

"Yes, I'll meet them in the lobby," he says.

He hobbles back to the side door, which requires a key he doesn't have. I hear him swear as it remains locked, balking him. He curses and lurches off toward the hotel entrance.

I remain where I am, making myself count to three hundred. When he doesn't return and nobody else comes, I crawl along the side of the building and emerge from the back of the hedge, in the rear lot near the dumpster, where I parked my car. Once I'm in it, with the doors locked, I strip off the pink wig and baseball cap and tuck them under my seat. I drink a whole liter of water without stopping, since I am hellishly thirsty as well as nauseated. I open my glove box and take out the half a granola bar I found on a table at the travel oasis this morning, break off the exposed end in case there are germs, force myself to eat the rest. William's tour and extracurriculars are expensive as well as exhausting.

I drive slowly through the lot, like any hotel guest leaving for home. I so wish that's where I were going. It's not that I have any great love for my sh*thole studio. It's just a container for me to live in while I do what I have to do. But right now the idea of being there, in the air-conditioning, lights off, face-planting onto my own futon, seems like heaven.

It's not going to happen. Sam Vetiver just had to push it by showing up today. Gosh damn her! I exit the lot, passing a Portsmouth, NH, sheriff's car coming in. Lights off, naturally. They'll take William's statement, but there's no emergency here.

In the way of most corporate chain hotels, this one is near an office park. I take the first turn I see and pull into a spot beneath a tree from which I can see the Marriott entrance and Sam Vetiver's Jeep, yellow in the sun as a child's rubber duckie. And William's SUV, with its bike and roof racks and stupid Mary Oliver bumper sticker. There's no way Sam Vetiver or William will be able to leave without my seeing them, and in the meantime, my only job is to stay awake, to watch and wait.

CHAPTER 9

FORT CONSTITUTION

T hat," said William, "was the Rabbit."

They were driving—somewhere, Sam didn't know where. William navigated through Portsmouth as if he had a destination in mind. He'd said very little since he'd returned to the Marriott lobby, limping like Captain Ahab, to confer with two of New Hampshire's finest. Sam had sat nearby on a couch, eavesdropping-not-eavesdropping; William's voice had grown so low with fury, it was hard to hear him. At one point, Sam had heard him growl, *Yes, it's all on record, which you'd know if you looked! Jesus Christ, I know she has to murder me in my sleep before you people take action, but at least do your basic job.* Now he was grim-faced and less voluble than usual but calm. If this was William enraged, Sam could take it.

She'd been checking out his car as he drove—it was like seeing a man's house for the first time; it told you so much. William's car was the luxe but unflashy small SUV people drove when they had money but didn't want to show off. It had a bike rack on the back, a Thule container on top, and a bumper sticker that read *Honk if you're letting the soft animal of your body love what it loves*. Inside, it smelled of his cologne, and the interior was clean, no crumpled fast-food wrappers or crumbs, just William's seersucker suits hanging from the dry-cleaning hook and a carton of breakfast bars on the back seat. Tour life, male version.

He stopped at a light and turned to Sam. He was wearing aviators, like every boy she'd gone to college with. "Thank you for coming to see me."

"Thanks for having me. I hope it's okay that it was the Darlings instead of a book event."

"Very okay, if a little below your pay grade. But I apologize for the drama."

"It's not your fault," said Sam. "I saw that woman before, at your Boston reading. She had curly blond hair then."

"She has many different looks," said William. "She keeps the wig industry in business. She's been stalking me for years."

"Seriously?"

"Dead serious. She comes to most of my readings. Tails me on the road. I strongly suspect she's been to my house."

"That's horrible!" said Sam. "Can't anyone do anything about it?" But she knew the answer. She'd grown up watching Lifetime Movie Network.

"No. It's all on record, I've reported every incident. But she has to threaten or cause me bodily harm before I can get even a restraining order. And she's too smart for that."

"Who is she, do you know? What does she want?"

William turned onto a road paralleling the ocean. "What does any stalker want? As a beautiful woman, as an author, you must have been through this. You know."

Sam nodded. For each book, she'd had readers send uncomfortably personal emails that, when she responded to say thanks, grew in length and intimacy. She'd learned to let her replies dwindle and wink out. But one recent gentleman had been persistent, flooding her in-box with commentary on her writing, analysis of the sexy passages, imaginings of what Sam had been thinking when she wrote them, descriptions of what they made him do. When she blocked his email, he'd popped up on social media, leaving paragraph-long comments on her posts and DMing photos of himself, naked, with her books. When she reported him, he started texting and calling—and Sam did not give out her number. The pièce de résistance was when he mailed a nude sketch of Sam to her apartment, with a note saying he could be there in 4.52 hours if the traffic wasn't bad. Sam never posted her address or identifying information of her home. She reported the incidents to the police, who of course could do nothing, and changed her locks.

"I did have a stalker," Sam said. "But he faded away."

"That's a mercy," said William. "And I'm sorry you had to go through it, though not surprised. I've come to think of it as a professional side effect: We invite readers into our imaginations in the most intimate way, invoke their strongest feelings . . . and then, when they close the cover of the book, it's all over. The most fragile ones can't handle it. They've formed what they think is a relationship."

"Like the celebrity stalkers who confuse the actor with the role," said Sam.

"Exactly. It could be considered a compliment, if it weren't such an annoyance."

"As long as that's all this woman is," Sam said.

William drove into a parking lot, passing one of the wooden National Parks signs Sam loved: FORT CONSTITUTION. "So far, yes. And it's been years, so I don't think she's going to escalate. In fact, she might be getting better. She used to send emails . . . "

Oh! thought Sam. She felt a small shock, as though she'd shuffled across the carpet and touched a light switch. She'd totally forgotten until now about the message she'd gotten via her website a few nights ago, from somebody named bibliogirl081569:

STAY THE F*CK AWAY FROM WILLIAM CORWYN. IF YOU KNOW WHAT'S GOOD FOR YOU.

At the time, Sam had been startled, then annoyed, then bemused. Whoever bibliogirl081569 was, she didn't know it took a lot more than that to scare a writer. Sam had received far more profane emails from aggrieved readers. And she'd been kind of charmed by bibliogirl081569's delicately skewed sensibilities, sending a threat but not wanting to spell out the curse word. Sam had filed the email in her Angry Randos file, spent an hour on William's social media trying to spot bibliogirl081569 among his commenters, then given up. It had to be somebody from the Boston event, because that was the only time Sam and William had been publicly together, but that could be one of a hundred women. Someone with a crush and a violent way of expressing herself online. Now Sam thought: Probably the Rabbit.

Sam considered telling William, but why? He couldn't do anything about it. And apparently she was all sound and fury, signifying nothing. Sam didn't want some irritating but harmless pest ruining the first chance she'd had at a viable relationship for the first time in . . . ever. It was only an email. If it happened again, she'd tell William about bibliogirl081569—or Sam would handle the Rabbit herself.

As William pulled into a leafy parking space near some picnic tables, Sam thought of something her mom, Jill, used to say, during her stint as a realtor between husbands three and four: *If a property has one thing wrong with it, buy it; more than that, run.* William had the Rabbit—but that wasn't his fault; anyone could attract a stalker. And Sam thought of another front seat, long ago: She'd been driving, Hank riding shotgun, and she'd just picked him up from the motel after the owner called. He'd passed out again, and he smelled like the bottom of a garbage can, cigar and vodka and blood—it was the first time she had known addiction had a smell. She'd poked him awake in front of the emergency room, and Hank had come to and said blearily, *Well, I guess we better go in.* He protested against Sam coming in with him because he didn't want to expose her to the gashes on his wrists when they unwrapped the towels—as if Sam hadn't already seen them in the motel, as if her sneakers hadn't made squelching noises in the carpet soaked with Hank's blood. She'd driven home by herself after leaving him at the hospital, which was the hardest thing she'd ever done, and cleaned up and put on a red turtleneck and gone straight to a book club at Barnes & Noble, where she'd concentrated as hard as she could to smile and understand her readers' usual small talk—*I loved your book!, Will you sign it for me?*—all the while thinking, If they only knew. Worrying the whole time that although it was impossible—she'd showered, she'd changed—she still had a comma of Hank's blood on her cheek, dried under her nails.

Now here was William, in his beautiful clothes and expensive car, with his extra suit and healthy snacks, smiling at Sam. Taking her hand. Saying, "Everything all right?"

"Sure," said Sam. "Why?"

"You just seemed a hundred miles away," said William. "As you are right now, in fact. Far too distant from me. Come closer."

He tugged her braid, and then they were kissing. William cupped Sam's breast, ran a thumb back and forth over the hard nipple beneath the cloth. She gasped and reached for him across the seat. Why were gearshifts in such awkward places?

"Jesus," said William against her neck.

He detached from her and put his glasses back on, then opened his door and got out to come around to Sam's. Sam heard gulls crying, the pound of waves, smelled the damp and salt.

"Walk with me, milady? I'm craving air. And hand me my briefcase, please?"

Sam retrieved it from between her feet, and William extracted a prescription bottle. He shook out a pill and swallowed it. Painkiller?

"You hurt your knee," Sam said, for he was limping.

"Skiing injury," he said. "It's why I no longer run. Except to chase stalkers."

He took Sam's hand and folded it into his elbow as they walked slowly through the empty parking lot to the fort. It was a big heap of crenellated stone, hanging out over the ocean as forts tended to do. It was closed, the entrance chained, and for the first time Sam wondered if it was quite wise, coming to an abandoned site with a man she didn't really know, not having told anyone where she was going. She'd texted Drishti from the hotel—HEY, D, YOU THERE?—but gotten distracted. Was it too late to take out her phone and start sharing her location?

Yes, because William was helping Sam up onto the narrow walkway that led them around the fort to the ocean. Sam clung to him as the waves crashed beneath them onto very large, pointy rocks. William guided them to a nook beneath an arrow-slit window, then stepped behind Sam and put his arms around her. The sun was setting, the ocean in front of them dim, nothing between Sam and death except William's arms. Along the shore she could see lights coming on in other, more horizontal beachside venues.

"This might be a good time to mention I'm terrified of heights," she said.

William's hold tightened. "I've got you," he said, and rested his chin on Sam's head in a way that had already become familiar. Sam leaned back against him.

"Why do you call her the Rabbit?" Sam asked.

"Hmmm?" said William into her hair. One of his hands remained firmly on Sam's stomach, pressing her safely against him; the other was on the move, stroking her nipple, then down her rib cage, then lifting her shirt.

"Your stalker," said Sam. "Why do you call her the Rabbit? Is it because of her teeth?"

William's hand stopped, a starburst of heat on Sam's hip.

"Good Lord, no," he said. "That would be cruel. It's because I imagined a woman who looks like that doesn't enjoy many lovers, so I wished for her a good relationship with her rabbit."

"She has a rabbit?" Sam said. Then she got it. "Oh. You mean her vibrator."

"Yes, exactly!" said William, and Sam felt him laugh. "The best pet a girl can have."

He rested his chin atop Sam's head again, swaying them slightly.

"The world can be so unkind to ugly women," he said. "But you wouldn't know anything about that, would you, lovely Simone?"

He eased out from behind her, obscuring the darkening view.

"Watch out!" Sam said.

"I'm safe," said William. "So are you. There's plenty of room—see?"

Sam peeked at him standing on the very edge of the walkway, then squeezed her eyes shut and shook her head.

"That's right," William said. "Don't look, if that's easier." He kissed her. "You're safe with me, Simone. I swear it to you."

Sam felt him kneeling. "But your knee," she said—middle-aged hookup problems.

William chuckled against her stomach. "My knee's fine."

He paused, fingers inside Sam's waistband. "Okay?" he said.

Sam opened her eyes. She could barely see him in the dusk, the glint of the last of the light off his glasses, his hair corkscrewing in the wind. "Okay."

William yanked Sam's capris and boy shorts down in one fluid movement. "I always thought that should have some accompanying sound."

"Like—Zoop!" said Sam, shivering not from the breeze but the sudden exposure.

"Zoop, yes, very good!" said William, laughing. "Zoop," he said, stroking Sam lightly, opening her up, his tongue following where his fingers led. "Zzzoooooooopppp," he murmured, the consonants reverberating in a most pleasant way, and then he stopped talking.

Sam leaned her head back against the fort, thanking God William had shaved his goatee and gripping his hair for dear life—this was why she never dated bald guys. Although her first professional writing job out of college had been the Penthouse Forum letters—*Dear Penthouse, I never thought it would happen to me!*—and she'd written about sex on boats, under waterfalls, and in treehouses, she'd never really enjoyed it outside. Nature was too distracting. But with William, that turned out not to be true. Sam remembered something an older and very famous writer had once said when they were both totally hammered in the ladies' room at a festival party: *Dearie, if you have a man who's good with his tongue, nothing else matters.* Sam found, as she writhed against the rough rock of the fort and scraped her skin against it and cried out again and again and still William kept doing what he was doing, his hands pinning her in place, that this was absolutely true.

The Rabbit

He takes her to a fort. A fort, for f*ck's sake. Why can't they just do something normal, like another restaurant or a beach? There must be plenty of nice flat sandy stretches around Portsmouth, NH. But noooooo. This is William we're talking about here. I suppose I shouldn't be surprised. This is a man who does polar bear plunges. And snowshoes and cross-country skis and does Ironman triathlons, or used to, for fun. Of course he's going to take Sam Vetiver to some abandoned rock pile hanging over an ocean, only inches between them and empty air, only empty air between them and the slippery jagged rocks below.

Which I happen to know are extremely dangerous because I am currently inching over them like a sea snail, the right side of my body squashed against the base of the fort. This is so much worse than the rocks along William's causeway, where the worst thing that could happen is falling into a cold lake. I am so not cut out for this kind of surveillance. Did I mention I am a bookseller? My exercise comes from unloading books onto shelves. Which is not nothing, but it's not this. For one thing, it's safely indoors, whereas here spume sprays up into my face, and seaweed washes over and between the rocks I'm navigating like dead women's hair, a reminder of what will happen should I lose my footing and fall. Thanks, Mother Nature. I needed that. Nor are my sneakers optimal for navigating slimy boulders at high tide—when I go to William's, I wear my Goodwill hiking boots, which have much better gription. I did not expect this athletic bullsh*t today. With each wave that crashes against the wall, with every placement of my feet, I close my eyes for a second and pray.

Physical hazards aside, it's also extra risky for me to be here because I was already spotted once today. I'm not exactly on game. If William did get photos of me at the Marriott and then he catches me here, that's grounds for harassment at least. I think. Which might carry stiffer penalties than stalking. So it was a little foolhardy to follow them in his car, to tail them through the parking lot. And then, when I realized William was taking Sam Vetiver to the fort over the ocean like he was acting out the I'm King of the World! scene in *Titanic*, to climb over these f*cking rocks so I can station myself beneath them and hear what they're saying and doing.

Which I can't, really. The crash and gurgle and suck of water prevents me from hearing anything but snatches of their conversation, drifting down to me. But it will have to be enough. I already screwed up once today, because I was sloppy. Now I have to be sure. What if Sam Vetiver is chasing William? What if the interest is only on her side? What if they just did some smooching in a café booth but he sees her mostly as a new literary pal and nothing more? Unlikely, but it could be the case.

I have to know. I have to ascertain whether it's reciprocal. Whether Sam Vetiver really is William's next love interest. The new chosen one.

I have to be 100 percent before I level up.

I flatten myself against the wall, feet wedged into a crack between rocks and palms uselessly pressing wet stone, and listen with all my might.

"—rabbit," I hear William say, and I cringe. Yes, I know he calls me this. Has he seen me? My foot, my shadow? For a terrible second I'm overcome with vertigo, and I fear I might pitch forward and fall into the sea.

Then I hear Sam Vetiver say something in an interrogatory tone, and the deeper timbre of William's voice as he answers. I hear him laughing and know I'm safe. For now. I force myself to look at the horizon and breathe through my mouth, the way you do when you're seasick.

"—ugly women," I hear as the wind carries his voice down, and I know he's still talking about me. I squeeze my eyes shut. "But you . . . Simone . . ."

Simone? Who the f*ck is Simone? Either they're discussing Nina Simone, the jazz singer, who is one of William's favorites, or it's Sam Vetiver's real name. I remind myself to check online. I can't afford more than $10 on www.moreinfo.net, but it gets you a decent amount of information.

Then I hear noises that are not ocean, or gulls crying, or anything other than unmistakably what they are. William is putting the moan in Simone. I don't know how he is managing to balance on that walkway while he's making that woman make those sounds, with his bad knee yet, but he's the athlete, not me. Well. At least now I know.

Now I'm sure.

Now there's zero doubt about the nature of their involvement.

Now I know what I have to do.

While they are occupied, I start to slip away. Either it's easier going back or I've gained some confidence from knowing William and Sam Vetiver are too busy to see me. Once I've climbed up to level ground, I peek around the corner of the fort and see exactly what he's doing to her. It doesn't look 100 percent safe for him to be kneeling on the ledge that way as she pushes herself into his face with her pants around her ankles, but it explains why I heard only her, not him.

On the way back to my car, although I've eaten only that half a granola bar today, I detour and throw up in a National Parks trash can.

CHAPTER 10

THE CO-DEP GROUP

S am's codependency support group was, like every other recovery meeting she'd been to, in a basement. This one was in a church, in a room they shared with a Sunday school, so the walls were covered with drawings of lambs, loaves and fishes, and Jesus. One December afternoon, they'd come in to find the invisible children had been extra busy: From the ceiling dangled dozens of tinfoil stars. It also meant the chairs were tiny, so the group members sat with their knees scrunched up by their chins or directly on the Noah's Ark—patterned carpet. KK, their sunny, septuagenarian group leader, said the tiny chairs were a reminder to be humble before one's Higher Power and also to laugh at oneself. Today, after another terrible day of writing, of procrastinating by trying to find the Rabbit on the internet and coming up blank, Sam needed both.

It was a small meeting, since it was six o'clock on a summer Friday: just KK, Sam, Drishti, Linda, and a newcomer who looked like Red-Haired Barbie, with such a tiny waist it seemed possible she'd had ribs removed. She frowned at the tiny chairs as if she were being punked.

"Is for midgets?" she said, in an accent Sam thought was Russian.

"No," said Sam, "they're for us. But you can sit on the floor, or there's a beanbag you can drag over."

The Russian's brow furrowed further over the word *beanbag*. "I take floor," she said, and folded herself gracefully down.

"Welcome, and let's get started," said KK. She passed the basket, and when it returned to her, she took the stopwatch out of it, the old-fashioned silver kind with a fob on top, and led them in the serenity prayer. *God, grant me the serenity to accept the things I cannot change, the courage to change the things I can, and the wisdom to know the difference.*

"I am told this is not religious group," the Russian whispered. "I do not believe."

"You don't have to," said Sam, and KK, overhearing, added, "Your Higher Power can be God, or Goddess, or Nature, or Source, or nothing— whatever you hold it to be."

The Russian didn't appear persuaded. Sam smiled at her. She remembered how it had felt to attend her first meeting, in the Berkshires; how the moment she'd opened her mouth to introduce herself, she'd started to sob from the sheer relief of being in a room full of people who all knew what she was going through, of not having to pretend everything was okay when it wasn't. How she'd known she was in the right place when a dozen hands reached toward her with tissues. There was no better place to have a meltdown than in a meeting of recovering codependents.

KK smiled around the circle. "I'll start. I'm KK, and I'm a codependent."

"Hi, KK," they all said obediently, except the Russian, who leaned toward Sam and said, "What is codependent?"

"It's someone who's focused more on other people and their problems than her own life."

"But hotline lady tells me this is meeting for women with drunk husbands."

"Yes and no," said Sam. "Many of us start coming because we live with addicts, but we stay to focus on ourselves."

The Russian sat back, mystified. Sam felt for her. She remembered, too, how skewed the equation had seemed when she'd gone to that first meeting, wanting to know what to do about Hank going completely off the rails, only to be told, *Nothing. You can't do anything about him. What about you? What are you going to do about your own life? What do you want?* Sam snapped, *What do you mean? How can I do anyfuckingthing about that while I'm living with this man? I don't care about my own life!* Then she'd put her hand over her mouth when she realized what she'd said.

"I'm really worried about my stepdaughter," KK was saying. "She was doing so well until she moved back in with her boyfriend, and now we're afraid she's using again. I'd love to go over there and beat the stuffing out of that little S.O.B., let me tell you. Anyway—"

"Why do you not do this," the Russian interrupted.

"No cross-talk," Linda said tiredly.

"She means no commenting on what other people are saying," Sam translated.

"But why not get daughter from boyfriend's house, have husband beat him up, teach him little lesson," suggested the Russian. "Then no more problem."

KK smiled beatifically. "It wouldn't change anything. She'd just go back for more."

"It would be enabling," Drishti added.

"What is that?" asked the Russian.

"It means doing for somebody else what she should do for herself," KK said. "We can't control persons, places, or things. Today I'm grateful for what I *can* control, for you girls, and for my rooftop herb garden. Thank you."

She handed the watch to Linda.

"I'm Linda," said Linda, "and today I'm batshit because my Sully's arraignment is tomorrow, and this judge is known to be extra harsh on dealing, and Sully's not a juvie anymore so he's probably gonna go up the river and I'm going out of my frigging mind. Thanks."

She handed the watch to Drishti.

"I'm Drishti," said Drishti, "yeah, that's my real name, it means the fixed spot you look at to keep yourself balanced during yoga. I'm a Sicilian from Charlestown, but in case you couldn't tell, my ma was a hippie. I'm good today, just maintaining, so I'll pass." She handed the stopwatch to Sam.

"I'm Sam," said Sam, "and I'm here today because I met a man . . ."

Despite the no cross-talk rule, KK winked, Linda genuflected, and Drishti smirked.

"Great job not talking, guys," said Sam. "Chef's kiss. Anyway, I met this amazing man—"

Drishti pretended to cough. "DICKMATIZED," she said into her cupped hands.

"*Hey*," Sam said, and elbowed her. Drishti raised her palms: Sorry, sorry.

"But even though a certain sponsor should be QUIET, she's not wrong," said Sam. "I do tend to get dickmatized. That means," she said to the Russian, "when you're in the early stages of a relationship, in the sex and love haze, and you can't see anything wrong."

The Russian nodded somberly. "I, too, have been dickmatized."

"Happens to the best of us," said Sam. "But I've always been ashamed of it, how easily I get tractor-beamed in by some guy and don't see red flags. Or I see them and overlook them. It's classic Unreliable Narrator."

This was the only literary term Sam had taught her group that stuck because it was so useful. It meant selective perception of one's own life. Of course, everyone was a U.N., because people could see things only from their own points of view. But in Sam's case, whole chapters had been blanked out, memories missing until somebody said, *Hey, remember that time when . . . ?* And then she did. It was the psyche's response to trauma, Sam knew. Mostly she was used to it; it was just a minor annoyance. But it also made her susceptible to bad decisions, which was why Drishti and the group were so helpful.

"I'm the girl in the movie who you'd be yelling at, *Don't open that door!* and I do it anyway," she finished. "So this time, I'm trying to be honest and accountable, open yet grounded. That's why I'm here. Thank you."

She handed the stopwatch to the Russian as KK silent-clapped and Drishti gave Sam the *I'm watching you* forked fingers. Sam gave it back. The Russian sat holding the stopwatch, thinking, then clicked the fob.

"Okay," she announced. "I am Svetlana, and I need to know how to keep focus on self while living with husband who I think is just nice man when we meet on internet but now is wet-brain alcoholic. He is crazy, even the doctor says this. For instance, last night he comes in the kitchen and he says, Svetlana, make me eggs, and he is so drunk and wearing only socks, like Christmas cartoon man, how do you call him, the Grinch. And I say, It is one in the a.m., I am getting warm milk, I am not making eggs, and he says, If you do not make eggs I will call government to deport you and also I will beat you, and I tell him, If you beat me, I will use this frying pan and make eggs with your alcoholic wet brain, and do you know what he does? His eyes roll up in his head and he passes out, BOOM! on the floor. I want to go to my sister, but she is telling me he is my husband and I should lie in my bed. Thank you. You are very nice women."

She handed the stopwatch to KK and looked at her expectantly.

"Well!" said KK after a pause. "Thank you, Svetlana. If you want to chat, I have some hotline and counselor numbers I can give you. Everyone else, good shares."

While they were laboriously getting up from the tiny seats, Drishti said to Sam, "Wanna grab a beer?"

"Sure," said Sam. One of her favorite things about group was the drinking afterward. The first time she'd attended this meeting, newly divorced and parched from years of abstinence around Hank, she'd asked, *Does anyone want to go get a cocktail?* There had been a terrible needle-scratch silence while Sam wondered if she'd committed the world's biggest faux pas—and then a dark-haired woman so weirdly gorgeous Sam couldn't believe she was an actual person as opposed to a movie star playing a nurse had said, *Hell yes, I do!* That was Drishti.

"You're buying, right?" said Sam.

"Hell no, sponsor never buys," said Drishti. "But I'll be a cheap date, since my ballgown's in the shop," and she gestured to her Crocs and scrubs.

"Favorite place?" said Sam.

"Yup," said Drishti. "LFG."

CHAPTER 11

THE WORLD ACCORDING TO DRISHTI

Their favorite place in summer months was the beer garden in the Esplanade, the greenway that ran the length of the Charles River. On a gorgeous August evening like this one, it was mobbed. Bostonians strolled, dog-walked, jogged, roller-bladed, skateboarded, and biked the paths. People picnicked on the grass, perched in the trees with takeout and beer, swayed in jewel-toned hammocks like caterpillars in cocoons. Sailboats swarmed the river, gondoliers glided along the canals, and a haze of pot and good nature hung over everything. The buildings of MIT and Harvard glittered gold across the water in the descending sun.

Sam and Drishti got beers from the truck and carried them to one of the docks. It was as covered with people as a hive with bees, but they found space at the very edge and sat dangling their feet over the water.

"Good job back there," Drishti said, toasting Sam.

"Thanks," said Sam, touching her red cup to Drishti's.

"I take it you're well and truly dickmatized."

"DRISHTI."

"C'mon, kid. Gimme the deets. I gotta live through you." Drishti had been engaged for almost ten years to a large, practically mute man named Franz. Once, when Sam had inquired about wedding plans, Drishti had said, *Don't fix what ain't broken.* Sam had not asked again.

"Spill," Drishti said, kicking Sam's ankle lightly.

"No way," Sam said, and smirked at the water.

"Oh boy. Never even fucking mind. You are SUPER-dickmatized. I can tell."

Sam smiled into her beer. Could you be dickmatized if you hadn't experienced the appendage in question? After the fort, where Sam had come so many times William literally had to hold her up, he'd simply gotten to his feet and led her back to his car. Was it a control thing? Was he one of those guys who had to give the woman fifteen orgasms before he had even one? Or could William, as Tabby had speculated, not get it up? Sam considered sharing this with Drishti, then decided not to. There were some things even a sponsor didn't need to know.

"No red flags?" said Drishti. "You going U.N. on me?"

"I don't think so," said Sam. "Except—William does have a stalker."

"Yeah," said Drishti, "you," and she laughed, her glossy dark curls bouncing.

"No, I mean besides me. This woman follows him everywhere. She sent me an email."

Drishti turned her mirrored sunglasses on Sam. "How did she get your email?"

"Everybody has my email. It's on my author website."

"Oh yeah," Drishti said. "What did it say?"

"It said stay away from William."

"Ooooooo, scary," Drishti said, and made a jerking-off gesture.

Sam laughed. "That's what I thought too."

"I guess that's a yellow flag. But didn't you have a stalker once? If you're a public figure, that's gonna happen. Just keep an eye out. And text me the code if you need to."

"LOL, I will," said Sam.

Drishti turned back to the water. "Here's what I want you to think about: What if there's nothing really wrong with this guy? Beyond, like, those crazy curling parrot toenails or irritable bowel or ED or something."

"Thanks, Drish."

"You're welcome. What I mean is, maybe he's just got the usual fucking annoying things all humans have, but nothing crazy. How will you handle that?" Drishti tipped her cup at Sam. "You've been through a war, kid. Your survival instinct's kicking in. But your PTSD overthinking is just as bad as not seeing danger signs. Did you ever think maybe this is just a good guy?"

Sam looked away, scrunching her face to keep from crying.

"You could just be happy," said Drishti. "For people like us, that can be the hardest thing to learn." She pushed Sam with her shoulder. "You want another beer?"

Sam nodded. Drishti stood and clopped off in her Crocs.

Sam took several deep breaths, watching the buildings across the water flame and waver like candles. It was so hard to believe in the happy ending—maybe because Sam wanted to so badly. More than anything in the world. She'd thought she'd found it with Hank; when they were first together, Sam had lain in bed next to him and said prayers of gratitude. For their paths having crossed, for finding the place she belonged. Then one afternoon she came home from the gym, grocery bags dangling from her hands, and smelled smoke, and she'd looked out the window over the kitchen sink to see something so wrong it took her a few moments to realize what it was: Hank, sitting in the baby pool in his Wayfarers and boxers with a fifth of vodka while their garage blazed with fire. *Come on in, girl,* he'd said, toasting Sam when she rushed outside. *The water's fine.*

Sam lifted the hem of her T-shirt and wiped her eyes. Maybe Drishti was right. Maybe Sam *was* paranoid. How could she assess anyone's behavior after what she'd been through? Maybe she just had to be open, and honest, and trust.

Drishti came back and handed Sam a beer. "Thanks, D. I owe you."

"Yeah you do."

They drank. "How's the book going?" Drishti said.

"It's not," said Sam, which was true. Every morning she sat dutifully at her desk, trying to produce *something*: a few wooden paragraphs of *The Gold Digger's Mistress*, blocks of scenes that were technically competent, the characters moving from one place to another, and completely lacking in motivation or heart. What was the point of this chapter again? she'd ask herself, once she'd backed out, and then: Oops. I forgot to put that in. "Because I don't *know*," she said to William in frustration, during one of their nightly calls. He was almost weirdly patient during these circular conversations, perhaps as behooved a man who ran a writer support group, offering over and over to hear her out on story arc, plot points. "I'm a good sounding board," he said. "Try me. I'm a giver." But Sam was still deeply hesitant to disclose specifics, and the book felt dead in the water.

"William says he'll help me with it," Sam said to Drishti now.

Drishti rolled her eyes. "Of course he will. But that's your side of the street. The book is YOUR responsibility. Keep him out of it. Figure your shit out for yourself."

"You're probably right," said Sam. "Thanks, D."

They drank, swinging their feet over the water. "Do you ever wonder why we are the way we are?" Sam asked.

"You mean hot and awesome?"

"I mean codependent. Why we chose the wrong men to begin with." Sam knew all the textbook reasons. Her mom, Jill, and the six husbands: modeling. Her dad, Ethan, the only parent actually interested in parenting, who'd died too young: grief. Sam's retired therapist, Stuart, a man she'd loved, had looked at her one day like a sweet bearded owl and said, *Isn't it sad when understanding can do so little*? And Sam had said, *Yes*.

Drishti shrugged. "We are how we are because it's how God made us, or our parents, or some dickhead flashed us on the T, who knows. It doesn't matter. What matters is deciding who we want to be, then being that thing. Every day."

Sam laughed. "That's it? The World According to Drishti?"

"That's it," said Drishti. "Don't say I never gave you anything."

"I'd never say that," said Sam.

Her phone started vibrating then, pushing itself around on the weathered boards. "Oh Jesus please us," Drishti groaned, "that's gotta be Mr. Dicktastic. Just go ahead. Answer it."

Sam smiled. "Sorry," she said. "One sec."

She flipped her phone over. But it wasn't William. It was a photo of herself and Drishti, sitting on the dock drinking their beer. Drishti in her scrubs. Sam in her red T-shirt. And a text from a blocked number:

YOUR NURSE FRIEND IS RIGHT, SIMONE. YOU'RE SUPER-D*CKMATIZED. STAY THE F*CK AWAY FROM WILLIAM CORWYN BEFORE IT'S TOO LATE.

The Rabbit

Well, that was satisfying. It was worth years of my life to watch Sam Vetiver jump up like her @$$ was on fire and swivel her head in all directions, trying to figure out who'd sent those texts. She looked like the girl from *The Exorcist*. I laughed so hard I had to bite my arm so she wouldn't hear me. I almost fell out of my cocoon.

She's gone now, though. She and her pretty, foul-mouthed nurse pal hightailed it out of here shortly after Sam Vetiver got my texts, and as they passed me I heard the friend say something like "cops FFS." Fine. Great. Let them go to the police. A message from a blocked number, showing a photo of two women. A text with a strongly worded suggestion but no threat of physical harm. A communication from nobody. That'll get them far. Meanwhile, Sam Vetiver will be out of her apartment for the next few hours—nonemergency law enforcement protocol rarely moves quickly—so I can go ahead with Step 2 of my evening's plan. Meanwhile, I lie here and giggle until I cry and my cocoon shakes.

Except it's not my cocoon. I feel somebody push me gently through the slippery thin fabric, and when I sit up, they are back: the two kids I rented this hammock from, giving them a ten-dollar bill an hour ago. Looking at me curiously. Young urban dwellers about the same age as the baby publicist who gave me Sam Vetiver's number, who I found on Sam Vetiver's publishing house website, the most junior person at Hercules, and called. *Hi, I* said, *I'm Cathy Auerbach from the* Boston Sun, *and I'm doing a Round-Up of the Summer's Hottest Authors, can I get Sam Vetiver's contact information, please?*, and she said *Hold on, her publicist's at lunch but let me put you through to her voicemail*, and I said what a shame because I had to file my story in an hour, I was on a hard deadline, and I'd hate to leave Sam Vetiver out, was she sure she couldn't just give me the phone number? I felt a little bad about it, manipulating youth, but really somebody should have trained her better. *Thanks*, I said once I had the number, *you've really helped me out.* Which was true.

These young people are peers of that baby publicist and also so alike they're interchangeable, students maybe, boy or girl or in between, I can't tell. They remind me in the nicest way of Thing 1 and Thing 2 from Dr. Seuss's *The Cat in the Hat*: They both have nice round faces with scatterings of acne they haven't grown out of yet, multiple piercings, identical choppy haircuts except one is dyed purple and one bright blue. They're wearing tiny shorts and shirts that expose lots of flesh in a way I never could have done as a kid, even if I'd wanted to. My mother would have locked me in the closet. For starters.

"Hi," they say, and the purple-haired one says, "We'd like our hammock back now please. We let you have an extra half hour actually."

"Sure," I say, and collect myself to roll out. Of course, since I'm not used to cocoons, I fall and land awkwardly on the ground, my whole left side now covered in goose poop. I wait for the sweet young Things to laugh, but instead they help me up, one on either side.

"You okay?" says the blue-haired Thing.

"Oh, yeah," I say, brushing at my butt. "Plenty of padding."

I wait for them to laugh at me. They smile uncertainly and exchange a look.

"Well, thanks again for letting me use your hammock," I say. "I loved it. It was so peaceful. Like being in a cocoon." As I'm walking away, I turn back. "Say," I add, as if the idea has just occurred to me, "you wouldn't want to *sell* it to me, would you? Because I love that cocoon." It enabled me to get so close to Sam Vetiver and yet stay hidden, observing in plain sight, and that could come in handy. Plus although it wouldn't be safe at rest stops, it would be much cheaper than motels and more comfortable than my front seat on rural overnight surveillance trips, for instance if William and Sam Vetiver went to a beach or mountain resort.

If Sam Vetiver hasn't wised up by then and moved the f*ck on.

The sweet young Things look at each other again. "You know, you can just order a hammock," the purple-haired one says. "Online."

"Yeah, they're like ten bucks," says the blue-haired one.

"Oh, really?" I say. "Thanks. That's good to know. I'll definitely invest in one. Well, have a nice evening now."

"You too," they say.

I feel them watching me as I walk away, and when I turn back, I expect them to be snickering. Instead, they both just wave. I do too.

As I head through the golden evening past people who are walking with their dogs and baby carriages and running and biking and throwing Frisbees and sitting with picnics and books, the first thing I do is open my burner phone and text a reminder to my regular phone to order a cocoon. In fact several of them, for my bookstore. We should carry them. Our customers will love reading in them. We could even offer a summer bundle.

The second thing I do is throw the burner phone in one of the lagoons. I feel bad about it, the nondegradable plastic lying at the bottom of this Boston waterway with broken bottles and condoms until the end of time. But there's sure as hell no way I'm going to let anyone find it, and this is the safest place. "Goodbye forever," I say as the phone arcs through the air, and a guy zipping past on a bike says, "You tell him, sister!" and dings his bell.

People are so nice here. As I leave the Esplanade for my car, which is parked at a very expensive meter, so I can get the gloves and tape I need for the next step of my plan, I think, Why? Is it that people have enough money and time in this city that they don't have to be constantly worried, that they can ride bikes or swing in hammocks? What if I'd been born here instead of Aegina, in the more accepting era of the sweet young Things? What if instead of my mother, I'd known people who were happy and kind? What if I'd been able to be a different person, and who would I be?

But that's the thing about the writer's favorite game, which I learned in my program with William: You can only play What If forward, not backward. In reverse, it's called regret.

And it's all pretend anyway.

I am who I am, and I know what I know. I'm on track now. There's no going back. I'm a little sad as I say goodbye to the pretty green waterfront park where people are so pleasant, goose poop notwithstanding. Sam Vetiver's apartment is only a few blocks away, according to the address I memorized. I didn't even need to ask the baby publicist for it, although she probably would have given it to me. It's amazing, the things you can learn at the Registry of Deeds.

CHAPTER 12

THE FUTURE PERFECT

S o this is your apartment," said William.

He and Sam were lying naked on the floor of Sam's library, Sam's head pillowed on William's chest. All around them their clothes lay where they'd been shucked, peeled, and ripped off in great haste, as if the people in them had exploded, then been raptured.

"I'm a little disappointed," William said. "I thought there'd be more books."

Sam laughed. William gently dislodged her and stood to prowl her shelves. Sam watched happily. He had a few days' worth of scruff now, glinting with silver and long enough to be soft. And she really enjoyed observing him stroll around naked. Aside from liking big guys, Sam didn't care much about the nude male form—she'd never oohed and aahed over six-pack abs or bulging pecs or tight ends in sport uniforms. To Sam, it was a man's mouth, the way he smelled, the intersection between his mind and sensuality that mattered. His attentiveness. His sense of naughtiness and play. She was thrilled to find that she and William were pitched in exactly the same key this way, more than anyone Sam had ever met, so she knew almost before she did it that if she touched him *this* way, he'd groan; *that* and he'd get a devilishly intent look that meant *Watch out, girl, I'm about to throw you down.* It was uncanny how well they fit.

William wasn't thirty; he had the usual scrapes and dings from the decades, maybe more because he'd used his body hard and well. Watermelon-pit scars around his right knee from surgery. A translucent circle the size of a peach pit on one hip, a toe banged permanently crooked. Scratches and bruises of indeterminate origin. He had a slight paunch that he hated and slapped with a scowl, and the hair on his chest was silver—but the erectile matter Tabby had mentioned and Sam had wondered about after the fort? A nonissue. William had popped a pill with dinner, and Sam had said, *All the better to ravish me with?* He'd looked confused, then smiled. *Oh, this isn't Viagra, honey, it's for my ticker. I take these for arrhythmia.* He'd slid his hand up Sam's thigh under the table. *I don't need pharmaceutical help to do this,* he'd said, thumbing her thong aside. *I can take care of you all on my own.*

"Impressive collection," William said now of Sam's books. He held out a hand to help Sam up. "Show me the rest of the place? And don't you dare put any clothes on."

Sam walked him through the apartment. "Kitchen. Bathroom. Sleeping loft, which maybe you'll see if you play your cards right—though so far you seem to be a man allergic to beds. And this is my study." She hugged herself, feeling almost more naked than she had when William had first hoisted her against her foyer wall and yanked up her skirt.

William explored this room, too, squinting without his glasses. "Nice ego shelf," he said of the display of Sam's first and foreign editions, the covers with women in red. "Pretty maids all in a row." He bent to peer at Ole Nielsen. "Is this your stubborn protagonist? Handsome." He straightened. "But where's the rest of it?"

"What do you mean?"

"It's immaculate in here," he said. "The walls should look like a crime scene breakdown. Please tell me you're the neatest writer who ever lived. Because otherwise you're more blocked than I thought."

"I'm completely blocked," Sam admitted.

"Oh, sugarplum." William pulled out her desk chair, sat, and patted his thigh. "Come."

Sam went, leaning into his reassuring solidity. William combed his fingers through the remains of Sam's braid, untangling the snarl their energetic lovemaking had made of her hair.

"I know you said you don't discuss your work in progress," he said, "but if there's one thing I've learned from the Darlings, it's that talking it through might help."

"I'm good, thanks."

"Are you, though? When's your delivery date?"

"Five months—no, four," Sam said, her stomach sinking.

"That's a minute from now. Please let me help you. What if we just brainstormed? Not about your current book. But other ideas. What if you think laterally: Do you have other books you might want to write?"

"I have *no* books I want to write," Sam said, and laughed. "That's the problem. I think I might be done."

William skimmed his fingers up Sam's obliques in a way that made her squirm and swat his hands. "I'm going to keep doing this until you take it back. You are not allowed to be done."

"Okay, fine. I'm not done. I'm just fucked."

"Yes, you are," he said, his voice dropping into the low growling register Sam was becoming familiar with and to which she had an instant, happy anatomical response. "And you will be again. Soon. Meanwhile, I'm serious. Do you have other concepts in the bullpen?"

Sam sighed. "Just wisps," she said. "But before Ole, I thought I might write about . . . a rumrunner. Dual timeline, the woman who runs a boardinghouse now and her great-grandmother. Both of them married to alcoholics. The great-grandmother's husband is the rumrunner . . ."

"Now *that*," said William, "is pure historical fiction gold. Why didn't you pitch it?"

Sam shrugged. "It didn't feel ready yet."

William drew Sam's detangled hair to one side, exposing her neck. "What if," he murmured against her nape, "you set Ole aside and we work on this rumrunner idea?"

"I can't," said Sam. "I'm under contract for *Gold Digger*."

"That's horseshit. It means nothing. They don't care what you hand in, as long as you hand in *something* that's the same genre."

"Is that true?" said Sam. "I've never done that before."

"It is true."

"Says the man who switches genres with every book."

"How do you think I get away with that?" William said. "I tell them I'm going to write one thing, and then I write another. Nobody has ever said boo." His hands began to rove. "I bet your editor won't even notice."

Sam thought this was untrue; Patricia would almost certainly remark on the fact that her gold miner had morphed into a rumrunner. But it wasn't a bad idea. "Are you sure?" she said. "It's kosher for me to just kill this darling?"

William had been tiptoeing his fingers between Sam's thighs, but now they stopped. "Do not use that malapropism around me, please. I loathe it."

"What?" said Sam, confused. "Kosher?"

"No. Kill your darlings. Did you know that most common piece of writing advice is also stolen? It was originally murder your darlings. Billy Faulkner appropriated it."

"I never heard that," said Sam. "Who said it first?"

"The fellow's name escapes me now," said William. "Which only proves how easy it is for one's literary legacy to be obliterated once somebody else purloins it. My greater point being, I hate a thief."

"Okay," said Sam, thinking, Now there's a trigger. "Noted."

William's hands recommenced their stealthy southward slide. "What if we work on this new book idea together? I'll help you. I'll be your writing Sherpa and sex toy."

"You're so generous," Sam said.

"I'm a giver," he agreed. "Let's give it a try, what do you have to lose?"

Matters progressed. The chair rolled dangerously beneath them. William stood and turned to set Sam on the desk, then dumped her suddenly on her feet.

"What is this?" he said, bending to retrieve a greeting card from the rug. The card featured Hemingway at his typewriter, above the caption: *I have learned a great deal from listening carefully. Most people never listen.* That was not what William was asking about. He held out the paper that had slid from the card, which said:

YOU'RE NOT LISTENING, SIMONE. WHAT DO I HAVE TO DO TO MAKE YOU LISTEN? STAY THE F*CK AWAY FROM WILLIAM CORWYN.

"Oh," said Sam. "That."

"Yes. This. What is this, Simone?"

"It's nothing," said Sam. "It was taped to my apartment door when I came home last week."

"It was *inside*?"

"No, no. The outer door. It's fine." Although the thought of the Rabbit waiting in the bushes outside Sam's building like a rat and then darting in behind some delivery person was not pleasing.

"It is in no way fine." William set the note on the desk and began to pace. "I hate that she's targeting you."

"So you think it's the Rabbit too."

"Likely."

Sam watched him stalk her study. "Then that's okay, right? Because you said she never does anything. Just leaves notes."

"She never does anything to *me*," said William. "Who knows what she's capable of with someone else."

He came to Sam and took her hands.

"There is one other possibility," he said. "I had . . . a complication a month or two ago. Not a relationship, although she seems to think it was. I thought we were just having some saucy fun. But when I broke it off, she was wildly angry." He sighed. "I'm not proud of myself. I crossed a boundary. She was from the Darlings."

"Oh, William," Sam groaned.

"I know." William rubbed his emerging beard. "It was a grave error in judgment. She's fragile, so I was gentle with her, and I thought ignoring her was the best course of action. But she's been contacting me, and I think I must talk to her again, more emphatically. I'm sorry if this hurts you to hear."

Sam blew out a ball of air. "It's not my favorite," she admitted. "But I get it. Life is messy."

"Thank you." William gazed down at her. "Meanwhile, Simone, maybe we should stop seeing each other for now. I'd rather mourn the loss of you than put you in harm's way for even a moment."

"*No*," Sam said, feeling the free fall of panic. She smacked William lightly on the bicep. "I refuse. Why should some poor deranged girl have the power to decide what we do? I can't believe I'm saying this, but— honestly, I can see this really being something serious, William."

William ran his thumb down Sam's cheek. "Same. It's perishingly rare, what we have."

"Yes," Sam said. "I'm in if you are."

"Have you told anyone about the threat? Reported it to the police?"

"Of course," said Sam. "I took it right down to the station. They can't do anything—as you know. But it's all on record."

William cinched his arms around Sam and propped his chin on her head. "At least," he said, his voice a rumble against her cheek, "if we're together, I can protect you."

Sam laced her fingers behind his back, grateful he couldn't see her face. When was the last time somebody had said this to her? Exactly never. She thought of visiting Hank in inpatient, the winter of his suicide attempt. The cubby in which she had to stow her phone, her jewelry, her boots because they had laces. How she had to be buzzed into the unit. How Hank's clothes had been replaced by mint-green scrubs and the smell of his skin by rubbing alcohol. How slow and slurred his speech had been. And how, when she drove home, the sun was low over the bare trees and she sat in her study by herself, paying bills and making dinner in the Crock-Pot because somebody had to. Maintaining.

"What if," said William into Sam's hair, "we *do* go the distance? Do you remember what I said to you at the fort, Simone?"

"Zoop?" said Sam.

William laughed and drew Sam down onto the rug.

"Yes, Zoop. But also that you're safe with me. Do you remember? Do you believe it?"

"I'm trying to," Sam said.

William knelt above her, swept Sam's legs apart with his knee, bent over.

"What if you come to my house in Maine?" he said. "What if you're naked all the time. Venus de Milo—ing around the grounds. What if you slept with me every night . . . and I brought you coffee every morning . . . and I made you a study where you could write? What if I were your in-house sounding board? What if you didn't have to do it alone? What if you were so happy and cared for and sated . . . you wrote that damned book in a month?"

What if. Every fiction writer's magic wand, the necessary plot-conjuring device. Could it survive the transition to real life? What if it did? What if indeed?

Sam moaned. William pulled out and flipped her over.

"Your back, Simone," he murmured in her ear. "Your shoulder blades are made for angel wings. What if . . . we're making the future perfect?"

The Rabbit

There's an old saying: You can tell a lot about a woman by spending time in her closet. Actually there isn't, I just made that up, but I can verify it's true. I know a lot more about Sam Vetiver than I did when I first got trapped in here an hour and a half ago.

I know Sam Vetiver has a f*ckton of red clothes, dresses and pantsuits and shirts, and at first I thought it was a weird fetish until I remembered that the women on her covers wear red so it must be a #DressLikeABook thing. Which I have to admit, grudgingly, is kind of a smart idea.

I know from the perfume clinging to these clothes what she smells like, chocolate and salt.

I know that most of what she wears is from discount stores, which is kind of a surprise.

I know that even though she might not be as rich as I thought she was, Sam Vetiver still lives in an apartment that looks like f*cking Hogwarts in a neighborhood so picturesque we sell postcards of it in my own store, even though we're over 150 miles away, for f*ck's sake.

I know that Sam Vetiver has never shopped for hair dye in the discount bin at the Dollar Store or used EBT/SNAP stamps for food while everyone else in the supermarket line watches with impatience or disgust or tolerant smiles; that she's never had to decide between rent or a car payment so her vehicle got repossessed and she had to walk to both her jobs in the sleet. That she's never slept in the kitchen with the gas stove on because her landlord has turned off the heat, and that she's had enough money to get her teeth fixed, so all her life people haven't popped up in her line of vision smacking their lips and saying *Meeeehhhhh, what's up, Doc?* and then dying laughing like it was the funniest, most original thing they'd ever heard.

I know if I had a dollar for every time I'd heard that, I could buy a place like this.

I know that even though rich people live here, this building was surprisingly easy to get into, that for all its ivy and architecture, they forgot the most important thing—oops! No doorman! Or security. The first time, last week after I saw Sam Vetiver and her pretty nurse friend on the Esplanade, I trotted right over here with my pizza box and my bandanna pulled over my face like a bike delivery girl who didn't want to get asphyxiated by exhaust and gloves on like a germophobe, and I rang all the doorbells, saying "Pizza for Number Three" until some crabby old guy said "Just leave it in the vestibule next time, it'll serve her right," and buzzed me in. Which only proves that money doesn't guarantee kindness, but I already knew that. What I didn't know was where Sam Vetiver kept her spare key, but I knew she had one, because that's one thing about us single girls: You always hide a key outside your apartment, because if you get locked out with nobody to let you in, you'll be sleeping outside. I finally found Sam Vetiver's taped to the inside of the building radiator outside her apartment, and I pocketed it and took out the note I'd printed at FedEx: YOU'RE NOT LISTENING, SIMONE. WHAT DO I HAVE TO DO TO MAKE YOU LISTEN? STAY THE F*CK AWAY FROM WILLIAM CORWYN, then stuck it to her door. I put it in a Hemingway card I permanently borrowed from my store, which I thought was a nice touch.

I know she got it, because it was gone the next day when I visited.

And I know she ignored it, because today I followed William to a waterfront seafood place here in Boston and watched him and Sam Vetiver being seated outside and knew I had a few hours to return to her apartment in my Bugs R Us exterminator suit, which is really just a coverall I got from the hardware store bargain bin and sewed a custom patch onto—you can get anything on Etsy—with my cover story ready just in case: that Sam Vetiver had hired me to spray for a cockroach infestation. No neighbor is going to question that.

But nobody was around, so I just let myself in.

And that is how I know how f*cking easy it is to get trapped in this closet, that a person could be just innocently planning a special surprise for Sam Vetiver and then get distracted by going through the refrigerator, way too much tofu but I finally found some mac and cheese way in the back, and maybe checking out some makeup, a little Sephora addiction going on there but the copper eye shadow was surprisingly flattering, and perhaps trying on Sam Vetiver's clothes, like the most elastic of the red shifts, which I got halfway on even though she's like a size negative 12. And I may or may not have been sitting in Sam Vetiver's desk chair grinding my teeth and thinking, How dare she. How dare she? How dare she, because she has the life I want, the only life I've ever wanted. Lanyards from every writing conference ever, signed first editions from all my heroes, photos of her with her arms around authors whose words saved my life. In *The Stand*, one of my favorite books, an inscription: *To Sam, Keep swinging for the fences. Love, Stephen King.* The photo on her desk of a man typing: When I turned it over, it said, *Dad, 1979.* Sam Vetiver was born to this life, has probably never questioned it for a second, has everything I ever dreamed of, and now she wants William too.

How dare she. Greedy little b*tch.

I may have been running my thumb over and over the Stephen King inscription when I heard the key in the front door and Sam Vetiver say "Honey, we're home," and the only thing to do was throw myself in the closet, and here I sit, wondering who the f*ck spends a f*cking evening indoors on a night like this, a beautiful evening when all Boston is outside?

Sam Vetiver, that's who.

And William. The greedy little b*tch had the audacity, after all my warnings, to bring him to her house. And a f*cking evening is exactly why.

Another thing I know: It's about ten thousand degrees in this closet. I know I can survive this. I've done it before. If anyone knows how to pass time in a closet, it's me. Thanks, Mom. But it's a pain in the @$$, and the first thing I'm going to do when I get out of here is pee like a f*cking racehorse in the back alley.

Which please God will be soon, let them go up to her sleeping loft, super comfy mattress BTW, and do the other thing people are supposed to do there, as opposed to in the living room where I can hear them now. Which is why I've been trapped in here for . . . I risk a look at my phone . . . 2.14 hours now.

Come *on*. I know William is f*cktastic, but the man is practically a sexagenarian! Which PS means sixtysomething, not marathon f*cking machine.

But no, I can hear them talking and laughing now, after the other noises I am all too familiar with from the fort, and William's house, and long ago. They must be done with the f*ckfest for the moment, because to my dismay I hear their voices coming into the study where the closet is. The door is open a crack and I don't dare shut it, so I see William's long flipper feet with the broken third left toe and Sam Vetiver's much smaller ones, her toe ring and nails like little pink shells, that woman is groomed for a new lover for sure. They stop right outside the closet.

"Nice ego shelf," I hear William say. "But where's the rest of it?"

As stealthily as I can, I push myself backward verrrry slowly until I'm pressed against the wall behind the clothes, inhaling dust and Sam Vetiver's perfume. Their voices are muffled, but when I strain I can just make out that they're discussing the book she's not writing and what she should do about it. "I'm completely blocked," I hear her say, and even through the fabric I can hear how sad she is.

Boo-hoo, poor you, I think, rich writer girl problems. But actually it is terrible to be a writer who's not writing. I should know. I wouldn't wish it on anyone. Not even Sam Vetiver.

Then I hear William offering to help, which of course he does, he's such a giver, and sure enough a few seconds later he says, "I'm a giver." I'm so f*cking sick of hearing him say this. I'm wondering whether she will take this bait when they start arguing about the card I taped to Sam Vetiver's door and the note inside it. "Maybe we should stop seeing each other," William suggests, and I think: Yes. *Yes.* Now's your chance, Sam Vetiver. Pull the cord. Jump. But stupid girl, she doesn't do it. Nobody here is surprised. He's sunk in her like a fishhook already.

They seal the deal with another f*ckfest—don't these people ever use a f*cking bed?—rhythmic slapping and sighing and moaning and William's voice, low and intimate and guiding her through it, the way he does, the way I can't forget and wake up mornings still feeling in my body, sometimes. He says something about her back and angel wings.

And then I can't. I just can't. I make myself into a little ball, as small as I can, hands over ears. I cry without making a sound. I'm good at that.

Can't I just give this up? What if I can't do this anymore? Because this is no way to live. Whatever I've done, I don't deserve this. Do I? It hurts. It hurts so much. What if I just walk away? What if I just stop this now and become somebody else?

But I can't. I made a promise a long time ago that I swore I would never break.

I also made a promise to myself, and although many promises have been broken to me, I will not break this one.

So I will wait. I'll wait until they're done with their selfish f*cking and get their filtered water and take it up to the sleeping loft to sleep naked in each other's arms and I will slink out of here like a cursed thing in a fairy tale and go back to my lair and make my plan. What I did with the last girl, what I'm doing with Sam Vetiver now, it's obviously not enough.

I'm keeping my promise. I can't give up now. I'm in for the duration.

I'll do whatever it takes.

CHAPTER 13

DO NOT PANIC!

From: Mireille Levenge

To: Sam Vetiver

Date: August 27

Time: 11:31 a.m.

Chère Sam,

I have been trying to reach you, but *quelle surprise*, you are screening! I hope this means you are working happily on *Gold Digger*. Let me know if I can help.

I spoke with your beloved editor Patricia this morning, and she asked again about pages. I'm sure you read in *PW* that Hercules, like other houses, has let go of some of its people, including authors. Do not panic! Patricia is not one of them. Nor are you. For now, your contract is intact.

Sam, I must stress what a good time this is to provide proof of your latest masterpiece, so Patricia can bring it to the Hercules team. Patricia believes in you 100 percent. She said she would contact you to set up a lunch, which, although I cannot tell you what to do, I would accept. And I would arrive with pages in hand.

As much as you are my Author Who Could, I am your Ride or Die Super-agent. Send me anything you have, and we will go over it, *d'accord*? Let us show Patricia, Hercules, and the world that you are producing another Sam Vetiver blockbuster.

Call *moi*! Any time, day or night. On my mobile if you have to.

Bisous, my favorite.

From: Mireille Levenge

To: Sam Vetiver

Date: August 29

Time: 12:14 p.m.

Chère Sam,

Again, *c'est moi*. I am sorry to be blowing up your phone and now your email. I wanted to be sure you got my last messages and that you are not curled in the fetal position. Please set an agent's mind at ease. Call.

From: Sam Vetiver

To: Mireille Levenge

Date: August 29

Time: 1:30 p.m.

Dearest Mireille,

I'm so sorry to have worried you. Yes, I got your messages, and although I am not curled in the fetal position, it did occur to me to go drink heavily under a bridge. I did not; I'm still at the desk. Of course I'll have lunch with Patricia, and I'll bring her the best pages I can.

Is there any way, just for the sake of argument, that I might present Patricia with an alternate idea? In case *GDM* continues to be stubborn? I know sometimes authors receive a contract for one book and then write another. Just a thought. Merely to explore options.

Love and gratitude,

Sam

From: Mireille Levenge
To: Sam Vetiver
Date: August 29
Time: 1:38 p.m.

Chère Sam,

Merci bien for confirming you received my messages. I am very glad you are not drunk beneath a bridge. May I suggest retail therapy, or at least a pedicure.

As for your question re: an alternate idea, I would say let us not even go there at this point. Sam, you are four months from delivery! And given the reorganization at Hercules, as at other publishers, it is not a good time for a roll of the dice.

That is my two cents. Of course I cannot tell you what to do, I am merely the agent. Call *moi* if you want to discuss.

Love,

Mireille

From: Sam Vetiver
To: Mireille Levenge
Date: August 29
Time: 1:45 p.m.

Dear Superagent,

I hear you loud and clear. Thank you for your candor and always having my best interests at heart. I've never defaulted on a deadline, and I won't start now. Back to work.

Love, Sam

From: Mireille Levenge
To: Sam Vetiver

Date: August 29

Time: 1:46 p.m.

    Bien. Send me whatever you have before you see Patricia.

From: Sam Vetiver

To: Mireille Levenge

Date: August 29

Time: 1:47 p.m.

    You are the best.

From: Mireille Levenge

To: Sam Vetiver

Date: August 29

Time: 1:48 p.m.

    Non, you are.

From: Sam Vetiver

To: Mireille Levenge

Date: August 29

Time: 1:48 p.m.

    No, you.

From: Mireille Levenge

To: Sam Vetiver

Date: August 29

Time: 1:49 p.m.

    Stop checking your email and get to work.

From: Patricia Miller

To: Sam Vetiver

Date: August 30

Time: 4:55 p.m.

Dear Sam,

Checking in to say I'm thinking of you. As you may know, I had lunch with Mireille. I wish we'd had better news with *Sodbuster*, but sales are soft for everyone except the heaviest hitters right now. I still think it's a hell of a book.

Meanwhile, we've got *Gold Digger* on deck. I'm sure you've heard Hercules, like every publisher, is tightening its belt. But I'm placing my bets on you. Let's make *Gold Digger* the next runaway bestseller. Do you have a sneak peek you could give me? I've got some schedule openings the first two weeks of September. How about a good old-fashioned editor-author hobnob? Come on down. Martinis on me.

Love,

Patricia XO

From: Sam Vetiver

To: Patricia Miller

Date: August 30

Time: 5:01 p.m.

Dearest Patricia,

Thank you so much for your lovely email. Yes, Mireille told me about your meeting. I too wish *Sodbuster* had done better, but onward! I'd seize any excuse to have lunch with you and gratefully accept. Thank you.

Love,

Sam XOXO

From: Patricia Miller

To: Sam Vetiver

Date: August 30

Time: 5:02 p.m.

Good, that's what I hoped you'd say. Let's get after it! I'll have my assistant send you some dates.

L, P

From: Sam Vetiver

To: Patricia Miller

Date: August 30

Time: 5:03 p.m.

Wonderful! Thank you so much, Patricia. You're the best.

XOXOX S.

From: Sam Vetiver

To: Sam Vetiver

Date: August 30

Time: 5:04 p.m.

Fuck. Fuck, fuck, fuck, fuck, FUCK. Fuck.

CHAPTER 14

A COCKTAIL OF NOVELISTS

I f a bunch of cardinals is called a radiance, turkey hens a harem, and crows a murder, then a roomful of novelists, Sam thought, should be called a cocktail. She made this observation every Wednesday night, when she stepped off the elderly elevator that stopped, disconcertingly, four inches above or below the top floor of an old building overlooking the Boston Common and heard her workshop all the way down the hall. They'd been put in the last classroom to minimize disturbance to the other writers, but it was futile. It wasn't the memoirists, poets, or the Writer Moms Mafia making all the noise. It was Sam's novelists.

She paused outside the door, smiling. From within came a kind of froth and roar: the writers shouting, laughing, bellowing past each other, and somebody—probably Cleo Whittyre—belting opera. These were Sam's people. She had been teaching this class since she'd gotten her MFA, and she'd never missed one. Not even when she'd been living in the Little House in the Berkshires with Hank; not when he was in jail or on benders or on the ward. Sam had made the six-hour round-trip drive because she knew how rare it was to find others who got it; who understood how important it was to sit in a room alone and download imaginary people and their stories; who believed in each other's characters and made them real. There had never been a time, no matter what else was happening, that Sam hadn't walked into her classroom and walked out again feeling better. When they were all gathered around the table, the power of faith was levitational, and Sam sometimes looked around and thought: This is what love is.

Sam went in and unpacked her laptop. Nobody paid the slightest bit of attention. The novelists went right on laughing, talking, shouting, singing. They were wearing skull-and-crossbones eye patches, and it took Sam a minute to realize why: The heroine of tonight's historical novel was a pirate. Sam's workshop took support to a new level.

"AVAST YE, NOVELISTS," she called, and toggled the light switch near the door. This got results, and the novelists began sifting down into their chairs.

"Hi boss," said Tabby, sliding an eye patch down the table to Sam. "I ordered them from the giant bookselling conglomerate that shall not be named."

"That was thoughtful," said Sam. She put on her eye patch. It stank of rubber and the elastic cut into her cheek. "Are these for children, by any chance?"

"Yep. Sorry. I couldn't find any adult ones."

"That's surprising," said Iowa Jones.

"Is it, though?" said Daisy.

"Sure! Think of all that pirate porn," said Iowa.

"And a new niche industry is born," said Cleo. She and Iowa high-fived. Sam was grateful Iowa and Cleo hadn't shown up in bawdy wench costumes.

"Where's Amelie?" Sam asked. Amelie was the author being work-shopped tonight.

"I was about to ask you that," said Tabby. "It's weird she'd be late to her own workshop."

"Maybe she's late *because* it's her workshop," suggested Joe.

"Har harrrrr," said Sam. She helped herself to some Pirate's Booty and parrot-shaped frosted cookies. Workshop was fattening. "Has anyone heard from her?"

The novelists checked their phones and laptops. Demurrals all around. Sam was surprised and a little concerned. She'd been late, partly because of sending William the pantsless selfie he'd requested as she left her apartment, which took thirty seconds to snap and five minutes to airbrush for cellulite, but mostly because, mindful of her stalker, Sam had taken a roundabout route. She knew that if the Rabbit or William's complication really wanted to get to Sam, they would, but she'd thought: You want to tail me? Fine, I'll make it hard for you. She left her building by the rear door, navigated her neighborhood through a network of alleys, snuck into the Ritz via the staff entrance, and popped out into the Public Garden, through which she zigzagged to class. If anyone was following her, Sam had given her a run for her money.

Workshop started at six, and it was now six thirty. The novelists were sometimes late because of traffic or parking, and once the guy being workshopped had shown up so inebriated that Sam had to escort him out. But never, in Sam's sixteen years teaching, had a writer missed class the night her novel was on the table.

"Let's give her a few more minutes," Sam said.

"I have an idea in the meantime," said Tabby. "Let's go around and vent, like I did at this amazing support group I went to that's run by . . . drumroll . . . our teacher's new beau!"

"Wait wait wait," said Jake. "Bow?"

"*Beau,*" said Lavinia, laughing. "As in love interest."

"Oh," said Jake. "I thought you meant bow as in crossbow."

"Or bow-tie pasta," said Chuck.

"None of you has any romantic soul," said Tabby.

"I do!" said Sunny, clasping her hands beneath her chin. "Who's the beau?"

"Yeah, who's the lucky man?" said Cooper.

"Oh my God, you guys," said Sam.

"Wait for it," said Tabby. She cupped her hands around her mouth and stage-whispered, "WILLIAM. CORWYN."

Daisy squinted. "Isn't he that uber-bestselling dude who writes as a woman?"

"You're dating a cross-dresser?" said Joe to Sam.

"Noooo," said Lavinia. "His *protagonists* are women." She turned her laptop to the room, the screen showing William's Wikipedia page.

"Ohhhhhhh, that guy," said Daisy. "Yeah, I've heard of him."

"Me too," said Sunny. "Isn't he pretty famous?"

"This is not a good use of our workshop time, people," Sam said.

"Hair, acceptable, check," said Iowa. "Teeth, check. Stern yet pensive expression, check."

"Bro has like 14K reviews on Goodreads for his latest book!" said Jake, eyes popping. "And it just came out this month!"

"And some not very nice ones," said Cooper. "*I hate the way this guy writes—did he swallow a dictionary? One star.*"

"*I didn't actually read this book,*" read Daisy, "*but I don't think I'd like it. One star.*"

"*My copy arrived damaged!*" read Birdy, laughing. "Oh, buddy. One star!"

"But thousands of good ones," said Jake. "And *The New Yorker* calls him The Virtuoso."

"Oh *my*," said Sunny, fanning herself.

"Virtuoso, play my heartstrings!"

"Virtuoso, tickle my ivories!"

"*Arrrr*, that's for piano."

"Oh yeah."

"You are all beyond help," said Sam, as the novelists continued their William roast. "I'm going to step out and call Amelie. Stalk amongst yourselves."

In the hallway she permitted herself a snicker and pulled out her phone. There was a text from the man himself: THANKS FOR THE DELECTABLE PHOTO, SUGARPLUM. YOU KNOW WHAT'S MISSING? MY HANDPRINT, RIGHT ON YOUR—Sam swiped this away before she could get distracted. Nothing from Amelie. Sam looked up Amelie's number—unlike the rest of her novelists, who'd worked together for years, Amelie was a recent addition to class. All Sam knew was that Amelie was mid-forties-ish, quiet, with tattoo sleeves and black hair so shiny it looked oiled, and that her historical pirate series had been published by a small press before it went under. Her goal was to bring her buccaneer to the Big Five, and Sam thought it was possible. Amelie had talent.

Amelie's phone went straight to voicemail. Sam scrolled quickly through Amelie's social to see if she'd taken an ill-timed road trip. Amelie's profile photo showed her wearing a leather bustier and clenching a cutlass between her teeth at something called PirateCon. "Whoa," said Sam. Apparently shy Amelie had a whole different life outside of class. But the conference had been a year ago, and Amelie's last post, about a romance panel, was a month old. Sam went back into the classroom.

The novelists had tired of William and were now playing that ever-popular game, The Top Ten Things Writers Least Like to Hear at Parties. *What's your book about? . . . Have you written anything I might have read? . . . Are you any good? . . . Can I buy your book in stores? . . . Can you actually make a living as a writer? . . . I always wanted to write a novel, but I never found time . . . Maybe you could write my novel for me! . . . I have a book for you to write!* Sam smiled around at the bright, beloved faces. If they only knew! What would they say, her people, if they knew how paralyzed Sam was, that even after over twenty years of being in this business, her position was so precarious? Not just because of the industry but because of her own doubt. Although Sam of course had not mentioned it to Mireille or Patricia, *The Gold Digger's Mistress* felt pretty much DOA. William's idea—or rather Sam's upcycled concept, the historical novel about the rumrunner—that might have legs. Sam wasn't sure. She'd started kicking the idea around with William, on FaceTime and on the phone, test-driving the ideas while he listened attentively. *What if it's near the Great Lakes, so the rumrunner is importing moonshine from Canada? What if it were set during Prohibition?* It was productive, and yet Sam still felt uncomfortable, as if she were wearing ill-fitting clothes. She just wasn't sure what she was going to do, which novel she would bring to Patricia at their New York meeting, and that meant she might be on the verge of torpedoing her career.

"What's up, boss?" said Jake, and Sam realized the room had gone quiet.

"Just checking again to see if I'd heard from Amelie."

"Anything?" said Chuck, and Sam shook her head.

"I hope nothing *bad* happened to her," Birdy said with vigor. "Should we go check?"

"I will if I haven't heard from her by tomorrow," said Sam. "Meanwhile, it's almost eight, so why don't we adjourn to the Park Plaza and do some readings?"

"Thank God," said Jake, ripping off his eye patch. "This thing was squeezing my head."

He stopped by Sam's chair as the novelists were packing up. "Hey, boss, you sure you're okay?" he asked quietly. He regarded her keenly from beneath the brim of his baseball cap. "You seem a little . . . something. New love?"

Sam smiled. "Just a lot going on."

"Listen," said Jake. "I know you're a grown-ass woman and big-time author and all, but know this: If that Corwyn dude's a player, I got you. We all got you."

"Thanks, bro."

Jake squeezed Sam's shoulder and headed for the door. "See you at the bar," he called.

"You mean the barrrrrr," said Iowa, and they all filed out.

CHAPTER 15

AT AMELIE'S

B ut it wasn't until the following week that Sam went to check on Amelie. She had, quite honestly, forgotten. After Amelie's no-show, Sam had sent an email: HEY, AMELIE! WE MISSED YOU IN WORKSHOP. PLEASE GET IN TOUCH TO RESCHEDULE—AND LET ME KNOW EVERYTHING'S OKAY. Then Sam had gone back to writing *The Rumrunner*, or rather writing *about* that new novel, and exploring it further with William—including a meeting on the Cape before one of his events at which they admittedly did more body-surfing and naked frolicking in the dunes than talking about the book. Which was fine with Sam, since she still had an unsettled feeling about it and couldn't tell exactly why. Was it the fact that she was cheating on her contract, sneaking around with the rumrunner when she was supposed to be with the gold miner? Was it that the idea was too connected to Hank's alcoholism, and she hadn't gotten the requisite distance to write about it? Was it that Sam wasn't used to collaboration, or that William was, ever so charmingly and with the best of intentions, pushing her? Sam wasn't sure, so it was a relief to turn from her own screen to this week's manuscript for class—whereupon, as soon as she settled into her chair with her pen, she thought: Amelie. Fuck!

Now Sam was in the vestibule of her missing novelist's building in Fort Point Channel, a harborside neighborhood as different from Sam's historic district as it was possible to be. The Point was all industrial warehouses converted to, initially, artists' lofts; Sam had come to grad school raves here where the only light was old films flickering on the walls and everyone was on X. Then the area was gentrified, the creatives forced into the exurbs. Amelie had to be doing pretty well at her graphic designer day job if she could afford to live here.

Sam buzzed Amelie once, twice, not really expecting a response and not getting one. If Amelie wasn't returning texts or emails, why would she come to the door? There was a management company listed, so Sam tried them next.

"I've been trying to reach my sister for a week," she said to the gruff-sounding man who answered, "but she's not picking up, and I'm worried. Is there any way you could let me in?"

"Sorry," the man said. "Can't. Security."

"Not even if you come in with me?"

"No can do."

"Please?" Sam persisted. "I think it's an emergency."

This time the man's voice sounded softer. "Look, if you really think she's in trouble, call for a wellness check. You know what that is?"

Sam wanted to smack herself on the forehead like a cartoon character. Of course she knew what a wellness check was. She'd used them for Hank—twice. On the second occasion, the emergency crew had reached him just in time.

"I'll do that," she said. "Thanks."

"Good luck, hon," the man said.

Sam called 911 and was routed to the appropriate line. Did she think her friend might be in mortal danger? Yes. Were there drugs involved? Maybe. Mental illness? Ditto. The dispatcher said they'd send somebody ASAP.

Sam stepped outside to wait. The vestibule was a sweatbox, the streets not much better. It was Labor Day weekend, and the sun was an angry orange ball, the sidewalk Sam was standing on literally steaming. The air smelled of garbage and brine. Yet Sam's arms prickled in goose bumps as she realized how alone she was in this maze of old buildings.

Was the Rabbit watching Sam right now? Or maybe it was William's complication: William had ruled her out; he'd spoken with her, he said, and been quite firm, and he felt very strongly that she would not bother Sam. Sam wasn't so sure. Women in love could be deceptive. And dangerous.

Whoever the stalker was, she could be anywhere: in that doorway, behind that dumpster. Sam hadn't received any more emails or notes, but she had an ominous feeling that it wasn't because the woman had given up, it was that she was re-strategizing, recharging and planning a next-level offensive. All it would take was one good bonk on the head and a push, for instance, for Sam to disappear forever into the dark water of Boston Harbor.

She was relieved when a delivery guy arrived on a Vespa with a sack of chicken so she could slip behind him into the air-conditioned building. Ha ha, who's the Rabbit now? thought Sam. Amelie's elevator was an industrial cage à la *Fatal Attraction*—one of Sam's favorite movies as a teen, which probably explained a lot. She didn't trust the contraption now, so she took the metal staircase, which shook and clanged disturbingly, to the top floor.

Amelie's door was bright purple. Sam knocked without much hope. "Amelie," she called, "it's Sam from class. Are you there?" She disliked the way the words bounced around the stairwell and echoed: . . . *am* . . . *ass* . . . *err* . . .

No answer from within. On a lower floor, though, there was a *clank clank clank!*, as if somebody were hitting a pipe with a hammer . . . or coming up the stairs. Sam rubbed her arms and looked around for a weapon, an umbrella, a rolled-up newspaper. There was nothing.

"Jesus, girl, get a grip," she muttered. Then there was a BANG!, and something flew at Sam's face. She wheeled around, fists up in her old boxing stance. But it was only the shadow and noise of the elevator coming to life.

The cage rose into view, containing two Boston police officers, one carrying a pry bar. "Ms. Vetiver?" said the other, whose name tag read HAYES. "You call for a wellness check?"

Sam said she had and showed her ID. Officer Hayes banged on Amelie's door. "Ms. Stutz," he called, "Boston PD. Open up, please." He did it again with the same result. Meanwhile, his partner took to the stairs, and Sam heard him knocking on neighbors' doors. He returned, shaking his head.

"Ms. Vetiver," said Officer Hayes, "you believe Ms. Stutz is in mortal danger?"

Sam prayed Amelie was not just away on vacation, and if she was, that she would forgive Sam for what was about to happen. "Yes," she said.

"Stand back, please," said Officer Hayes.

The other cop rammed the bar just above Amelie's doorknob. The noise was terrific, and Sam covered her ears. The door popped open, releasing a flood of brilliant light into the hallway, along with the smell of incense and something meatier, like dead mouse.

"Give us a few," said Officer Hayes. "We'll look around, let you know what we find."

Sam paced the hallway to the chicken-wired window at the end, which overlooked an air shaft. More shadows stirred above: pigeons, waddling over the skylight. Sam knew she should reach out to Drishti or William; the time you least wanted to ask for support was the time you most should. But she didn't. She had a very bad feeling.

She thought of her hand on the doorknob. In the motel. How it had smelled of smoke and wet metal even outside the door, in the hallway. The ruined rug.

The elevator banged and descended, and this time when it came up there were two EMTs in it, with a gurney. Sam covered her mouth. "Oh my God," she said.

Officer Hayes came out of Amelie's apartment, removing his cap. "Ms. Vetiver," he said, "I'm very sorry to have to tell you, Ms. Stutz is deceased."

Oh, Amelie, thought Sam. I'm so sorry. "Was it—how did she—"

"We'll do a more thorough investigation, but we found several empty bottles of prescription medication. It seems pretty conclusive Ms. Stutz took her own life."

Sam nodded. She bent and put her head between her legs.

"Can I get you some water?" said Officer Hayes.

"Yes please," said Sam faintly.

She concentrated on her five senses, a behavioral therapy trick Hank had taught her. Static of police radios, squeak of EMT Crocs and gurney wheels. Taste of blood. Smell of sandalwood and dead mouse. Sam should have known. Should have come sooner. She knew Drishti and her group and Hank and even his group would say there was nothing Sam could have done, but Sam didn't buy that. She never had. What if she'd persisted, called Amelie again, asked her what was wrong, why she had missed class, could Sam do anything? Did Amelie want company, another heartbeat in the house? Sam knew what it was like to live alone. What if she had just come to sit quietly on the couch so Amelie knew somebody was there? Instead Sam had been at the fucking beach with William. Literally, the fucking beach. They'd probably been banging their brains out while Amelie was pouring that final glass of water or wine. Whatever anyone said, Sam had been through this before. She should have known. She should have come.

Can you hear me? Open the door!

You'll have to pay for that carpet, you know.

Ghost voices from another room, a place that was never really very far away.

The EMTs emerged wheeling the gurney, which had a shape on it zipped into a gray bag. "Oh my God," Sam moaned. She reached out as if to touch Amelie but did not. I'm so sorry, Amelie, Sam thought. And, as the cage carried Amelie down: Why? Why did you do it?

Officer Hayes brought Sam a glass of water, which she drank gratefully, her stomach hitching at the iron taste. "Was there any evidence of foul play?" she asked. She sounded ridiculous to herself, like she was on some true crime show.

"None."

"Did she leave a note?"

"Not that we saw. You're welcome to take a look around if you don't disturb anything."

"No, that's okay," Sam said, and stepped over the threshold anyway.

The first thing that struck her was the reason for all that light: two walls of windows overlooking Boston Harbor and the skyline. Tugs, the Tea Party schooner, boats of all kinds swooping back and forth: No wonder Amelie wrote about pirates, Sam thought inanely. Amelie's small-press book jackets, blown up to poster size, lined the walls: pirate queens wielding swords, standing on prows, kissing half-dressed men in ripped pantaloons. Oh, Amelie, Sam thought again. Why?

She walked around gingerly, scanning surfaces for a note. Refrigerator, coffee table, Amelie's desk—an enormous teak thing piled with ledgers and a cutlass letter opener: nothing. Nor were there any photos of people. No family, no PirateCon pals, not even a parrot. Had Amelie succumbed to killing loneliness? Was that why she had done it?

Because the loft was an open floor plan, Sam didn't realize she was in the bedroom until she came upon the bed, a wooden four-poster with a canopy like sails and a long dark stain down the center of the duvet. Sam backed away—she knew what that meant. The dead mouse smell was stronger here too. The officers had collected the prescription bottles, but nothing else was disturbed. Sam tipped her head to read the book titles on the bedside table. *Moby-Dick; The Wreck of the Whaleship Essex; The Bell Jar*; the poems of Emily Dickinson. Had Amelie had depression? *What Billy Styron called* Darkness Visible, Sam heard William say.

"Ms. Vetiver," Officer Hayes called, "we're about to lock up."

"Of course. Is it all right if I use the bathroom?" Sam realized only as she asked how badly she had to go.

"Sure. Just don't touch anything."

In the bathroom, the only room with a door on it, Sam tried not to look at the pink and purple bras on the shower rod, the mini-skyline of toiletries on the counter. An octopus-sized fern stretched fronds toward a skylight, and Sam felt so heavy with sorrow she could barely breathe.

Who would take care of the plant? Her dad, Ethan, had died when Sam was six, so she was familiar with death but not with its apparatus. Would Sam have to sign anything, do anything? But she had already done nothing. Now it was too late.

Something buzzed on the counter, making Sam jump: Amelie's phone, in its bedazzled skull-and-crossbones case, pushing itself around amid the cosmetics as if it wanted Sam's attention. Sam watched it. It would be wrong to pick it up. Invasive. Probably illegal. Instead Sam reached over and poked it with one finger, flipping it as if it were a rock that might have something nasty underneath. The screen was deeply cracked, as if Amelie had stepped on or thrown it, and on it, beneath a text inviting Amelie to receive $5 off her next noodle bowl, was a stack of messages from somebody Amelie had named MR. DELICIOUS POISON.

Huh, thought Sam. Maybe it hadn't been mental instability or loneliness but heartbreak. Had Amelie been grieving Mr. Delicious Poison? Was that why she had done it? Sam picked up the phone by the edges and carried it out to Officer Hayes, who was standing patiently in the kitchen with a roll of yellow DO NOT CROSS police tape.

"Sorry, I touched this," Sam said. "I thought you might need it."

"Just put it over there," said Officer Hayes, nodding toward the counter.

Sam thanked him and left the apartment, kissing her fingers and pressing them to where a mezuzah would have lived, had Amelie been Jewish, for protection.

This time Sam used the elevator, and as she cranked the gate closed and hit the black button for the ground floor, she felt so weighted with sadness, in that familiar and despairing way, that she could not move. She descended, the skylight receding above her. Why? Why had Amelie done it? Sam had been told over and over that if somebody really wanted to take her own life, there was nothing anyone could do—that person was the captain of her own soul, and that responsibility belonged to her alone. Still. If Sam had reached out. If she had brought Amelie to group or William's Darlings. Would that have made a difference?

And . . . what if it hadn't been Amelie's choice? Sam was quite sure this wasn't true. The officers were right about the cause of death. This was an old game Sam was playing with herself because it was easier than the reality. But . . . what if Amelie hadn't been alone at the end? What if somebody had been with her? What if someone had been sitting on her big wooden bed, nodding kindly and training the gun on Amelie as she took the pills?

Suddenly Sam knew, as surely as if lightning had struck her from the skylight. The human part of her felt terrible about it; the writer nodded and said: *Yes.* Sam might never know why Amelie had done it, but as the iron cage carried her down through the heart of the building, she knew exactly what to write. Sometimes a novel was a question that in life had no easy answer. It was not what Sam had expected to write; it was neither the rumrunner nor the gold miner; it was a pivot, a complete departure, the greatest literary risk possible. But: The dead writer had just given Sam her next book.

The Rabbit

I know why she died.

The Darling Factor

A THRILLER BY SAM VETIVER

Book proposal

New York Times bestselling author of *The Sharecropper's Daughter* and *The Sodbuster's Wife* Sam Vetiver takes an exciting new direction in *The Darling Factor*, a thriller that investigates the dark undercurrents of writing fiction—and how literary ambition can turn deadly.

Spanning three decades and multiple settings, from the exclusive ivy-covered writers' workshop at Triton College to the publishing skyscrapers of Manhattan to tract housing on the wrong side of the tracks, *The Darling Factor* follows a group of writers from their graduate school days to the top of the bestseller lists. The Darlings, as the young writers call themselves when they first meet, are tight-knit, competitive, and haunted early by tragedy; halfway through their second year, one of them, a promising prizewinner named Piper, disappears. The Darlings believe it's suicide—or do they? Piper's best friend in the program, Cassie Quentin, is never quite sure. She investigates Piper's death while they are all still at Triton but can turn up no evidence, so she puts the death on her emotional back burner while navigating her career as a contemporary novelist. But when her former graduate school cohort starts dying one by one, Cassie returns to Triton to find out once and for all the answer to the question: Was Piper indeed the first victim? Or is someone else the killer—and why?

Showcasing the psychological deftness and depth of understanding that hallmarks her historical fiction, Sam Vetiver contributes a new layer of insight into the artistic psyche—and how some creatives might do anything, including kill, to keep their own careers alive.

PART II

William

CHAPTER 16

AT THE CONFERENCE

I'm at a conference when my new paramour calls. Or rather, I am on my bed naked in the hotel room and she sends me a FaceTime request. I am marginally annoyed, as I was busy. But I sign out of the website I was in and take the call.

"Hello, jellybean," I say. "Where are you?"

A superfluous question, as it is immediately evident Simone is on the Acela. The seat behind her, the triple chime as the train approaches a new stop, the sun and shadows playing over her pretty face as the movement propels her forward. Toward New York. Toward our publisher, although today Simone is not going to Hercules House but to the Southampton Authors' Luncheon in Long Island, where she is tomorrow's speaker, a sort of vestigial post-tour event. We're such a literary power couple. A new experience for me. The reception is sporadic: Simone freezes, unfreezes. Freezes, unfreezes. By my estimation, this means she is somewhere in Connecticut. I have made that trip many times. With my battered brown briefcase on the seat next to me, containing my next bestseller. Whether it's the satchel or its contents, I have been unbelievably lucky thus far. It has never failed.

"I'm somewhere in Connecticut," Simone says, pixelating and unpixelating.

"I thought as much," I say. Again I try to quash my irritation. Why would she wait to call me until this part of the journey, when the reception is spotty? How inconsiderate. Simone might have called me from Massachusetts. Or better, from her hotel in the Hamptons—although I might not be available to answer then. Regardless, somewhere where she is stable.

"Would you like to see where I am?" I ask, and pan the camera down over my body. I am nude as the day I was born, and my previous activity, the one Simone interrupted, has left me half turgid. My penis rests against my left thigh, still engorged, slightly purple.

"Holy God," Simone says, fanning herself. "That's so unfair."

"Quid pro quo," I say.

"I'm on a *train*, William."

"Just the girls then?"

Simone hunches forward and furtively lifts her blouse so I can see her breasts, attractively packaged in a black bra. I am not much of a tit man, I must confess. I prefer asses. Something I can smack with my hand. And if I were left to gravitate to my own tastes, which unfortunately I can't always do, I would choose very slender women. Who knows why—some crush on a little gymnast on the back of a cereal box when I was a child, perhaps, some girl buried in the sands of time. Whatever the reason, I like them taut and tight, muscle and bone, no cleavage to speak of so their nipples protrude like pebbles on a flat expanse, growing when I tug on them.

Simone has more flesh on her than I'd prefer. Admittedly, she is most men's ideal, small but rounded, with the 36-24-36 curves *Playboy* trained us to love. I have to admit she is prettily made. I can work with it. I have many times before. And our chemistry, I was relieved and astonished to discover, is startlingly electric, perhaps the best I've ever known. Imagine my surprise: There I was, steeling myself to go through the movements, and instead in her mouth, in her hands, in her hottest tightest wettest space, I found nirvana. It's as though I'd gone through my whole life having a mild distaste for chocolate and suddenly could eat nothing else.

"There you are," I say, smiling at Simone's breasts before she lets her shirt drop. "Hello, ladies." I keep my camera pointed down so she can see me stroke myself.

"William, stop," she says. "This is cataclysmically unfair."

"I will on one condition," I say, not stopping. "Tonight, when you're in your hotel room, after you've eaten your room service cheeseburger and removed your red dress and Spanx, when you're getting ready for bed, I want you to stand for a few minutes naked. Touch yourself. Wherever you please—your choice. Imagine it's me. Then take a photo and send it to me."

"Deal," she says. The color has risen in her cheeks. "Even better, do you want me to FaceTime you?"

"There's nothing I'd like more, but I'll likely be tied up," I say. This is true. "You know how these things are. The real work isn't done at the podium but at the parties."

"True. How's the conference so far?"

"Fine," I say. "Typical. I'm being hit on every thirty seconds." I laugh. This is also true. Our profession is not known for being full of hetero men, or at least not virile ones with hair, teeth, and a sturdy erection. The odds are in my favor.

Simone does not laugh, although she offers a pained smile. "I hope you tell all those hos you're spoken for," she says, and I can hear her straining to say it lightly.

"I tell them my lover is a literary powerhouse with the body of an odalisque," I say, and now she does laugh, and then I see her recalculating as she realizes I didn't answer her question. *Wait a second* is practically emblazoned on her forehead.

"I've got to jump soon, sugarpants," I say. "I'm on a panel about defining genre in fiction."

"Of course you are, Virtuoso," she says. "Though don't you mean *defying* genre in fiction?"

"I like what the word *Virtuoso* makes your mouth do," I say. Simone has wickedly pillowy lips, especially the lower one. I feel myself harden again. "And I suppose I'm on the panel to provide the exception to the rule."

"Because you are exceptional."

"As are you, honeybun." I am growing impatient with all this cooing. "How's our favorite rumrunner? Are you getting work done on the train? My favorite place to write—no interruptions." Unless you're procrastinating by calling a hardworking man at a conference, I do not add.

"He's fine," says Simone, and I'm disturbed to see a secretive expression flit over her face. My current beloved is a pretty one, with her strawberry-blond hair and green eyes and spray of freckles, rather like a pornographic Nancy Drew. She also wears her thoughts on her face, which is handy for me. I do not care for the looks of this one.

"The rumrunner's still drunk," she adds, trying to play it off. I do not smile.

"How's the outline going? Last we spoke, you were breaking the historical section into chapters?"

"It's a little balky," she admits. "Lots of question marks where the scenes should be. Especially in the murky middle."

"I'm looking forward to getting back and helping," I say. "Ever your obedient Muse."

"Same," she says, as I carry the phone into the bathroom and prop it up on a stack of towels. "I miss—" She dissolves and reassembles.

"What's that?" I say. "You're breaking up."

Simone garbles something, freezing with her mouth open. What I wouldn't do to be able to stick my erection through the screen. "Don't forget your promise," I say on the off chance she can hear me, "the naked photo, and also I'll expect that outline by the time we're both back. Wait'll you see what I've planned for your reward." I bend tenderly toward the screen. "Adorations," I say, blowing her a kiss.

"Can't hear—" she says, and then she is gone.

I shower and shave, trying not to dwell on that shadow I saw pass over Simone's face—an expression that looked, for all her womanly face paint, like a little girl caught doing something wrong. Or trying to hide it. But perhaps I am being too suspicious. It has happened before. Simone may be beavering obediently away on our idea even now, as I dry off and pat my bespoke cologne on my face, my chest, my balls. The throes of a new idea is always an uncertain place. Our historical blockbuster is gelling in that bright mind of hers; she just needs a helping hand. Which I will happily provide when we next meet. I'm a giver that way.

Meanwhile, I have other contributions to make here at this literary conference. I dress in my post–Labor Day tour clothes—blue button-down Oxford, khakis, suit jacket, tie; I cannot abide my fellow male writers who present themselves for literary events in burrito-stained T-shirts. Such disrespect for the readers. But I fibbed to Simone. I already had my panel today. The event this evening is a cocktail party, and as I descend in the elevator to the hotel lobby, I can already feel it, the tingle that accompanies a hunt. This is nothing serious, of course, just a little sportfucking. Merely a maneuver to keep limber. But I feel great satisfaction when I spot my quarry before I even reach the revolving door at the hotel entrance. It makes everything so easy.

She is at the bar, a pallid young woman with long, unbound sandy hair, in an ill-fitting navy dress she probably hopes looks sophisticated, poor dear, and a name tag that proclaims her to be part of the conference. There she is, my evening project. I will help her with her confidence by tending to her, by making her feel she's the most beautiful creature in the world. What woman would not want that? She'll be walking differently tomorrow because of me.

I stroll to the bar to stand next to her, take out my phone, swipe away a text from Simone, shake my head sadly, and turn to the young woman, who is eyeing me. AVA HALLAM, DEBUT AUTHOR, her name tag says. I incline toward her as I almost always have to, as I am tall and she is petite. She has dark freckles that I know form constellations beneath her clothes, and I look forward to making alternate patterns on her skin.

"Hello," I say. "You're here for the writing conference as well? I have no signal in here. Can you remind me where the cocktail party is, please?"

CHAPTER 17

MILLE-FEUILLE

The next time I see Simone is at the White Lion Inn, in the Berkshires. She is not a guest of the inn; she is ensconced at Woodstock Hill, a nearby writers' retreat where our publisher is now putting her up so she can make progress on her novel. God bless Simone's editor. Although Simone is, thanks to me, now working on *The Rumrunner* instead of *The Gold Digger's Mistress*, she's so flighty and easily susceptible to distraction in the city where she lives, her teaching and her so-called codependents' support group and what have you. Literary lockdown for her is imperative.

I know Woodstock Hill, a charming white farm of the colonial era, repurposed for the housing, feeding, and coddling of writers trying to jump-start, revise, or complete projects. I myself once spent a very productive few weeks there—which is why I can't return now to rendezvous with Simone. The rules mandate monklike silence throughout the day, no socializing until evening, and there are always a handful of writers tempted to violate the sanctuary with fraternization, a walk or conversation on the grounds, or activities of a more boisterous and salacious kind behind closed doors. Again, I know. I have partaken. I cannot repeat my past indiscretions, and my presence there, especially as I am between projects, would be disruptive.

Therefore I have rented us a prohibitively expensive room at this eighteenth-century inn, with its deep front porch and line of Adirondack rockers surveying the mountains, its historic staircase with alarmingly narrow risers and its creaking slanted floors. The wallpaper is toile, the air museum-musty, the laboring AC unit—certainly not a fixture in George Washington's time—failing to dispel humidity. There is a replica antique bed whose four posts I intend to put to good use. Ours is a top-floor suite for which I paid extra so my sweet can make all the noise I can make her make, and before the door even closes behind us I am upon her, lifting her shirt, stripping her pants, undoing her bra with one hand, an ambidextrous talent of mine, even as I'm biting her nipple through the lace. It has been a week since we last saw each other.

Once our initial thirst has been slaked, we stroll around the grounds exchanging catch-up conversation: My tour travels—with some salient details omitted; her room at the retreat—which has no bedposts, sadly, but does feature a gas fireplace—and the other writers she knows there. One of them, Simone says, arrived with her own mattress, kombucha brewer, and meditation instructor, and has mandated that a retreat employee visit a local farm every morning to fetch fresh goat milk. We both know who this woman is. I laugh at Simone's impression of her—"Are you sure this milk is fresh? Was it *squeezed from the goat this morning?*" Unlike some of the other women I've been involved with, Simone is really very funny. It's not a requisite, but it is refreshing.

We eat dinner by candlelight in the inn's restaurant, with its stone fireplace and original floorboards, pretending to be like all the other genteel, genial couples dining there, although my hand is busy under the table the entire time. Simone is as wet as a fountain, whether from earlier or now. This is another characteristic of hers I appreciate; it makes my situation so much more pleasant. When we're done with dinner, I suggest we sit on the rockers and watch the moon rise; I want her to read whatever progress she's made on *The Rumrunner*, but Simone is ready to go back upstairs. This is another thing about Simone that I have not found in another woman: Her sexual appetite matches mine. And she has no shame about it. It's astonishing, really.

A man doesn't want to be rude, so I follow her back to our chamber, contemplating the black lace thong she is wearing beneath her demure sundress and feeling myself hardening again, which proves two things: (1) I continue to be a not-very-imaginative, typical heterosexual adult male, easily titillated by straps and lace—a cheap sexual date, if you will; and (2) the pill I took this afternoon is still in effect. God bless pharmaceuticals.

By the time we are done, the moon has risen above the mountains and is peering through the nearest window. We are parched and both drink a bottle of the water the inn has provided. I check my watch; it has been eight hours since I last took my medication, so I fetch the prescription bottle from my satchel and take a pill. Just to be on the safe side. Simone watches from her pillow, naked now, as God intended.

"That's for your heart, right?" she says.

"Yes." I get back in bed, and she nestles next to me, her head on my chest.

"Do you mind if I ask . . . what the condition is, exactly?"

I put my other arm behind my head. I'm feeling expansive. I am genuinely fond of Simone, and there's no harm in her knowing. It's a pretty moment, actually, our bodies sated and happy, the ceiling glowing blue.

"When I was a boy, I had a fever," I say. "Rheumatic fever. It sounds like something from a children's book, doesn't it?"

I feel Simone nod. "Like *Heidi*," she says, "or *Little House on the Prairie*. But that was scarlet fever. I don't know rheumatic fever."

"It's a form of strep," I say, "or rather it's a reaction to the bacteria that causes strep. Other children get it and just have sore throats. I contracted it, maybe on the playground, and . . ."

. . . and for a moment I am in my boyhood bedroom, which unlike this one was dark as a cave and to which the door was always locked. I remember the pain in my throat, and trying and failing to call for help, so it was not until the following morning that my sister, Penelope, Pen, unlocked my door and found me unconscious on the floor with a 106-degree temperature.

I relay all this to Simone. "It took my father—he was a surgeon—a few tries to diagnose what it was," I continue. "At first he suspected tonsils, so they came out." At home, I do not add. "When I didn't improve, he treated me for strep. By that time the bacterium had infected my heart, and I was in bed for a year."

I feel Simone's head shift on my chest as she looks at me. "I'm so sorry, William. That's horrible."

"It was," I agree. "I was in bed like an old man. An invalid. I used to try to get out, but if I was caught, I was punished. So I stayed in bed until my father pronounced me well, and my sister, Pen, brought me books from the library. She sat with me and read to me, *Tom Sawyer, Robinson Crusoe*, all the Narnia and Oz books—have you read the whole series? They are hair-raising. And imaginative. And it was then that..."

I stop. Simone looks up at me again.

"Then that what?"

"I started to write," I say. "I wrote my first story. It was about, predictably, a sick little boy whose imagination took him everywhere, and it was published in the local paper. Pen submitted it to a contest for me. That's how I got the writing bug, via the bug that causes strep. So that little schoolyard bastard who gave it to me really did me a favor."

Some of this may actually be true. How much, I don't know. My life until I reached college is shrouded in a kind of mist, from which only certain memories emerge like deadly promontories. I recall the pain of my throat, monstrous and searing. My father did remove my tonsils. I was always locked in my room at night, purportedly to cure me of sleepwalking. The rest is a fiction.

My heart is fine. There was no playground; Pen and I were homeschooled. I was not the natural writer in the family; Pen was. Nor did she bring me anything from the town's public library, as my tale implies; we were not allowed off the mountain to visit it, although my father had a den from which Pen habitually and at her own peril snuck books. And I did eventually and secretly mail a submission to the town newspaper, and then to a popular children's magazine, and things grew from there.

It used to trouble me, my cloaked past and the necessity of invention, but now I think it's like writing novels. Realities get layered atop each other in a mille-feuille of experience, and often I find myself wondering: Did that really happen, or did I write it? And: What does it matter?

Simone is quiet for a few seconds longer, then sits up. Her face is serious in the moonglow, her unplaited hair a curtain. During the times I'm not with her, I have begun finding strands of it everywhere, on my clothes, in my car, like some magical traveling cobweb.

"Thank you for telling me," she says. "That's horrendous. I'm so sorry that happened to you. Although I'm not sorry you became a writer. The world has greatly benefited from that. But . . . your heart now? It's still affected?"

"Negligibly," I say. "The walls are thinner than they should be, that's all. Sometimes I have some defibrillation. Don't worry, Simone," I add, because her face is now a tragedy mask. "It's not going to kill me. Unless you fuck me to death."

She doesn't laugh. Her mouth wrenches to one side, and she looks away. "It's not funny."

I reach up and thumb away a tear that is tracking alongside her nose. "A poor joke. Apologies, sweetheart. I didn't mean to upset you."

"I just can't lose any more people I love," she says. "So keep taking your medicine, okay?"

"Yes'm," I say. "I promise." This statement is certainly true.

She slaps my chest lightly as if I've disagreed, then lies down again. I pull her in closer.

"How about you," I say, "when did you become a writer?"

"I've always been a writer," she says. "My dad was a writer. My very first memory is of sitting under his desk while he wrote. I felt so safe."

"And what is it he wrote? Anything I might have read?"

"No, he wrote for children's TV." She names the show, a broadcast populated by puppets, so iconic that even I, sans offspring, am aware of it. "Every so often they'd need a kid for a segment and I'd get hauled into the studio for the day." She laughs. "It was amazing, now that I think about it, but at the time it was just strange. The greasy pancake makeup, and the costume changes, and the hot lights. They were the first ones to put my hair in a side braid, and it became my *lewk*. And to see my dad there, in a skyscraper in New York, was surreal. I was so proud of him."

"I'm sure he's more proud of you."

"He would be," Simone agrees. "But he died when I was six. He was going to a broadcasters' convention in Chicago, but he never made it. Car crash on the way to LaGuardia. My mom never admitted it, but I know it was intentional. I saw the death certificate, and I remember looking up *suicide* in Webster's."

Ah, there's the rub, I think. All of my women have something sad about them—as who doesn't, but they have some special thorn of pain they carry in their core, no matter how bright their smiles. I don't know why I'm drawn to damaged birds, but I have accepted it's my DNA. Concealed by her brave red clothes and authorial bravado, this must be Simone's wound.

"I'm sorry, Simone," I say. "Do you want to tell me more about it?"

"Not really," she says. "But thank you."

She sounds dreamy, which means it is the perfect time to ask the question I have been waiting to introduce all night. "Then tell me, how is it going with our pal the rumrunner?"

There is a pause, and I wonder if Simone has fallen asleep and whether I should joggle my shoulder to rouse her when she says, "Actually, I've been working on something a little different."

I feel a dash of alarm. "What do you mean?" I ask.

That is when Simone tells me—I can barely believe it!—that although our publisher is generously footing the bill for the Canyon Ranch for writers so she can produce an historical novel, and although I have contributed my own time, energy, and creative largesse by coaching Simone *at length* about our rumrunner's story—hours upon hours listening to her develop that idea; saying *Mmmhmmm* and *Home run!* and *Now you're cooking* as she babbles on about dual storylines; nodding attentively as she breaks the one-page synopsis into parts and chapters; holding an expression of deep focus as she says *But what if? But what if? But what if?* . . . despite all of this, Simone is disobediently, stubbornly, willfully writing *something else.* Something she has been keeping from me, despite my having sacrificed my own firepower to develop *our* historical novel about the rumrunner.

Now, with the temerity to actually look proud of herself, Simone opens her phone to read to me the proposal for the atrocity she is contemplating writing, a *familiar* atrocity entitled *The Darling Factor.* Which features a graduate program like mine, with a cohort like mine, with a woman who commits suicide as my original darling, my fiancée, Becky, did . . . Except in Simone's perverse, twisted, *derivative* "thriller," it's possible the woman did not take her own life but was murdered.

"This may go nowhere," Simone adds. "And I'm sorry about the rumrunner—it's a great concept, and I might return to him for the next book. But—and I was kind of afraid to tell you this—for whatever reason, I didn't feel quite right about it. Maybe it's too close, or not baked yet, or—I was supposed to be doing something different. And then, after my poor novelist Amelie committed suicide, this came to me like a thunderbolt. You know how that is. So rare. I've started working on it, and for the first time in a long time I actually feel plugged in. So . . . that's what I'm doing this week at the retreat. Walking out over the abyss. Ta-da!" She flourishes her arms, then sets her phone on the nightstand and snuggles back into my armpit. "William? Are you asleep?"

I am not asleep.

"We have a problem, Simone," I say.

"What?"

"Appropriation."

"*What?*"

I shift my shoulder from beneath Simone, so her head thumps onto her own pillow. She heard me. She knows what it means. Everyone in publishing knows what appropriation means. It's our industry's hottest buzzword—and greatest fear. Once upon a time, it was considered perfectly, well, appropriate to write about somebody else's life, another person's experience. We called that act of imaginative empathy *fiction*. Now, however, an author has to be very careful that he—especially if he is a he, and especially if he is a white he of a certain age—does not trespass on another writer's story. If he attempts to picture life, anecdotes, moments, from outside his own culture or gender, it can choke the oxygen from the writer who is rightfully entitled to it from birth, from having lived those experiences.

It's true that we white male writers have enjoyed the home court advantage in the literary world, for several centuries, in fact. I acknowledge the importance—the necessity—of making space for others to tell their stories. I've also thought the concept of appropriation was complete horseshit: If we wrote only what happened to us, wouldn't that be autobiography? What would happen to fiction? What about the noble attempt to get out of one's skin and into another, attempting to understand what it's like to be human from another person's point of view, gender, ethnicity? And thereby building understanding and commonality among us? Why else would I write from the female point of view but to show my great love for women? About appropriation, if it wouldn't end my career, I would have said: *Bah humbug.*

Until now. When it is happening to me.

"You know precisely what I mean," I say to Simone. "We've discussed literary thievery. I will not allow you to appropriate my life for fiction."

"William! What are you talking about!"

But that furtive tone is back in her voice.

"My fiancée? Her suicide? At my graduate program? *The* Darling *Factor*? Are you clueless or just malevolent? This is a thousand times worse than Billy Faulkner taking careless credit for a writing adage. You are *deliberately* repurposing my personal tragedy for your novel."

Simone sits up. She switches on the lamp and peers at me. "William.

You can't be serious."

"Serious as a lawsuit, Simone."

"*What?*"

"You heard me."

"You're really going there? I don't appreciate being threatened."

I sit up too. "It's not a threat. It's a promise." I get out of bed and start to dress.

"Where are you going?" she asks.

"For a walk," I say.

"It's two thirty in the morning."

"I need some air. There's less danger to me out there than there is in here."

"What is *that* supposed to mean?" She has the audacity to sound exasperated.

"Out there, there may be stalkers. Or bears. In here I'm trapped with a vampire."

"William!" Simone laughs and shakes her head. "What are you even *talking* about?" she says again. "Stop. Please, stop a minute and look at me. Do you think you're the only writer who ever went to grad school? I have my master's, too, you know. Or that you're the only person who ever lost somebody to suicide? In my college, it was so common that they offered a four-point-oh GPA to the surviving roommate, to compensate for the trauma!"

"We are not talking about apocryphal, *fictitious* people, Simone," I say. "We are talking about your stealing my *personal* pain."

"It's not just your pain. It's mine too. I just lost a novelist from my workshop. Did you forget that? I went to the Hamptons straight from her memorial!"

I don't bother answering this. Of course I remember that sad lost-soul writer. The world is full of these women. What does Simone think I have been trying to do my whole life, via the Darlings and such? All I do is help. I step into my shoes.

"Oh my God. *William*. Wait. Please." Simone gets up and walks toward me, unabashed or unaware that she's naked, and again I admire her despite myself. Despite her effrontery. Who does she think she is? She puts a hand on my arm, and I look down at it.

"I'm sorry if I triggered you," she says. "I didn't mean to. I know you suffered a terrible loss. But I have to write what I have to write, you know? It's the number one rule of writing. You have to be free to write about what's most important to you."

"No, Simone," I say, "the number one rule of writing is to write what you know. This is *mine*. My territory." I bend toward her, raise my eyebrows for emphasis. "I *hate* a thief."

I remove her hand with my own, very deliberately, as if I'm unbuckling a seat belt, and place it back at her side.

"I am going for a walk," I announce. "When I come back, I'm going to sleep. You have kept me up late enough as it is, and lest you forget, I am still on tour. We can discuss this further or never revisit it again, as you wish. But know this, Simone: As fond as I am of you—and until tonight I had *extremely* high hopes for us—if you write this book, our story ends here."

"William," she says. She's shaking her head. There are tears in her eyes. "That's not fair."

"You are hardly qualified to speak of fairness in this moment, Simone," I say. "Think about it while I'm gone. Sleep on it. Let me know your decision in the morning."

She squares her chin. The flush has risen on her face, her breastbone, hiding her freckles like a rising storm front obscures stars.

"I'm a writer," she says. Her voice is wobbling, but I can't tell whether it is passion or fear. "So are you. I'd expect you to be more understanding."

"I'd expect you to have more character," I say.

I open the door. "I was just about to tender an invitation," I say. "To my island in Maine, after my tour. I had a plan. I *calendarized* it. I wanted to let you into my home, writing sanctuary, my private life. But I can't be with a woman I can't trust. Think it over, Simone. It's your choice. You decide."

I leave and stand outside the door. I hear nothing. Simone is not cry-ing. I am annoyed. These tactics would have worked with the others. Not with Simone. Damn her. How could I have been mistaken? All this investment, wasted. But it is possible I am overreacting, especially af-ter the shock of hearing her plot. Perhaps by morning, Simone will have seen the error of her ways. I walk down the stairs and out into the night, as I said I would do; Simone, like the others, will come to understand that I always mean what I say.

CHAPTER 18

ON THE LAKE

'm in a kayak in the middle of a lake near the inn when the texts start coming in. I can hear them rattling my phone in the dry bag the innkeepers thoughtfully provided with the boat. God forbid we should be without our devices in this age of documenting as we live, perchance to make others jealous. For me, the phone is also marketing; I'm sure my readers would appreciate a shot or two of where I am now, the red kayak on the blue water of this lake, in a bowl of mountains, surrounded by pine trees so crisp they could be used as a scratch-and-sniff. The white clouds, the late-September sunshine. And, bonus, a selfie of my shirtless chest, glistening and seal-slick postswim. **intermission**, my caption would read, with my characteristic e. e. cummings brevity and lowercase punctuation, or **wish you were here**. Responses would come pouring in: **I wish I were there, too! . . . WTG taking some down time! . . . when are you coming to MY bookstore? . . . nice pecs lolz! . . . #inspiring #smokeshow #faveauthor**. If they could see I am completely naked, as I believe in being as much as possible, it might break the literary internet. **sun's out, buns out!** It's unlikely my publisher has numbers correlating what Simone once referred to as "writer man meat" with book sales, but I have no doubt the connection exists.

Alas for my readers, I have the phone with me for a different reason today, and that is Simone herself. I am waiting to see if she expresses adequate contrition. I am not yet sure what she would have to do to weasel back into my good graces, but she sure as hell had better start trying. I stayed away from our room until 5:30 a.m., when the bird orchestra was tuning up outside. Simone was asleep when I let myself in, or more likely pretending to be. She was deft at it. She breathed with little snorts and sighs while I stood watching her. Cogitating. Weighing things.

She "woke" quickly, however, when I got back into bed with her, and she slipped a warm hand into my briefs, which I had kept on to signal my displeasure. I let her fondle me for a few moments before I deliberately moved to my own side of the bed. I then slept; I am blessed by being able to slumber in any circumstance. I don't know whether Simone did or not. When I woke, I didn't say a word but instead slid under the covers and lapped her with my tongue until her yells became yelps became yips—tending to Simone is often like being in an X-rated Dr. Seuss book—then got up, showered alone, dressed, and extended my arm. I walked her to the inn's dining room, where we had breakfast, croissants and jam. We strolled around the grounds, and I praised the chest-high wildflowers, the preponderance of bees in the designated pollinator areas.

I could feel Simone watching me, her small but powerful mental engine churning as she tried to deduce, from my behavior, what to say. Whether to apologize; whether to further defend or explain herself— which would have been a grave mistake; whether my prebreakfast meal of her meant I had forgiven her; what would happen next. When I accompanied her to her car to return her to her retreat, she ventured, *Are we okay?* I leaned in through her window and kissed her. *That's up to you*, I said. I tapped on the roof of her car to send her on her way.

Now her texts, for of course they are from her, indicate significant distress.

Hi, William. 🖐 Well, it must be Mercury retrograde or something, because in addition to our disagreement, when I got back to the retreat, my room

had been broken into. Everything was tossed and my laptop was missing—
which makes unfortunate sense because it was the only thing of value.

I could be grateful, because thanks to my being with you, my wallet and
phone weren't in the room, but of course if I'd been there, the break-in
wouldn't have happened.

I feel like the past 24 hours are a terrible dream I'd like to wake up from.
I can't tell which upsets me more, honestly, the theft or our argument. It's
probably a toss-up. Can we talk, please?

I bob gently in the kayak as I read these messages. I could point out the irony of Simone being burgled after she so wantonly proposed stealing my life story. This might constitute, in her mildly woo-woo view, karmic redress. Instead, I type:

Esclknfakre70379rujklscnklaefih;;;

. . . and erase it without sending, so she'll see the three dots rippling, then ceasing.

I put the phone in the dry bag and paddle to another part of the lake, an inlet next to a large rock with sheltering pines growing from it. It's amazing that in my afternoon here, there have been no speedboats or Jet Skis to blast top country hits or kick up disturbing wake. Perhaps because it's a September weekday, the kids back in school, but still, a minor miracle.

The dry bag is silent. I can practically feel Simone quivering as she tries not to check her phone. I take mine out again.

Hi Simone.

I'm sorry to hear about the break-in. That must upset your equilibrium
considerably. From what I recall of my time at the retreat, the owners
are very conscientious. I hope they're able to assist you in locating your

laptop. Have you/they called the police? Is it insured? I assume you've backed up your files.

I assume no such thing. In fact, I've verified the opposite is true. So many writers don't save their work. Superstition, or a fear of making something seem like business when they believe it's a magical act. I myself back up religiously, but not to any drive that might be stolen; instead, I email myself my work via a password-protected account under a pseudonym. Simone, however, is one of the careless ones. There were no thumb or zip drives in her apartment, and she's superstitious. When I asked her about it, she told me she never shows her work until a first draft is done—*past the point of miscarriage,* she said. She works within one document and several handwritten journals. She doesn't back up.

The response dots are rippling; of course they are. Before her next message can come through, I write:

I don't know what Mercury retrograde is or what it might have to do with anything, but as far as we are concerned, I meant what I said this morning. And last night. Assuming you were actively listening and not merely attempting to defend an indefensible position.

Simone, I'm embarrassed to admit how much I've already planned our life together. I have pictured you on the small island I call home, wandering the shoreline in the morning with a mug of coffee I have made for you in your hand. I have pictured us stargazing on my dock, holding you on my lap beneath the Milky Way. I have thought about where we could set up shop in my house, where I could offer you a space that provides both a view and privacy. Of course, I have imagined us in our bed.

The three dots have disappeared. I can feel Simone scanning my messages, collating them through that quick brain of hers. Holding her breath.

I have permitted myself to wonder if you are the partner I have searched for my whole life. Now, since you confessed the topic of your new novel, those dreams are dashed.

Not only have you used me, my time, creative passion, and yes, my love, to develop a project you discarded like yesterday's lettuce—I am speaking, of course, of our rumrunner—you have shown the greatest insensitivity about Becky. Did you even know her name? Becky Bowman, my first Darling. Did you ever ask me about her? A single question? You did not because to me she was a person, is a person, whereas to you she is a character, a pawn to be moved around the fictional board as it suits you.

Now the dots are rippling. Again, I am too swift for her.

You will no doubt protest that it's fiction. That your characters bear no resemblance to the people I lived with and treasured. I sincerely doubt it. Even the title, as I mentioned last night, is a dead giveaway of your plagiarizing my past.

After this essay, I take a quick plunge into the refreshing water of the lake to give her a chance to assemble her *mea culpa*.

Oh, William. I'm so sorry. I didn't mean to be disrespectful to you or Becky, and no, I did not know her name. First, I'm happy to change the title. You're right, it's way too on the nose. I'm lousy with titles, and I just grabbed it because—I guess it was in my mind after I visited your support group. My bad. It's gone. My editor would likely have changed it anyway, even if you didn't have a problem with it.

And second, at the risk of further upsetting you, the novel IS fiction. You know how this goes, too: something sparks inspiration, and then the rest of the project takes off from there, in a new direction. This has nothing to do with your life.

I shake off water, comb my hair back with my fingers, and type:

**You're mistaken, Simone. I do not agree. I am a person, not your "spark."
I don't exist merely to light your fire.**

**But there is still a slim chance. I am in your hands. We are. The future
perfect. All our gorgeous potential. Should you choose to kill this new
project for the historical novel you were working on—and in which I
had considerable creative equity, by the way—there's room for another
conversation.**

I set the phone in the bag and lean back, closing my eyes. The sun has
dipped toward the horizon and I can feel the mineral chill wafting off
the big rock as I float half in light, half in shadow. The sun on my legs is
warm. I hear a loon call and another answer.

The dry bag rattles. I listen to the loons for some time, and perhaps
doze off, for when I open my eyes I have drifted back onto open water. I
yawn, finish my electrolyte drink, and flick open my screen.

*I hear you, William. Likewise, you're very important to me, and I'm
processing all of this. Are you still at the inn? I can skip the author dinner
here tonight. Can you come to the retreat? Or shall I come there? Any
challenging conversation is better had in person, and I would rather have
this one with my foot on yours, or holding your hand.*

She's right, of course, under normal circumstances. These are not
normal circumstances.

I rapidly peck back:

**Honey, my schedule is not flexible. You know what it's like on tour. I'm
right in the middle of something.**

I don't feel it necessary to mention it's the middle of a lake.

I can't get away right now. Why do you think I didn't answer you sooner? When I don't respond, it's because I'm engaged in something crucial.

The three dots. Pause. The three dots again.

Okay. Understood. And yes, I know what it's like on tour. I have a few days left here, so as rattled as I am, I think I'm going to stay and work longhand. I need to give a statement to the police anyway, and with your permission I'm going to mention the Rabbit.

I mark this with a thumbs-up and wait, floating.

If you change your mind, if you get a break in the schedule, I'll be here. If not, let's please coordinate a meeting, okay? I'd really like to see you and talk this through. I've fallen for you, William. I hope it's not too much to say that. I have great hopes for us too. And again, I'm sorry.

One of the loons pops up right in front of the kayak and regards me with his red devil eye before disappearing again.

I hear your apology, Simone. Let's see if you actually back it up with action. If you make the right decision about your book, you know how to find me. Otherwise, I'll be in touch when—and if—I'm ready. I require some space to nurse my sore heart. XO

The three dots, then Simone sends xoxox. A minute later, 🖤.

I don't respond. Nor do I put the phone back in the dry bag. I set it in my naked lap, squinting into the sinking sun and letting small waves carry me where they may. Thinking.

It's a little astonishing to me I'm not just bringing the axe down. Perplexing, really. But Simone has always been an outlier. She's so different from the women I've normally sought. She's published, for one thing. She's relatively well known. She's got a readership—at least, she did. She's the only one who's been anywhere close to my level of success. Not that most writers ever get here. I've been very lucky. Still, my other romantic possibilities have been unpublished. Aspiring. Grateful for my assistance. Call it what you will, ego or a savior complex, or perhaps I'm simply softhearted: I've always been drawn to women who need my help. I'm a giver that way.

Simone was a risk, no question, as a pattern change always is. Yet there was something about her that struck me ever since I was perusing social media before setting off on tour, idly scrolling in the bath, as one does. I had a list of women from the Darlings that I was cross-sectioning with profiles. Simone had not then been to the group, but one of her students had, a former journalist named Tabby, and when I tugged on that string, it led me to Simone. From the instant I saw Simone holding up a mic in her profile photo, I was intrigued. Simone was *piquant*. I fancied I could see the hopeful eight-year-old beneath her painted face, and I thought: *Yes. It's you!* I was concerned that she was published, by Hercules no less—but due diligence proved that only her first novel had done very well. Perhaps she was a one-hit wonder, and since then her literary star had lowered book by book. If it was beneath the horizon, she might welcome my guidance.

I was delighted to discover that my instincts were correct: Simone is in as much need as any of the others. Hapless. Floundering. Flaky—tossing away a potential book contract, and for what? Because she doesn't *feel* it? Amateur move. Luckily for her, she's had me to help her. She's got a decent mind, and I could feel the engine starting to churn, the pistons revolving, as she produced her idea and I helped her refine it. The rumrunner piloting his boat across Lake Superior, ferrying moonshine in his Tin Lizzie; the injuries to his wife and family; the ways they echoed through the generations: This is good stuff. But underdeveloped as a negative forgotten in a chemical bath, and now useless. How careless, how criminally thoughtless, of Simone to turn her back on a project we created to flit off to something else unspeakably base, commercial, and based on . . . me.

However. Simone might still be swayed back to historical fiction. We might still make amends. I've heard makeup sex is fantastic; I wouldn't know, I've never had it, since if a woman offends me, gives me the slightest trouble, I just amputate. But I'm willing to pay out some rope in this case. There's a chambermaid here at the inn whose shy smile is at odds with her wickedly flashing tongue ring; I'll spend another night here finding out which speaks to her true nature. Clearing the pipes. Then I'll visit Simone at the retreat tomorrow and we'll have a conversation.

Meanwhile, a prudent man always has a backup plan, and a backup for his backup. In case my romance with Simone does not continue, even after I give her another chance . . . I remove my phone from my dry bag. No more texts from Simone, just a puzzled, injured silence I can almost feel smoking from it like dry ice. Good, she's taken my point. I swipe open my social media and visit a few of the other profiles I have bookmarked for this occasion. I send a message here, drop a wave there. *Luminous!* ⭐, I write on one post; *Bewitching!* 🌚 on another. Then I secure my phone in my dry bag a final time and, with the shadows growing long and the loons calling mating songs to each other, I stroke back toward shore.

CHAPTER 19

INTO THE WOODS

I magine my surprise, then, when I arrive at the Woodstock Hill retreat at noon the next day, armed with good intentions, only to see Simone . . . leaving.

She is coming trippingly down the front steps like Humbert Humbert's tongue pronouncing Lo-Li-Ta, her bright plait bouncing over one shoulder. I would recognize Simone anywhere, from any distance, because of that braid. I'd also recognize her because: Simone.

Naturally, I duck back into my car and follow her ancient yellow Jeep onto the road. Where is she going? The rules of the retreat mandate staying at the retreat, sequestering in one's room or taking soul-clearing walks on the grounds or getting a synapse-stimulating massage or releasing writer's block in downward dog or doing what the writers are actually there to do, which is write. Leaving the property breaks the spell. Are you cuckolding me, dear? I think at Simone's little head, which I can see through her rearview. *Perfidy, thy name is Simone.* What's good for the gander is good for the goose, like my chambermaid this morning? (Tongue ring won.) But I don't think so. Simone is no sportfucker; most women aren't, and I've come to recognize the mutant subspecies who are by the fried, feral miasma they emit and, like any wise man, stay far, far away. More likely Simone is heading to the nearest city to buy a new laptop.

Whatever Simone is doing, she's done me a favor, I realize, by drawing me away from Woodstock Hill. I wasn't planning on sauntering brazenly through the common areas, instead stealing up the maid's staircase to Simone's room. But I had not thoroughly thought this through. Writers return annually to this retreat, and there may be someone here from my time who might remember not only me but my May-November romance with poor sad Kaelynn. Not that there was anything untoward about it. Not at all. But the cultural landscape has shifted, and an established male writer in his prime having a dalliance with an unpublished aspirant two decades his junior, though *de rigueur* and even sought after then, would not be viewed so favorably now. There might be . . . retrospective questions.

Poor Kaelynn, the human Eeyore. Honestly, I haven't thought about her much in the intervening years. Occasionally an especially droopy twentysomething at the Darlings might bring a Kaelynn memory to mind, as well as a brief fantasy of secretly placing a memorial to her on the Woodstock Hill grounds. In the pasture where we had our first literal roll in the hay, for instance. But it passes quickly, leaving only a greasy residue of relief and gratitude. Poor Kaelynn, looking like a convenience store clerk with her dull blond pageboy and acne-spattered forehead, in torn T-shirts featuring rock bands I'd never heard of, limp in bed as in life. There was only one situation that animated her: talking about alternate galaxies, in which case she never shut up. That was the gift she gave me: Kaelynn introduced me to science fiction, and at Woodstock Hill my third novel, *The Space Between Worlds*, was born.

I'd just come off my year-long tour for *You Never Said Goodbye*, which was still on the *New York Times* list in hardcover, and my editor Jayne decided I was suffering from something she called "blockbuster paralysis," a diagnosis to which I meekly copped, although I don't believe in it for a second. Any writer who can't handle success should be buried with his pen through his heart, in my opinion. But despite my actual literary Achilles' heel, which I've never disclosed, not to Jayne, not to anyone, I have two authorial superpowers: I write fast and well, and I can tell what's going to hit. They say don't ever write to please the market, that a book takes a long time to complete, and by the time it's done the zeitgeist will have shifted, so authors should write only what moves them. I couldn't agree less. I came to Woodstock Hill knowing dystopian sci-fi would be the next big thing. Just as I know historical fiction, however editors moan about the market being saturated, is huge now.

I therefore owe poor sad Kaelynn for introducing me to the genre, and perhaps I should have dedicated *Space* to her instead of *to all women exploring new frontiers* . . . Especially given what happened to Kaelynn after her tenure at the retreat. But it would not be wise to resuscitate recollections of that time. I don't even really want to revisit them myself. So I blow that tragic girl a kiss, wherever she may be, and follow Simone farther from Woodstock Hill. Wherever she might be leading me.

Which turns out to be into the woods, via a municipal road that turns into a rutted logging track. About a mile in, Simone's brake lights come on; she pauses as if checking directions, then gets out and unhooks a chain connecting two wooden posts. A sign is nailed to one of them: 1415; 1415 ½. POSTED. NO HUNTING. TRESPASSERS WILL BE PROSECUTED. Simone drives through, reattaches the chain, and continues out of sight.

I continue on a ways, conceal my car in a pullout, and hoof it back on foot, wending through the forest Simone has disappeared into instead of taking the drive. I'm used to navigating woods from strolling my island in Maine every day and from hunting as a boy. I hike up through a birch and maple forest, which segues into an apple orchard, which opens into a meadow at the top of which sits an Airstream trailer. This must have been Simone's destination, for as I conceal myself behind a big pine near the Airstream, she emerges from it bearing two glass bottles of Coke. I am close enough to see straws striped like barber poles. How nice— whatever recluse Simone's visiting in the woods, he or she is a regular Martha Stewart.

He, for there he is. Simone's host comes out of the trailer with two red folding chairs. I size him up: mid-fifties-ish; short—shorter than I am, anyway; stocky, with wire-rimmed glasses, plaid shorts, and white T-shirt, porkpie hat, barefoot. Who is this happy asshole? The urge is all but overwhelming to stride into the clearing, hand extended, smiling, and say, *Good afternoon, I'm William Corwyn! Who the fuck are you?*

"This is so nice," says Simone as they settle into the chairs. "It's like you landed in heaven. How'd you score this again?"

The man clips the end of a cigar, lights it. Of course he does. The filthy habit of little men who need to appear bigger.

"Remember Dave, from rehab? The guy who bailed me out? The main house up the road is his summer home. His caretaker had MS, so . . ."

"That's too bad," says Simone. "For him, not for you."

"I'll tell you what, Ms. Vetiver, I must have some good karma. I feel unbelievably lucky."

"Because you are," she says. She sips soda through her straw. "Do you get lonely here? It's pretty far from everyone, especially without a car."

"After the halfway house? Are you kidding? Besides, I'm making friends with the bears. I'm putting food out for them."

"For fuck's sake. Please tell me you're kidding. That doesn't even work with mice—as you might remember from our house, or do you need me to remind you."

He laughs, a deep sound from his barrel chest. He's probably a scrapper in the ring, but I could take him. "How could I forget the mouse condo? It scarred me for life."

"Then I highly recommend you don't feed the bears. They will kill you and eat you."

"You think?" he says. He blows a smoke ring. "But you're still pretty cute when I'm yanking your braid."

"For fuck's sake, Hank," Simone says, and rolls her eyes. Coke rattles in her striped straw.

Hank. Why does this sound familiar? The penny drops: This is Simone's ex-husband, the wastrel alcoholic starting his life afresh. How's that going? I think. Nice trailer, buddy.

"How's that feel?" Simone asks, nodding at the pale circlet of flesh around his ankle. "No more house arrest. You're like the players who take their wedding ring off but can't hide the tan."

He scrubs a thoughtful hand over his grizzled stubble. "I don't think I want to," he says. "It's like a battle scar. Something I went through and survived."

"And it'll fade quickly," she says. "Unlike . . ." She touches his wrist. I imagine the raised white ridges of flesh, horizontal if he wasn't serious, vertical if he was. For the second time today I think of poor sad Kaelynn, and long-ago lost Becky, and some others who, if God is merciful, are at rest . . . *Lord, hear our prayer.*

"You want to hear something really crazy?" he says. "I almost miss the monitor. I felt less lonely when I had it on. Somebody always keeping tabs on me."

You poor bastard, I think, at the same time as Simone says, "I get it."

"How fucked-up is that?" he asks, and they say in unison, "Soooooo fucked-up!" This has the timing of an old private joke.

"Remember how she used to say that?" says Simone. "That couples' counselor—Joanna? Hannah? She did *not* know how to handle you."

"Nobody did," he says. "Because I was soooo fucked-up. I put you through a lot, girl."

"You did," Simone agrees.

He slides her a glance Simone doesn't see, because she's looking out across the apple orchard with a thousand-yard stare. Wasps hum in the fallen fruit. "Can you forgive me?" he asks.

"I have," says Simone. "Mostly. I'm working on it."

The poor fool leans toward her, and I tense involuntarily, but he just plants a kiss on her cheek. Simone smiles to herself. I consider stealing away, not because I'm disgusted by this display but because it's not worth my time. Simone's not here to sleep with this toothless junkyard dog; she'd be legitimately stupid if she did, and I don't misjudge people that badly. She's here for comfort, like a child clutching an old binkie. That's fine, but I have more important things to do.

Then he says, "So what made you hit the fire alarm today?"

"Somebody broke into my room at the retreat. Trashed it and took my laptop."

"That's terrible! Did you report it?"

"The owners did. They were mortified. They said they'd never had a break-in before." Simone sighs. "They don't have a security system beyond locking the doors at night because they host only writers. What're people going to steal?"

"Um, laptops?"

"Well, we know that *now*."

"Please tell me you backed up your work."

"Sort of," says Simone. "I keep forgetting to use my thumb drive, but I've been emailing myself what I'm working on at the end of every day."

I grind my knuckles into the pine bark. *Fuck*. Not only is she appropriating my past, she's stealing my backup method. And she didn't tell me this. It's unwelcome news. It means her new purloined abomination still exists out there somewhere.

"That's a relief. And you can always get a new laptop."

"I'm going to have to. I found the old one by the duck pond. It looked like somebody had run over it with a truck."

"Wait," says the ex. "That makes no sense. If someone stole it to fence it, why would they destroy it?"

"Because they weren't going to pawn it. It was a warning. To me. I think from this insane woman who's been stalking me ever since . . . I got involved with another writer. A guy, I mean." Simone glances at him. "Sorry, do you not want me to talk to you about this?"

"It stings a little," he admits. "But go on."

Simone tells him about the Rabbit. "It's probably her. Although it also could be another woman, an ex William tried to break it off with, who's maybe not taking no for an answer . . ."

"Let me get this straight," he says. "This guy has not one but two women stalking him."

"Not him. Me. And it's probably only one. I just can't tell which one. But I'm pretty sure she, whichever it was, is the one who broke into my room at the retreat and trashed it. Nobody else's room was touched."

"Did she leave you a note this time?"

Simone pauses. "No. Come to think of it, she didn't. Unless I just didn't see it . . . I was upset, so I didn't look that closely."

"I'll bet. Sam, I don't want to overstep, but I have to say: This guy sounds like bad news."

That is a bit of an overstep, pal, I think.

"Not overstepping," says Simone. "Caring. It's not his fault, though."

"I'm not sure I agree. You said not one but two women. It sounds like a pattern. And patterns don't make themselves. He either didn't stop them—or he's actively encouraging it."

Simone laughs. "That's dramatic."

"It's a dramatic situation. Stalking? Notes in your apartment? Now a break-in? Good grief, why are you staying with this guy?"

Simone sighs. "I'm not sure I am with him. We're kind of on the outs right now. Not because of the *dramatic situation*. Because of the book."

Simone tells him about our contretemps and my ultimatum. I listen carefully for any note of derision, but she simply recites the story. "He feels I'm appropriating his life for material," she says. "And it makes him not trust me. So we're at a stalemate at the moment."

"Of course you're appropriating. That's what writers do, borrow from life. Isn't that what you've always told me?"

"I mean, sure. Little bits and pieces, anyway, and then we change it. The story becomes its own thing. And he knows that, of course. But he was really pissed about it, I clearly hit a nerve there, and no matter how much I apologized, he can't hear me. So now I have an impossible choice to make: Man or book?"

"You want to know what I think?"

Not in the slightest.

"Of course," says Simone.

"Nobody worthy of you would put you in that position. Why would you dump the book? It's the first time I'd heard you excited about your work in ages. Dump the guy."

Cicadas whir while Simone considers her answer. Her ex smokes serenely, continuing to pollute the orchard. It just seems so dangerous, putting a recovering alcoholic in charge of a property, especially one who smokes. Don't they say an addict never really recovers, that he must be vigilant every day? And isn't isolation poison to them? What if this poor bastard, stranded here without a car, grew so lonely he took his emergency handle of vodka from its hiding place, in a high cabinet or in the dry grass near the Airstream's tires, and poured himself a shot? And another and another? And what if he lit a cigar while drinking and passed out with it in his hand? What if? Anything at all could happen to a drunk living alone in the woods.

Finally Simone says, "I don't think William and I are over . . ."

I smile behind my tree. Good girl.

"But I'm not ready to give up on the new thriller idea, either," she admits.

Wrong answer, Simone. *Very* wrong answer.

"Is it bad I'm hoping it goes badly with him?" he says, and she laughs.

"It's human," she says. She stands and stretches. I watch him eyeing her breasts beneath her thin T-shirt as she arches her back. Behold 'em and weep, you poor sucker, I think. They used to be yours. Now they're mine. If I want them.

"I'd better go," Simone says. "I want to hit the road before dark."

He stands, too, and hugs her. "Remember when we talked about getting an Airstream just like this and driving around the country? And I'd take portraits of people while you wrote and sold pies out the back window?"

Simone laughs. "I remember you having a fantasy about this that I in no way partook in."

He draws back to look at her. "You sure you don't want to reconsider?"

"I'm good, thank you," she says. "Besides, you seem like you're in a solid place now. With your friends the bears and all."

They embrace again, and now I do make my silent departure. Let them have their tender moment.

Eight months, is what I'm thinking as I make my way back to my car. I have a two-book contract, *All the Lambent Souls* being the first, and the second is due in eight months. I have only that long to deliver it. Is it worth continuing with Simone? It's starting to seem like a lot of work for diminishing returns. It is very sad, but I didn't hear the answers I was hoping for today. So Simone didn't bang her dumpster fire of an ex; bully for her. I'd rather she fuck a platoon than say what she said. *Not sure which book to write* indeed. It's imperative I be with a woman who supports my creative needs, not tears them down. How can I be with one who shows such disrespect? I cannot.

Back in my car, I wipe pine sap and blood from my knuckles and retrieve my phone from the glove box. There are responses from the messages I sent yesterday. Good. *Hello, backups!* I'm reading them when I hear Simone's Jeep coming and slide down in my seat. There's a pause, as if she's idling at the end of the drive while I sweat here. A text from her pops silently onto my screen:

I miss you.

She drives off. I'm about to do the same when another vehicle comes up behind me and I have to duck again. What the hell? This is a lot of traffic for a private road. Is it the owner of the big house, or some guests he's hosting for dinner, perhaps? Then I see who it is and start to laugh. Simone and I might be done, but she won't be lonely. As the Rabbit barrels past me in her rustbucket, I see beneath the brim of her ballcap the unmistakable overbite.

CHAPTER 20

VENN DIAGRAM

THE DARLINGS
FEEDBACK FORM

Attendee Name (if you prefer to remain anonymous, please leave blank):
Cyndi Pietorowski

Email (if you prefer not to be added to our mailing list/newsletter, please leave blank):
cyndipwrites@gmail.com

Date/location attended (if more than one meeting, please list most recent):
Portsmouth, NH, July

=====   **YOUR DARLINGS EXPERIENCE**   =====

How did you hear about us?
Article in The Boston Sun :D

On a scale of 1–10, with 1 being least helpful and 10 most, how was your experience?
9! But only because I was too shy to talk to anyone :D

On a scale of 1—10, with 1 being least helpful and 10 most, how likely are you
to return?

10!

On a scale of 1—10, with 1 being least helpful and 10 most, how likely are you
to recommend The Darlings to a friend?

I don't have a lot of writer friends, in fact I don't have any :(
which is why I came to the group, but if I did, 10!

If you are already involved with a writers' community, what does The Darlings offer you that the other group doesn't? (Not trying to puff ourselves up;
we genuinely want to make sure we're satisfying your literary needs!)

I've never been to a writer meeting, but now I'm so glad I did!

Did you connect with other writers at the meeting? Why or why not?

Not this time, see above :(

Additional comments/thoughts/suggestions:

I honestly can't think of anything you could do better. Next time
I will try to share! William is amazing! THANK YOU for starting and
hosting this group!

YOURSELF

Approximate age group (if you choose to share! We aspire to serve writers of
all ages, and we know beliefs and methods often vary by decade):

20s 30s (40s) 50s 60s 70s 80+

Do you identify as male, female, nonbinary?

female

Please describe your current writing project:

I'm writing a novel (eeeee, I can't even believe I'm saying that!) about my great-x-9-grandmother, Margaret Scott, who was one of the accused at the Salem Witch Trials . . . No. 16 to be condemned and executed :(

Please describe your position related to the publishing industry. Are you:

1. a writer

②an aspiring writer

3. a published writer (please feel free to list your works here!)

4. affiliated with the industry in some other way (Editor, agent, literary magazine, educator, etc.)

5. N/A

Please tell us a little about your writing history (if you are just starting out, that's fine! Welcome! :))

Thank you! I'm a total newbie. I left my corporate job last year to start writing about Margaret Scott (see above), my ancestress. I have no idea what I'm doing, but I'm obsessed!

What genre would you place your work in? (If multiple, please feel free to list)

Oh my, genre! :) I feel so official. Fiction novel, and since it's set in the 1600s, I guess historical?

What are your aspirations for your current project?

Again, I'm blushing! But I would LOVE to see my novel on the shelf. (Eeee!) I want the world to know Margaret's story! So I guess to get it published, by the big New York publishers or Amazon or self-publishing? As long as Margaret gets to readers.

What are your aspirations for your writing career?

Eeeee! Even MORE than publishing Margaret's story? I never even thought about it! Maybe I would keep right on going with the other Salem women's stories? Crazy to even think about it! :)

Please describe how The Darlings can help you:

You are already helping me just by existing and making me fill out this questionnaire! (Well, not making me. You know what I mean.) I feel more like a writer now just because I have been to this group. You are giving me hope! Thank you!!!!

I would in future meetings LOVE to learn more about how to get published. I looked up other programs online, and they can help me finish my book, so maybe I should do that first? Listening to the other writers in this group talk about how they write has been so, so helpful. But no other group will tell you how to ACTUALLY get published. So that would help!

Thank you for attending! It is our honor to support you and your writing.

—————— CYNDI PIETOROWSKI, SOCIAL MEDIA PROFILE ——————

ABOUT

Pronouns: She / her

Work: Writer at Self, 1 year

Work: Paralegal, Frohling & Hanley, Esq., 12 years

Work: Attorney, Gomez & Yountz, 4 years

Education: J.D. Suffolk Law School

Education: B.Sc., North Shore Community College

Lives in: Salem, MA

MURDER YOUR DARLINGS

Places lived: Boston, MA; Salem, MA

Friends: 112

Birthplace: Salem, MA

Relationship status: Single

Birthday: November 10, 1980

Bio: direct descendent of Margaret Scott, No. 16 "witch" hanged at the Salem Witch Trials. Consultant on Sarah Jessica Parker's episode of NBC's "Who Do You Think You Are," exploring SJP's Salem ancestry. Native Salemite. Former attorney and newbie book writer. Practicing Wiccan. Proud Mom to 19 cats.

SOCIAL MEDIA DIRECT MESSENGER

William Corwyn

Sept. 20, 8:32 a.m.

Dear Cyndi—if I may—

Hello! Permit me to introduce myself (although obviously this mode of communication gives it away up front): I'm William Corwyn, the founder of the Darlings writers' support group you attended this summer. Please forgive me for not having responded sooner. I've been on book tour, which has an adverse effect on being a human being. I'm mortified that I've left a fellow scribe hanging for so long.

I read your feedback form with great interest. Kudos on coming to the meeting! That takes considerable bravery, especially when you don't think of yourself as a writer yet. (May I whisper a secret? If you're writing, you're a writer.) I'm glad you joined us and found it helpful.

I'll also confess to an ulterior motive, my dear. I am fascinated by the fact that you're writing historical fiction, which I have never attempted to do (who is the neophyte now?), and that you are the direct descendent of Margaret Scott. When I read this, I sat straight up as if struck by the proverbial thunderbolt and thought: My God. I must meet this woman. Because I have been intrigued since boyhood by the Salem Witch Trials. I know many people have, they speak directly to our sense of history and injustice, but although so much has been written about them, it has all been so . . . dusty (a la *The Crucible*) or fatuous and academic, and too often by men. (Who did Arthur Miller think he was, anyway, appropriating such a story?)

Although it is nearing its conclusion, my tour brings me near Salem next week. I'm wondering if you might be free Wednesday for a walk or a coffee (or an alternate beverage of your choice)? I'd love to hear more about what you're working on. And, of course, to offer assistance any way I can.

Either way, please know you have my respect, and I hope to see you back at the Darlings soon.

Ever your admirer,

William

Cyndi Pietorowski

Sept. 20, 8:51 a.m.

OMG!!!!!! Hi!!!!! Of course I know who you are, Mr. Corwyn!!!!!!! Not only have I read everything you've ever written, I am so grateful to you for starting The Darlings. It's the first time I ever felt like a real writer. This is the second, although hearing from you feels more like a dream!!!!!!

I would love to meet you, again, and I'm happy to share about Margaret and what I'm writing. Except are you sure?!? You are so important, and I can't imagine you would want to waste your time with a total newbie like me.

William Corwyn

Sept. 20, 9:10 a.m.

It would be my pleasure to meet with you, my dear. You would be doing me the favor. If you'll indulge me, I'll spin a little yarn that explains why.

When I was a young man (more years ago than I care to confess), I was laboring away in my undergraduate creative writing workshop when one of my colleagues bet me $5 that I didn't have the . . . well, the courage to submit my novel-in-progress to a New York City publisher. I took that bet. I used my laundry quarters to photocopy the manuscript in the student union (that alone tells you how old I am), popped it in a box (ditto), and spent the rest of my monthly student loan stipend to send it to an editor whose name I chose from Publishers Marketplace in the library (which back in those olden days was an actual book, the size of an encyclopedia and twice as heavy).

I promptly forgot about it and went back about my business, which was writing and drinking beer, so you can imagine my surprise when a week later, the phone in the closet at the end of my hall rang (more horse-and-carriage-era tales) and an editor, Jayne Wetzel, asked if I was the author of *The Girl on the Mountain* and, if so, would I be able to come to New York? She would send me bus fare.

That bet was the best $5 I ever spent.

Ever since that day, which marked the start of my extraordinarily fortunate career, I swore that if there were anything I could ever do to help an up-and-coming writer, especially one with such a passion as yours, I would do it. Please, allow me to walk with you.

But I do have one condition: You must call me William.

Cyndi Pietorowski

Sept. 20, 9:15 a.m.

Oh, Mr. Corwyn! Sorry. William! (Eeeek!!!!!) I am sitting here with tears in my eyes. What a beautiful story! Thank you so much for sharing it with me. And for reaching out to me. Of course, I would be honored to meet with you. Thank you!!!!!!

William Corwyn

Sept. 20, 9:27 a.m.

Tremendous. I'm looking forward to learning more (I won't say "pick your brains"; do you loathe that phrase as much as I do?) about you and your ancestress Margaret. My free window is Wednesday; I have a reading in the evening, but I could swing by Salem in early afternoon; would that suit? Where would you like to meet?

Cyndi Pietorowski

Sept. 20, 9:28 a.m.

That works great! Do you know the Blue Trees? Say around 1 p.m.?

PS, I still can't believe you are writing to me! Eeeeee!!!!
PPS, "pick your brains" is gross!

William Corwyn

Sept. 20, 9:29 a.m.

Great (unpicked) minds. I don't know the Blue Trees, but how poetic. Rest assured I shall find them on Wednesday and be very happy to do so. Thank you. Thank you.

Sam Vetiver

Sept. 20, 9:30 a.m.

Hi, William. I don't know the Blue Trees either. That does sound poetic, but I have no idea where they are . . . or is it a bookstore?

William Corwyn

Sept. 20, 9:31 a.m.

. . .

Cindy Pietorowski

Sept. 20, 9:35 a.m.

I'm so excited!!!! Thank you again. See you at 1:30 on Wednesday. Eeeeeee!

William Corwyn

Sept. 20, 9:35 a.m.

. . .

Sam Vetiver

Sept. 20, 9:40 a.m.

William? Are you there?

Sam Vetiver

Sept. 20, 9:43 a.m.

Okay, I'm going to guess that last message wasn't to me. Whatever the Blue Trees turn out to be, I hope you do find them and they indeed make you very happy.

Also, are we ever going to talk? Get together? I miss you terribly, and I'm so confused about where we are. I'm having a hard time being left hanging. Are we done? As in done-done? I pray we aren't. After everything we talked about—your house, the future perfect? Can we please have a conversation?

William Corwyn is offline

CHAPTER 21

THE BLUE TREES

The Blue Trees are, indeed, blue. Electrifyingly, eyeball-vibratingly blue. I assumed, since they are in Salem, that they in some way commemorate the women and men of the witch trials, who were accused, condemned, and executed. I was mistaken. A plaque in this park where the Blue Trees form a strange, surreal little dreamscape explains that they are an art installation and have been doused in eco-friendly paint to draw attention to climate change. How the Trees are supposed to do this, exactly, what connects their shocking lapis trunks and the declination of the planet—that I do not know. It's an equation for greater minds than mine.

I'm not trying too hard to figure it out. My attention is on other things. Every car that stops, every woman I see coming down the path—I stand at attention, I smile. *Is that you?* This isn't just some little tongue-ringed chambermaid or debut author, bookstore staffer or literary luncheon volunteer. A man cannot live on sportfucking alone. Unlike many men, I've always had a yearning for a stronger connection. I'm a hopeless romantic that way.

So with each new person on the path, I crane forward, eyebrows rising in happy anticipation, a bouquet of daisies in one hand. Every time I am disappointed. Cyndi is late. By half an hour, and the sun is starting to take on a cocktail-hour slant. I conceal my growing irritation; tardiness is not a habit I tolerate. It shows devaluation of a man's time. I'm paying her out some rope, though; perhaps something happened to her, a car accident, or . . . Well, that really is the only justifiable excuse. Serious injury or death. I scroll my phone, refreshing the feeds every few minutes, to see if Cyndi's sent me some sob story via Messenger (no); checking my Amazon author rank (#11 this morning); how *All the Lambent Souls* is doing (#9 in Fiction; #1 in Family Saga). And not answering Simone's texts and calls.

It's difficult. To my horror, I miss Simone. It's unprecedented, it's shocking, but I do. We haven't communicated since she visited her ex on the mountain. I considered training her instead, the way I discourage overzealous readers from writing to me: responding with fewer and fewer sentences before I wink out altogether. Withdrawing the food supply. But Simone would recognize the technique; she's used it on her own overly familiar fans. So I thought it kinder to sever contact in one swift slice. Simone is smart, was my rationale. She'll know what silence means.

Or so I thought. Instead, Simone has proven herself to be as desperate as all the others: The less I respond to her, the more ardently she tries. My phone has been buzzing day and night. If I were still corresponding with her, it'd be to tell her to knock it off. It's hard for a man to track his book's progress and be in touch with his fans with such constant uninvited bombardment.

Today, with the unerring spoilsport instincts peculiar to her gender, she tries to torpedo my meeting with Cyndi by choosing this very moment to send me a video. When I click on it—I know I shouldn't, but I can't help myself—there is Simone languishing on a couch somewhere, her face red and swollen to almost unrecognizable proportions from crying, black makeup trickling down the bloated landscape of her cheeks.

"Hi, William. I kind of hate myself for sending this video but I'm trying to find *some* way to get through to you, and this is so important. After everything we discussed, our future, me being at your house . . . this is so unfair. It's the worst thing in the world, having to choose between a book and the man you love—I hope it's okay to say that. Because I do. Love you. Fuck. This is not the way I wanted to say that. But it's true, and I really want to work this through with you. There has to be a solution. Because this—this *amputation*"—she stops to hyperventilate with sobs, and I watch her breasts heaving—"it's *awful*. So wasteful. And not to sound paranoid, but are you already connecting with other women? Like with that weird DM that I'm fairly sure wasn't meant for me? If so, we *are* done . . . but if not, I want to try and save what we have, because you know how hard to find it is. Okay. I've debased myself enough but please, let's talk in person—"

She freezes mid-sob, and the video ends. I shove my phone in my pocket and adjust my trousers, swearing under my breath. Sabotage successful, Simone. Her beautiful wicked mouth was so puffy from crying that all I can think about now is how it would feel to shove myself inside it.

Of course, I won't reply. I must protect myself from a woman who'd steal from me, who'd excavate tragedies from my past, who might—worst of all—derail my own creativity. Still, I'm astonished to find I miss Simone like a phantom limb. My throat aches. My eyes feel gritty. I yearn for just one glimpse of her bright little head amid the trees. That side plait of hers that spoke whimsically and deceivingly of a regressive temperament, making me think she might be tractable as a child. That braid lied. She transgressed. And yet I wish the woman approaching me now were her.

She is not. This is definitely Cyndi walking toward me, smiling tremulously. I know her instantly because I know so many women like this. They come to me at readings, sidling up to the signing table with manuscripts they hope I can pass on to my editor, my agent. They attend the Darlings meetings, sometimes once, often more. They are widows, perhaps, or empty-nest divorcées of a certain age, flesh wrinkling and sagging like that of a past-prime peach. Or they are lifelong loners. I picture them at their kitchen tables with their solo mugs of coffee, their laptops, their diaries and pens, birds pecking at the feeders outside. They want to write their stories. They yearn to connect. *I took a memoir class . . . I was hoping you could read this . . . I just finished this book about my trip to Nepal and . . . I know you must be so busy but . . . If you only could . . . I've tried so hard to get published and . . .* On and on.

To be fair, Cyndi has never asked me for anything, only attended a Darlings meeting. I do not remember her. But she fits that fingernail-slim Venn diagram of traits I look for in a potential partner: early forties, single, no children. Small and blond—she could be Simone's cousin. She's got the body type that pre-Simone, damn her, I gravitated to, gymnast-slim, bendable and flippable as a puppet. Cyndi's a writer, or trying to be, and unpublished. She's working in the genre I'm interested in: historical fiction. Finally, in person she's button-cute—thank God—with honey-colored hair and big blue eyes, jeans and sandals and a T-shirt that says WICKED. A little more careworn than her profile photo made her look, but who among us does not airbrush? *Vive la Cyndi!* Cyndi Pietorowski may be just the woman I need in this next chapter of my life.

I bow slightly toward her. "You must be Cyndi," I say. "I'm William Corwyn."

"I *know*," she breathes. "I can't believe I actually get to meet you one-on-one like this! Eeeeee!" She flushes strawberry. It's a pretty trait. "I mean . . ."

"As I said in my embarrassingly long-winded messages, the pleasure is mine." I hold out the daises I had the presence of mind to pick up at a Price Chopper. "For you, my dear. A small token of my appreciation for your time."

She wrings her hands. "It's *so* nice of you. But I can't take them. They're dangerous for cats."

"I'm sorry," I say. "I didn't know that. How so?"

"If they eat them, they die."

What stupid cat would eat daisies? I think. "What idiot would bring daisies to a cat mom?" I say, and toss the flowers over my shoulder, hoping to make her laugh. Instead, she looks alarmed.

"Oh no, don't waste them!" she says, and scoots past me to retrieve them. As she bends over I assess the rearview: as I thought, not a scrap of meat on those little bones. It'll be like fucking a chair. Oh well. It's nothing I haven't done before.

"We can bring them to the witches," Cyndi says.

"Why didn't I think of that," I say.

She peers hopefully up at me. Her eyes are the largest, bluest, and saddest I've ever seen, like an orphaned forest creature in a Disney movie. *Bambi*, I think—one of my memory promontories looming suddenly from the mist. The one movie I saw as a child: I don't know why we were off the peak, but we were, and I remember the scratchy plush theater seats and the smell of popcorn. And the fire, which killed the mother deer. While the other children shrieked and sobbed, I was riveted. Finally, I thought, somebody understands my life.

"Have you been to the memorial before?" Cyndi asks.

"I haven't," I admit. "I'm hoping you'll be my guide."

She clasps her hands. "I would *love* to."

I check my watch. "I'm afraid I have only an hour before my event. I hope that gives us enough time." I scan her face for remorse about having kept me waiting. She goggles winsomely back. I suppress a sigh. "Take me to your leaders."

We leave the Blue Trees side by side, Cyndi clutching the bouquet of daisies like a bride going to the altar. People smile at her as we walk through Salem, past brown and blood-colored houses with historic register plaques and tiny mullioned windows, squatting directly on the street.

The memorial is not far, and it surprises me: Given the commercial circus Salem has made of its gory past, I expect something subtle like a giant gibbet, or a bronze sculpture of screaming women chained to a pyre. Instead, we enter a small park ringed with old stone walls, from which protrude what look like benches—except they are gravestones. There are nineteen of them, each inscribed with a name, birth and death dates, and the manner of execution.

Cyndi separates from me as soon as we enter, heading toward one stone with the air of somebody on a sacred mission, so I leave her to it and wander. Almost all of the condemned went by rope; only one, an unfortunate fellow named Giles Corey, was "pressed"—crushed to death between millstones. I grimace. Hard way to die, friend, I think, pausing to extend my condolences. Around me, tourists lick ice cream and vape and take photos of the inscriptions, sometimes uttering soft noises of horror or pity. I'm surprisingly moved by this little park, its palpable sadness so at odds with the peace of its sun and shadow, its old trees.

I return to Cyndi, whose eyes are closed and lips moving.

"This must be your ancestress," I say, when she's done.

"Margaret Scott," she says, patting the stone in front of her. She's set my daisies on it next to a semicircle of burnt tea lights and a withered rose.

"How much do you know about her?" I ask.

"I know *everything*," Cyndi says. "She came to me and told me."

Sweet Jesus, I think, but I have to know. "Please, tell," I say, leading Cyndi to a normal wooden bench by the park's entrance. We sit. "How lucky, to have a literal visiting Muse. And one you're related to. How did it happen?"

"I was at work," Cyndi says, "preparing a brief, and I went to the break room and there was Margaret. Standing by the mini fridge in her cloak and bonnet. I knew her instantly. She looked just like my gram."

"That is . . . " I say, fishing for the right word. *Insane.* "Astonishing. Were you frightened?"

Cyndi shakes her head. "Maybe I should have been, but I wasn't. She said, *Verily, child, thou must write my story.* So I did. I gave notice that afternoon."

"True dedication. Was that a difficult decision?"

"Oh, no. I mean, I missed my colleagues. And I felt bad about handing off some of my cases. But it was . . ." She squints into the trees.

"A calling?" I suggest.

"*Yes*," she breathes.

"Every career writer feels that way, my dear," I say. "Otherwise we'd all be doing something else, something more pleasant, like digging ditches." Or law. "What is your process?" I give her a tender look. "Do you mind my playing twenty questions? I'm just—bewitched."

Cyndi groans at my pun and gives me a little push. First physical contact she's initiated. "I wouldn't say it's a *process*, exactly. That sounds so grand, more for actual writers like you."

"Don't put yourself down," I say sternly. "Remember what I said? If you're writing, you're a writer." She nods. "So Margaret—dictates to you, is that what it's like?"

"Kind of. Margaret told me her story all at once, so I wrote it down and now I'm filling in the blanks. Like . . . writer *Mad Libs*?"

"Writer *Mad Libs*, that's very good. It sounds like you're a plotter, then, rather than a pantser?"

Cyndi wrinkles her pert little nose. "What does *that* mean?"

"Sorry. Shop talk. Plotters have an outline," I explain. "Pantsers create the story as they go."

"Oh! No, I work with an outline. Margaret gave it to me. And all those years of law school, I'm trained that way, I guess." She looks worried. "Is that bad?"

I lower my voice and lean in. "Don't quote me, but I one hundred percent approve. It's *so* much better to use an outline. You waste so much less time." This is completely true. "And how are you actually writing—using Scrivener? Word? A quill pen?"

Cyndi laughs. "Margaret would love it if I used a quill pen! I should have thought of that. But no, just regular Bics and legal pads."

"You write longhand?"

"I do. Is *that* wrong?"

"Not at all. It's infinitely preferable." This is also true. "A lot of writers are returning to writing that way. It's a more direct creative conduit—at least for those of us who were raised to the pen. The indelible connection between mind and hand." I take Cyndi's petite paw with its bitten nails and turn it over so the vulnerable palm faces up, noticing as I do a semicolon tattooed on her wrist.

"That is serious commitment to punctuation," I say, smiling. Cyndi looks down at our conjoined hands, cheeks flushing again. I lift her inked wrist to my mouth and press the lightest kiss upon it.

"Forgive me," I say, "is it all right I did that? I should have asked."

"No, it's fine," she whispers.

I gaze at her like a shy boy in a Norman Rockwell painting, but I release her hand. Something tells me to be extra careful with this one. She looks yearningly at me as I stand.

"I must away, milady," I say, extending my arm. "Would you see me to my car?"

We retrace our steps through Salem, past tourists buying witch paraphernalia, having tarot readings, getting pierced. It's a beautiful mellow September day, bees humming in the wastebaskets, the sun the bright white of an unshaded bulb. The season is turning, in more ways than one. Maybe I can put Simone behind me. Maybe Cyndi can help. She's seemingly pliable and sweeter than syrup. Also, she's certifiable. But who cares, as long as our romance is fruitful? What writer is not a little nuts?

When we reach the Blue Trees, I say, "Such a fruitful sojourn. Thank you. And still I have so many questions. May I see you again, my dear? Maybe when I come back through town, in about a week?"

She beams up at me. "That would be *lovely.*"

"And perhaps I could see your place? It was Margaret's house, yes?"

"I wish," she says. "The original house was bulldozed long ago. But the land is the same."

"Either way," I say, "it's where the magic happens." I open my arms. "More anon, okay?"

As we hug, I realize there is one way Cyndi is like Simone: She's short enough that I could rest my chin on her head. But I don't. It feels like a sacrilege. Instead I absently cup her skull beneath her honey-colored hair, learning the shape of it, gazing through the Blue Trees and wondering what the world has done to her, why she had this sudden break with reality. Not that it really matters, but still. It is a curiosity. Simone was wounded, too, I know. That story about her father, and now she is adrift. There are so many lonely women, so many ways in which they've been hurt. It could break your heart.

Then I do see Simone, flitting among the trees like a wraith or a fairy. Or a witch.

Simone? I glimpse the bright blond of her braid between two blue trunks; I even think I see light glinting off the fountain pen she keeps tucked in it. *It's you!* I scan the street for her yellow Jeep, see a flash of sneakered sole—she always wears sneakers—and then she is gone. Or has ducked behind a tree. Or maybe, I think as I detach Cyndi's face from my previously pristine blue shirt, maybe Simone was not there at all. Maybe I wanted to see her badly enough that I dreamed her up.

CHAPTER 22

AT CYNDI'S

The afternoon I go to Cyndi's condo is the first day it feels like fall. October is a deceptive bitch that way, smiling at you with her lazy warmth, then parting her skirts and blasting you with cold. When I leave my hotel in the morning, there's frost on my windshield, and there's suddenly credence to the pumpkin everything I've seen for a month: coffee, candles, hand soap, bread. Orange leaves on all the bookstore sidewalk signs, and the new big books of autumn replacing summer blockbusters on the front tables. Though thankfully *All the Lambent Souls* remains. If the trend continues, according to the numbers my editor Jayne forwards me every week, my latest novel will remain on the bestseller list well into the holiday season. Huzzah! No humbug here.

Still, I am inching ever closer to that second-book deadline, and that means I am ready to be home. The road is wonderful, and it is tiring: all those accolades, all that smiling up at readers from the signing table and making small talk about their lives while trying to spell their names right; all the unknown female bodies and unfamiliar beds. Plus all the harrowing drama with Simone. I'm not Father Time, but I'm not twenty anymore, either, and I do best churning out pages when I'm back in my study, in sweatpants and HARRINGTON T-shirt, getting up from the desk only to feed the fire. It's physical, this yearning for my house, the only sound the occasional coyote or crack of ice on the lake. There's just one thing I have to do first.

Cyndi's home is a triple-decker in Witchcraft Heights, squeezed in among a row of others, their lawns cluttered with toys and cordoned by chain-link fences. Cyndi's Victorian is painted those lugubrious historically correct colors; *Look for the purple house,* she told me, and indeed it is, lavender with mustard, maroon, and forest-green trim. It looks exactly as you'd expect a house to look if the woman who owned it believed herself to be the descendent of witches, with a mansard roof and dormer windows from which harpies might fly on brooms. Although Cyndi lives on just the top floor, she told me, and rents out the others. It makes sense. No writer can survive on savings alone.

Cyndi is late answering the door. Her tardiness is habitual, then, not an aberration. This is a problem. We'll need to have words about it, how she left me shivering on the porch with a bag of catnip. I press the buzzer again, counting to thirty before I release it, and canvass the street as I wait. There's a yellow Jeep at the end of the block. *Simone? Is that you?* I squint, but I can't see the driver. Get a grip, man, I tell myself. Ever since I severed communication, I've been seeing Simone everywhere. It's like when I had an infestation of mice at my home in Maine, how constantly in my peripheral vision there was scrambling movement. Until I put down poison. But this is not real. *Do you know how many yellow Jeeps there are in the world?* Not many, actually. *But why would Simone be following me?* Because she can't let me go. Because she's desperate. There are women for whom the love of William Corwyn was not a good thing. If Simone is tailing me, all the more reason to cut her off. Simone, the Rabbit, the others: How many of these deranged stalker women is a man supposed to take?

I'm striding down the steps to confront her when the door opens behind me. "Oh, no," Cyndi groans, putting her hands to her cheeks and making an Edvard Munch face. "I'm so sorry! The bell is broken."

Nice of you to tell me, I think. "No worries at all," I say.

"Your hands are freezing," she laments. "You must have been waiting forever!"

"Only about a hundred years," I say, smiling.

"I was writing and I totally lost track of time," she says, ushering me up a dark stairwell. "Thank goodness I set my phone alarm to check the porch!"

"That was smart," I agree. "But I'm so glad the writing was flowing; that's more important than my comfort." This is true. Almost. The smell of pumpkin spice candle and cat litter grows stronger as we approach her door. I thought Cyndi was exaggerating about the number of cats she had, but I'm starting to get a bad feeling.

"Do you really have nineteen cats?" I ask, as we enter a foyer that seethes with sinuous shadows, coiling, twining, leaping from high places. My eyes burn. Is this even legal? If I were allergic, I'd be dead.

"I do!" Cyndi says. "One for each of the murdered accused. Every time one cat crosses over, I get another from the shelter."

"That makes sense," I say, concealing my dismay. I'm not *against* animals per se; it's more that I was not raised with them as pets. They were in service to science, and never allowed inside the house.

Cyndi ushers me into a living room dominated by a magnificent mausoleum of a fireplace. It's hard for me to stand up straight in this garret under the eaves. I have to hunch unless we're in the center of the room. It's a mess, a hoarder's nest of books and melted candles and charred clumps of sage and bundles of yarn and discarded sweaters. The windows are tiny, the walls painted eggplant. God save us from creative paint colors, *plum* and *saffron* and *sage* and *yolk*. A home should offer respite from the world outside, including visually, and in mine the walls are white, or bookshelves, or windows. Of course, every inch of this room is infested with cats. If I lived here, I'd be mad too.

Above the mantel is an oil painting of a dour bonneted woman whose eyes would follow me around the room if I could move. "Goodwife Scott, I presume," I say.

"Yes, that's Margaret! My relative."

"Please tell her to turn away," I say, "so I can do this," and I'm bending to kiss Cyndi when something sinks hot needles into my calf. "What the fuck!" I say, lashing out with my foot.

"Oh, Reverend!" Cyndi says. She detaches a large gray cat from my pants, leaving tufted holes. It inflates and hisses at me. "That's Reverend Burroughs. He's usually better behaved."

"Perhaps he senses my impure thoughts," I say.

"Cats *are* psychic." Cyndi looks around in distress. "I meant to tidy up before you got here."

"It's fine," I say. "Cozy. A perfect aerie for writing." But Cyndi dashes around ferrying detritus from one side of the room to the other. I watch her curiously. There's a motor running in her that wasn't turned on when we last met, nor during any of our FaceTime calls this week. She's as disheveled as her house, hair mussed as though she's been yanking it all morning, long mirrored skirt crooked, feet bare.

"There," she says finally, putting her hands on her narrow hips and *foof*ing out air, although the room looks just like it did before. She goes to a portholed swinging door that I suspect leads to the kitchen, fording a river of cats with her feet. "Can I get you anything? Coffee or tea? I have a special brew I make for when I'm writing . . ."

What I really want is a hazmat suit and a flamethrower. "Is the tea hallucinogenic?" I ask.

Cyndi giggles. "No. It's mint."

"*C'est la guerre*. Well, I'll have that."

"Be right back," she says. "Make yourself comfortable."

This is obviously impossible, but I blow her a kiss and, the moment the door swings shut behind her, start my investigation. The only thing I can't find in this room is the most important, which is the legal pad Cyndi says she writes on. I shoo a fat orange creature from a knitting nest on the coffee table. A pill bottle rolls from beneath it: LORAZEPAM, its label says. Ah. Antianxiety. There's another, Lithobid, which I believe is lithium, and a third, Risperidone. I don't know that one, but I quickly look it up on my phone. It's an antipsychotic. This explains much, including why Cyndi would have left a legal career to take dictation from an apparition. Poor girl. Poor sweet fragile girl—deceitful, too; she mentioned none of this during our chats this week. I feel a stab of anger and the usual disappointment. Is *no* woman trustworthy? But I'll give Cyndi the benefit of the doubt; she did open up to me about her time in what she called *the system*, which I thought meant libraries and then learned meant foster care, to which she was relinquished after her gram died. At least I now know what Cyndi's vulnerabilities are. I tuck the bottles beneath the yarn as Cyndi backs through the door, carrying a tray.

"Allow me," I say, and take it off her hands. I persuade a pair of cats off the couch with my foot and set down the tray, upon which is a pretty Japanese tea set and a fan of orange cake slices.

"Did you make this, kitten?" I ask. "Is there nothing you can't do?"

Cyndi flushes. "It's nothing. Just a family recipe. Do you like pumpkin spice?"

"Who doesn't? I wish it could be Halloween all year."

"So do I," she breathes as we sit.

I fill the small earthenware cups and hand her one, putting mine to my lips and pretending to sip as if I'm at a child's tea party. "Do you know what a group of cats is called?"

"A coven?" Cyndi guesses hopefully.

"A clutter," I say, which certainly seems appropriate. "Or more historically, a clowder."

"Ooooo, a *clowder*," she breathes. "I *love* that! It's so Salem-y."

"I thought you might," I say.

I lean over to kiss her, deeply this time. Dry lips, eager pointy little tongue. I try not to think of Simone's luscious slippery mouth and playful sensibilities. I come up for air first and pull Cyndi's feet into my lap. They're dusty-bottomed, with fat piggies and blue nails.

"Oh," she groans, as I begin kneading her soles. "That feels amazing."

"I put myself through grad school as a reflexologist," I say. I have no idea where this came from, but it could be true. I am good at foot rubs.

I work the knots in Cyndi's arches. "Relax," I order. I contemplate Cyndi as her head lolls back, eyes closing, throat so trustingly exposed. She looks so peaceful. My whole life I've pictured exactly this, coming up from my basement study to find a woman like Cyndi on the couch, reading, lights on and soup on the stove. Taking the book from her hand and asking *How was your day?*; telling her about mine, massaging her feet as snow falls outside, or autumn leaves or dogwood blossoms. Then perchance the hot tub, then bed. This is all I've ever wanted—this, and to keep writing bestselling books. How has this common-place goal, a partnership, eluded me? Dolts, madmen, the stupid rich, the street-sharp poor, the drug-addled, pious, wicked, confused—even homely women: Most everyone has someone. I'd hoped it would be Simone, I think with a lance of pain. But maybe it's Cyndi. Cyndi could be the one.

"Do you always write in this room, kitten?" I ask, cracking her toes one by one.

"Mmmhmm. That feels *so* good," she moans, as I massage her paper-thin Achilles tendons.

"I always have a fear while I'm mid-book that something will happen to me, and it'll be irrevocably lost. Do you have that?"

She tips her head, squints. "Not really."

"Do you back up your work? Photocopy it"—I laugh—"or scan it? Send it to anyone?"

Cyndi screws up her face. "I don't. I know I *should*. But every time I think about bringing it to, like, Staples or something, I feel like that'd let all the magic out. Is that stupid?"

"On the contrary," I say. "Margaret would approve." I ease her skirt up to rub her calves, then inch it higher. Her legs are white and spindly, with silver lines on the thighs that I think at first are stretch marks. This would be a turn-off. Then I realize what they really are: a skein of scars like a spider's web. Poor girl. I skate my fingers over them, barely a whisper of a touch.

"Where *is* your magnum opus, kitten?" I murmur.

Cyndi looks around, frowning. "That's funny. It has to be in here somewhere."

"We'll find it," I say. I lower myself carefully on top of her. "What if," I whisper in her ear, tonguing it, "what if you come to my house in Maine? See where *I* write?"

"I'd love to," she sighs, as I slide my hand to the scant meat of her breast. "But the cats."

"Obviously, they'd come with you." I almost laugh, trying to imagine how big that cage would have to be. "What if they stay in my barn?"

Cyndi's eyes pop open in alarm. "Oh no. They're indoor cats."

"A barn is indoors," I say reasonably. Unless somebody were to leave the barn doors open and they got out, to fend for themselves in my woods with the coyotes and eagles and foxes.

"I don't think they would like that," Cyndi says stubbornly.

"Then what if we build them their own house? The cathouse. With nineteen rooms. A birdcage in each one." I trail my fingers up Cyndi's marred thighs.

"That sounds perfect," she says, sucking in breath as I pull her underwear aside and test her warmth and wetness.

"It's settled, then," I murmur. I sit up, leaving her exposed, and smile.

"Kitten," I say, "would you please find Margaret and read to me?"

Cyndi shoves herself up on her elbows. "*Now?*"

"I'd love nothing more," I say truthfully—although the prospect of further exploring what's beneath her flowered briefs is also appealing. Later. Priorities. "I want to help you. I want to hear your work. I want to know *everything*. About Margaret, about your book, about you—"

I must have uttered some magic incantation of my own, for Cyndi launches herself at me, mewling. Before I know what's happening, I'm on my back with her straddling me, little hands scrabbling to undo my belt and zipper, yanking me out of my briefs—"Careful, sweetie, it's not a gearshift," I warn—and impaling herself on me. The next thing I know, she's started to ride.

Well! I think. That was unexpected. I hadn't planned for this to happen until our next meeting. But if she wants to accelerate things, who am I to argue? I reach for her hips to guide her along, faster deeper more, and she slaps my hands away. Apparently Kitten has her own ideas of how this should go. Fine. It's a bit like being in a churn, but it's not unpleasant. Thank God I took my own medication before getting out of the car.

As Cyndi's bouncing away, head thrown back and eyes closed, I have an unwilling flash of Simone doing the same but facing the other direction, reverse cowgirl, her beautiful back flexing. How I'd said *Yeehaw!* and felt her internal muscles clenching on me when she laughed. *Stop it. For God's sake. Focus.* I look around for the legal pad. As Cyndi said, it must be here somewhere—

Then I spot it. Of course, it has been a foot away all along. On the floor under the couch. Tucked beneath a giant Maine coon, who stares balefully at me and switches its tail.

I'd like nothing more than to extend my leg and shove the cat away, then kick the legal pad fully beneath the couch, from which I'd retrieve it once Cyndi is finished and I send her into the kitchen for more tea. As it is, I'll have to wait. At least her handwriting is large and legible. She's speeding up now, moaning toward her conclusion, and as I begin my narrative, *That's it, kitten, do you know how beautiful you are right now, aglow, luminescent,* I look toward the window and my freedom, the cat-hair-less air I'll be inhaling an hour from now, when I'll be jogging down the front steps having set up our next meeting, at which, I'll suggest, we read to each other from our WIPs, our works-in-progress, perhaps in the bath. So I can hear the whole story. And help her. *Come for me, kitten . . . you feel it building! . . . inescapable . . . delicious . . . ,* and as I say *You're on the edge!* I wonder if that yellow Jeep will still be out there when I depart, and as I say . . . *Now! Do it now!* and Cyndi yowls and scratches my chest hard enough to draw blood, I have two thoughts simultaneously: Why must all women be crazy? and Dear God, the things I do for my art.

CHAPTER 23

EDITORIAL CORRESPONDENCE

From: William Corwyn

To: Jayne Wetzel

Date: October 15

Time: 6:34 a.m.

Dear Jayne,

How are you, my dear? I'm writing from Brattleboro, where, as you know if you've been keeping up with my travels, I'm keynoting at a literary festival. The organizers have put me in a B&B overlooking a lively stream, which recalls one of my fondest memories: you and I playing hooky after the Sanibel Island Writers' Conference and going fishing in the Keys. You were the better fisherwoman, as you are my superior in every way.

Good news: This event marks the end of my official tour. Many thanks to Hercules for sending me on the road in bravura style. After this, I will be hunkered down at my place in Maine to write, except for one more stop: to *you*. I want to swing by the publishing house to present the idea for my next book. Even though it's far out of my way, and although it's counterintuitive to yo-yo south before traveling north, I'm feeling extremely enthused about it and can't wait to share it with you. How about lunch on Thursday? Or shall we make dinner plans?

Since all work and more work makes William a happy boy, I'm wondering if you might also arrange a reading for me at the 92nd St. Y while I'm in town. Perhaps even in conversation with another author, although I'm fine taking the mic on my own. I know you will admonish me about the importance of downtime, but I'm happy to do an epilogue event to keep *Lambent Souls* front and center; holiday sales are around the corner.

Looking forward as ever, dear.

William.

From: Jayne Wetzel

To: William Corwyn

Date: October 15

Time: 11:15 a.m.

Hey Billy! Great to hear from you. Congrats on being in the home stretch. Man, we put you through the wringer with this one. I'm surprised you're still standing. We've all been applauding your progress. I've been joking we should create a William Corwyn Tracker like the Santa app.

It'd be a treat to have you here, we'd roll out the red carpet, but don't feel the need to add to your mileage. Why don't you go home and get some sleep and we can discuss your idea via videoconference or the old-fashioned way, phone. I'm sure whatever you've come up with is phenom. Can't wait to hear. Call me early next week.

Love,

Jayne

From: William Corwyn

To: Jayne Wetzel

Date: October 15

Time: 11:20 a.m.

My dear, you talk as though I'm some old geezer who's unable to get out of bed without assistance. I assure you it's the opposite: My tour has galvanized me, and much as I yearn to be home writing, I'd be delighted to shake a few more hands, sign a few more books, and most of all see you. Thursday? That would be best for me.

P.S. Let me know, please, about the 92nd St. Y.

From: William Corwyn

To: Jayne Wetzel

Date: October 15

Time: 12:45 p.m.

Dear, did you receive my last message?

From: Jayne Wetzel

To: William Corwyn

Date: October 15

Time: 1:45 p.m.

Hi Billy, yes, sorry, I was at lunch. You know that's where editors do most of our business. I'll check availability at the Y. I'm sure they'd be glad to have you back, but they usually book out well in advance, and you did read there last year, so their audience might be saturated. Maybe the Strand? With only a week's notice I can't promise, but I'll ask. And again, I can't wait to hear what your brilliant Billy brain has come up with for this next one.

   X J.

From: William Corwyn

To: Jayne Wetzel

Date: October 15

Time: 1:48 p.m.

Hi Jayne, it's hard for me to believe an audience might be saturated from one prior event a year ago, but if it's too much of a hassle for you to arrange,

I can skip the reading. I do think it's imperative for me to talk my book idea through with you in person. Please let me know about Thursday so I can make sure to hold the date. Thanks.

From: Jayne Wetzel
To: William Corwyn
Date: October 15
Time: 1:52 p.m.

Sure thing, but are you sure you don't want to call or email it to me? I'm heading to Frankfurt next Friday for the book fair (schmoozing your foreign publishers), and much as I'd love to see you, I hate to think of you coming all this way. Especially when I'd rather think of you at your desk . . . writing.

From: William Corwyn
To: Jayne Wetzel
Date: October 15
Time: 1:58 p.m.

No, I think in person is best. Frankly, I am surprised you would even suggest email. Are you not concerned about security? In an age when anyone could hack in and steal my idea?

   I require an answer about Thursday, if you can fit me in before your trip.

From: Jayne Wetzel
To: William Corwyn
Date: October 15
Time: 2:03 p.m.

   Thursday lunch is *wunderbar*. See you then.

"I know who you are," she says, and I'm revising my opinion of her just slightly when she nods to my avatar and says, "You're pretty ubiquitous around here."

"As it should be," I say. "My ubiquity pays your salary. Let Jayne know I'm here, please."

While I'm waiting, I take visual inventory of the lobby. As downstairs, the walls are comprised of spotlit glass shelves featuring the first editions of Hercules authors going back to when the publisher was founded, beginning with Fitzgerald and Dreiser and continuing through Styron, Roth, E. B. White, to the ladies: Toni Morrison, Ann Patchett, Donna Tartt. Good company. I do see one of Simone's novels, only her first, *The Sharecropper's Daughter*, which did so nicely for her and the house. *Too bad, Simone. If you'd played your cards right, you'd be here with me.* In contrast, all of my books are featured, from *The Girl on the Mountain* to *Medusa* to *Lambent Souls*. There are several editions of my first major bestseller, *You Never Said Goodbye*, hardcover and domestic paperback and all the foreign editions. This, too, is as it should be.

Jayne comes striding into the lobby, and we hug. "Admiring yourself?" she says.

"Admiring my placement," I say, grinning. "Thanks for making time for me before your big trip to Frankfurt." I wink to let her know she's forgiven. "*Ich bin ein Frankfurter.*"

Jayne laughs. "You're some kinda hot dog, all right." She squeezes my arm affectionately. Jayne's about ten years older than I am, tall with a great rack, a real Valkyrie, and I've often imagined if we had met when I was still a virgin, we could have had a Mrs. Robinson situation. Jayne would have eaten me alive, and I would have died happy. She's still attractive, in her energetic, perpetually untidy way, with light eyes and graying sandy hair and excellent teeth, the kind of woman you'd more expect to see on a Thoroughbred than in an office. In fact, she does retreat in winters to her horse farm in Florida. Jayne is not at all for me, but she has come to occupy a much more important place in my life than a romantic snack: my editor. Without her having plucked my manuscript out of the slush pile while I was still an undergraduate, if she hadn't then summoned me to New York, my career, and hence I, would not exist.

"Let's go back," she says. "Did you just get in? You're impeccable as usual, Billy. Next to you I always feel like I just spilled coffee on myself. Which actually I did." She brushes in disgust at the stain on her sweater. "Speaking of which—coffee? Tea?"

"Coffee with cream, dear, please," I say to the receptionist, not because I really want it but to give her a chance to redeem herself.

I walk with Jayne into the inner sanctum. Contrary to what most aspiring writers probably dream, the guts of the publishing house look like any other corporate office, a maze of cubicles where the junior editors and assistants sit, carpet, overhead lights, file cabinets—and more books. Shelves and shelves of them, hardcovers and paperbacks and galleys, oh my, and stacks of paper everywhere, manuscripts, even in this age of digital submission. The walls are lined with framed posters of the more famous authors' book covers, Gabriel Garcia Marquez and Pat Conroy, Andre Dubus and Jodi Picoult. The senior editors have offices with doors that shut and multimillion-dollar views, and as I accompany Jayne to her corner suite, I notice an addition to the decor: more of me, avatar Williams appearing at intervals. The first one is plain, simply greeting whoever comes back into the house, but another, next to a cubicle, is wearing a lei and a Hawaiian shirt. A third has a Yankees cap on, a fourth sports a beret and pencil mustache, baguette jammed into the crook of his cardboard arm. By the time we get to the William holding a bouquet of dead flowers and a sign that says EVOLVED WHITE MALE AUTHOR, I'm feeling a little steamed.

"What's with the avatars?" I ask, as I enter Jayne's office, which at least is gratifyingly wall-to-ceiling with my book covers. She grins.

"Don't you just love them?" she says. "Marketing overordered, and we decided to keep them. We call them the Flat Williams. You're our favorite two-dimensional character!"

She's laughing as she drops into her desk chair, *ha ha ha,* until she sees I am not joining her but instead smiling thinly, standing with my hands clasped behind my back.

"Oh, come on," she says. "Don't tell me you've lost your sense of humor. I'll send you home with some." She beams up at me as the receptionist comes in with my coffee. "Now tell me the fabulous book idea."

"Thank you, dear," I say to the girl as she leaves. She's spraddle-legged, which is too bad but also lends itself to some interesting possibilities.

Relenting, I sit and launch into my elevator pitch for the new novel, which I admit is unformed yet, but I know I can execute and polish. "So there you have it," I finish. "Still under construction, but basically: historical fiction, dual timeline, revenge across the centuries. With a clowder thrown in for good measure. That's the working title, by the way. *The Clowder.*"

Jayne has been listening with rapt attention the entire time I've been speaking, tugging on her earlobe. Now she asks: "What's a clowder?"

"A group of cats," I say. "In this case, an ironic nod to the thing men have always called women. A certain part of their anatomy, anyway. And a love letter to those women, my angry female readers. Like the ones in the pink knitted hats."

Jayne stares at me a minute longer, then claps. "Bravo. Billy Corwyn plus histfic is every editor's dream."

"Plus cats," I remind her.

"Plus cats. You're going to reinvent the blockbuster."

I bow my head modestly.

"Frankly, I'm relieved," Jayne adds. "I know I can count on you to pull a rabbit out of the hat last minute, Billy, but this time you were cutting it close."

"I just like to keep things interesting."

"Well, cut it out. I'm too old for that." She grins, her full-wattage white smile. "You writers are a major pain in the ass between books. Hangry vampires looking for a fix. You'll do anything for a new idea."

We both laugh merrily, *ha ha ha*, as if what she said weren't completely true.

We go over a few business details: the numbers on *Lambent Souls*, extremely pleasing, no surprise there, I've earned my bonus and then some. It'll be a merry Christmas! I promise to deliver a written synopsis for *Clowder* by next week—"I'm not a hundred percent on the title," Jayne admits, "I want to run it past marketing. I don't want people to hear it as *Chowder* and think it's a cookbook. But conceptually? Grand slam home run." 500K print run to start. Pub date this time next year. I'll lead the catalog as always. Of course I'll continue to work with my current publicity team, all the senior publicists and book reps. This is all satisfactory. "Good Jayne," I say when we're done. "The best Jayne. Now, the really important question: When's your next vacation so I can take you fishing?"

"Let's talk about it after the holidays," she says. She glances at her watch. "Crap, I forgot to order. What are you hungry for?"

"I'm good," I say, to Jayne's surprise. "Go go go."

"Are you sure?"

"Get out of here. Go charm foreign publishers."

As we stand, I say, "Is Patricia in?" I mean Patricia Miller, Simone's editor, and I know very well she's in because I follow her on social media. Like Jayne, Patricia will be in house until late tonight, putting out every fire she can before setting her away message and jetting across the pond to Frankfurt.

"She should be back from lunch," Jayne says.

"Great, then I'll just say hi on my way out," I say.

Patricia's office is literally next to Jayne's, and the door is partially open. I rap on it with a knuckle. "Knock knock," I say. "Guess who's here."

Patricia is at her computer with glasses on and frowning as she looks up, the screen mirrored in her lenses, but she takes them off as she stands to greet me. She's as elegant as Jayne is messy, an Erté lithograph come to life. Smooth black bob, ever-red lipstick, Chanel No. 5. *Tres soi-*

gné. This office is where all the posters of Simone's book covers live, and I avoid looking at them, instead bending to hug Simone's diminutive editor. Air kiss, air kiss.

"This is a pleasant surprise," Patricia says in her husky voice.

"You look edible, as always," I tell her. "Adorable! Editorable!"

"Same old Billy," she says. "What are you doing here? I thought you were on the road."

"Just finished. And came in to bend Jayne's ear about my latest idea."

"Which is *en fuego*," Jayne says from the doorway.

"I'm not surprised," Patricia drawls. She looks me up and down. "You're looking well, Billy. Handsome as ever. Touring agrees with you."

"Don't tell him that," says Jayne. "I need him to sit his handsome ass down in the chair and write."

"I'm going, I can take a hint," I say. "I just wanted to pop in and say hello."

"It's always good to see you," says Patricia, and she's turning back to her desk when I say, "By the way, I met one of your authors when I was in Boston with *Lambent Souls*. Simone Vetiver?"

Patricia blinks. "Oh, Sam. Right. I always forget her real name is Simone."

"She's charming," I say. "And your ears must have been burning. She thinks the world of you."

"Mutual," says Patricia. "She's a gem."

"That she is. I finally read her this past year and saw what all the fuss is about. Completely merited. Good job, you."

"Well, it's really her, you know," says Patricia. "But thank you."

I lower my voice. "I don't want to be the bearer of unhappy news, but she did say something that concerned me a little. Gravely, actually."

Patricia's brows rise. "Oh?"

"Yes. When we had dinner, she confessed she was struggling with her latest book and said she was going to try her hand at a thriller instead. I'm sure you're aware of this?"

"We discussed it recently, yes."

"Yes. Well. You understand why I was concerned for her. It's usually a bad bet for an author to switch genres. Unless"—I laugh and gesture to myself—"you've made a whole career of it."

"You are one of a kind, it's true," says Patricia.

"I'm sure you discouraged her from trying it."

Patricia sticks the stem of her glasses in her mouth and chews thoughtfully. "The pivot isn't for everyone. And Sam's done well with her historicals. But sometimes, with a fresh idea, it can work."

"Not in this case," I say firmly. "I would *strongly* discourage her, Patricia. Between you and me, and you know I hate to tell tales, but Simone doesn't have a strong grasp on this new genre. In fact, it's sadly shaky. And, from what she read to me, I'm sorry to say it's . . ." I pause for emphasis. "Appropriated."

Patricia frowns. "Now that is a serious allegation. Appropriated from whom?"

"From me," I say. I sigh. "Maybe it wasn't intentional, it might have been the heat of the moment, but Simone airlifted a situation directly from my own life. One I told her about in confidence."

"Is that true?" says Jayne from behind me. I'd forgotten she was there. "That's a big deal, Billy."

"Oh yes, it's true," I say. "Remember my little support group I run, the Darlings?" Both women nod. "And the genesis of it? That's a lesser-known story . . . and it's hard for me to talk about. Suffice it to say I founded the Darlings after the death of somebody I loved, and that is what Simone's writing about. She's"—I start to say *perverted*—"she's 'borrowed' it," I say, making air quotes, "as the basis for her murder mystery. It's so hurtful. It's reopened a very painful wound."

"I'm very sorry to hear that," Patricia says.

"Thank you. I'm sorry to have to tell you. But I'm sure you appreciate why this upsets me. I'd hate to have to bring legal into this. Especially since we're all one big happy Hercules family."

"Of course," Patricia says. "I understand. Thanks for telling me. I'll look into it."

"You'll talk to Simone?" I persist.

Patricia glances toward Jayne, and I feel something pass in the air between the two editors. I'm sure they'll have words about this after I leave the office. For a moment, I almost feel bad about derailing their crowded pretravel schedule. "I'll definitely talk to her," Patricia says.

"Thank you, dear." I bend toward her again. Air kiss, air kiss. "So good to see you. *Gut Reise*. Dominate those Germans. They've had it coming for years."

I reverse my trajectory, saying *auf Wiedersehen* and good luck to dear Jayne in the lobby, finger-tipping the receptionist, taking the elevator down into Gotham. I step through the revolving door into the busy afternoon: steam rising from the subway grates, smell of pretzels, pigeons cooing, the usual cacophony of conversation and cell phone chimes and horns and sirens. My publisher's tower gleams at my back.

That visit was a smash success by anyone's standards. I take out my phone, then realize there's nobody to call. As always. The first time I came here, reeling out of the building with my satchel and the almost unbelievable news that I was going to be published, I wanted to call Pen. But I couldn't. I went across the street to a deli instead and had a cheese omelet as big as a football that made me sick all afternoon. Now, though I yearn to text Simone, I can't, for many obvious reasons. I could call Cyndi, flavor of the moment, but to tell a self-published novelist about this meeting would be boastful and cruel. I consider phoning back upstairs and asking the splay-legged receptionist whether she wants to play hooky for the afternoon.

I decide against it. I'll go see the new exhibit at the Met, then hop a train back north. No more silly games; it's time to concentrate. I accomplished what I came here to do. I pitched my own idea—not that this was ever in doubt—and poisoned the well of Simone's thriller. Now I need to get to work. I have my own book to write.

CHAPTER 25

THE HAWTHORNE

The Hawthorne Hotel in Salem is as historic as they come, a handsome brick edifice flying its standards over the town's cracked sidewalks. Inside, the Oriental carpets are thick; there are grandfather clocks, fresh flower arrangements, numerous oil paintings of whalers. There's rumored to be an entire captain's cabin on the top floor, an homage to the building's original use as the Maritime Society. The air smells of lemon wood polish and fried food from the tavern. This is exactly the kind of luxury hotel I'd enjoy staying in under normal circumstances, that I request from the Hercules team when they're booking my accommodations. Unfortunately, I'm no longer on tour, and today is Halloween Eve, and Salem is a boiling cauldron of insanity.

"It's been like this all month," the clerk at the front desk confides as she's validating my parking, which, stunned by the hysteria outside, I'd neglected to do when first checking in. She hands me back my license and room key, which surprisingly is plastic. I would have thought no tacky digital cards for the Hawthorne, rather a big heavy brass thing that slips into a lock, but at least this one has a watercolor of the hotel on it. "The Chamber of Commerce actually tells people *not* to come here in October. It's on the city website."

I give a curt nod. *Thank you, Lady Obvious.* I'm so annoyed I don't even bother to assess her fuckability. I practically sustained a black eye and broken ribs fighting my way through the black-clad purple-haired tattooed and pierced estrogen extravaganza outside. My suite tonight cost $1,200, which I'd attributed, silly me, to fall foliage season, and if it didn't come with a Privileged Guest spot, I'd be parking in the sea.

As I'm tucking away my wallet, the clerk says, "Wait, aren't you that superfamous writer from Maine?" Somewhat mollified, I'm about to say *Yes, yes I am,* when she adds, "You wrote the book about that haunted hotel! I should've given you Room 612." She taps rapidly at her keyboard. "Too bad, it's taken. Are you here to"—she lowers her voice—"channel something?"

"You must have me confused with someone else," I say, "I'm just a regular warlock," and I storm across the lobby, elbowing through the Wiccan wildebeests. I take the elevator up with a gang of teen ghouls who disperse into the third floor, leaving me with a gray-haired granny whose V-neck says PROUD CRONE and a WITCH IN TRAINING in a stroller.

"Going to 612?" the CRONE asks when I re-jab the button for the sixth floor.

There's no way in hell I'm telling her my room number. "Why do you ask?" I say, eyeing the WITCH IN TRAINING, who is violently shaking her juice box upside-down.

The CRONE winks and leans over the stroller bar, exposing an expanse of crinkled cleavage I'd give a month of my life not to have seen. "So are we," she says in a hoarse whisper. "Going to see Miss Bridget. Though she's more active at night. So we'll come back then too."

"Sounds like a party," I say. The doors open, and I push the Close button as I slide through. "Oops! Sorry about that!"

The top floor is mercifully quiet. I look up *Miss Bridget / Rm 612 / Hawthorne* and discover that the hotel is built on the former apple orchard of the first woman to be hanged in Salem, Bridget Bishop. Of course it was. And that she is said to roam this floor in a white nightgown. As one does. That's why all these lunatics are here, to commune with the likes of Miss Bridget. What do they expect will happen on Halloween, exactly? The resurrection of the witches, scarlet A's bursting into flames on their bosoms? The midnight ride of headless Nathaniel Hawthorne? Every deranged shrew in the country is rioting on the streets outside, hoping to assuage the emptiness of their lives through some pathetic sorceress power fantasy. Good fucking luck, ladies. After this one night it'll be back to casting spells in your lonely living rooms, cats your sole companions, vibrators your only magic wands. I'm still muttering to myself as I locate my suite—*not* Room 612—and turn the key in the lock.

Why didn't Cyndi warn me about this? It was her idea to come here. Or rather, it was mine to meet somewhere other than her cat-infested hellhole, after I spent a night there following my visit to New York and one cat scratched me so badly I needed stitches, and another pissed in my shoes. *Kitten,* I'd said, once Cyndi was satisfied, *how about our next rendezvous, I take you on a trip?* This was what I'd planned anyway; it's how it always goes, meeting at their place, then a few overnights, then—if they prove trustworthy—my home. Except no woman has ever lasted more than a night there, just long enough for a little sportfucking, because they always let me down. But never mind. I remain hopeful, ever the romantic optimist.

Cyndi was reluctant. *That's a* lovely *idea,* she said, *but I don't know if I should travel. The cats.* I'd thought she was kidding the first time she'd said this; did she never really leave her home? *Can't the downstairs tenants take care of them?* I suggested. Cyndi had screwed up her dear little face, thinking about it, closing one big blue eye, then the other. *I guess. But also, it's almost Halloween.* I laughed. *What happens on Halloween, kitten? Do you go trick-or-treating? If you show me a trick, I'll give you a treat.* Cyndi did not laugh. *It's when the membrane is thinnest between this world and the next*, she said firmly. *I've never been away from my altar. Margaret might visit.* I detached a cat from my head, where it was sinking claws into my scalp. *What if,* I said, *we bring your altar with us? It's portable, no?* Cyndi thought about this some more. *You know where I've always wanted to be on Halloween?* she said finally. *Tell me,* I said. *The Hawthorne,* Cyndi said. *It's supposed to be a portal!* Her big eyes grew round, as if she were an orphan viewing a feast through a window. *We could have a séance,* I suggested. Cyndi clapped. *Ooooh! We could summon Margaret!* I ran my thumb down her clavicle. *I'm sure she'd come, especially if we read your book in the tub.* Cyndi squeaked: *Eeeeee! Yes! But . . .* Her face fell. *I've* never *been able to get a room there. It's too expensive, and especially not on Halloween. I'm sure it's been booked for months.* I discreetly propelled a cat across the room with my foot, hiding a smirk. My poor dear Kitten, so unaccustomed to the perks of wealth and status. *Leave it to me,* I said.

I did not understand at the time, nor like any sane person would I ever have guessed, what a broiling brouhaha Halloween is here, but the suite consoles me somewhat. It's as peaceful as the streets are psychotic, with thick carpet, medallioned wallpaper, a writing desk by the window that might have pleased Nathaniel himself. I'll be putting that to good use later, along with the four-poster bed I requested and the claw-foot tub. Although the view isn't directly of the harbor, there's the sense, as always in seaside towns, of light bouncing off water. A luxurious, well-appointed cocoon. Except for Cyndi's battered red rollaway, which she's abandoned in the middle of the room—why?—and the squirrel's nest of items that, I am beginning to suspect, accompanies her everywhere: on the couch a cardigan inside out, a half-eaten apple, a brush choked with blond strands; on the coffee table tarot cards, a Ouija board, a candle, the crow under glass. Of course she had to bring him with her. At least there are no cats. That I know of. I set my briefcase on the desk.

"Kitten," I call, wheeling Cyndi's suitcase to the bedroom—why must women always overpack? We are here for one night. Canopy bed, as promised. I recall against my will Simone performing an endearingly clumsy but arousing striptease on a similar bed, swiveling out of her sundress and thumbing down her thong, and thrust the memory away with a growl. *No. Go away.* The Hawthorne may be haunted, by Bridget Bishop and God knows who, but the only ghost I believe in is Simone.

"Kitten, where did you go?" I call.

No answer from Cyndi. But there's the zapping sound of somebody unlocking the main door to the suite. I return to the living room, frowning, in time to see the handle flipping from horizontal to vertical. Housekeeping? This late in the day? Or a guest who's mistaken the room for his own—but then why would he have our key? Is it room service; does complimentary champagne come with the suite? For this price, it should.

"We don't need anything, thank you," I call with irritation. "And don't you knock?" For the door is already swinging open. I go to block it with my foot—

—and it's Simone.

"Simone?" I say doubtfully. "Is it you?"

She pushes past me, corporeal enough. I smell the cold wind in her hair and on her skin, and there's a half-dead maple leaf caught in her braid. She's in her yoga pants and sneakers and a suede jacket, and I think stupidly that I've never known her in fall. She looks around, breathing hard, her cheeks flushed as if she's run up the stairs.

"Cyndi?" she calls. "I'm here!"

"What are you doing here?" I say. I'm still so bewildered by the presence of actual, three-dimensional Simone after weeks of being haunted by her that I'm slow to calculate. My body is happily responding to her, her scent, her chest rising and falling—I took my meds in the car, and boy are they kicking in. I want to go to her, thrust my tongue into her mouth, reach into her shirt and twist her breasts. I don't know whether to fuck her or shake her.

Then I realize she's called Cyndi by name.

"Why are you here?" I ask again. My scrambled brain coughs up an unlikely but happy answer—a threesome? Did they plan this? Do they think it's my birthday? How does Simone know Cyndi? I move toward Simone, but she sidesteps me, bristling.

"I'm here to verify what *you're* doing here," she says. "And so is she. Hey, Cyndi! Where are you, girl?"

She's across the room before I can catch her, but finally I start functioning again. "No," I say furiously, snatching for her and grabbing only air. "You can't just come in here and *maraud*." For she's racing around like a greyhound, rampaging through the bedroom. I lunge for her and catch her elbow. "Simone!" I grip her arm. "What the fuck are you doing!"

Simone glares at me. Her eyes are lurid with tears.

"I'd ask you the same question," she says, "but I think we already know. Where's Cyndi?"

Before I can decide whether to say *Who?*, or *Mind your own business*, Simone stamps on my foot. "Let *go!*" she spits. It doesn't hurt, but it surprises me enough that I let out an exclamation and relax my grasp, and Simone wrenches herself free and scrambles to the one room of the suite she hasn't yet investigated, the bathroom. Whereupon I curse myself again for being so slow-moving, so taken by surprise, so susceptible to Simone that I was too weak to stop her, for the next thing I hear is her scream, not a piercing one but the kind of high wheezy noise a person makes when she's so startled and scared she can't take a full breath, and all I can do is think if only I had held on to her, for now she will never unsee, and I, joining her, will never unsee, and indeed there is no way to ever unsee, or undo the trauma of seeing, a woman dead in a bathtub full of her own blood.

PART III

SAM (and the Rabbit)

CHAPTER 26

NOTES

THE EVE OF ALL HALLOW'S EVE

HAWTHORNE HOTEL

To Whom It May Concern (and to William C., who probably found me, sorry!),

I, Cyndi Pietorowski, am going to join my great-x-9-grandmother Margaret Scott, who was falsely accused, condemned, and executed for witchcraft not far from this site in 1692. Margaret appeared to me here as I was setting up for a séance to reach her. I guess she couldn't wait to summon me!!!! (PS, fellow Wiccans, there is DEFINITELY a portal in this hotel.) Margaret said that my time here is complete, and my parents, as well as my gram and all my great-aunties and uncles, await me on the other side.

This life has been interesting but not very kind to me, so I am not afraid to go. I am happy!!!! I will leave signs for anyone who wants to contact me via ritual.

The only concern I have about leaving this realm is my cats. My last Will and Testament is in my home at 327 Hill Street in Salem, in my bedside table drawer. It is recent, signed, and notarized. My Executrix, Heather Yountz of Gomez and Yountz, my former place of employment, has a copy. Whoever finds this, please direct her to immediately put my house on the market and use the proceeds to relocate my cats to the Popoki Cat

Sanctuary in Hawai'i. My savings should be enough to hire a sitter while these arrangements are being made and to pay for their transport as well as lifelong care. Please give my furbabies kisses from me and tell them I will see them on the other side.

With appreciation for the gifts of this dimension,
looking forward to the next,
Cyndi Pietorowski. XOXO

SALEM POLICE DEPARTMENT

Transcript: interview with William Corwyn,
Hawthorne Hotel Skylark Conference Room, Oct. 30, 3:26 p.m.

Recording officer: Joseph Moldover, Badge No. 1923

Thank you, I'm comfortable enough. Yes. I consent to being recorded. I'm going to record on my phone as well. So we're clear, this is an informal interview, correct? Not an official witness statement? Let the record show you have not read me my Mirandas.

Very good. If there's evidence of foul play, I'll provide a follow-up interview. With my attorney present.

All right. [Sighs.] Ms. Pietorowski. Poor girl. I didn't know her very well. She was a new friend, you could say. I was trying to help her with her book. She's writing—was writing . . . [inaudible] Thank you. I'd love some water.

She was writing a novel based on her ancestress Margaret Scott, who was hanged here in Salem. She wasn't yet published, so I reached out to see if I could be of assistance—

Yes, it *is* unusual for an author of my stature to help a newbie. But I believe in, what's the phrase? Paying it forward. I've been very fortunate with my career, so I try to help however I can. I run a writers' support group called The Darlings, and Cyndi came to one of our meetings. That's how we connected. I realized from her feedback form that she had unusually scant resources. So I offered a helping hand.

I wouldn't describe it as *dating*, exactly, but yes, *her* interest was romantic. It was a very recent development, I'd say only a couple of weeks, and I was uneasy about it because although she seemed so sweet, she was such a lost soul. I have a bit of a Pygmalion complex; that's a—oh, you know what it is? Really? Very good! I don't think of most police officers having English degrees. Yes, *Pygmalion*, the Shaw play about the professor rescuing the flower girl. It's not a popular thing to admit now, but I tend toward partners who are not quite . . . of my standing. I suppose it's that giving proclivity again. [Clears throat.] More water, please. Thanks.

Today? I arrived at the hotel around 1:30. The front desk clerk should have a record. I met Cyndi here. It was difficult to even access the lobby because—well, you know what it's like outside. It's a melee, to put it politely. I don't know how you cope with this insanity year after year.

We checked in—yes, I rented the suite. The poor girl couldn't afford it, and she had always wanted to come here. She said the Hawthorne had a portal and she wanted to channel Margaret. [Sighs.] I have to admit I agreed partly because I didn't want to meet at Cyndi's house. She has nineteen cats. No exaggeration. So I humored her. I said let's have a séance at the Hawthorne. If only I hadn't encouraged her fantasies, maybe . . . I knew she was unstable, I saw signs, but—

Specifically? The best way I can describe it is that her energy seemed variable. She boomeranged from quiet and calm to amped up and lascivious. I found medication at her house, antianxiety pills, and lithium, and antipsychotics—yes, like the ones by the tub. She didn't talk to me about her condition or conditions—as I said, we didn't know each other that well. But she never mentioned suicide.

Today she seemed rather frenzied. I attributed it to her being excited that she was at her so-called portal—and also, if I may be candid, to my company. We met in the lobby, got the room keys, and were en route to the suite when I realized I'd left my briefcase in my car. I'm never without it, not just because it has my WIP in it—that's my work-in-progress—but because of my own medication. Well. You're a young man, but you can guess what I mean. [Lowers voice, inaudible.] Yes . . . that, and beta-blockers, which I take for my heart. I have a condition—A-fib, atrial defibrillation—that I need prescriptions for, and it's not wise for me to be without them.

It was a real job to reach my car. The streets are jammed with so-called witches. Some madwoman elbowed me in the thorax, and another one nearly stuck me in the eye with a broom handle. Again, hats off to you for handling this annual madness.

When I returned to the hotel, I got my parking validated, spoke with the desk clerk, and went to the suite. I'm not sure how long I'd been gone, maybe . . . a half hour? Forty-five minutes? Long enough for . . . [inaudible]

Thank you. Please excuse my distress. This is just such a shame. I wish I could have done—something. Even if I didn't know Cyndi very well, I wish I had seen . . . I lost a fiancée many years ago to the same illness, so this cuts me to the quick.

Oh—right. Ms. Vetiver. I'd estimate she arrived about five minutes before we found Cyndi. Actually, Ms. Vetiver—Simone—found her. She went into the bathroom and made the awful discovery. But I was seconds behind her. Of course, she was hysterically upset.

We had met before this. She's also a novelist, published by my publisher. And . . . yes, I did know her in a more intimate way. We had a fling earlier this year. I stopped seeing her after I learned we had . . . irreconcilable artistic differences. To be blunt, she tried to appropriate material from me. In . . . early September?

We haven't spoken since I jettisoned her. Until today. I have no idea why she was there. Possibly Cyndi was in Simone's novel class? Or they'd arranged some Wiccan writer ritual and Simone got the time wrong?

You're not suggesting ... No. That's ludicrous. Simone would never harm anyone. Even if there were motive. Well, yes, I suppose you're right. Jealousy is powerful. And I have been its object before. Women do tend to form strong attachments to me. But if this were a crime of passion, wouldn't that be a very different death? More—well, passionate? Impromptu, violent ... I can't imagine, given the pills, the razor, Cyndi's note, that this was anything but a suicide.

Then again, I don't have that kind of mind. It's why for all my range I've never written a thriller. Nor do I aspire to. You'll think I'm an old softie, but I just can't stand the blood.

If you *did* suspect foul play, I'd take a look at my stalker. I've filed numerous complaints about her. They're in all the law enforcement databases. I went to graduate school with her, and she became obsessed. She's only ever tailed me, however. Not threatened me physically. She's too wily for that; she knows it would get her in real trouble. But perhaps this time ...

I don't know her name. I know that sounds absurd, but I have no idea. I know what it *used* to be, when we were in the program together. But she's obviously changed it, because when I hired an investigator to find her—the police have been pathetically useless, no offense—her trail had gone cold. She'd just vanished. I'm sure she's operating under a pseudonym. But yes, I'm sure it's the same woman. You can't mistake her appearance. She has a pronounced overbite.

Ask Ms. Vetiver about her. She's received written warnings, as have my other paramours over the years. Ms. Vetiver has filed her own reports and been told the same thing I was: Nobody can do anything.

So I'd concentrate my efforts on the stalker, if I were you. IF Cyndi's death is anything but what it appears ...

Yes, if you have more questions, feel free to get in touch. You have my number. Although please be advised I'm about to start my next novel, so I may not always be readily available. But I will try my best. Thank you, officer, for your sensitivity and empathy. Under other circumstances, I'd say it's been a pleasure.

JENNA BLUM

SALEM POLICE DEPARTMENT

Transcript: interview with Simone Vetiver,
Hawthorne Hotel Pickman Conference Room, Oct. 30, 3:31 p.m.

Recording officer: Kimberly Lowrance, Badge No. 1756

Thank you. I'm okay. I don't need water. [Crying.] This is so terrible. Sorry. I'll get it together. [Sobbing.] It's just such a shock.

Sure, you can record. Can I record too? And I don't need my attorney for this, right? Otherwise you'd read me my Miranda rights?

Okay. [Sighs.] I got here this afternoon around 2:00. I was supposed to be here earlier, but it was so nuts out there. I was a half hour late. I'd told Cyndi 1:30 . . . [Blows nose.]

I didn't know her very well. We'd met only once before this, at Gulu Gulu in Salem—yes, the café. I set up the meeting on social because I thought she was seeing William, the guy who was upstairs with me in the suite—oh, duh, of course you already know this. Sorry. I'm still so shocky.

So what happened is, William and I had been dating, and it was serious, like marriage-level. He kept talking about a life together. And I was literally ecstatic we'd found each other. We met when he was in town on tour for his latest novel—yes, *All the Lambent Souls*, did you read it? [Sighs.] Of course. Everyone's read it. And loves it. Say hi to your book club from me!

Anyway, when we got together, it was like planets colliding. Being a writer is so strange and isolating, and we really bonded over that. He was talking about our future even in our first correspondence . . . The future perfect. [Sighs.] After only two months, we were already talking about my coming to his house in Maine.

Then we had a fight, *one* fight, and he got weird— Oh, weird as in offended, super-affronted, unable-to-get-over-it. The fight was about . . . Well, I started working on a new project that was *very* loosely, as in the *teensiest* bit, inspired by William's losing his fiancée in grad school. I mean not even. Just inspired by actual events, as they say on TV. Not the plot or the people, just the original idea, like that spark that comes off a Zippo, you know, when you're trying to light it. You put that together with the What Ifs of the story and that's how novels are born. William knows this, of course. But he was so angry he couldn't hear me, and he stayed so mad that—

Nononono, just angry *verbally*. That's all. Not physically. He gave me an ultimatum, the book or him, and while I dealing with that—*thank* you, it IS the writer's *Sophie's Choice!*—he disappeared. I texted him and emailed him and called him and . . . crickets.

So I started to wonder *Hmmm, is there somebody else?* I know you must be thinking I'm a moron, it's not like I'm the first woman to get dumped, but I just had this feeling. So I started scrolling his social, and I saw him making flirty comments on a bunch of women's posts—all writers, all my age-ish, they all could've been related to me. I was like, *Huh. Does this guy have a type or what.* Most of them responded just casually, but this one, Cyndi Pietorowski . . . [Sighs.] God. Poor Cyndi. She put hearts on all his posts, and wrote a jillion comments with egregious amounts of exclamation points, and then William mis-messaged me on social, sending me an invitation meant for her about meeting at the Blue Trees. Yes, the art installation here in Salem. Like, *Whoopsie!* You fucked up, dude. So I went to the park when they'd arranged to meet and I saw them—

No, I didn't confront them. I just watched. And then, and I am not proud of myself, I looked up where she lived, and I went to her house—

Oh my God no, not to say anything to her! Honestly I had no idea why I was going. I just—went. I think to make it real, you know? So I was sitting in my car and I got lucky, or unlucky, however you want to look at it, because William pulled up. I recognized his car instantly because who the F else has a Mary Oliver bumper sticker?

No, I still didn't do anything. I guess I'm way too cowardly to be a Real Housewife of Salem. I just sat there and watched him hug her and go inside and I felt seriously sick. Like I might throw up. So I waited until it passed and I went home. That was it.

Except I'd previously sent Cyndi a DM on social that said, *Are you seeing William Corwyn?* And when I got home I saw she'd answered, and she said he'd offered to help her with her book.

Of course he did. God, I was so angry. I mean, sure, it's William's pre-rogative to help whoever he wants. And he does run a writers' support group, The Darlings. He's just *such* a helpful guy. But a week before he'd been talking about marrying me and already he was "helping" [subject makes finger quotes] a woman who looked so much like me and mean-while not returning my calls or emails or texts? His side of the street was *not* clean. His relationship hygiene was terrible, to put it mildly.

So I arranged to meet Cyndi at Gulu Gulu—I guess about two weeks ago? I'll check the date for you on my calendar. And again, I'm not really sure what my motivation was. Maybe to warn her about this guy. Maybe to find out what was really going on. I hate the word closure, but it would have helped to have confirmation.

We had lunch, and she was such a sweetheart . . . [Sniffles.] She reminded me of a puppy at a shelter. I know that sounds terrible and I don't mean to be disrespectful, especially not when talking about the—the deceased . . . but it was just the way she looked at people. Me, the server. She was just so hopeful. And self-effacing, she kept putting herself down, saying she couldn't believe I'd make time to talk to her, or that William had. She seemed truly confused about why he'd contacted her. She said they'd connected over her book and that otherwise she was sure he was just being nice . . .

[Deep breath.] . . . which I did not in any way believe, and I told her I thought he was playing me, potentially us, and she was like, Oh, I hope not, how awful. So I said, Want to help me out? and we made a plan to lure William to a place where we'd be there together to confront him and see what was really up. Which leads us to today.

[Drinks water.] I got my key from the front desk, Cyndi had left me one, saying I was her sister, and I went up to the room, and there was William—

About 2:00 . . . 2:05? I'd guess? Maybe 2:10?

No. No. Definitely no sound or sign of struggle. Not then and not before I came in. Just William saying What the hell are you doing here,

Simone, and I was like, We want to ask you the same question, and I called for Cyndi but she didn't answer, so I went looking for her, and— [Sobbing.]

I'm sorry. It was just such a shock. Although maybe it shouldn't have been. I saw signs, when we were at the café—she took meds at the table, and one of them was lithium. Plus I saw the semicolon tattoo on her wrist, and I know that means the person has had suicidal ideation or past attempts. As in, *My sentence could have ended here, but I keep going.* It's a suicide survivor thing—my former fiancé has one too. He got it after his release from the psychiatric hospital.

So I'm shocked but not surprised that she took her own life. Are you—do you suspect it could be something else? I guess you can't say, but . . . I just want to clarify for the record that if it IS foul play, I do NOT think it's William. He'd have no motive, and as mad as I am at him, I think he's seriously sketchy about women but not more than that.

There *is* one other possibility you could investigate *if* you think it's foul play. There's a woman who's been stalking me—actually she's William's stalker, but I inherited her. The Rabbit, he calls her. Because . . . Never mind. I don't know her real name. She started following me and leaving me threatening notes while I was dating him, but since he ghosted me I haven't heard from her.

No, I didn't save the notes because I turned them in to the Boston PD, but they would have them on file. Nothing too gory. Just stay away from William Corwyn if you know what's good for you, stuff like that.

Nothing physically violent, or I would have gotten a restraining order. Still, I would ask William about her. He'd know more. There was another supposedly disturbed woman he mentioned, too—a complication, he called her, though God knows what the real story was there. As I said, his relationship style was hot mess. And women in love can be crazy.

Of course. I'm happy to help. Well, not happy, but you know what I mean. If I think of anything else, I'll let you know. [Sighs.] I'm sure Cyndi's death is what it looks like. But I would check out the Rabbit, if you can figure out who and where she is.

The Rabbit

Here I am in Salem, and the good thing about it is, it's crowded AF. Easy for a girl to get lost on Halloween, especially if she's gone to the Dollar Store and gotten a fake nose piercing, a packet of supposedly silver rings that are already leaving green circles on her fingers, and purple barrette feathers for her hair. I blend right in here, or at least I would if I were clinically insane. There are witches in capes and hats, witches with twig brooms, witches with actual live ravens on their shoulders, witches with pentagram tattoos, pouring into the city in vehicles that all have the same bumper sticker: *My Other Car's a Broom!* They're setting up tents in the parks and parking lots, including this one I'm sitting in now, on a broken chair I found behind the Hawthorne Hotel dumpster. I admire their commitment and some of them even look bad-@$$ but who the f*ck has the time and money for this?

The bad thing about Salem is, it's crowded AF, which means it's hard for me to maintain a clear sight line on the back door of the Hawthorne—until the emergency vehicles show up. Here we go. They part the crowd like Moses, moving slowly through the lot with their flashers on but sirens off. The witches make way reluctantly, at first turning to see what's happening and then going back to their business, which I assume is preparing to summon spirits tonight or some such. They're not really interested in seeing who is newly, actually, physically dead.

Myself, I am quite interested. I drift through the crowd until I'm near the back door where the ambulance is parked. It takes a minute, of course it does, the authorities have to investigate, they have to officially pronounce her deceased. I hug myself in the chilly wind coming off the harbor. I almost wish I had some big velvet witchy cloak. Eventually the door opens and the EMTs bring out the gurney with its enclosed passenger. Cyndi Pietorowski. Poor girl. So many William Corwyn love interests, so many body bags.

Some of the witches look up from their cell phones and books of spells or whatever, and one chants something in a long-dead language. Somebody else hits a gong, which spooks the ravens, one of which splats on its irate owner's shoulder. I'm not religious, but I say a prayer in case Anyone is listening. This one was certifiably nuts. Poor little Cyndi. But she was so sweet. And I am sorry. I'm genuinely sorry. I'm so, so sorry for what has happened to her. Even though it's William's fault for choosing her in the first place. But it is definitely my fault too.

The ambulance proceeds in reverse. The police vehicles remain. So do I. I didn't see William's car in the lot, but I know he's in there somewhere. And I know if he leaves the hotel, which BTW is about fifty times nicer than any I've ever stayed in, he'll want to avoid notice and do it through the back door.

But guess who comes out with a female police officer? Not William. Sam Vetiver! I can't believe it. F*cking Sam Vetiver. She's like a yeast infection you thought was gone but that never goes away. What the hell is she doing here? I mean, obviously she's here because William is here. And I knew she was stalking that poor Cyndi. I knew because I tailed Sam Vetiver for a while to make sure she and William were done, which is how I knew she was spying on them in that weird park with the blue trees, and then at Cyndi's house FFS, although Sam Vetiver just jumped around in the bushes for a while in a totally ineffective way trying to see through the windows and then went and sat in her yellow Jeep and cried, then drove home. Which is also how I knew William had ditched her, had done that William thing of promising her the world and then pulling the football away. I knew he'd ghosted her because why the hell else would a grown woman be acting like such a lunatic. I watched Sam Vetiver through her apartment windows scrolling social media all hours of the night, her face underlit with screen glow, and I knew she and William were over, that he'd kicked the chair out from under her and let her twist.

So I thought she was no longer a threat and I switched to the Cyndi channel instead. But somehow I f*cked up, because here Sam Vetiver is, released from police questioning and wandering through the insanity like some orphan child in a Nat Geo photo shoot about a natural disaster, her face smeared with makeup and tears.

I elbow through the witches, saying " 'Scuse me pardon me 'scuse me" and following Sam Vetiver to the train station where her yellow Jeep is parked. How did I miss it? I was focused on Cyndi, is how. So f*cking sloppy. Sam Vetiver gets into her Jeep, and I bolt for the waterfront warehouse where I've been parked and sleeping for the whole last week. Wherever Sam Vetiver goes, I go, and I've got to get to my car.

CHAPTER 27

THE RUNNING OF THE WITCHES

Sam Vetiver was lost.

Metaphorically, not literally. In actuality she was sitting in her Jeep behind the Salem train station, being buffeted by hundreds of turbocharged Wiccans. Sam had never been to the Running of the Bulls in Pamplona, but she imagined it was much like this, except with witches instead of large angry bovine creatures. From the surfeit of estrogen and patchouli alone, Sam would have known where she was with her eyes closed.

Emotionally, she was as lost as she'd ever been in her life.

She didn't know what to do. She was in no condition to drive; she didn't even remember how she'd gotten to her car. One moment she was in the conference room at the Hawthorne, the next she was here. Huddled in her driver's seat with the heater cranked all the way up, unable to get warm. It wasn't the cold, damp wind whistling off the harbor or the gunmetal sky, Sam knew. It was shock. She'd been here before.

She couldn't stop seeing Cyndi—this was another PTSD symptom, her therapist had told her. Invasive thoughts. So that every time Sam blinked, she saw Cyndi in the tub. Blink: Cyndi's big blue eyes staring blindly at the ceiling. Blink: her hair fanning in the maroon water. Blink: her T-shirt and jeans molded to her body—who wore clothes when she slit her wrists in the tub? Cyndi, that's who. Because she was such a sweetheart she wanted to spare whoever found her the extra shock of her nudity. Blink: how leached her skin was, her lips gray, an unseasonable fly washing its legs on her dead arm next to the pill bottles on the tub's edge.

Sam should have known. She remembered the Family Day group leader at Hank's psychiatric ward saying, *What's the number-one thing you should know? It's not your fault.* Sam had nodded. She was sure this was true, and yet she'd never believed it for a second. Not at all.

She should have stopped Hank. And Amelie. And Cyndi. And her dad. Sam was 0 for 4. She should have known.

And this time maybe Sam was directly responsible as well as clueless, because hadn't she known Cyndi had a condition? She had. She'd watched Cyndi count out her meds at the café table—*Sorry*, Cyndi had said, smiling sweetly, *if I don't take these at the same time every day, they're not as effective.* Had noticed the semicolon tattooed on Cyndi's wrist and thought, Oh, honey. Had seen how Cyndi's eyes gleamed when she talked about William: *He reached out to help me with my fiction novel! I was so surprised! I mean, somebody like you, I could understand him talking to. But me, why?* And how that light in Cyndi's face had gone out when Sam described how William had treated her, said Cyndi should be careful, suggested they confront him together. *Sure*, Cyndi had said. *I'd be happy to help.* But she had drooped and gone quiet. What if Cyndi had been depending on the What If fantasy of life with William, even more than Sam had, and in puncturing it, Sam had tripped her wires?

Sam should have stayed away. Maybe then the next time she'd seen Cyndi would not have been dead in a bathtub, with William in the next room.

William.

And what was *wrong* with Sam that all she wanted to do, the only thing in the world, was talk to William?

She had been utterly unprepared for the instant surge of animal relief she'd felt when she opened the suite door and saw him standing there: *It's you!* Or for the joy that had flooded his face, probably mirroring her own, swiftly replaced by confusion, then anger, then frustration as he chased her through the rooms.

Or for the hot, damp solidity of his body as he restrained her when she lunged, howling, toward the bathtub—screaming *No, no! No!* His ferocious growl in her ear: *Don't, Simone! Stop it. You can't help her. She's beyond that now. And don't touch her. You can't disturb the scene.*

She'd thought he might offer some commiseration, some touch or reassurance, when she sat shuddering on the couch while he called the front desk. His voice so calm as he said *There's been an incident in Room 620, I need the police*, but he'd been pulling down the skin under his eyes as he spoke, turning his face into a grotesque Halloween mask. When he hung up, he'd been remote as a stranger, standing in the middle of the room with his hands at his sides, muttering a most familiar refrain: *I should have done something. I should have known.*

And when the detectives arrived after the manager and EMTs, William had spared Sam only one glance, the kind he might give a pedestrian on the street, before they escorted him from the suite.

Of course, he'd been under terrible strain. As Sam was. They'd been in the same room with a dead woman. They'd found her together. Maybe that was why Sam's need to see William, to talk to him, was like a fever. Even though he'd dumped her and ignored her, even though he'd taken up with a woman a decade his junior who was emotionally unstable, even though Sam's subsequent behavior had turned her into someone she didn't like, was actively ashamed of, who called him and messaged him and stalked him and eventually set a honey trap in desperation— after all this, William was the only person in the world who knew exactly how Sam felt right now. How terrified he might be blamed. How scared that there might have been third-party Rabbit involvement. How guilty that, if Cyndi's death was the suicide even the police seemed to believe it was, he might have done something to prevent it.

Sam's phone buzzed. Drishti. Sam hadn't told Drishti beforehand that she was going to the Hawthorne, nor, later, about finding Cyndi in the tub. Sam had texted only SOS, CAN I STAY WITH YOU GUYS TONIGHT?, because the thought of being in her own apartment, visited by spectral Cyndi or perhaps the actual Rabbit, was insupportable.

But it was time to tell Drishti what had happened and come clean. Sam flipped her phone.

The text said: HI SIMONE. WHERE ARE YOU? ARE YOU ALL RIGHT?

CHAPTER 28

TRAUMA BOND

Hi, William. No, I'm not all right. Are you?

No.

Did you give a witness statement?

Yes. You?

Yes. It sounds like they think Cyndi's death was a suicide.

What else could it be? Occam's razor: The simplest explanation is usually the right one.

Agree. But it could have been the Rabbit?

Unlikely. But possible. I told them that.

So did I.

Has she troubled you lately? Contacted you?

No. Not since we stopped . . . No.

Thank God for small mercies.

I guess.

. . .

. . .

God, that was devastating. I'm sitting in my car shaking and I can't stop.
Can I tell you something I've **never** told anyone?

Yes. Tell.

I found Hank.

. . . Forgive me, I'm confused. Was he lost?

No. I mean he had a suicide **attempt**. When he was drinking. I found him.

Oh Simone. Honey. You never said.

Maybe I should have **mentioned** it.

Yes, you should.

Can I tell you now?

Please.

It was when we lived in the Berkshires. He was on a serious bender, the
one after he set the garage on fire. I asked him to leave. I told him he had
a choice: I could drive him to the nearest motel or I'd call the cops. He
chose the motel. I drove him there. William, the hardest thing I ever did
was leave him there in the middle of the night. I drove away watching him
in my wing mirror, walking into that motel room with his porkpie hat on,
and I had no idea if I'd ever see him again.

Oh, Simone. I'm so sorry.

Thank you. I had a bad feeling. And I was right. The motel owner called
me around 4 AM. She'd smelled smoke coming from Hank's room. He'd
cut his wrists. And taken pills with vodka. His cigar had rolled onto the
rug. Good thing he smoked, right?

What a terrible ordeal.

The motel owner was so pissed. She kept saying, *You'll have to pay for
that carpet, you know.* Meanwhile I took Hank to the ER and they got him
patched up. He wouldn't let me come in because he didn't want me to
see the cuts. After that he went to the psych ward. Inpatient. And that
saved his life. They got him the right meds. But it was the hardest thing
I've ever lived through.

What you did was an incredible act of courage and kindness, Simone.

Not at all. I loved him. And he was a human being who needed my help. I'm sure you'd do the same.

I would have, if I'd gotten the chance.

OMG. Right. Becky. I'm sorry, that was clumsy of me. Of course you know how I feel. How did she, if you don't mind my asking . . .

Pills. Like Cyndi. But without the wrists.

Oh God. And you found her?

I did. In our apartment.

I'm so sorry, William.

Thank you.

And maybe this isn't the right time to bring this up. But I want you to know I meant you and Becky no disrespect with my novel idea.

. . .

William? Are you there?

Here. Thinking.

Okay. Well, I needed you to know that.

I heard you, Simone. I heard you the first time. You tendered an apology and I thanked you. It was not good enough. You didn't say you'd give up the book. You were considering going ahead with the thievery of my story. I had to protect myself.

By getting involved with Cyndi?

. . .

Hello?

I was typing, Simone. Would you like to know what I was typing? I was asking you what you were doing there. At the Hawthorne. How did you know Cyndi?

Honestly? I got in touch with her because I thought you were dating her and I couldn't stand it. Especially because you and I had no real closure.

243

It was making me crazy. So I'm not proud of it, but we met to discuss you. Which, speaking of which, what were YOU doing there? Were you two dating?

Not dating per se. She was obsessed with me, Simone.

What do you mean, obsessed? In what way?

In the obsessed way. She reached out to me after attending a Darlings meeting. Asked me for help with her novel. I acquiesced, although I was very busy with the end of my tour and also reeling from your betrayal. She would not leave me alone. I made a grave error by going to her house to work with her, and she seemed to think we were in a romantic arrangement. Perhaps I should have been more blunt, but she was so vulnerable, I was afraid to hurt her. Do you know what I mean?

Yes. I saw it too. She was on serious meds.

Her antipsychotics. Yes. And the cats.

I didn't meet the cats.

Count yourself lucky. They are a nightmare. The best thing that could happen to those poor creatures is to be shipped off to a sanctuary in Hawai'i. Cyndi's house was a hoarder house. She was very unstable. But also tenacious. She pursued me hotly. When she begged me to come to the Hawthorne, I stupidly went. I thought maybe I could make it clear to her that I was interested in her as no more than a helpful editor. I got there minutes before you did. You know the rest.

Yes. I'll never forget it.

Nor I.

. . .

  . . .

Hi, Simone.

Hello, William.

I have missed you.

Have you?

Yes. I've been haunted by you.

Well. That's nice. I feel the same. But your ghosting me made it hard to tell.

I did not ghost you, Simone, if we must use juvenile vernacular. I stepped out of our relationship out of self-preservation. Perhaps I overcorrected, and if so, apologies. But I was angry and bereft over your carelessness. Do you know how badly you hurt me with that book idea? Do you feel any repentance? Have you thought more about your decision?

. . . What decision? I thought we were done.

Whether we are done or not depends on your decision whether to write your book. Your so-called thriller.

. . .

No answer, Simone? Wrong answer. I'd better get back on the road. I'm at a rest stop to have this conversation, but I see it's perhaps not worth my time.

Wait! William. Stop. Sorry, I was processing. I didn't know there was any possibility left for us. This is new information for me. And I want to respond mindfully because this is such a fraught topic for both of us.

True. Take your time. I'll wait. Respond wisely.

I'm not working on that book right now.

How do you feel about that?

. . . I don't know.

I feel relieved, Simone. It means you've taken that thriller idea out behind the barn and shot it. It means you've learned the difference between empty equivocating and meaningful action. It goes a long way toward repairing us. But I also hate the idea of you not writing.

Me too. Thanks.

What if . . .

What if what?

What if we were having this conversation in person? There's much I think we still have to clear up. And much we could say to each other.

Agree.

Where are you now?

Still in my car. In Salem.

Remember when I was going to invite you to my house in Maine?

I remember.

What if I re-tendered my invitation? What if I gave you the coordinates to my house now? Would you come?

The Rabbit

Movin me down the highway, movin me down the highway . . . movin ahead so life won't pass me by . . .

This is what I'm singing as I drive up the interstate. My car has a CD player, but it never worked, and I don't pay for any of the subscription music services. So I'm singing this song from memory, as I do whenever I'm on the road tailing one of William's girls. It's the only happy memory I have of my mom, dancing with her to it in front of our stove, which we pretended was a fireplace because it was our source of heat. Some guy had left the record behind and it was scratched so it skipped and stuck . . . *highway . . . highway . . . highway . . .* and still we had fun dancing to it. Later I realized my mom was drunk as sh*t, but a girl has to take her happy memories where she can.

Today it's not life I don't want passing me by but Sam Vetiver. I keep one car between us as she zooms along in the fast lane. I'll say one thing for that old Jeep of hers, it's good it's that obnoxious yellow, because otherwise I might lose sight of it. That thing moves surprisingly fast.

But then again, I know exactly where she's going. I could drive to William's in my sleep.

She turns off the highway, and so do I. We cruise along for a while. This is the point at which you can tell you're getting into the north country. The interstate is developed, has office parks and condos and malls. This two-lane is hemmed in by forest. There are leaping deer signs, and moose. I thought they didn't really exist, were just a myth the locals made up to titillate and scare the tourists, until one dawn I was following William to Albany and saw a mama and baby standing by the side of the road. Just hanging out and chewing breakfast in the mist, like something from a movie.

There are mountains now, and curves. And trees. So many of them. Dense on the road on either side. Choking off the light. So much forest.

There are fewer vehicles, too, and I drop back so Sam Vetiver won't spot me. Not that she would probably recognize me. My vehicle, unlike hers, blends in. It's an old sedan, which is one of the two kinds of cars people drive up here, the other being some big SUV or pickup, sometimes with truck nuts and often with dead deer in the bed, heads lolling and eyes glazed.

We drive ever farther inland and north. Bear signs join the moose and deer. About an hour later she turns onto the dirt road that will take her to the logging track to William Island. I'm starting to get sleepy now, I pulled an all-nighter staking out her apartment, so thank goodness we're almost there. The sky has a low, heavy, gray look too.

When Sam Vetiver finds William's private road, I peel off. Give her some time. It's too isolated here for me to get too close. I snooze in the drive of an abandoned hunting camp.

By the time I wake, I figure it's safe. I drive to my usual hiding spot, conceal the car. I'm lucky, there's some snow, but it's so cold it's frozen solid. I won't leave significant tracks.

Now comes the hard part, navigating the rocks along the causeway and around William's gate. The pillars are for show, they're not attached to anything, their bases are just sunk into the lake. Which isn't fully frozen yet, I can still see bubbles like somebody's trapped under the dark ice. So I hug one of the pillars, spreading my body like a starfish, and make a calculated jump—landing safely on the other side. Welcome to William Island! It's a challenge to get here, but I'm used to it.

What I'm not used to: seeing Sam Vetiver's yellow Jeep behind the gate, parked in the driveway. It's like coming into my sh*thole apartment and finding a snake. My stomach lurches.

I can hear them carrying on all the way from the yard. *Oh! Oh! Oh!* Gosh damn Sam Vetiver. I wedge myself in between the bushes and the house, beneath William's bedroom window, waiting, trying to decide what to do. I shift around silently, flex my mittened fingers to stay warm. The temperature is dropping wickedly. I could get into the house through my secret window, but I'm too sad. After listening to as much of their post-f*ckfest nonsense as I can stand, I decide to risk driving back to my sh*thole and returning tomorrow.

As I'm following the causeway back out to where I hid my car, crawling over the rocks, I hear the garage door rumble up, the sound carrying across the ice in that long-range flat way that's possible only in winter. I pause, clinging to a boulder, and pop my head up just enough to see William in the robe he usually reserves for hot tub use, a big thick forest green one as if he's at a luxury spa, and his boots. Sam Vetiver is watching him from the garage in just his sweatshirt, jumping up and down on the cold cement and laughing.

He opens the tailgate of her Jeep and lifts out a suitcase the size of a coffin. And another. Wheels them both through the garage into the house. Sam Vetiver darts out and grabs a backpack from her front seat, squealing as her bare feet hit the frosty driveway.

She runs inside. The door rolls closed.

The house is quiet now, lights shining against the cold dusk. In the black woods even the birds have gone silent.

F*ck. This is not normal.

This is not normal at all. How long is that b*tch planning to stay?

A long time, from the looks of it.

This is cataclysmically bad.

This has never happened before.

"F*ck," I say out loud. "F*ck!" I say to the darkening sky.

Then I continue crawling over the icy rocks to my car. I've got a lot of work ahead of me now. It's time to do the thing I hoped I'd never have to do but I have a plan for nonetheless. It's time to pull the trigger on Operation Rabbit Hole.

CHAPTER 29

THE SCRIPTORIUM

William's house was not what Sam had thought it would be. For one thing, it was on an actual island surrounded by a massive lake. At least there was a causeway to it, so she didn't have to go by boat. At the end of the drive there was an iron gate with spikes, upon one of which was impaled a stuffed Peter Rabbit whose fur ruffled in the steady wind. Had William put it there? A warning to the Rabbit? To children? What *was* this place? Sam texted, HERE! William didn't answer, but the iron gates parted in the middle to allow her inside, the rabbit swinging on its spike, its flat black eyes tracking the sky as Sam passed.

And there, in the doorway of a house that looked like a ski chalet had a baby with a cathedral, was William. He was in socks and sweats, and—how had he grown a beard so quickly? Unlike his goatee, it was almost completely gray. Maybe he really had been suffering the loss of Sam. Or the shock of Cyndi. He came to greet Sam without even putting on shoes, his face red either from wind or crying, since his eyes above the bristling beard were full of tears.

"It's you," he said.

"It's you," Sam said.

He crushed her against him so hard she could barely breathe.

"Thank God you've come," he said.

He took her hand and led her inside. The house was magnificent and scary. Its walls were all glass, offering a panoramic view of the lake. There was a double-sided stone fireplace that soared to the ceiling. Two worn leather couches faced each other as if in conversation, Pendleton blankets slung over their backs. Where there were slivers of wall, they were hidden behind bookshelves. Next to the mantel, an enormous black bear reared up on hind legs, snarling out at the room.

"Wow," said Sam. "Who's that?"

"That's Ernest."

"After Papa, I assume. He looks combative. Did you shoot him yourself?"

"No, I read him drafts until he died of boredom." William laughed. He knelt in front of Sam to unlace her boots, now dripping on what was probably a priceless Turkish rug. "Welcome home, sugarplum," he said, sliding off one, then the other, then her pants. "*Zoop!*"

He led her via spiral staircase to his bedroom, as beautiful and impersonal as a hotel suite, but they were too impatient to make it to the bed and got reacquainted on the carpet. Quick and rough and necessary, giving Sam rug burn and a sense of release. Was this all there was to it? Were they reconciled? Were they actually doing this? Could she relax now? She cried when she came and lay in stunned wonder afterward, blinking at the icy shimmer through the faraway clerestory windows. They had another quickie overlooking the yard, and afterward, cleaning up in the master bath with pine-smelling soap, Sam watched a doe step delicately across the ice outside and wondered if the deer had been responsible for the snapping noises she'd heard while she and William were making love—or was it other animals?

"Hi!" said William when Sam emerged. He'd been waiting for her, holding up his sweatshirt for her to wear. Sam wondered if this was a whole new William who, instead of being elusive, would follow her around puppylike all the time, and how she would feel about that. Right now, she liked it. He toured her down through the ground floor, all space and light and lake. The kitchen had a Viking range, granite countertops with embedded fossils, a fruit bowl with actual fruit in it. A pineapple, a mango. A mango! thought Sam. The dining room was governed by an oak table that could seat twenty, crowned by candelabra almost as tall as Sam. A den with an Eames lounge chair, another woodstove, more piles of books. Skylights everywhere. It was all gorgeous, tasteful, and impeccable, and it made Sam deeply uneasy. It was all the glass. She felt—watched.

Sam shivered. "Are you cold?" William asked. He was holding the hem of her shirt, his shirt, like a child afraid to get lost in a department store. "I can add wood to the stoves—or turn on the boiler. Let me know if you get chilly."

"I'm good at the moment, thanks," said Sam. "And this place is gorgeous. But don't you get scared, living out here by yourself?"

"Not at all. The isolation is the whole point of it," said William. "Occasionally a fan figures out where I live and makes it to the gates. Hence poor Peter Rabbit out there—I keep meaning to take him down, but I think he makes quite a nice sentry, don't you? Not to mention an effective warning to our special friend, if a little on the nose. But don't worry. Nobody ever gets in."

He opened a side door with a flourish. "Ta-da," he said, "the Scriptorium!"

Sam stepped out into the open air—or so she thought at first. This room was a glass box. The walls, the roof: They were all invisible. Except for the flagstone floor and the card table and chair in the center, it was like being outside, in the drifts sloping to the vast white-and-gray lake, the dark density of forest on the periphery.

"Wait until you see it at night," William said. "When it's clear, the ceiling is a frenzy of stars. The floor's heated. And this room's a sauna when the sun's out. Perfect for writing naked."

"This is where you write?" Sam asked. "In the nude?"

"No, this is where *you* write in the nude," William said, grinning. "At least, that's my diabolical plan. Welcome to your new study!"

Sam gave him a raised-brow look. She tentatively approached the table and stood resting a hand on it, testing the vibes. It was very sweet of William to have given Sam this space. But she had never written in a room like this. She preferred actual walls, and if she faced a view, she drew the curtains so she wouldn't be distracted. So she could focus on only what was in her mind's eye. This was so—exposed.

She turned to find William observing her with a frown. "Do you like it?" he asked. "As soon as you confirmed you were coming, I set it up for you."

"It's stunning," said Sam sincerely.

"Of course, this is rudimentary. I expect you to make it your own. We'll go to Augusta later this week, and you can pick out whatever your creative heart desires."

"That would be lovely," Sam said. She would wait to tell him this wouldn't work for her, that she'd rather write in a guest bedroom upstairs or even a big walk-in closet. She'd just gotten here an hour ago. It was a little early to be lodging complaints. In a few weeks, if all went well, please God, and they were more established, she'd suggest it.

"Would you like the rest of the tour now? Or shall we . . ." William slid his hands over Sam's breasts beneath his shirt. "I don't think this room has ever been properly christened."

"Maybe tour first?" Sam asked. "I want to see where *you* write."

"Ah. Milady wants to see the dungeon. As you wish."

William pulled away from Sam to look down at her. "There's just one house rule, Simone. I want you to feel this is your home, too, all right? But you are not to go into my study. Ever. Under any circumstances. Do we have an understanding, Simone? I will not have my sanctuary invaded. Any violation, and you'll be on the road."

Okay, Bluebeard, thought Sam. William was taking his new facial hair a little too seriously. She nodded. "I hear you."

"Do you?"

"William, come on. If anyone gets the need for creative privacy, it's another writer."

"Your track record has proven otherwise, Simone."

Sam sighed. "That was different. It was an *idea*. And I'm not working on that book anymore."

"Swear it."

Sam drew her finger over her breastbone. "Cross my heart and hope to die."

William smiled. "I doubt it'll come to that. Deal. And I'll consider this space inviolate as well. I'll never come in without permission. Although I can't promise I won't stand outside and press this up against the window," and he placed Sam's hand on his erection.

"That's so nice," she said. "Not at all distracting."

"Lead on, Macduff," William said, shuffling forward with Sam still clutching him. She laughed and led him from her new writing room, but as they walked past the floor-to-ceiling windows in the den, the hallway, the great room, her flesh crawled. She could not get over the feeling she was being watched.

The Rabbit

It's 3:00 a.m. and I'm creeping up the causeway, trying to make no sound in my secondhand snowshoes and carrying the final supplies on my back. I've humped a lot of equipment to this place over the years, preparing for just this scenario. It occurred to me one afternoon at my bookstore how I could do this when I had to, if William ever hooked up with a really persistent woman. I was working the register and chewing it over when a customer brought me the memoir everyone was reading that year, the one with a boot on the cover, about how a writer I loved had hiked the whole Pacific Crest Trail even though she was basically an imbecile about wilderness survival, and I thought: Aha.

After that I started doing my research and buying things in cash from the Camping section on Craigslist, bringing them here one at a time. Freeze-dried food rations. Mattress pad and insulated sleeping bag. My Luggable Loo, a 3.5-pound portable toilet that is the only item I did not buy used. Solar chargers for my phone, headlamp, and, most importantly, space heater. It's really amazing how ingenious and eco-friendly camping can be.

Tonight my backpack contains duct tape. A balaclava. Gloves. My trusty box cutter, which I got at my first bookstore and am never ever without.

I've made it around the gates and onto the island, fitting my feet into William and Sam Vetiver's snowshoe prints. There's no moon—I checked the *Farmer's Almanac* to make sure—and I don't dare risk my headlamp, so I'm sort of feeling my way along. It's so cold the snow is noisy underfoot, *creak creak creak*, and I hope if William and Sam Vetiver wake they'll think I'm one of the critters who lives here, the coyotes I hear howling and cracking branches, or maybe it's wolves.

I cross the yard to the front door, noting that Sam Vetiver's Jeep is still in the driveway. It looks like a dead mastodon, buried under snow. Yup, that b*tch is here for the duration. My mission is necessary and well-timed. I jump into the bushes from the doormat so I won't leave tracks and crawl through them to my basement window. I've oiled it every few weeks with WD-40, so it makes no noise as I ease it open. I take off my backpack and drop it inside, then hold my breath. This is always the tricky part, when I fear I'll get stuck half in and half out of the window like Pooh Bear. But somehow I don't. I push myself through with only a little rip in the butt of my snow-pants, and land on the dirt floor.

I get up, brush myself off, switch on my headlamp, and look around. My new home is a stone-walled root cellar off the storage room across from William's study, its tiny door hidden behind a bookshelf like something in a fairy tale. I bet he's forgotten this room is here, if he ever even knew. This, the Rabbit Hole, is about eight feet by ten feet, so I can extend my arms, and the ceiling is high enough I can almost stand to my full height, which is five foot five. This isn't so bad. It's much bigger than the closet under the stairs my mother used to lock me in when she went out, sometimes forget-ting that I was there.

I'll be cozy enough here. The only sad thing is that I had to take a leave of absence from my job. *We'll miss you, Sparky*, Tim said, when I told him my mom was terminally ill. I wish. Who knows what the woman is actually up to. She's too mean to die, and she drinks so much her insides are probably pre-served like snakes in formaldehyde. *I'm coming back*, I said. *As soon as . . . as soon as it's over.* Tim arranged his big blunt features into an appropriately sad expression. *Please do*, he said. *You'll always have a place here.*

I pray to Whoever's listening that he wasn't lying. I love my job. I love my store. I'd hate to lose either of them. Maybe this will be quick. Maybe I'll be able to drive Sam Vetiver out in a week. Maybe I won't have to resort to stronger measures, the ones I used on the other women. I don't know, be-cause I've never done it this way before. I've never lived in William's house with him and one of his b*tches. Because none of them has ever stayed here. It's totally unprecedented.

And it's so much more dangerous. Living so close to them, it'll be so much easier for them to catch me.

But it must be done. Finishing the job here will rely on luck and timing. For now, I've done as much planning as I can. I stand on tiptoes to fasten the basement window, taking a last look at the moonless night, and say "Goodbye, outside world." Then I shut myself into the Rabbit Hole.

CHAPTER 30

VALENTINES

I t was Valentine's Day, just before midnight, and Sam was happier than she'd ever been. She normally loathed this holiday—so many people did, grumbling about consumerism when really it was the way the date pressed the bruise of already almost untenable loneliness. Last year on February 14, Sam had watched *The Shining*. The year before that, she'd also been alone because Hank was in rehab. Prior Valentines he'd been on the psych ward, on a bender, or incarcerated. This year, Sam and William had rung it in as God intended: doggie-style, a candle throwing puppet-show shadows on the walls and the only sounds their animal noises and the movement of creatures outside. *Who cooks for you*, a barred owl called to its mate. "Good night, Valentine," said William when they were done, and he clamped his heavy legs and arms around Sam and went instantly to sleep.

Sam lay awake, as was her new habit, marveling that this was her life, that she was actually living The Future Perfect. It was so much better than she could have imagined. It was companionship. Safety. Love. Home. It was the comfort of wearing William's clothes, her own still in suitcases in the closet, her feet in his socks, his sweatpants falling off her hips. It was Thanksgiving morning, Sam streaking naked through the house gobbling like a turkey and daring William to catch her, then both of them being too weak with laughter to do anything about it when he did.

It was hiking out into the forest and choosing a pine tree, which William sawed down and dragged back and which they decorated for Christmas with white lights and cranberry-popcorn strings Sam taught him to make, which she'd read about as a child in the *Little House* books.

It was waking in the chilly house at night and running to the bathroom, then diving back into bed, where William functioned as a furnace. The cold eye of the moon peering through the skylights. It was waking to the gold tracery of ice on the windows and William bringing Sam coffee in mugs with bookstore logos on them after his predawn writing stint, sometimes pulling off his clothes and climbing back into bed with her, Sam squealing at his cold hands. *Good morning, Pop-Tart,* he said, grinning.

It was suiting up and snowshoeing the grounds while their morning muffins baked, checking to see if anything had changed during the night, noting the animal tracks William was teaching Sam to identify. The gray-and-white landscape punctuated by red-and-blue flashes that were birds.

It was going their separate ways to their writing desks and meeting in mid-afternoon to cross-country ski on the lake, something Sam was slowly getting better at, though she was still on her back more than her feet. It was her toppling over and yelling "I've fallen and I can't get up!" William face-planting next to her, the two of them making snow angels and laughing. It was returning to the house with their thighs red as freezer meat and jumping into the shower, with attendant shenanigans. Drying each other off before one of the many fireplaces, then having Scotch and reading there together.

It was making dinner, Sam chopping onions and tomatoes and peppers while William tended the fish or chicken, him turning to *Zoop!* her sweats down and set her on the counter and be inside her with one thrust. It was eating at the long oak table in the glow of the candelabra, woodstove white-hot and her feet on William's under the table. It was never being in a room together without touching.

It was hot tub before bed, Sam sitting on William's lap and her floating breasts solarized silver in the moonlight. It was lovemaking before sleep, then drifting like Chagall lovers into the starry sky.

It was everything Sam had ever wanted and better than she could have dreamed.

There was only one problem, and it was this:

Sam wasn't writing.

She had tried. Every day when William returned to his study, Sam went obediently to her desk in the Scriptorium. She took care of correspondence, opened a new document, and put her hands on the keyboard of her new and relatively unused laptop. Nothing happened. At first she wrote a sentence or two and erased it, starting and deleting, but eventually she simply sat dreaming, gazing out at the lake through the glass wall with her coffee growing cold in its mug beside her and her chin propped in her hand.

As far as Sam's career was concerned, it wasn't a problem—yet. Because she hadn't told anybody. Her last email from Mireille read, *Chère Sam, a little bird has told me you have flown north to live with Monsieur Corwyn. C'est vrai? Is this why you have been so quiet, you are trapped beneath a heavy man?* 😄 *This would not be my choice, but if you must stay in your love igloo, perhaps you can find out his secret of how he writes all those female-centric blockbusters.* 😎 *As long as you are writing absolute genius for your new April 1 deadline, which as superagent nonpareil I have secured for you, ahem ahem you are welcome, all is well.* Patricia hadn't said anything at all. Hopefully she didn't know.

As far as Sam's identity went, it was a big problem. Sam could not remember a time when she hadn't been writing. Her first memory was sitting beneath her dad's desk making block letters with her Magic Marker, her childhood and adolescent mornings spent writing in her notebooks. Sam's entire personal and professional life had been calibrated around her authorial striving, then success. But what if she couldn't do it anymore? What if, as in the Hans Christian Andersen fairy tale about the mermaid who gave up her tail so she could walk on land, every step a knife, to be with her prince—what if Sam had traded her writing for this happiness?

"What even am I if I'm not writing?" she asked William one night as they lay reading by the fire, William threading his fingers through Sam's unraveling braid.

William tented the thick tome he'd been reading, a history of the Massachusetts Bay Colony, on his chest and looked pensive. He had been giving Sam small assignments every day—*what if you write this, what if you try that*—but not pushing her.

"Happy?" he suggested.

"I'll tell you what you are," Drishti said, "you're his little love ho." Drishti had been bugshit ever since Sam told her on Thanksgiving she wasn't coming back, which made their conversations rather unpleasant. "Of *course* you're not writing. You're totally dickmatized. You gave up your whole life. Your apartment, which PS probably looks like a frat house now because of that kid you rented it to. Our group. Your class, Sam!" Sam grimaced. She had tried at first to teach online, but William's Wi-Fi was slow, and the novelists ended up freezing like war correspondents with bad connections, and eventually Sam said, *Let's all just meet for an in-person retreat in the spring!* "You're basically Codependency What Not to Do 101. You gave up everything that made you you. Remember you? The you who was a kick-ass writer? The you who wasn't living in butt-fuck Nova Scotia or wherever you are with some guy who ghosted you and then fucked that poor dead girl in the bath? Not that he fucked her *while* she was dead in the bath. But who even knows with him. He'll probably chop you up in little pieces and make you into soup in his hot tub when he's on to his next ho, and Jesus please us," Drishti said in disgust, "I'm here for you, kid, text me the code if you need to, but what a balls-up stupid fucking idiotic thing to do."

Drishti made some good points. And there were things Sam missed about her life in Boston: food delivery, wearing pants and lipstick, the moving postcard view from her apartment that had actual people in it.

Her novelists. But those things didn't add up to a life, and Sam had been so unbearably lonely. William assured her the writing might come back once she adjusted, and what if this one imperfection was the flaw in the design, the thing that proved everything else was real?

William murmured something into Sam's neck and clutched her more tightly. She shut her eyes and willed herself to sleep. But she couldn't, because this was the one other thing that was wrong, less provable than her writer's block, an intangible that nonetheless felt like a certainty: They were not alone. Her skin crawled with the knowledge. They were being watched. Somebody else was in the room.

The Rabbit

They look so perfect, lying there asleep. William not on his back the way he used to be, snoring his invisible feather up off his lips, but engulfing Sam Vetiver as if protecting her. She curled in his arms like a stupid little naked cocktail shrimp. Scott and Zelda. Anaïs and Henry. Hemingway and every-body. The literary Valentines.

F*ck I hate this holiday, which in my store begins the day after Christmas. All through the start of the New Year we lug Romance to all the front tables, setting it out on the end caps. I gain fifteen pounds from the impulse candy, even the gross chalky hearts saying B MINE and UR LIT. I'm never so happy as I am on February 15, tearing down love and taping up shamrocks.

Suddenly I have a terrible thought.

What if this is for real?

William's never let any woman stay for a weekend, let alone for months. Sam Vetiver has clearly moved in. They have *routines*.

What if I'm looking at William in love—with somebody other than himself?

What if this time is different?

But I cannot afford to think this way. I can't even allow myself to consider it. I need to take control of this situation before it gets worse.

I run my thumb over the release button of my trusty box cutter. It's a good one, I got it my very first day as a bookseller and have carried it from store to store, as well as on other errands. I feel bad for it because of how I might have to use it here. It's meant to slice only cardboard, to liberate books that will bring people joy. But it can do other jobs too.

The blade is very sharp. Skin under the chin is like butter. Slice the jugular first, a quick bleed-out if I'm lucky. Then an artery or two to be sure. This is the fastest, most painless death.

I don't want this. I'm really a very peaceful person. I'm so bad at killing. When I have to stomp mice in my sh*thole, for instance, when they're struggling in the glue traps, I throw up.

But Sam Vetiver is leaving me no choice.

I was so hoping she'd take the hints I've been leaving her. Tossing her earbuds in the snow. Emptying her expensive salon shampoo. Throwing her phone under the couch. Peeing in her boots. Raising her discomfort level to the point at which she might go back to the city. Not that I had much optimism. As I suspected from the start, she's a tough one.

And I can't leave this to chance. They're getting closer by the day. Which just makes everything that much harder. The sooner the better. I'd do it tonight if I could. But there are two of them to one of me, and William is so big. He would overpower me if I didn't play it just right. And I don't need to take care of them both. Just one.

I'm rehearsing the moves and using my superpower, which is seeing how people will look dead, like big dumb surprised dolls, when Sam Vetiver's eyes pop open.

F*ck! She's looking right at me.

It's a good thing I know this place so well, even in the dark. By the time I hear her scream, I'm already downstairs.

And I'm in the basement when I hear William's voice, along with his heavy footsteps and Sam Vetiver's lighter ones. I'm scrambling through the storage room with the water heater, past the army of Flat Williams and shelves of William's swag, all the merch his publisher sends to influencers and reviewers with advance reading copies. T-shirts with his covers. Hair product baskets for *Medusa*. Glow-in-the-dark putty for *The Space Between Worlds*. "Love-scented" *You Never Said Goodbye* candles. Magnets and keychains, tote bags and notebooks: Does anyone ever actually use the sh*t that comes with books, or do they just toss it all in the trash?

At the back of the room there's an actual-@$$ billboard, William holding all his novels beneath the command Read The Virtuoso! I have no idea how he even got it in here, but as I move it aside and push behind the bookshelf and squeeze through the tiny Rabbit Hole door, I'm grateful. I'm thinking something no woman has said ever: *Thank God this man's ego is so big!* Because I can hide behind it. And plan my next step.

CHAPTER 31

CAUSEWAY

Y ou don't believe me, do you," Sam said.

She and William were tromping along the shoreline in their snowshoes, as they did every morning, but this time they were looking for different prints. Rabbit tracks. William was a few feet ahead of Sam, posture alert, head thrust aggressively forward like an explorer investigating a hostile continent. He'd shaved off his beard the day after Sam arrived, since it was unkind to the more sensitive parts of her anatomy, but he'd since been experimenting with muttonchop sideburns, and in the early dawn light, he looked like a retired 1970s porn star in a plaid hunting cap. He leaned over to inspect something in the snow, then pointed silently.

"Whitetail," Sam said. "Bobcat."

William nodded and crunched onward. There were plenty of snowshoe tracks, too, which he and she had made; if a third person had been there, there'd be no way to tell the difference. Sam labored to keep up. She was still not very proficient on the snowshoes. William could *wait* for her. He usually did. And why was he not talking? Sam had never known William to be quiet for so long, not even after he'd chased the Rabbit unsuccessfully in the Portsmouth Marriott.

She floundered up behind him as he trekked up the hill toward the causeway. They'd combed the house attic to basement with flashlights

after Sam saw the Rabbit, then searched the yard. Warmed up with coffee and carbs at dawn and come back out for a more thorough sweep of
the island, though William had said, *You can go back to bed if you want.*
Sam said *No, I'm good* as she stepped grimly back into boots that felt
squashy and smelled weird. She'd never had sweaty feet before, but
maybe snowshoe boots were different. She'd look for disinfectant products next time they were in Augusta.

"I swear I saw her, William," Sam said now. "She was *in* the house."

William held up a hand as he stepped onto the lake near the gate pillars, then gestured to Sam that it was safe. Sam edged out onto the ice.
The rising sun dodged in and out of low clouds, brightening and darkening the morning around them.

"I'm not loving the silent treatment," Sam said. "Are you mad at me?"

"That's not the word I would use," said William without turning.

"What then?" William didn't respond. "Annoyed? Frustrated? Hu-
moring me? Because you *really* don't believe she was in our bedroom.
Right?"

Now William glanced at her. "I believe *you* believe it. I believe you
think you saw a—" he cocked an eyebrow—"*wascally wabbit!*"

"It's not funny," said Sam.

"No, it isn't," William continued, proceeding across the ice. "You
rout me out of bed while I'm on a deadline, when you *know* I need my
sleep and every minute counts, just because you had a bad dream—"

"That's *not* what it was."

"I hope that *is* what it was, Simone. Or similar. Because I'm starting
to wonder..."

"What?" said Sam.

William climbed onto the causeway, now an elevated snow-covered
plateau bisecting the ice. Sam stood on the lake with her arms crossed.

"What do you wonder? Just spit it out," she said.

William looked down at her, his expression calm, even flat, and Sam
felt a moment of danger, not to her but to them, as if the ice she was
standing on were mushy and unsafe after all.

"Never mind," he said as if to himself. "You're not that Machiavellian." He held out a gloved hand to Sam to help her. She ignored him, crawling up over the invisible boulders on all fours.

"It's your brilliant Simone brain," said William, forging down the causeway toward the logging road. "You're a writer who's not writing, and your mind is like an hyperactive puppy. If you don't give it something to chew on, it'll destroy everything in its path."

"Whether I'm writing or not, and thanks for that dog analogy, by the way—" Sam began, and then her right snowshoe caught on something and tipped her sideways and she tumbled off the causeway. It wasn't more than a few feet, but the wind had been strong in the night and scoured away much of the snow. She landed badly and hit her head on the ice.

"Ow," she said. "Fuck."

William was crouched at her side instantly, pressing her in place.

"Oh honey," he said. "Stay still for a minute. Do you feel dizzy?"

"No."

"Nauseous?"

"No. Just stupid," Sam said. She laughed. William didn't. He pulled off her hood and wool hat and very carefully felt her head, Sam wincing when he found the tender spot.

"Nice goose egg," he said. "We'll keep an eye on it. I'll take you to Augusta if you're concussed, or we can call for a medevac. Although it'll take them an hour to get out here . . ."

"I think I'm fine," Sam said. "Just clumsy."

"Not clumsy. Unpracticed. This is what I've been telling you," William said, sitting next to her. His cheeks were bright red, tiny ice crystals in his sideburns. "This is why you must *never* go out without me. You're not used to it here. This doesn't look like a bad fall. But if it had been . . ."

"I'm not a child, William. I lived in the Berkshires. And I'm learning."

"I know you are. I applaud what a sport you've been. But experienced countryfolk get in trouble out here. Even ones born into these conditions. Look what happened to Pen."

Pen? thought Sam. His sister? She was about to ask, What *had* happened to Pen? when William said, "I'm being too hard on you, I see that now. Let's get you back to the house. I'll continue the hunt on my own. I keep forgetting how new all this is to you. You're acclimating. That's why you're seeing things."

"I am not—" Sam started to argue, but instead, as he helped her to her feet and dusted her off, she changed tack and asked, "What about security?"

"What do you mean?" William said. He guided her along the ice back toward the house, holding Sam's hand now, though she could feel nothing in the insulated Mickey Mouse gloves they both wore.

"I mean do you have any security here, in addition to the gates?" Which they were passing now, navigating back around the pillars. The stuffed rabbit was still affixed to one of the spikes. He'd lost an ear, and his fur had molted off in patches.

"There's ample security," William said shortly. "Do you see where we live? Do you know how hard it is to get here in the winter?"

"But there's no security system per se," Sam persisted. "Right? Like no cameras or alarms that alert the police or anything?"

William laughed. "Simone, sweetheart. The difficulty anyone would have getting here to do us harm is the difficulty anyone would have getting here to help us. How long do you think it would take the sheriff to reach us on an unplowed road? Even a plowed one? If we had a fire, the house would burn to the ground long before the fire department could get here. We are *unincorporated*."

"Oh good, I feel so much better now," Sam said.

"I won't minimize the risks, Simone. We face real dangers here. But *I'm* your security." William pulled her up onto the snowy shore of the island. "I know it's hard for you to suspend disbelief," he continued as they trekked toward the house. "How can you trust, after what you went through with Hank? But I am not some poor feckless addict. You're safe now." He put a hand on Sam's heart. "*Believe*," he said emphatically.

Sam stared at him, unblinking.

"Work with me for a minute," she said. "Just *pretend* the Rabbit was in the house. What if she comes back? What if she gets in again?"

William gazed out across the lake. He was in profile to her, the icy light turning his closest eye into a translucent marble. It shifted back and forth as if he were dreaming. He's not here, Sam thought. Where is he?

"Let the Rabbit come," he said, distantly, almost casually. "I welcome it. I've prayed to catch her in my house. Because that would be a clear case of self-defense. I'd end her."

Sam squinted up at him. His hair, more gray now than brown, whipped around the ear flaps of his cap. "Are you serious?"

"Very," said William, still in that remote tone. "I'd try to disable her first. Humanely. And permanently, so she couldn't pull any more stunts. Then turn her over to the authorities. But if things get out of hand in the moment, well . . . she'll bring her fate upon herself."

"Whoa," said Sam. "I'm not sure if that makes me feel better or worse."

"I can't tell you how to feel, Simone. It's simply what'll happen."

Sam turned away to stare out, too, at the uncompromising vista that was all rock and ice and pines and snow, the only movement an eagle circling and circling, seeking prey for breakfast. She felt dismay at the turn this morning had taken: William's dismissiveness; their lack of an actual alarm system, and now this, his cold-blooded predetermined plan for the Rabbit. But he had been living with the reality of this threat for years, and he was under deadline pressure, and Sam had woken him screaming in the night. Neither of them was exactly at their best.

"Can we at least change the locks?" she said finally.

William seemed to return from wherever he was. "Yes, if you don't mind handling it. I really need to keep on top of the book."

"Done."

"Deal," said William.

He looked down at her then and seemed to remember who Sam was, smiling for the first time that morning. He bent to kiss her, his nose an icy blade. "Let's go get warm," he said. "I have some ideas."

The Rabbit

I'm near the entrance to the glass box they call the Scriptorium, watching Sam Vetiver write. Supposedly. What she's really doing is nothing. She's just staring out at the lake. I know writers do a whole lot of that. I used to do it myself. But that woman has not written more than four words since she's been here. I don't know why she even bothers to come to the desk. Her writer brain is basically toast.

You'd think losing her authorial self-respect would be enough reason for her to leave. Or maybe seeing a woman in the bedroom closet at night with a box cutter. But no. That would be something a sane person would do, and we are not dealing with a sane person. We're dealing with a woman under the spell of William Corwyn. The D*ckmatizing, the gaslighting—I'm sure he's told Sam Vetiver I don't exist, she dreamed me up, like Scrooge telling Jacob Marley he's just a bit of potato. Dickens and Alfred Hitchcock have nothing on this guy.

Well, I'm not a figment or a spud. I'm here and I'm real, and if Sam Vetiver's not going to leave on her own, I'm going to make her. I thumb the blade in and out of my trusty box cutter, psyching myself up. She's in here alone. William's in his study, actually writing. If I do this right, she won't make a sound.

The problem? I can't make myself move. This part is not fun. It's so hard. I've been slapped. Punched. Kicked. Screamed at. Pepper-sprayed—that's how I found out I'm allergic to chilis. It took days for the swelling to go down enough for me to see, let alone until I stopped looking like a goggle-eyed goldfish. I had to hide at home in my sh*thole, I lost a whole week's work at my store. And those are the encounters that have gone well.

Plus it's extra risky here. Unlike in the outside world, there's no quick escape off the island. The snow and ice will slow me down, make me easy to track. Even if I'm fast, I'll be more visible.

But this f*cking woman. As I feared, Sam Vetiver is stubborn. And just because she's a pain in my @$$, just because she's made it harder for me by moving in with William, it doesn't mean I can break my promise.

I size up the room. Who would choose to write in a glass box like this? It's so creepy how the walls are invisible. Like being outside. A sitting duck. But whatever. Luckily it's a cloudy day. There won't be any reflection to let Sam Vetiver know I'm coming. And I'll make no sound on the slate floor in my socks.

I focus on the hollow at the base of Sam Vetiver's skull, exposed by her stupid side braid with the pen in it, above the top knob of her spine. Slide one foot over the threshold. Then the other. Clutching my box cutter like a rabbit's foot for luck, hot in my hand. Blade out. Rehearsing what I will say. *Don't move, and do* not *scream—*

"Simone? I'm making a sandwich. Do you want one?"

William, pounding through the great room. I hit the floor just in time. Scrabble backward on hands and knees to beneath the dining room table.

"Jesus," Sam Vetiver says as he bounds into the Scriptorium. "You startled me! I should make you wear bells around your neck."

For once I one hundred percent agree with Sam Vetiver.

"That would be one place for them," he says. He tweaks her dumb braid and smacks a kiss right on the spot I was just looking at, then guides her hand into his sweats. "I know another."

As they get going again, I creep back through the house toward the basement. It's my own fault for being such a weenie. The longer I wait, the more entrenched Sam Vetiver gets, and the harder it is for me to do my job. This is not like the previous times with the other women. This is worse. And even if it does go badly, I have to risk it. Because my vow. Next time he's really distracted. Next time she's alone. I'll take the first chance I can get.

CHAPTER 32

ORION

The next evening Sam was in the hot tub alone. Usually William accompanied her, got in first, and held out his hand to help her. But tonight he'd gotten a phone call he wanted to take in his study—*Do you mind, sugarplum? I'll join you ASAP*—so Sam was on her own beneath the dark trees, watching the phantasmagoric swirl of the northern lights, flinching at every CRACK! of branch or ice, and clutching a big rock.

It was probably stupid, Sam knew. Not because she hadn't seen the Rabbit. She had. But because if the Rabbit was still here and intended Sam harm, Sam's rock wouldn't make much difference. The Rabbit had a knife, Sam was pretty sure of it, and in the game of Knife versus Rock, Knife won every time. But Sam might have the advantage of surprise.

She tipped her head back. At least the lights were fantastic, shimmering green and shooting flares across the Milky Way. Sam remembered from her research for *The Sodbuster's Wife* that Scandinavian settlers thought the lights were a good omen, whereas some Native Americans believed they were spirits of ill-tempered giants kicking a walrus skull around the sky. Either way, they were said to be departed souls, crossing over—

"Bubble bubble toil and trouble," said William from the dark, and Sam screamed, hurling the rock in his direction. She felt more than saw him duck and swear.

"Simone," he said, looming up next to the tub in his spa robe with her rock in his hand. "What is wrong with you?" On his face in the green light was a look of almost insane rage, and for a second Sam feared he might smash the rock into her head. Then it was gone, so quickly Sam wasn't sure she'd seen it at all.

William threw the rock into the snow and took off his robe. "You could have really hurt me," he said, lowering himself into the steaming water.

"You scared the hell out of me," Sam said.

"I just came out of the basement bulkhead door, that's all. You really do have the most pronounced startle reflex."

"Sorry," Sam said. Sorry not sorry, she thought. Perhaps she had a pronounced startle reflex because there'd been a woman hiding with a knife in their bedroom closet, but she didn't want to open that argument again.

William settled into his usual position facing the lake. He scooped water onto his face and sighed.

"We have a problem, Simone," he said.

Sam's stomach dropped. She had the feeling she always did at these moments, as if he'd opened a trapdoor beneath her that even she hadn't known was there. Please don't end it, she thought. Don't send me away.

"What is it?" she said warily.

"You're too far from me. Come here."

Sam slid over to her customary spot between William's knees. He rested his chin on the tendon between her neck and shoulder.

"There," he said, settling her back against his chest. "Isn't that better?"

"It doesn't suck," Sam said.

There was another CRACK! and Sam flinched. William's arms tightened around her.

"I've got you," he said. "And it's just the ice."

Sam nodded. There had been a thaw that afternoon, the temperature rising into the twenties from subzero, and the ice was expanding, producing its usual symphony of weird noises. Booms, space lasers, deep moans. When Sam first arrived, she'd said to William, *I know this is ridiculous, but do you have* . . . whales *here?* Sometimes the ice sounded like those big creatures communicating to each other underwater, the tenderest and most forlorn sound Sam had ever heard.

"Here's our problem," William said. "I've done everything I can to convince you that you're safe here with me. And it's not enough. You still don't believe me, do you."

Sam shook her head, reluctantly. "I don't. I'm sorry. It's not anything you've done or not done. You've been a splendid host. And I do love it here. It's otherworldly beautiful. It's just . . ."

"You don't feel safe."

"Right. I don't."

"Then that's a dealbreaker," said William. "We can't go on this way."

Oh God, Sam thought. Here we go again.

"What if . . ." William paused so long, Sam turned to look back at him. "A minute, beloved. This scares me a little. It's hard to say."

Sam felt him breathing beneath her, his stomach like a bellows.

"What if we look for another house? Together?"

"Seriously? Do you mean it?"

"I do," he said.

Sam twisted fully around in the water. "Oh, yes," she said. "Yes, William! Yes yes!"

He grinned. "I love making you say that. What if we both come up with a wish list of what we want in a living space, then compare? I won't live in a city, Simone. That's not for me. But I would consider a university town—provided we had adequate privacy."

"That's perfect," said Sam. "Thank you. You don't know what this means to me."

William moved her off his lap so he could submerge fully, then burst out of the water with a *Pah!* He slicked his hair back, looking like the world's most elegant nude headwaiter, and pulled Sam to him in the center of the tub so they floated nose to nose.

"Don't look now," he said, "but we *are* being watched." He turned them so they faced the horizon. "That guy there, see him? Orion the mighty hunter. He shows himself only at this time of year." With a dripping finger William traced the celestial giant's limbs and sword, his arrow permanently aimed at the Bull.

"The world's biggest Peeping Tom," said Sam.

"Exactly. Think I could take him?"

Sam laughed. "Absolutely."

"What if I get one of his stars for you?" William squinted and pointed. "Like *that* one, that brightest one there. What if I pluck it from the sky and put it on your finger?" He reached for his robe and took from its pocket a black velvet box.

"What if," he said, "we got married? Would you feel safe then?"

Sam stared at the box. William was moody, arrogant, prone to not taking responsibility for his actions. Paranoid about his study and his past. Vain about facial hair. Vituperative when angry. And Sam loved him. She loved him with all her heart.

"Please, Simone, open it," said William.

Sam did. The ring was emerald cut, a skating rink on a platinum band. The diamond glimmered green from the fantastical lights above.

"What do you say?" William said. "Will you marry me, Simone? *Come, madam wife, sit by my side and let the world slip / We shall ne'er be younger.*"

Sam put her palms on either side of his wet face and kissed him.

"*Yes,*" she said, "*I said yes I will Yes.*"

The Rabbit

Oh no. No no no no no. He went and did the thing, held out the ultimate bait, and the dumb-@$$ b*tch went for it. First he ruined yet another chance I had to take a crack at Sam Vetiver, I was just about to put my trusty box cutter on her throat and tell her to drop that silly rock, and William popped out of his study like a d*ck-in-the-box and f*cked that up. And now this abomination, Sam Vetiver squealing like a pig and William saying "Well, now, Mrs. Corwyn, I like the sound of that," and Sam Vetiver saying, "And it's such a *beautiful* ring!" This is so bad. Not only are they talking about getting another place in a more populated area, which will make everything harder than it already is, but they'll be even more joined at the hip than they are now. I've got to finish this before they move. It's not checkmate, but it's definitely check, and as I go through the bushes back to the Rabbit Hole and seal myself in, I look at the big hunter man in the sky with his show-off sword and say, "You f*cker."

CHAPTER 33

HARRINGTON

The weight of the ring was still unfamiliar on Sam's finger when she drove off the property later that week. Everything was strange: the height of her Jeep; bumping up the causeway and the logging track, which had taken William a full day to plow out. Just being off the island was surreal. Since their pre-Christmas shopping trip to Augusta, Sam hadn't left once. She felt like an Amish girl on Rumspringa, marveling at her speed, travel plazas, other cars on the highway. And she kept checking her rearview to make sure nobody was following her. The Rabbit, for instance. Intent on driving her off the road.

But the farther from Maine Sam got, the more those unpleasant fantasies faded. Sam was heading to Harrington, William's graduate alma mater, to teach a workshop for the MFA program. He'd been going to do it and then got offered a last-minute, irrefutably generous keynote opportunity at the San Diego Writers' Conference when their headliner got food poisoning, so he'd passed the workshop to Sam. *See if you can spot the ghost of Young William quoting e. e. cummings in the halls*, he'd said, grinning, and although Sam didn't want to see ghosts of any sort, she was excited about the opportunity to teach. It had been far too long.

By the time she drove onto campus, it was her life with William that seemed like a dream. Sam felt like herself again, slammed back into her author body. She stopped at the entrance to take a photo of the guild sign—HARRINGTON COLLEGE, EST. 1824—and texted it to William, then navigated to the guest parking lot. How often had Sam done just this, parachuted into some unfamiliar college or university to give a lecture, run a workshop, teach? She applied lipstick, grabbed her bookbag, and stepped out of her Jeep, the heels of her leather boots gritting on pavement in a way she hadn't heard in months. "Showtime," she said to herself.

Harrington was pretty, a typical liberal arts school with stone buildings, big old trees, snow-covered quads bisected by icy paths. Sam located the English Department on the map the assistant had sent, and the graduate program director, Dr. Zahra Alaam, came to greet her. Sam just had time to slough her coat in Zahra's office and use the bathroom before she was escorted to a room she would have recognized in her dreams: oak paneling, mullioned windows, the students sitting in a circle. Sam smiled at the aspiring writers, remembering what it was like to be one of them, a twentysomething slouching in her black leather blazer, reeking of cigarettes and trying to appear both ambitious and blasé—i.e., literary—yet having only one question in mind. She was therefore not surprised when, after Zahra introduced Sam, a student raised her hand and said, "How did you get published?"

After workshop, Zahra took Sam to the student union for quinoa bowls, which they brought to Zahra's office. With the exception of a large red beanbag chair and the leg lamp from *A Christmas Story*, the space was like all academic offices: small, cramped, overheated, crowded with books and papers. "That was so much fun," said Sam, sitting in the non-beanbag chair across from Zahra's desk, taking the lid off her eco-friendly bowl. "Thank you. I haven't taught in months."

"You are very welcome," said Zahra. "They loved you. But your website says you teach a novel workshop?"

"Oh yes, I do. I'm just taking a little break. An intermission."

Zahra smiled. She was an East Asian woman in her mid-fifties, Sam guessed, in leather pants and a purple cashmere sweater, a nose ring, peacock earrings Sam greatly coveted, her hands covered with the red tracery of *mehndi*. Zahra's debut novel, *The Woman with Delicate Skin*, had been a New York Times Notable Book, and she had published a few more since, including a memoir about linguistic diaspora. "It can't be too serious a break," Zahra said, patting her own hair. "You have a pen in your braid."

Sam's hand rose. "Ha! I always forget about that. Habit. I've been doing that since I was in my *Harriet the Spy* days."

"Ah, Harriet. She was a great mentor to so many of us."

"She was. Besides, you never know when you might need a pen."

"That is true," Zahra agreed. "And how is it going, your intermission?"

"It's weird," said Sam, and they both laughed. Sam thought about it as she speared roasted vegetables and tofu prepared by a stranger. Her last months on the island seemed as harsh and lovely as a Russian fairy tale, all snow and passion and wolves and the Rabbit.

"I did this crazy thing," she confessed to Zahra. "I stepped out of my life in Boston without a second thought."

Zahra ate a forkful of kale. "That sounds like a novel waiting to be written."

"Maybe. Except I think Anne Tyler already did it. Or Anna Quindlen."

"Probably. The Annes and Shakespeare have already written everything. What is your new life like? Is it liberating? Exhilarating? Frightening?"

"Mostly happy," said Sam. She couldn't begin to think how she'd explain the Rabbit, even if she were inclined to. "A bit disconcerting sometimes."

"I can imagine. How are you spending your days?"

"Not writing," Sam said, and laughed. "Spending time with my fiancé, who *is* writing." She smiled. "It's the first time I've called him that. We just got engaged."

"Congratulations! First marriage?"

"For him. Second for me."

"The happy one. Come on, let's see it."

Sam held out her hand. The ring fractured rainbow light all over the office.

"That is a *rock*," said Zahra. "True congratulations. If your betrothed is a writer, he either is very successful or has a trust fund. Or a secret life of crime."

Sam squinched up her face, puzzled. Did Zahra not know who William was? Did she not remember she'd gotten Sam's name from him? But then, maybe William had presented Sam as a professional colleague instead of saying they were together. Their engagement was so new. It would take time for his privacy policy to erode.

"Actually, he's an alum of your program," Sam said. "He was the one who recommended I come teach for you today, because he had a conflict. William Corwyn?"

Zahra blinked and sat back in her chair. "I see."

She didn't make a face, but her sudden impassivity was such that she might as well have. "What is it?" said Sam. "Is something wrong?"

"No, certainly not. I know William. He was in my years here."

"Oh, I didn't know you were a Harrington alum as well. That's so funny. And so great. Congratulations yourself!"

"Thank you."

"So," said Sam, "you must know all the young William stories. Give me the dirt!"

Zahra did not smile, and Sam felt her own grin wilt. "Wait. Is there actual dirt?"

"I would not feel comfortable talking about this," said Zahra. "It is not my place."

"Zahra," said Sam. "Please." A shiver rippled across her skin despite the stuffy office. "I know we don't know each other, but you're right. My first marriage was not happy. Or rather, it was not wise. And if I'm making a mistake with this one, if there's something I should know, please. I'm asking woman to woman. Tell me."

Zahra was silent a moment longer, then got up and shut her door, which had been open a few inches in case a student came by.

"You attended an MFA program, am I right?" she asked, sitting back down.

Sam nodded. "In the late nineties."

"So you remember what they were like. Cutthroat. Mercilessly competitive. Like the Roman arena. Especially then. Especially for women."

"Mine was more like Wendy and the Lost Boys," Sam said, and recounted for Zahra her experience as the only woman in her graduate program—how she'd had to prove herself via belching, swearing, drinking, ruthless expurgation of adverbs and adjectives, and participating in the workshop torture ranking system: How bad had the author's experience been while in The Box, unable to speak?, tickling, slapping, punching, waterboarding, or the worst, Zahra should forgive her, the anal pear? How all the guys wanted to be posthumously famous and Sam wanted to be on Oprah, and how her friend Jean said *God save us if Sam gets published, she will be all the more insufferably bourgeoisie*, and how, when Sam did sign with Mireille, they had hauled her to the student pub and toasted her with tequila shots: *To Sam, the fucking bitch!*

Zahra smiled faintly at Sam's description. But still she did not laugh.

"You were lucky," she said. "Our program was not like that. We had the dick-swinging, of course. Women as well as men. But it was not friendly. It was vicious. It was designed to push out the weak. And I am sorry to say William was the worst of them. The ringleader of the lads. A real bully."

Oh God, Sam thought. "How so?" she asked.

"Nobody's writing was ever as good as his. It was not good, period. He was very charming about it—at first. The iron fist in the velvet glove. He would begin with praise, citing a real skill or talent or pleasing turn of phrase the author had. Then he would cut that person down. Mercilessly. A sword to the ankles. The things he called the stories! Jejune. Perfervid. Execrable. As flavorless as overmasticated gum. A sleeping potion he wished were deadly. A literary lobotomy. On and on."

"That's awful," said Sam through numb lips.

"Yes. He had a flair for the dramatic as well. Once he threw a story into the center of the room and did the *hopak* on it. Another time, he made one into a paper airplane and sailed it out the window. He set one of my pieces on fire with a Zippo and burned it in the wastebasket. He made people cry. One woman had a nervous breakdown and left the program altogether."

"Oh my God," said Sam. "Why didn't anyone stop it? What were the teachers doing?"

"Smirking, mostly," said Zahra. "Sitting with their arms crossed. They said it prepared us for the real world, that as cruel as we were to each other, it was only a fraction as nasty as reviewers would be, or readers. That if we didn't have a thick skin, we ought not to be writers."

Sam nodded. She'd heard the same thing from her own workshop leaders. And unlike in the program, when people hit writers in the real world, in the papers or online, the writers were in the stocks. They couldn't punch back.

Zahra had turned to look out the window at the sullen white sky, her face contemplative. "I had a theory," she said, "that William was especially ruthless because he feared he had no real story. He was a copycat, you see. Each piece he brought in was different, and it was derivative of someone else: Hemingway, Faulkner, Carver, Joyce. William's first novel, that fluke published while he was still in college, *The Girl on the Mountain*, even the critics said it was just like Carson McCullers. But here at Harrington he could not get away with this. Our instructors called him out. Said he had to find his own voice. I thought perhaps he had none, that he was zero at the core. But then." She shrugged. "I guess he found his voice after all. And it was feminine. He has done quite well with it. Better than well. Good for him."

She turned from the window, set her lid back on her quinoa bowl, and smiled at Sam, who had been sitting quietly, collating all this information. There was a question she needed to ask.

"If you don't mind," Sam said, "did you know William's fiancée? Becky Bowman? She was in your cohort, too, right?"

Zahra closed her eyes briefly. "Yes. A tragedy."

"What was she like?"

Zahra sighed. "If I tell you, you must promise to keep it confidential. Nobody must know what I am about to say."

Sam cleared her throat. It was so dry in here. "I promise."

"Some of us thought it strange."

Sam leaned forward. "What was strange?"

"Their engagement, to start." Zahra took a sip of her tea. "William was such a ladies' man. The kids today would call him a player, or worse. He slept with anything that moved—as long as she was attractive." She gestured to Sam, as if in proof. "His tastes have not changed. The exception was Becky. She was not, and forgive me for speaking ill of the dead, a pretty girl. She was very sweet . . ."

Sam thought of Cyndi hunched in her booth in Salem, her shy and hopeful smile.

"But so quiet. Long hair, drugstore glasses, dressed like a PE teacher. Very shy. She wrote about love and sat in the corners. We called her Mouse."

Sam winced.

"I know. I am ashamed now." Zahra *tsk*ed her tongue at herself. "She seemed to blossom, initially, under William's attention. But then she became even more quiet and withdrawn. By our second year, when they had been together a few months, it was as though she had been erased. We thought perhaps drugs? Alcohol? She was a ghost. And then, a month or so after their engagement . . ." She shook her head. "I'm sure he told you the story."

"He mentioned it, yes," Sam said. She twisted her own new ring. It was loose on her finger. Her throat ached.

"We wondered," said Zahra, "if he had something to do with it."

"With her—death?" Sam asked, voice cracking on the last word.

"Yes. Perhaps. It sounds ridiculous now, an outrageous accusation. But you must remember we were students of creative writing, with feverish imaginations we were flexing overtime, on a rural campus with not much else to do. And the boyfriend is always the first suspect, is he not? Excuse me, the fiancé. Even if the death is a suicide. The college investigated, of course, and the police. William came up clean. But for a few months we speculated, particularly the mystery and thriller writers among us. What stumped us, and put an end to our macabre parlor game, was that we could come up with no motive. The difficulty of staging a suicide aside, what would his motive have been?"

Sam shook her head. She couldn't speak.

"It was a cruel pastime," said Zahra. "Really, I am a little surprised to look back and see how catty I was at that age. We all were. It was not fair to William. As harsh as he had been with us in workshop, he was devastated by Becky's death. He wrote that blockbuster novel for her, and I read he founded a support group in her name? That he still runs?"

"The Darlings," Sam whispered, realizing that William had not held a Darlings meeting since she'd moved in. Like her workshop, they had disappeared.

"Yes. The Darlings. That tracks. That was what he called Becky. His Darling. We thought he was being ironic." Zahra sighed. "However extreme our theories, I still wonder whether we persisted with them because we caught a whiff of truth. That although William did not cause Becky's death outright, he contributed to it by bullying and belittling her. Denigrating her behind closed doors. None of us thought to ask, to make sure she was all right. Nowadays we would call him a narcissist. But then, we did not have that language. We knew only that he was a charismatic bully who had chosen, for his own reasons, an introverted woman. We thought their pairing very strange and left it at that."

Zahra's phone chimed, and she rose. "I must go to my next meeting. If I've upset you, you are welcome to stay here and collect your thoughts. You are welcome to stay anyway."

Sam rose too. "No, I'm fine," she said. "I'd better go. I have a long drive back."

"We are more than happy to put you up at the inn," said Zahra. "It is not bad, actually."

She surprised Sam by taking her elbow on the way out, as if they were old school chums or little French girls walking to the *boulangerie*.

"Please try not to worry," she said. "We were children then. No older than those students you spoke to today. I am different from who I was then, definitely older if not wiser. I'm sure you are different too. You would not marry the man I described."

She waited until Sam nodded, then gave her arm a light squeeze.

"Surely, then, William has grown as well. With his writers' support group, his Darlings, he has done a great deal of good. Please extend to him my congratulations, on his career and your engagement. I'm certain you will have a lovely life." She shut out the lights and locked her office door. "Just perhaps," she added, "watch your back."

The Rabbit

There's an old saying: While the cats are away, the Rabbit will play. Actually there isn't, but there should be, because that's what happens. When William and Sam Vetiver go off on their respective trips, I wait an hour to make sure they're really gone, and then out of the Rabbit Hole I pop.

The first thing I do? Take a long-@$$ shower. I stand under the hot water until it goes cold, using up all of Sam Vetiver's salon-scented products. Then I cook myself a decent meal. I've been eating well enough, lots of peanut butter and beans, but it's amazing what a difference in morale it makes when food's hot. Next I wander the house, wrapped in one of those scratchy striped blankets William's had since grad school. I build a fire and take a nap next to the big stuffed bear. I read a few pages here, a few there. I go up to William and Sam Vetiver's bedroom and jump on their bed, then use their vibrator—why they need this I have no idea, I guess for variety—and flush all their lube down the toilet. Finally there's nothing left to do but fire up the hot tub and sit under the stars.

It's then that I realize how lonely I am. I don't miss William and Sam Vetiver's f*ckfests, but it is weird with them both gone, William at some Big Deal Conference and Sam Vetiver at, of all places, Harrington.

Harrington.

A coyote yips somewhere on the lake. A chorus howls back. I do too.

I'm almost glad my car battery was dead so I couldn't follow her. I hate even thinking about that f*cking place.

It all started so well. That's what I thought. I actually allowed myself to believe I'd made it, clawed my way out of Aegina by saving my paychecks from Barbara's Book Nook and going up the road to Upper Great Lakes Community College, then applying—and applying and applying—to Harrington, whose MFA program I'd seen in *Writer's Digest* while working in the UGLCC bookstore. I couldn't believe it. You could get a *degree* in creative writing? There were scholarships for it??? I'd finally gotten in after applying five times in a row, and here I was in this fancy seminar room with wood-paneled walls and tiny diamond-paned windows like at Medieval Times. With rich people who'd given up two years of their lives to be here, who said things like *Aspen* and *Choate* and they all knew what it meant. Maybe I could learn to be one of them. Maybe my real life started now. I was like Gatsby, if he'd been born a baby girl in a sh*tbox.

That fantasy lasted a week.

Then workshop started.

Here's what workshop is. You hand in a story, which is called submitting. Your classmates read it. The next week, you're put in The Box, which means they discuss you for three hours while you can't say a word. The Box is supposed to encourage "rigorous listening." What it really encourages is suicidal ideation, if you ask me. We actually had some people try that. And one succeeded. Others quit at break. But not me. I hung in there until The Incident, even though I realized the people I thought were writers were really wolves and William was the leader of them all, an alpha killer in a blue button-down and khakis.

He seized that position the first day, and we all went along with it because he was the only one who'd already been published—his novel *The Girl on the Mountain*, which came out while he was still in college. Never mind that it sold like fifteen hundred copies. Or that the *Washington Post* reviewer panned it, saying, "If Corwyn doesn't continue as an author—and that would certainly be my recommendation—he has a fine career ahead as a politician, because he is in love with the sound of his own voice." But *Kirkus* called the book "a luminous, poised debut," and *The New Yorker* included William in its *30 Under 30* issue. He was the only one who could throw around phrases like *my agent, my editor, my publicist, print run, foreign rights, film option.* In our program, he was king.

As I found out the first workshop, because I was first up. Our instructor had assigned the order, and I'd drawn the short straw. Not that I knew that at the time. All I knew was that I'd submitted my best story, the opening chapter of what I hoped would be a novel called *Aegina.* I read a page of it aloud, and then I went in The Box.

"*I* will," said William, when the instructor asked who wanted to start us off. "This author is really raw. She has *vim*," he said with emphasis, leaning forward and raising his eyebrows. Vim? I thought. What the f*ck is that?

"Agreed. She has potential," said Zahra, the woman with waist-length hair and red designs on her hands, and I swelled like a sponge in mopwater because I didn't yet know that *potential* was a slur, like *ambitious*, meaning you'd fallen short of what you'd tried to achieve.

Everyone was nodding when William added, "But the story is pure melodrama. The little girl locked in the closet so her mom can go out on the town? Forced to drink her own urine? Cheap shock value. Trauma porn."

"So tropey," said another writer, and someone else added, "It was contrived."

I sat with my face stinging as if they'd all slapped me, thinking, But it happened! It really happened! I couldn't say that, though, and besides, we were supposed to be writing fiction. So I just drew William in my notebook with a dagger sticking out of his mouth.

"I see what the writer is attempting," he continued. "But the writing has no grandeur. It's *commercial*," he pronounced, which I would come to realize was the worst insult of all, meaning your work would never be reviewed by anyone who mattered or nominated for the big prizes, only sold in mass-market paperback in spinning drugstore racks or next to the dog food and toilet paper in big box stores.

After workshop everyone went to the Castle, the student pub, except me. The second I was released from The Box I stuffed my notebook in my bag and ran from the room like it was on fire, although I found out later that was unnecessarily dramatic. William didn't actually hate me. He just had a very low opinion of my work, which matched his opinion of everyone's work, only with different adjectives. It was nothing personal. When it came to writing, William was an equal-opportunity f*cker.

As he was when it came to actual f*cking: That man screwed everything within d*ck distance, right across the disciplines. Even the poets. His one criterion was that the women had to be pretty in some way. The only ones he didn't sleep with that first year were me and the other quiet girl in the program, Becky, the Mouse.

Which was why I was so shocked one night the fall of our second year, when I was in the empty cafeteria filling my thermos at the milk machine and William came up next to me. He did his smiling and bowing thing and said "Moooooo," and I was wondering whether he was calling me a cow when he said, "We can do better than that, can't we?" and took the thermos from my hand. He said what a shame we'd been in workshop over a year but never gotten properly acquainted, and did I want to grab a beer at the Castle? and I looked all around and behind me to make sure there was nobody else there, that he was actually talking to me.

CHAPTER 34

CROSSROADS

S am stayed on the Harrington campus that night after all. She didn't want to drive after dark, contending with black ice and deer, so instead she checked herself into the inn. She didn't tell Zahra, not wanting the department head to feel obligated to take her to dinner. Sam needed to digest what Zahra had said. She wanted to be alone. And she didn't feel quite ready to go back to Maine.

She embarked on a quiet errand, stopping at a grocery store, then driving to an address William had texted her. The house was a duplex with olive-green siding and a deep front porch with student stuff on it: bikes, a grill, a plaid couch. It was near the train tracks behind mechanics' shops and take-out restaurants, the cold air smelling of grease. Sam took a photo for William and wondered what his readers would say if they only knew about his humble grad school lodgings, so in contrast to what he had become. She was a little surprised there was no plaque or marker, WILLIAM CORWYN SLEPT HERE, or offerings like the stuffed rabbit on its spike. She felt a terrible nostalgia for the William she would never know, a beautiful young man full of energy and ambition so great he would apparently hurt others for it, whether he intended to or not. She pictured him drinking beer on that couch, hosting readings, lying in bed with Becky and listening to the trains pass a block away. Sam got out of her Jeep, walked up to the cement porch, bisected by a tectonic crack, and laid her bouquet of supermarket flowers on it. *For you, Becky*, she said silently, but it was really for both of them, for all of them, for who they had been in their youth.

She slept badly that night and woke feeling as though she'd been beaten in her sleep. She got coffee from the campus convenience store and hit the road, saying "Thank you" to Harrington and Zahra as she left, though Sam wasn't sure she was grateful she'd come or not. She drove past dairy farms, the sun winking in and out, the snow tired in the fields, the two-lane road winding through small towns. After an hour she reached the interstate and stopped at a gas station. It had started to flurry.

Sam got fuel and more caffeine, used the bathroom. Back in her Jeep she checked the forecast, squalls on and off all the way to William Island, then sat and sipped her convenience store coffee and looked through the windshield at the highway. She had taken it north to William's house in November. She could, if she turned south, drive straight to Boston.

Sam was deeply troubled by what Zahra had told her about William, and saddened. She hated thinking of him being a bully in workshop. Of course, there had been a lot of bullies in workshop. Sam herself had been told she should choose another profession, that she was not a natural writer, that her stories were improbable, trite, clichéd, worthless. She didn't think the others had meant anything personal; it was just a kind of survival instinct. They all knew how slim the odds of making it as a writer were, that their instructors would never provide anything as plebeian or useful as connections, that an agent could glance at your query describing the book it had taken you three or five or ten years to write and pass in thirty seconds, or an editor could read the first page, toss it, and go out for lunch. The writers were scrambling to get out of the slush pile and kicking others in the face as they did it. The fewer of them there were, the better the chances.

William's behavior had been the norm. It was distasteful, reprehensible, but it was not a dealbreaker. And his workshop was decades ago. Even Zahra had pointed out how he must have changed, the Darlings a testament to how much. He used his own invaluable time to pay it forward. To help less fortunate writers. He certainly had been unfailingly supportive of Sam.

And yet.

There was something bothering Sam, something more than William's workshop behavior, something on the tip of her brain.

Mireille: *Perhaps you can find out his secret, how he writes all these female-centric blockbusters.*

Zahra: *William was especially ruthless because he had no real story. He was a copycat. He was zero at the core.*

Sam remembered what she'd thought the first time she went to hear William read: What writer switched genres with every book? No writer. Except William.

And why *did* he write only from the female point of view?

Sam scoffed. This was ridiculous. Of *course* William wasn't stealing women's stories for his novels. Surely Zahra hadn't meant to imply that. Zahra herself had exonerated William, saying nobody had found anything wrong with his conduct beyond the usual workshop douchebaggery. And bullying Becky.

But: *We thought their pairing very strange*, Zahra had also said.

And there was—had been—Cyndi, hunched in her hoodie: *He reached out to help me with my fiction novel! I was so surprised! I mean, somebody like you, I could understand him talking to. But me, why?*

Zahra: *I guess he found his own voice after all. And it was feminine.*

Had he, though? Or had William found somebody else's voice? Many somebodies? Female somebodies? That he had handpicked and curated? Culled from lectures, conferences, his own support group? Women who were isolated, by profession and also maybe by personality? The shy ones? Each writing in a different genre? Women who, if they then said *Wait, that's my story!* would be scoffed at and disbelieved, who didn't have the resources or reputation to confront a monolith like William Corwyn?

"This is *insane*," Sam said. What if Zahra had *intended* this, to plant this idea in Sam's head? Zahra could have had an axe to grind with William all these years—no doubt he'd treated her abysmally too. And Zahra had to be jealous. In Sam's program, a woman a year ahead of her had won the Pulitzer. Sam had always been so grateful she hadn't been in that writer's workshop. She wouldn't have been able to bear the envy. She might have been so discouraged she wouldn't have published at all. Look at Zahra: one quiet, well-regarded novel early on, then two that had dropped down the well, a memoir, and some articles. She'd achieved much in her professional life, but nothing like William's stratospheric, highly visible success. In Zahra's position, Sam might have wanted to smear William, too, sow discord in his upcoming marriage.

Still.

Sam watched snow spinning out of the gray sky. If she left now, she might beat William back to the house, especially if the weather got worse and delayed his flight. She could greet him with lights on, soup on the stove, a hearty blaze in the fireplace.

She could check out his study.

Or she could drive south. Stay with Drishti. Leave all this trouble behind. Including the Rabbit—in her new confusion Sam had almost forgotten the Rabbit!, who was probably lurking at the house right now, just waiting for Sam to come home alone. Ready to use that blade Sam had seen in her hand. Or bash Sam's head with a rock and drag her onto the ice, making it look like an accident. Or drown her in the hot tub. *He'll probably chop you up into little pieces and make you into soup.*

Sam twisted her beautiful ring. She could see it all so clearly. Marrying William in the backyard. Overlooking the lake. A small wedding, maybe even just the two of them and a judge, Sam in a white sundress, William in his button-down and khakis. Something simple because extravagance was beside the point: All they needed was each other. William leaning forward, smiling, to kiss her. *It's you.*

It wouldn't have to be forever. Sam could just visit Drishti to take a break, get some perspective. That was what a sane person would do.

Sam set her coffee in the cupholder and put the Jeep in drive. Pulled onto the service road. Signaled her intent. At the last minute, she swerved, bumping over the median, and took the northern exit instead. Toward Maine.

The Rabbit

They're back, both of them. They arrived on the island yesterday evening within minutes of each other, as if they'd planned it. I was so mad! I'd been lying in wait for Sam Vetiver, or rather crouching in the bushes as soon as I heard her Jeep on the causeway, but just as she got out William came bumping up in his fancy car with the chained snow tires. Then I had to listen to "Hi," and "Hi," and "It's you," and "It's you," and "Love," and "Love," and all manner of wubba-wubba reunion bullsh*t, including the mother of all f*ckfests that was so loud I could hear it down in the Rabbit Hole with my earmuffs on.

God forbid they're ever parted from each other for more than a few days. The world will blow up.

I look forward to making that happen.

Meanwhile, this morning, business as usual. William wakes before dawn and makes coffee, he writes in his basement study, he goes back up, they have breakfast. I assume the position, standing on a chair under the kitchen air vent. There's a smell of pancakes that practically makes me cry, plus plates clanking and silverware clinking as William says, "We're going to get a blizzard tomorrow," and Sam Vetiver says, "That's exciting!" and William says, "Spoken like a true city girl, they can be deadly. I'll go to Augusta for provisions. Want to come?" and Sam Vetiver says, "I may stay home if you don't mind, I've got some things I want to do here," and I think, Me too, Sam Vetiver, me too. I'm doing a silent happy dance about this develop-ment, final-f*cking-ly she'll be alone! William says, "Send me your shopping list, I know we need lube," and Sam Vetiver says, "I noticed that, I don't know what happened to all of it," and William says "Well, I do," and then they settle down to eat and are quiet.

Until Sam Vetiver says, "Oh, did you get that photo I sent you?"

"Of my lowly student digs? Yes, I did. Incredibly sweet of you."

"I wanted to see where you lived."

"A lot went down in that house," William says, and I think, It sure as f*ck did. "Thank you, sugarplum."

"Also, Zahra sends best wishes. And congrats on your career and our engagement."

A pause. "Who?" William says.

"Zahra Alaam? From your program? Didn't she invite you to teach?"

"No, it was arranged through my speaker's bureau. I don't recall any Sara."

"Not Sara, *Zahra*. Beautiful East Indian woman? Dark hair, mehndi—you know, henna designs on her hands?"

"Ohhhhh," says William. "I *may* know who you mean. It was so many years ago, but . . . I think I remember reading she published?"

"She did."

"But she's a one-hit wonder. Started strong, then fizzled out."

"I'm not sure I'd say that," says Sam Vetiver. "She's the program head now."

"*Is* she," says William. "At Harrington! Of our graduate MFA workshop?"

"Yup."

"Well," he says. "How about that. Good for her, making the best of it. You know what they say: Those who can't do, teach." His chair scrapes, and he adds, "Thanks for letting me know. I'll get in touch. Who knows, she may want me for a commencement address one of these days . . . And now, you luscious distraction you, I must away to the desk," and I scurry back to the Rabbit Hole, all the better to be hidden by the time he comes downstairs.

As if. As if William doesn't remember Zahra. Or Becky or me or his merry men, the guys who backed him up in everything he did. But maybe he doesn't. Maybe the only way William can live with himself is to forget everything the minute he does it, especially the horrible things. The ones that do the most harm. Even if, as I bet, he doesn't think they're hurtful at all.

Like what he did to me the night of The Incident, when he came up to me in the cafeteria, because of course he didn't approach me at the milk machine to talk Shakespeare.

That's why I was so shocked, because I knew what was going to happen. William had that reputation, but this would be like Brad Pitt sleeping with his cleaning lady. I kept thinking, Me? Are you sure? I wondered if William was drunk or on drugs, even having some kind of mental breakdown. But he wasn't. He knew exactly what he was doing.

He took me to the Castle, the student pub where I'd just started picking up extra cash as a dishwasher and which actually did look like a castle, with turrets and everything, and we went to the basement, where I sat on the customer side of the bar for the very first time, on a velvet stool, and William bought me a pint of cider I couldn't drink a drop of because I was so nervous I knew if I took a sip, I'd choke. I kept thinking, You don't have to do this. You don't have to treat me like a date you're trying to impress. I'll go to bed with you anyway.

But William was a gentleman. He drank his own beer, and he asked me what my plans were after I left Harrington. Of course, like all of us, I was planning to write. "The Great American Novel?" William said, doing his gazing thing. I could barely look him in the face, it was like staring straight into the sun. "Is that your aspiration?" I shook my head. "No," I said. "I just want to get published. To make a living writing." It was the first time I'd said it out loud, and to my surprise it didn't sound as foolish and conceited as it did in my head. It sounded doable. "You said yourself I was writing commercial fiction," I reminded him.

William looked surprised. "Did I?" he said. "Well, that's certainly more lucrative than striving for literary posterity. Here's to your enormous commercial success." He toasted me, and we both drank. "I remember now," he said, "you're the one who writes about that terrible place in upstate New York. Regina."

I thought my face would burst into flames right there on my barstool. I muttered something like "Aegina. Yes, that's me."

"They're very bleak stories," said William. "Suffused with hopelessness. But that's the stuff of literary fiction, like Cormac or Dubus, and it doesn't match your domestic content. Have you ever thought about writing romance? Something more *Bridges of Madison County* than *Blood Meridian*? It seems that might be more in line with your talents. And ambitions."

I ducked my head. I knew he was insulting me. Any sort of genre fiction was considered brainless, paint-by-numbers stuff, the kind of book that would be consumed on a plane or on a beach and instantly forgotten. Literary fast food. And romance was the worst of all. William himself had called it thumb-sucking tripe for sad housewives, the print version of a vibrator. Nobody in our program would have used it for toilet paper.

And in fact I did not want to write romance, because what did I know about love? I was in no way qualified, not even in my imagination. But I so badly did not want William Corwyn to stop looking at me like that that all I did was mumble "Yeah, romance, maybe," into my cider.

"I think romance gets a bad rap," said William. "What could be more important than love? We need more of it in our lives, don't you agree?"

I did brave a glance right at him then, and he smiled.

"You're just the person to do it," he said. "I've been watching you for months, and I suspect you're a woman of great passions."

He tucked my hair, which I'd just home-permed, behind my ear.

"There," he said. "I've been wanting to do that all night."

Of course we went to his house after that, the little green duplex by the train depot. And he f*cked me in his apartment, on his very neat bed with the scratchy striped blankets he still has upstairs. He had no curtains on the windows and I remember the way the moonlight and the orange streetlight fell across our bodies and how embarrassed I was and kept trying to pull the sheets up, but William stopped me. "No," he said. "Don't do that, sweetie. Don't hide from me. I want to see you." I threw my fists down by my side and squinched my eyes closed like I was at the gynecologist. I felt William's hand on my face. "Look at me," he said, and I did. He was raised up above me like some god. "You're beautiful," he said. "Do you believe me?" He waited, holding himself in his hand, moving it slowly up and down, until I nodded. Then he said, "Good," and drove himself into me. "Oh," he said, "you feel even better than I thought you'd feel," and "You are so juicy," and, swiveling his hips, "I knew how avid you'd be," because at that point I was making noises I didn't know a human being could make, let alone myself.

I wasn't a virgin before that night with William. There had been boys back in Aegina, the guy I worked the night shift with at the Kwik Trip and the guy I bought my car from and the ones who stuck their hands between my legs in the back row of the school bus or movies or in parking lots or at the quarry because they'd heard I was an easy lay. And I was. I was an easy lay. I let them push my bra up and grope me and push my head into their laps so I could suck them off and f*ck me with their fingers and then with their d*cks because I was hoping against hope that at some point I'd do something right and one of them would call me his girlfriend. Like the other girls. Wasn't that how they got guys? The ones who waited for them by the lockers and held their hands in the hallways and drove them places in their cars and gave them their letter jackets and talked about getting married after school? It was all I wanted, to be somebody's girlfriend, to get the f*ck out of my mother's house, to be loved. I thought this was how you did it. Except I must have been doing something wrong, because after every hookup not one of those guys so much as acknowledged me or gave me a cigarette or stick of gum. They looked right past me. As if I did not exist.

I thought William was different. The way he f*cked certainly was. He wasn't like three pumps and done. He was present. He was there. He actually seemed to care whether I was enjoying myself, was intent on me having orgasms, something I didn't even know I could do with another person. Many times, in fact. This must be what lovemaking is, I remember thinking. And afterward he actually held me as we were going to sleep. He petted my hair. I felt his big body close around me like an oyster shell around a pearl and I felt so safe, and I tried as hard as I could to stay awake, staring at the stack of books on his dresser, because all I wanted was for this moment, this night, to last forever. If I had died then, I would have been perfectly happy.

But of course daylight came, and William was up with the dawn, as the birds were chirping in the trees. I woke and felt cold because he was no longer next to me and saw him dressing. "Good morning, lambchop," he said when he saw my eyes open, and he used the long toes of his big foot to pick my panties up off the floor. He made little beeping noises like a truck reversing as he lifted them toward me. "You might need these," he said with his sunshine grin. "I have to get to work. The page waits for no man."

"Oh sure," I said, "I'll leave ASAP," and he said, "Stay as long as you want," and I said, hoping he'd talk me out of it and offer me breakfast, "No really, I should go, I need to write too," and he said, "Romance?" and cocked his eyebrow at me, smiling, and I said, "No, actually, I'm working on a thriller." I couldn't believe I'd said that, it was like a frog had jumped out of my mouth, I hadn't told anybody. Thrillers were almost as bad as romance in our program, the same mindless junk but with gore. "Not a thriller-thriller," I hastened to add, since William was standing there with one leg in his pants and one not, gaping at me. I was so embarrassed. I cursed myself for having admitted this. "Much more literary," I said, "like *The Shining*?"

William stared at me a minute longer, then said, "Godspeed." He came to me and kissed me on the forehead, like a priest. "Thank you for that gift of a night," he said, and walked out.

I don't know where in the apartment he worked, tucked away in a study or at the kitchen table, because I lay there for about fifteen minutes and then got up and wrote my phone number and *Thanks, this was fun!!!!* on a sheet of paper I ripped out of one of his notebooks. I considered adding a heart, at the end or over the *i*, but finally I decided against it and snuck out. The apartment was full of birdsong, sunshine, the smell of coffee.

That whole day I was in a daze, sore and sleep-deprived, replaying the night over and over in my head, trying to decide whether I'd said anything so stupid that he wouldn't call, remembering how he'd touched me, talked to me, how he'd actually kissed me—no man could do that and not call you, right? It was so different from before, any of the guys I'd known. I thought of that kiss on my forehead. That was tenderness. That was love. I checked my flip phone so much I practically sprained my wrist taking it in and out of my pocket. I skipped my seventeenth-century poetry class, which believe me was no sacrifice, and stayed in my sh*thole to write *Mr. and Mrs. Corwyn* hundreds of times in my notebook, his name and mine together. I kept looking out the window in case William was standing out there like Romeo, had looked up my address in the student directory. I was on fire with impatience to see him again, which was why I was so glad to hear his voice that night when I went to work at the Castle. He had come to see me! I was in the kitchen loading a tray of pint glasses into the dishwasher when I heard him at the bar, and I was taking off my hairnet and rehearsing what I'd do when I came out, would I play it casual and say Hey Hemingway, buy you a drink? or just lean over the bar and kiss him?, when I heard other voices and realized William was not alone, he was with Matt and Thom from our program. They were laughing about something, that goatish boy laughter I'd learned to dread because it was usually targeted at me or some other woman but was always bad.

I went and stood by the door to listen. Thom said, "It wasn't terrible, a little like f*cking a bag of mayo but any port in the storm, am I right?" and Matt said, "Speaking of which, Corwyn, someone said they saw you leaving here last night with the Rabbit."

"Who said that?" said William.

"Is it true?" said Matt.

"Maybe," said William, and Matt and Thom groaned.

"Jesus Christ, what the f*ck, man, are you desperate?" said Thom, and Matt said, "Did you finally f*ck your way through all the other p*ssy on campus?"

"Maybe," said William again, and they all laughed. "But seriously, what makes you think I f*cked her? Maybe I was just trying to help her."

"Yeah, trying to help her off with her size one hundred granny panties," said Matt, and my face burned, because I actually had been wearing bad underwear last night, waist-high and possibly with period stains, and how had he known this, had William taken photos or something? And Thom said, "Trying to help her finally lose her virginity."

"You have such a low opinion of me," said William. "What if I was trying to help her with her writing?" and one of them made a WAH sound like an airhorn and said, "Nice try, Corwyn."

"Oh all right," said William, "I might have thrown her a mercy f*ck," and they jeered.

"So kind of you," said Thom, and William said, "It was no big deal. I like f*cking ugly girls. They work harder."

"To Saint William," said Matt, "patron saint of ugly women."

"To Saint William!" and they clinked glasses.

"Thanks, boys," said William. "That's me. I'm a giver!"

I couldn't listen anymore then. I had been standing with my hand over my mouth but I took off my apron and hung it up and walked out the rear door of the Castle and never went back, and I never returned to my classes, either, especially our workshop, because how could I face William and those guys after something like that? That was the last time I ever wrote anything, too, thriller or stories or otherwise. The next day I packed up my things in my student housing sh*thole and drove away from Harrington and never looked back. I shoved it all into the back of my mind and tried my very best never to think about it, writing or William or Harrington, ever again.

Until a few years later, when something happened I knew would change everything.

CHAPTER 35

THE BLIZZARD

think the forecast's wrong," William said. "The blizzard's going to move in sooner than predicted."

On one hand, Sam wanted to know why William thought he knew more than professional meteorologists; on the other, she thought he was probably right. They were eating breakfast at the kitchen island, William spooning up oatmeal and squinting at the sky through the window wall. It was the color of lead above the tree line. Wind squalled from the north, stirring up powdery ghosts from the vast expanse of snow-covered ice.

"If you don't mind, sweetheart," said William, "I'm going to skip our morning walk. We won't make Augusta, but there's time to run to East Fork to grab a few provisions. Want to come?"

"No, I'm good, thanks," said Sam.

"Sure? We're likely to be housebound for a few days."

"I think I'm traveled out for a while. I'll stay here and do the tromp."

"No," said William.

"No?" said Sam.

"Simone, I don't want you out there by yourself. I'm sorry. I'm not being paternalistic. It's just too dangerous. You don't know the land as well as I do, and if that blizzard moves in, it's no joke. People have gotten disoriented and died within feet of their doorsteps. Even the ones born here."

Sam was about to tell him she knew this from the prairie research she'd done for *The Sodbuster's Wife* when William added, again: "Look what happened to Pen."

There was a beat. "What *did* happen to Pen?" Sam asked. "I don't think you ever told me."

William looked startled. "Didn't I?" he said. "Well. It's a very sad story. She went out during a blizzard on the mountain where we lived. She was very headstrong and could not be argued out of it. And by the time we found her, it was too late."

Sam looked at him sharply. He was staring across the other-planetary sweep of white beyond the window glass, rubbing one of his graying sideburns. "I'm so sorry, William," she said. "Thank you for telling me."

"You're welcome. It pains me to talk about, and I do so only to emphasize how serious the situation can be. You'll do what I say, then, sweetheart?"

"I promise," Sam said.

She saw him off, waving and blowing kisses as his car disappeared at the end of the causeway. William was likely right; the day beyond the glass walls had darkened considerably, the light more like evening than midmorning. The wind was hooting under the eaves with a mournful sound like somebody blowing across the mouth of a bottle, something Sam had never heard before, and the pines on the far side of the lake were thrashing uneasily.

William would be quick on his errand. Since he wasn't going to Augusta, Sam didn't have much time. As she opened the door to the basement, the light dimmed further and the first snow hit the glass walls, sounding more like sprayed sand.

Sam eased down the steps in her sock feet, through the main area of the basement and past the storage room. It was silly to be quiet, she was the only person around for miles, and still she was furtive as a burglar. The door to William's study was unlocked. *Believe.* Sam paused. This was such a violation of privacy, and not just because William had specifically requested Sam not come in here, had set a very clear boundary. It was an invasion of his creative space. Sam knew how this felt. Somebody reading your writing without your permission was a dealbreaker.

But Sam wasn't going to read William's work. She was looking for other people's.

What if he had stolen his books from women?

What if he hadn't?

Either way, Sam had to know. It was a matter of her future.

She opened the door and went in.

The room was shadowy and cold as a root cellar. Sam could see her breath. How could William write in here? But men always ran hotter, and William was no exception. *I have an excellent bedwarmer,* he said, when she asked him how he could sleep in their frigid room with all his limbs outside the covers.

Sam took a few steps forward and looked around in disbelief. She recalled William ribbing her in Boston for how disturbingly neat her study was, yet this room was monastic. On industrial carpet, there was only a chair and a desk. On the desk, three objects: an award, a banker's lamp, and a laptop. No books, no shelves, no papers, no filing cabinets full of incriminating manuscripts.

Sam picked up the award. It was a heavy glass thing shaped like a mountain, with jagged edges and the inscription MR. WILLIAM COR- WYN, MT. WASHINGTON POST FICTION CONTEST WINNER, 1986. Sam smiled faintly; this must have been his first writing award. She rubbed it on her sleeve and set it down. She switched on the lamp and noticed a single Polaroid taped to the wall: young William with hair curling over the flipped-up collar of his pink Izod shirt, red flash eyes staring into the camera. Behind him, laughing, a pretty girl with long, straight cinnamon-colored hair held back from her face with a whale-covered headband. Sam remembered those headbands. She'd had one. Who was this laughing girl—in, Sam realized, the only photo in the entire house? *Pen? Is that you?* It had to be. Sam considered taking the photo down to see if there was anything on the back, but that would be even more disrespectful, and besides, she was running out of time.

There was a thud overhead and Sam flinched—the Rabbit? There was nobody behind her, and when the lights flickered Sam realized it was probably a branch blown against the house. The wind was cranking up to gale force now, shrieking like a teakettle, then leveling off. If Sam was going to do this, she had to hurry. She thought, Please, don't let there be anything, and opened the laptop.

The screen glowed to life, showing a passcode bar against a gray background. "Fuck," said Sam. Although what had she expected? Even her own laptop was protected. Sam set her hands on William's keyboard and typed his birthday. The passcode bar shivered. She tried her own next, then theirs together, then *WilliamAndSam*, then *WilliamAndSimoneCorwyn* . . . Really, it was hopeless. *WilliamCorwyn#1*. *WilliamCorwynNYTBestseller. KingCorwyn—*

A gust of cold punched into the room. Sam turned, but it was not the door behind her that had blown open. It was the one beneath the bulkhead that led to outside. William stood there in his parka, plastered with snow, holding his axe.

"Simone," he said. "It's you." Behind him, the square of daylight was as gray and staticky as a dead TV screen with snow.

"I came back," William said softly. "The storm moved in even faster than I thought. It was too dangerous. So I drove home. I saw the light on in here, and I thought maybe there was an intruder. And I was right. There is."

Sam opened her mouth to say she was sorry, but nothing came out. She stood shivering and shivering.

"What did I say, Simone?" William asked. "What was the one request I made of you? What did I say I would do if I caught you in my study?"

They stared at each other, snowmelt dripping from William's nose and the blade of the axe. Outside the wind screamed like a hawk.

The Rabbit

When I wake up, the light in the Rabbit Hole looks weird, and I have no idea what time it is. I check my watch, and I'm flabbergasted to see it's late morning. I'm usually up at sunrise with William, both to keep an eye on him and out of habit, all those mornings opening my store. Now I realize why I slept so late: The basement window is completely blocked by snow. The Rabbit Hole is almost as dark as if it's night.

It also sounds like it's trying to take off. The whole house is. The wind out there is so crazy it's like I'm standing right next to a jet engine, not that I've ever flown, only heard them on TV. I thought I'd experienced blizzards in Augusta, but I've never heard anything like this.

It's not the wind screaming that woke me, though. It's William and Sam Vetiver, and it sounds like they're having one motherf*cker of an argument. I can hear them even over the storm. I crawl out of my sleeping bag and tiptoe through the storage room, all the while happily imagining what Sam Vetiver could have done to p*ss William off so much.

But when I pop out into the basement I almost die, because *they are right there*. William and Sam Vetiver, coming out of his study. William's face is turned away from me, he's saying something to her over his shoulder, or he'd see me. I drop and push myself back into the storage room, my heart pounding in my mouth. Jeez. No wonder I could hear them. They were only feet away.

And wait. Sam Vetiver was in the *study?!?!?!?!* I have to admit I'm impressed. I've heard them talking about it, William lecturing Sam Vetiver, in that very solemn you-must-not-play-with-matches voice you use with a toddler, how she is never to go in there, ever. What a breach it would be of his priceless privacy. An assault on his creativity. And so on. And Sam Vetiver agreeing, meek as a Mormon wife, *I hear you, William. I'm a writer too. I get it.* Which, I realize now, is not the same as her promising she won't do it. Maybe she has more in common with Mormon wives than I thought, because I bet under those skirts and head coverings are some bad-@$$ b*tches.

"I will not tolerate snoops," William is saying. From behind a Flat William's butt I watch him deposit his axe against the log rack and head toward the stairs. Since he has an actual furnace there really is no reason for him to chop so much wood, but William loves being a big man with an axe. "I was very clear about what will happen."

"I know," Sam Vetiver whines, following him. "I already said I'm sorry. What do you want me to do? I'd say it a hundred times if it'd help—"

"That won't be necessary," says William, stomping up the steps. "In fact quite the opposite. What I require now, Simone, is space. For my temper to come down. I won't take responsibility for what might happen otherwise."

"But—" Sam Vetiver says, as they reach the top of the stairs, and I think, Don't argue with a man with an axe, girl.

"What. Did. I. Say," he says. "You're not listening." And then the kitchen door slams and the argument continues above, muted now by the jet plane wind.

Huh. I sit back on my heels. This should be one of the best days of my life. Sam Vetiver going in William's study is a dealbreaker, so soon she'll hit the road. Forever! So he's said.

Then again, he's broken a lot of his own rules for Sam Vetiver. I don't trust it. Or her.

And something else is bothering me. What is it?

What was she doing in the study?

Then it comes to me, and I want to smack myself in the face. DUH! She was trying to get into William's laptop. There's nothing else in there. I know because I've been in multiple times. Of course, Sam Vetiver was probably looking for something other than I would—like trying to break into his social, see if he's writing to other women. Which I'm sure he is, or would've been before Sam Vetiver moved in here. Spinning his pretty webs of words.

But I know something else to look for. Something that will end this whole situation right now. The solution to the Sam Vetiver problem. I'm such a dum-dum. I can't believe I didn't think of it before. I've been trying the same old strategy I did with the others, but this has been in my face the whole time. Sometimes things are so obvious you can't see them.

The final piece of the puzzle snaps into place.

I count to one hundred, then two hundred, then dart into the study.

Aside from William's big wet boot prints on the floor, the room looks as it always does. Neat. Tidy. Weirdly sterile. The award on the desk. William and Pen on the wall.

And the laptop in the center of the desk, gleaming.

I flip up the lid and get the home screen with the passcode bar.

I don't bother with William's birthday, though I know what it is. That's too obvious. I don't try Sam Vetiver's, either.

I start with his ego.

The other birthdays. The important ones. His book birthdays. His pub dates.

I've memorized them all. I start with just digits, then spell out the month names, proceeding methodically. I try the latest book first, *Lambent Souls*, and work backward, but the whole time I'm thinking of William's first bestseller. And Becky. Poor dead Becky.

She was the only sort-of friend I ever had. I wasn't very good at making friends. I'd never gotten much practice. Having the girls at your school call you the Human Can Opener or guys finger-f*ck you in a men's room doesn't do much for your people skills. But Becky and I got to know each other a little, and it wasn't because we were the quietest and least hot women at Harrington, according to the Pig Scale. It was because of what happened in her workshop.

Which was what happened to everyone: She was massively humiliated. Her story was picked apart like a rotisserie chicken and called contrived and artless, and William tossed his copy onto the floor and said "Maybe I just don't understand plebian stories meant to appeal to the masses, but this is literary drool," and afterward, when everyone left to go to the Castle, Becky crouched on the floor, picking up her pages. Some of them had footprints on them.

I noticed she was crying, so I said, "Do you want some help?"

And she said, "No, that's okay, thanks. I'm just being a big baby because it's my birthday." I stood there a minute more because I wasn't very good at birthdays either, never having celebrated my own, but I knew you shouldn't leave a person crying on the floor, especially on that day. So I helped her gather up her story, and then I said, "I have an idea, if you want to come with me."

We went to the CamCo, and I used the last of my food points to buy a flat of cupcakes from the day-old table. It meant I wouldn't eat tomorrow, but the dining hall dumpsters were full of perfectly good scraps, you wouldn't believe how much food students waste. I held the cupcakes out to Becky and said, "I hope you like vanilla."

"Honestly? It's my favorite," she said.

We took the cupcakes to the big flat rock called Porcupine Rock because that was Harrington's mascot so there was all this graffiti on it, like Go Porks! PORKS RULE!, and we sat and watched the moon rise, a big yellow one, almost full, just a little misshapen on one side. I was shy about eating only the frosting like I usually do, but I saw Becky scraping hers off with her teeth and leaving the yellow cake, so I did too. I said, "I liked your story."

"Thanks," she said. "Also thanks for never saying anything mean."

"You too," I said.

"Honestly, why would I?" she said. "Writing is hard enough, and the world is even harder," and I said, "That's the truth," and we sat licking frosting off our fingers. "It's my fault what happened back there," Becky said. "It wasn't my best writing. My heart wasn't in it. But I can't hand in what I'm really excited about." "Which is what?" I said. "Why can't you?" and she said, "Don't tell anybody," and I said I wouldn't, and she said, "It has to be a secret," and I said okay, and she stage-whispered, "It's a ROMANCE novel."

Oh, I said. Gotcha. Of course she couldn't submit those pages. She'd be ridiculed right out of the program. If writing commercial was a crime at Harrington, romance was a sin. They might even revoke her scholarship.

Becky ate her third wad of frosting and threw the bald cake into the woods for the raccoons. "But I do want to publish it after the program, though," she said. "Do you think that's stupid? Like too lowbrow?"

"Not at all," I said, "or if it is, I'm with you. I want to write thrillers. Maybe we could be the Lowbrow Club," and I blushed because I had never said anything like that to anyone before, and why would anyone ever want to be in a club with me?

But Becky said, "To the Lowbrow Club," and I said, "May we both be huge bestsellers," and we mushed our final cupcakes together in a toast. Then I asked her what her romance novel was about, and I sat eating and listening and nodding while she told me the story.

After that we started hanging out a little, taking walks or sometimes meeting at the student union just to sit and read together, and the program swallowed us both up again and I forgot all about my thriller and her romance novel until years later, long after The Incident with William, when I'd left Harrington and was working in my first bookstore.

CHAPTER 36

THE JIG IS UP

After William had caught Sam in his study and stowed his axe, after he'd taken off his ice-encrusted parka and boots, they'd come upstairs and Sam had sat miserably in the great room like a guest as William built roaring fires in all the woodstoves and fireplaces—the power was out. "May I help?" she asked, but he said "No thanks." He stalked into the kitchen, and she heard him clanking around in there. Sam went and stood in the doorway, watching William fix dinner on the gas burner, which he'd lit with a match. Crackers and tomato soup. "Is there enough for two?" she asked.

"Help yourself," he said, and carried his bowl into the dining room.

Sam ate the leftovers out of the pot, although she didn't want it at all. Outside the wind shrieked and the window walls trembled and literally bowed inward, then hissed as they were blasted with snow. Sam would not have been surprised if they'd shattered and the roof flew off the house. The fire flattened and fizzed in the stove. It was amazing how moving air could sound like someone screaming.

She went back into the great room and found William making up one of the couches with the Pendleton blankets and his pillow from upstairs. "What are you doing?" Sam said.

"What does it look like I'm doing, Simone?"

"Would you like some company?"

"Does it look like I'm inviting your company?"

Sam sighed. "William. Please. I'm so sorry. What can I do to make it up to you? I'll never go near your study again, I promise. I was just—"

"I know what you were doing, Simone."

"What?"

"The jig is up," William said.

"What does that mean?" Sam asked.

"It means I know what you were doing in my study. You were digging. Digging digging digging in my past like a little mongrel bitch. Again. Looking for God-knows-what. Trying to discredit me. To bring about my ruination."

"*What?*" Sam said. She felt again the danger she'd had the morning on the causeway, a sensation like vertigo. Was this really happening? And she felt something else: Shame. He wasn't completely wrong. But she'd been looking for evidence to prove he was in the clear.

"That's ridiculous," she said. "I wasn't digging for anything. I was just curious—"

"You're lying, Simone. I know it and you know it. I've known it all along, how untrustworthy you are. I could no longer ignore it that morning on the causeway, after you woke me screaming in the night about some supposed phantom with a knife. And the way you run around half-naked all the time. Loll about the house like some Lolita, trying to lure me onto the rocks. To throw me off my game. Derail my deadline. Because I'm writing and you're not. You're trying to undermine me. You always have been."

Sam was shaking her head, no no no. "None of that is in any way true. I would never—"

"I suppose it was inevitable," William went on, tucking his blanket in around his feet. "I'm the more successful one. You're the dinghy to my ocean liner. I don't know if you're even conscious of your deranging envy. I suspect not. But everything you've done in this relationship is designed to destroy me."

Sam's eyes filled with tears of indignation, sorrow, and fear. She couldn't believe he was saying this. That he believed it. *Did* he believe it? Worse, had he believed it all along? It was so insane. Maybe it was just the heat of the moment. But he was breaking them.

"Please stop," she said.

"You showed me your true colors back in the summer. You're a liar and a thief."

"William," said Sam. Her voice wobbled. She forced herself to speak extra calmly. "All I did was go into your study. It was wrong of me. I violated a boundary and I apologize. But we have to be able to work things through—"

"It's my fault as much as yours," William said, as if Sam hadn't spoken. He removed his glasses, folding the stems and setting them on an ottoman, and pulled his striped blanket to his chin. "Fool me once, et cetera. I knew what you were, but I let you back in. I thought if I proposed I could bell the bitch, that you'd stop this mad campaign. I loved you. *Love*, Simone," he said, casting Sam a significant look. "But that's done. You can't leave now; you'll never make it to the interstate alive. But as soon as the storm is over and I've cleared the road, you're gone."

"William. You can't mean that."

"I do."

"But we're engaged! You just asked me to *marry* you."

"Leave the ring on the kitchen counter, next to the fruit bowl," said William.

"William, come *on*—"

"This conversation, like this relationship, is over," William said, and folded himself into his blanket, turning his back on Sam.

Sam stood looking at him, waiting for him to, if not change his mind and hold his arms out to her, then at least roll back over and say something. He didn't. She was still incredulous that this was happening, that he'd canceled their engagement, that he'd throw their life away, that he believed the awful things he'd said about her, that things had gone this bad this quickly.

Sam considered climbing onto the couch behind him, lifting her shirt and his, pressing her breasts to his back. Healing them with skin. But she feared what William would do, and she wasn't even sure what she meant by that, so after a few minutes of watching him pretend to sleep—or actually do it, since he could conk out that fast—and listening to the wind shriek and snow sandblast the glass walls and the fire pop and snap in the grate, she went upstairs alone.

Their bed was cold without William. Sam put on every extra blanket she could find and crawled in wearing all her clothes. She plugged in her phone, and nothing happened. Of course. The power was out. Sam had only 21 percent battery, and she'd need to conserve it for however long this storm lasted. Tomorrow, when it was at least light, she'd charge it in her Jeep. In the meantime, she couldn't scroll social or use the flashlight to read a book, and she was too cold to go find candles, so she switched on low power mode and set the phone aside, then pulled the blankets over her head and made a little cave in which she huddled, miserable.

How had she gotten to this place? Stuck on an island in rural Maine in the middle of a blizzard, with a man who'd dumped her again, this time breaking an engagement. She couldn't believe it. She really couldn't believe this was happening. Why had she gone into the study? What if she'd just left well enough alone? What if Sam hadn't disrespected William's one ask, hadn't snooped in his laptop, hadn't let Zahra get into her head? What if she'd dismissed as preposterous the very idea that her lover had stolen women's stories? What if she'd laughed it all off and turned back to her own work? What if, in reverse, became if only. Sam yearned to believe it, that in the morning there'd be some fix, that in the light of day over muffins and coffee there would be something, some magic thing she could say that would make William forgive her and they'd come up to this bedroom and make love and everything would be all right again.

But there was also this: She couldn't get past the things he'd said.

I know what you were doing. Digging digging digging like a little mongrel bitch.

Trying to discredit me. To bring about my ruination.

The dinghy to my ocean liner. A liar and a thief.

I don't know if you're even conscious of your deranging envy.

I thought if I proposed I could bell the bitch.

Sam wished to God he hadn't said them. She'd tried to ignore, to dismiss his earlier assessments of her character—*careless, untrustworthy, thief, vampire*—as barbs William just shot off when he was angry. But now she could no longer pretend they didn't exist.

This conversation, like this relationship, is over.

And what about the other women, the ones he might have stolen stories from? Even if William was fast asleep, if Sam could sneak past him without waking him, if the blizzard covered the sound of her creeping into the study, the laptop was locked. Sam had failed completely. She'd really screwed this up.

"God damn it," she said. She dashed away tears and sat up, throwing the covers back. She reached for her phone to text Drishti—not LOL but HEY D, COMING HOME FOR A VISIT, OKAY TO STAY WITH YOU AND FRANZ FOR A MINUTE WHILE I FIGURE SOME THINGS OUT?

But as Sam swiped the phone open, its screen lit up with a text from an unknown number. She read it and sucked in a breath.

"Holy fuck," she said.

The Rabbit

The text I send Sam Vetiver says HIS LAPTOP IS OPEN. COME DOWN NOW. And I'm hiding behind the water heater to see what she does. If she wakes William up and they hunt for me, I'm toast. If she doesn't, and she comes downstairs, well. She'll know what I know, and finally all this can end.

I've known for years. I figured it out the day the eighteen-wheeler pulled up to my first bookstore in Portland, Maine, almost three years after I left Harrington. Every month at that time there was one book chosen by the world's most popular TV talk show host for her book club, and there were so many copies printed, it had to be delivered by truck. We had to clear the whole front table for it, the most valuable one facing the door, and all the end caps and merch shelves. It was a big secret too. We never knew in advance what the book was. It was a great guessing game for most of the staff, but I hated it because I was always afraid the book picked would be William's. Please, please, I prayed every time the truck pulled up with the talk show host selection. Please don't let it be him. But that June, I sliced open the top box and there he was, smirking at me from the back of his new hardcover. A little older, he had some smile lines now, but same smarmy motherf*cker.

I didn't read it, of course. Not right away. Even though everybody raved about it, oh how they loved that f*cking novel. The booksellers clutched it to their chests and said they'd devoured it in one sitting and then turned back to the first page to start over right away, it had kept them up all night, it was the best thing they'd ever read. Bob, the GM of my original store, got tears in his eyes when he talked about it. Customers came in demanding not one or two but five, ten, twenty copies for their families and book clubs. We could not keep it in stock.

Finally one afternoon, in William's fourth printing, I couldn't stand it anymore. I snuck a copy from the Hottest Summer Reads table, not like anyone would miss it, and took it to the storeroom with my lunch, even though we weren't supposed to bring food in there. I didn't want to be in the break room or around any of the other staff when I read it, in case I had a reaction. Nobody at my store knew my history with William, or Harrington, and I wanted to keep it that way.

So I got myself settled on a box of new middle-grade books with my ham sandwich and my milk and I opened the novel. *You Never Said Goodbye*. From the very first sentence I understood why it was so popular, a worldwide phenomenon. It was so, so good.

And it was so, so familiar.

The language might have been all William, never a regular word when a hundred-dollar one would do.

But the story was pure Becky Bowman.

It was exactly the story she'd told me that night on Porcupine Rock, on her birthday. And we'd talked about it some after that.

I couldn't believe it. I got hot all over, then cold, then jumped up. I kicked my milk by mistake, and it spilled across the floor.

I raced to the nearest computer and frantically tapped out an email to Becky, using the last address I had for her. **DID YOU READ *YOU NEVER SAID GOODBYE*, WILLIAM'S NEW NOVEL? YOU HAVE TO. IT'S YOUR BOOK!**

I felt so jumpy and sick the rest of the day that I almost said I was ill and went home. But I'd never done that, so instead I just surreptitiously turned all of William's books face down and checked my email every half hour.

There was nothing. Not that day or the next. I tried again, several times. I was surprised. Becky and I hadn't been in touch since I'd run away from the program, but we'd been on good terms before that, so even if she'd been mad at me for leaving without, well, saying goodbye, she still would've written back. I thought.

On the night of the third day, in my sh*thole studio, I bit the bullet and looked up Becky's profile on social media. What I saw there made me run to my bathroom and throw up my mac and cheese.

Becky was dead.

Her whole wall was plastered with condolences from our cohort. WE MISS YOU, BECKY. THINKING OF YOU, BECKY. Elizabeth Bishop's poem "One Art," about all the things a person can lose in life. Where were all these people when she was alive, crying on the floor after they'd stomped her story?

The sad messages went back almost three years. She'd been dead that long, and I hadn't known.

Maybe even worse than being dead, she'd been engaged. To William.

Her profile photo showed the two of them, William hugging her from behind as Becky extended her hand toward whoever was taking the photo. There was a big joehonking diamond on her ring finger. She was grinning in a way I'd never seen, and I saw she was pretty after all. I'd give anything to have a smile like that.

I clicked on that photo and saw all the congratulatory messages. BRAVO, YOU TWO! CONGRATS! HAPPIEST LITERARY COUPLE SINCE SCOTTY AND ZELDA! The Shakespeare poem about *Let me not to the marriage of true minds admit impediment.*

The date of that photo was three years before.

So Becky and William had gotten engaged the spring after I left the program, right after winter break, from what I could tell.

By that summer, she was dead.

Two and a half years later, about the amount of time it would take for a speedy writer to turn an outline into a manuscript and for a publisher to fast-track a manuscript into a book, William's first international sensation came out.

Almost thirty years and three more monster bestselling novels later and here we are, and the code that cracked William's laptop was not his book birthdays after all. It was a death date. I started with poor dead Becky's, but it wasn't hers. It was that last girl, Cyndi, the most recent one, the sweet little cuckoo-bird with all the cats.

The door opens at the top of the steps, and I fade back until I see it's Sam Vetiver, not William, creeping down. She's holding on to the railing to distribute her weight so her feet won't creak on the wooden steps, even though the storm is howling. Extra cautious. Atta girl. At the bottom she glances in my direction, but maybe she's just looking over her shoulder, scanning the dark basement. Then she goes into the study, where the only light in the house comes from the laptop's open screen.

CHAPTER 37

END MATTER

S am had, of course, never seen William's screensaver. It turned out to be a photo of himself, laughing at the lectern of some conference—or awards ceremony, or fundraiser? Whatever the occasion, it was a big one, because behind William there was another, much larger William on a Jumbotron. In his seersucker. Mic in one hand, one of his books in the other.

Which interested Sam much more than his screen backdrop. William's novels. *Were* they his? Whatever entity had summoned her to the basement somehow knew of Sam's curiosity in this matter. This had much larger and more disturbing implications, but Sam didn't have time to think about them right now. Whoever had opened the laptop probably didn't mean to harm Sam, or it would have happened already. Even if it was the Rabbit. So Sam decided to think.

The important thing was that the passcode bar was gone, and Sam had full access. William's desktop was, like his study, pathologically neat. There were two folders: one marked THE CLOWDER and the other labeled BOOKS. Sam frowned. What the hell was a clowder? She clicked on that one first.

From the widow's walk Mindy could see the tiny winks of anniversary candles, flashlights, and phone screens in the dark, like little sparks

of souls released. They processed along the base of Gallows Hill and moved out toward Proctor's Ledge. What made Mindy shudder was the knowledge of how in Margaret's day, it would have been actual torches, flooding the Salem streets like a river as they paraded her toward her death: the good townsfolk rejoicing or at least enjoying the spectacle of the burning of Mindy's own blood, her great-ancestor. Margaret Scott, the witch.**

*** note to self: William, you dolt, don't forget to change name!*

That was the last document William had open.

"Oh God," said Sam. "Oh no."

William was writing Cyndi's book.

But maybe he wasn't. Maybe Sam was misinterpreting. She went into the subfolders: RESEARCH—more info than Sam had ever wanted to know about the Salem witch trials; DRAFTS—more pages, including from long-dead Margaret Scott's POV; and END MATTER.

What was end matter? Nonfiction had end matter: bibliographies, indices, author's notes. Fiction did not. Sam opened this.

There was page after page after yellow-lined page of a detailed outline titled "The Clowder." Penned in large neat female cursive. Scanned into William's computer.

Sam touched the fountain pen in her own braid. She remembered Cyndi commenting on it at the café, saying, *I write by hand, too, on legal pads. Rookie move, I know, but after all those years of law school, I guess I never broke the habit.*

Sam dragged over William's document and compared it side by side with the outline. Aside from his transposing the language from Cyndi's simple storyboard descriptions to William's filigreed vocabulary, it was identical. Plot twist per plot twist. Every point of character development tracked. All William was doing was fleshing out Cyndi's story in his own prose.

Sam left the outline and went to the folder in END MATTER labeled KITTEN. A survey from William's Darlings group, also filled out in

Cyndi's handwriting. That must have been how he'd found her. Correspondence between William and Cyndi, arranging to meet at the Blue Trees—"Oh yeah, I remember that," said Sam through clenched teeth. She read through it all: PLEASE, ALLOW ME TO WALK WITH YOU. BUT I DO HAVE ONE CONDITION: YOU MUST CALL ME WILLIAM. "She pursued him hotly, my ass," Sam muttered.

And finally, an obituary.

Cyndi Pietorowski, 42, of Salem, MA, died suddenly at the Hawthorne Hotel on October 30. Pietorowski, a Salem native and descendant of accused witch Margaret Scott, was an attorney at Gomez and Yountz and attended Suffolk Law School and Salem State University. Pietorowski's tenant says she had taken a hiatus from legal work to focus on creative pursuits. Pietorowski had no immediate family, but her 19 cats now reside at the Popoki Sanctuary in Hawai'i. Her death has been ruled a suicide.

The headshot of Cyndi, smiling sweetly in an incongruous power suit against a powder-blue corporate background, was a gut punch. It must have been her law firm photo. Sam kissed her fingers and touched it to the screen, then closed out of KITTEN, END MATTER, and THE CLOWDER.

She went to the main folder on the desktop, the one labeled BOOKS.

The Girl on the Mountain
You Never Said Goodbye
The Space Between Worlds
Medusa
All the Lambent Souls

Sam opened *Lambent Souls*, William's most recent bestseller, and went straight to END MATTER.

The original manuscript, which unlike Cyndi's was a Word document, had been written by a woman William called Faerie and whose name was Marta O'Leary, according to her title page, dated three years ago. There was a note from Marta to William attached: *Thank you so much for reading this! I can't believe you'd take the time to help somebody like me. I'm honored!*

"No," Sam moaned.

Marta O'Leary, 37, died suddenly on January 7 in her home, of an apparent overdose. O'Leary, an adjunct English instructor at Keystone Community College, had been taking medication for severe migraines and suffered from depression, according to a colleague. O'Leary leaves no family but is survived by cousins in County Cork, Ireland . . .

Medusa's original author was Eleni Panatagopulous, aka Goddess. She had died from carbon monoxide poisoning.

The Space Between Worlds had been written by a woman named Kaelynn Christianson, Stargazer, who had fallen off a roof. Presumably while stargazing . . . perhaps at Orion the mighty hunter?

"No no no," Sam said.

The author of *You Never Said Goodbye* was Becky Bowman— William's fiancée from grad school. His original Darling. She sure was. She had also been his Mouseketeer, and she had overdosed.

And finally, in END MATTER for *The Girl on the Mountain*, there was a folder simply marked PEN.

William's sister.

"Oh please God no," said Sam, even as she opened this. William's sister. His own sister!

Penelope Corwyn, 16, died Tuesday at Mount Washington Hospital following fatal exposure to the January 14 blizzard. According to her father, renowned neurosurgeon Archibald Corwyn, Penelope had left the house after a quarrel with her brother William and been caught in the storm. "By the time I found her, it was too late to resuscitate her," the senior Mr. Corwyn said. Penelope is survived by her father and her younger brother. Contributions may be made to the New Hampshire Humane Society.

On the last page of Pen's scanned manuscript of *The Girl on the Mountain*—written in loopy cursive on what looked like three-ring binder paper—was a note from William. Sam recognized his handwriting, tiny antlike all-caps script that was all but indecipherable unless you pressed your face right up next to the paper and squinted hard:

DEAR PEN.

I CAN'T BELIEVE YOU'RE GONE. I THOUGHT I'D SEE SIGNS OF YOU, THAT YOU MIGHT VISIT ME IN DREAMS, BUT YOU HAVE ABANDONED ME. WHY? ARE YOU STILL ANGRY WITH ME? IT'S SO CRUEL.

I WANTED TO TELL YOU THAT I'VE DECIDED TO PUBLISH YOUR BOOK. THE STORY WILL ALWAYS BE PURE YOU. BUT I'LL HAVE TO DRESS UP THE LANGUAGE. MY FINESSE WILL BE NECESSARY TO GET IT OVER THE PUBLISHING THRESHOLD.

I'M SURE IN TIME YOU'LL FORGIVE ME. PLEASE SEND ME A SIGN.

LOVE ALWAYS,

WILLIAM.

"She had a quarrel with her brother," Sam said. "Yeah, I bet. I'm so sorry, Pen."

She closed Pen's file and was about to click out of BOOKS when she noticed two more folders. Sam sucked in a sharp breath. One was labeled WENCH, and in it, typed in bolded red on Amelie's manuscript for *The Pirate Queen*, was the word DISCARD.

The final folder was labeled LOVE. On their original correspondence, which was the only writing Sam had shared with William, he'd written PENDING.

Sam closed all the folders. She was crying from rage and fear but only faintly aware of it. She opened William's email. Nothing happened, just the spinning wheel of death. Of course. The power was out. The computer was functioning on its own battery, and there was no Wi-Fi. Sam opened her phone to use it as a hot spot. It was at 11 percent. "Fuck," Sam said. But it worked. She keyed in her phone network name and password, and William's mailbox appeared on the screen, loading with agonizing slowness. His computer was also running on fumes, 9 percent battery. Sam addressed an email to Mireille and Patricia, cc'ing herself, and attached all the BOOKS folders. "Come on, come on," she said.

Her hands were shaking too hard to type, so she dictated a text to Drishti: COMING HOME SOONER THAN EXPECTED, LOL LOL LOL! The phone was unhappy about sending the message while it was also uploading William's bulky files, but finally Sam heard the little swish. "Thank God," she said. *All the Lambent Souls*, *Medusa*, and *The Space Between Worlds* had uploaded; now *You Never Said Goodbye* was at bat. A warning popped up on the laptop screen: *Your battery is at 5%! Charge now or your work will be lost!*

"Come on," Sam said. "You can do it." She could practically feel the others standing around her in the dark, a ghostly phalanx. Marta and Becky and Eleni and Kaelynn and Cyndi and Pen. A holy host of writers. The Darlings.

Your battery is at 2%! Place into charger immediately!

There was a sound from above like nothing Sam had ever heard before, a moan like the call of a mastodon, and then a CRASH! that shook the house. She looked up, terrified—it must have been a tree, coming through one of the glass walls?—then back at the screen. *The Girl on the Mountain* was uploading, with painful slowness.

"Simone?"

"No," Sam said. "Please God no."

William's footsteps pounded overhead. "Simone, where are you? Are you all right?"

He would go to their bedroom first, look for her there. Now was Sam's chance. She could slip up the basement steps to the couch in the den, say she'd been too scared to sleep upstairs alone.

But her phone. Without the hot spot, the Wi-Fi would not work. Without the Wi-Fi, the books and proof of William's murderous appropriation would not get out. And Sam didn't dare hope the hot spot would work from upstairs. She couldn't leave it to chance.

She heard William running back down. Descending.

"Simone," he called. The basement door opened. "I know you're down there. I know you're in my study, Simone."

"Please," Sam said to the uploading file. "Please please please."

Your power is at 1%!

Sam looked at her phone. It had died.

She turned to face the study door, terrified, trying to brace for whatever was coming at her. William had murdered all his darlings and taken their books. Now it was Sam's turn.

The Rabbit

I hear William coming down the stairs like FEE FI FO FUM and realize I've played this all wrong. I wanted to give Sam Vetiver a chance to look at the manuscripts and connect the dots and then text her: I'M HERE, I'M ON YOUR SIDE, PRETEND YOU DON'T KNOW AND AFTER THE STORM WE'LL GO TO THE POLICE. Because I didn't want her to scream and alert William. Because if I snuck up behind her without warning, she would. And because if she didn't see the evidence first with her own eyes, she wouldn't believe me. That was the mistake I made before. With all the other women. I provided no proof.

I did try to warn them. I tried so many times. As soon as I figured out what William had done to Becky, I went to the police. I took *You Never Said Goodbye* to my local precinct and slapped it down on a detective's desk and said, *Hey, this guy put the woo on my friend and stole her book and killed her and wrote it himself.* And they said, *Do you have evidence?* and I said, *Maybe? I'll try to get more, but meanwhile she told me the story and now here it is and she's dead, you should at least look into it,* and they said, *Okay, we'll check it out,* and anyone who's ever watched TV knew this was a kiss-off and sure enough, as I left, I heard one detective say, *That one's been bingeing too much CSI.*

I went back to the Harrington group on social and asked if anyone else had known about Becky's book, but of course nobody had, since they hadn't been friends with her until after she was dead. She was distant from her family and had no sibs, which I later figured out was a qualifier for William's women. And she'd been single until William put a ring on it. I had no idea where she might have written down any of her ideas, if she did. There was no proof. I'd hit a dead end, and now I knew why they called it that.

So I started following William and his darlings. I had to quit my job to do it and find another one closer to his house, and all my disposable income, such as it was, went to keeping on his tail. But I couldn't stand the thought he'd treat other women the way he'd treated me, except so, so much worse. Plus I had a debt to pay, to Becky. I'd had such a narrow escape. The only reason I was alive was that I'd said, in William's bedroom, that I was writing a thriller when he wanted a romance. Like Becky was writing. Otherwise I'd be dead too.

If the cops wouldn't listen to me, I figured, maybe William's targets would.

Nope. So much for the literary sisterhood. Not one of these chicks had heard of hos before bros. It was partly because William was culling the most isolated women from the herd so there'd be fewer family members or friends to get suspicious, and that meant they clung to him all the harder. I got it, of course. If I hadn't known better, if I hadn't known William Corwyn and he'd descended the mountain into my loneliness and said *You don't have to be alone anymore, my darling, I'm here!* I'd have done anything to stay in the dream too.

Plus nobody believes a woman who looks like me.

Get away from me, you crazy bitch, was what the Medusa woman said. And *Get your own man* and *Fuck off*, and *Stop bothering me, I called the cops*—that was the sad droopy one, Kaelynn, who then surprised me by flipping me the bird before she scurried away. The Irish woman had some fire, she tried to run me over with her car. Medusa also threw a drink on me and the pirate woman kickboxed me in the stomach. And I didn't even get a chance to warn this last one with all the cats because I was too distracted by Sam Vetiver.

Fail fail fail fail fail, and every time I failed another woman died, and if I had broken the promise to myself, which was I'LL NEVER LET HIM HURT ANOTHER WOMAN THE WAY HE HURT ME, I'd also made a vow after finding out about poor dead Becky that I'd never let William hurt anyone even worse, steal their stories and take their lives.

The ultimate appropriation.

And I've already broken that promise four f*cking times.

Not this time. Sam Vetiver is in the study and William's coming and he won't even have to use his gun, which is empty because like so much else about William it's just for show, but none of the women ever suspected that. Why would you? Somebody holds a gun on you, you don't say *Hey, sir, would you mind proving that's loaded?* They just did what he told them to, each woman wrote her suicide note before he fed her pills, like Marta and Becky, or locked her in a running car, like Eleni, or pushed her off a roof, like Kaelynn, or gave her pills *and* slit her wrists, like Cyndi. But it'll be much easier with Sam Vetiver because all he'll have to do is knock her out and haul her out into the snow, and her death will look natural. Like, maybe, Pen's.

I'm so scared. I'm shaking all over. My muscles have completely vapor-locked. I can't move. But if I don't stop him, he'll kill Sam just like he did the rest. I can't let that happen. I've worked all these years for this moment. I made a vow. So I count myself down: "Three . . . two . . ." and on *one!* I launch myself across the basement floor.

CHAPTER 38

INTO THE STORM

I n addition to fight or flight, Sam's therapist had once told her, there was a third option: freeze.

Which was what she seemed to be doing now. She was backed up against William's desk, hyperventilating, listening to William come down the basement steps saying "I've exercised heroic restraint, Simone, but since you obviously can't stop yourself from defying me, I'll have to do it for you," staring through the dark at the study door, waiting for it to swing further inward—

!!!!GO!!!!

Sam didn't know whether the voice was hers or all the dead writers, but she ripped her hands off the desk with such force she was surprised there was no Velcro sound. She dove for the door—not the one to the basement but the one to the bulkhead. The door to outside.

She yanked it open. She'd done a polar bear plunge one New Year's Day when she was with Hank. He sat on the lake shore in his parka, cheering, *You got this, Ms. Vetiver! Report back!* Sam was unable to report back. The shock of the cold had rendered her unable to breathe.

This was going to be like that. Except there was no Hank waiting with a towel and a thermos of coffee. This was going to hurt.

But whatever William had planned for her would hurt more. Sam had no doubt of that.

Even on the covered steps leading up to the yard, the cold was an assault. Sam cinched her sweatshirt hood tight and pulled the sleeves down over her hands. Thank God she'd slept in all her clothes, even if she had no hat or gloves. William's big boots were next to the door, and Sam thrust her feet into them, gasping. They were full of snow and eight sizes too large, like clown shoes. Sam flopped up the stairs as fast as she could.

The instant she reached the top, the wind scoured her face. It was like being sandblasted. The snow was not flakes at all but millions of grains of ice. Sam's exposed skin burned, then went numb. She instinctively screwed her eyes shut, then opened them and cried out in pain. The snow scraped her lids, her cheeks. The gale sounded like walking into the world's biggest blender, with gusts that punched her and made her stagger. She extended her arms and shuffled forward blindly, not sure where she was going. The physical onslaught made it hard to think.

But it was preferable to dying in the house. Sam was a baby about pain. She had to take Valium just for a tooth cleaning. William had so many weapons in there: knives, fireplace poker, awls, mallets, his axe. *That axe!* There was nothing more terrifying than a sharp blade, no negotiating with it. Freezing to death, in contrast, was supposed to be pleasant. Like going to sleep. The body just shut down—

Okay, Sam. Nobody's going to die here. Okay? Just find shelter. Hide. Sam turtled her chin and kept staggering forward, palms out, like Frankenstein. She couldn't go to her car, even if she had any idea where it was. It was the first place William would look for her, and he was probably much better prepared than Sam was for these conditions. Equipment. Ski goggles. For all she knew he had an infrared scope. Orion the mighty hunter. *All the better to track you with, my dear.* Sam could see or hear nothing behind her in the roar and scream of wind. But if he found her, she'd fight. She'd make it hard for him. And then she'd hope he'd make it quick.

But first she'd try to save herself. And that meant heading for cover.

The woods! Could she walk across the lake? Where even was the lake? Sam cracked her eyes a slit and saw nothing but white. She literally could be upside-down and she wouldn't know. There was no darker stripe where the forest might be. Still, she kept moving, not lifting her feet but shoving them along in William's boots as if she were on her cross-country skis. As William had taught her to do. If she got to the trees, she might have a chance. She might be able to see a little better. Could bundle some boughs. Crawl beneath them. Try to stay warm. Try to wait it out. Unless, of course, she wandered in the wrong direction, farther out onto the ice, and died of exposure. At least she'd probably freeze, not drown or be cut—

Her right foot slammed into something and she lurched forward. Yelped in surprise.

She slid her left foot. *Thud.* Something solid. She flailed her hands. Felt the object press against her knees, her thighs and belly. A structure— she'd walked into something waist-high. The tailgate of her Jeep? The hot tub?

Jesus, that meant she'd gone only a few feet from the house. The hot tub was next to the deck. Near the basement door. Sam had been walking in circles the whole time. What if William was right behind her, lifting the axe—

He'll probably chop you up in little pieces and make you into soup in his hot tub.

The hot tub!

Sam began to huff. Pulling the Arctic air into her warm, tender lungs. Which seared with ice, making her cough. It hurt. But the oxygen gave her the strength to do what she needed to do, which was sweep her arms like horizontal windshield wipers, pushing enough snow off the hot tub lid to expose the icy canvas. Then try to lift it. The lid was hinged so half of it could be opened at one time, and it was almost too heavy for Sam under normal circumstances. She hooked what she thought were her fingers beneath what she hoped was the lid and pulled up. Nothing happened. She tried again, grunting, straining, streaming tears of effort that hardened instantly on her cheeks. *Don't fucking cry. You'll freeze your eyelids shut.*

She felt the lid give. Lift a few inches. Sam pushed and pushed and got her shoulder under it and pushed more. The water was not superheated, of course. William set it to a hundred degrees before they got in and turned it off when they got out. But they had been in it last night, and the water would still be temperate, maybe even tepid, certainly warmer than what surrounded Sam now. If she could last only a little longer, maybe the snow would let up, maybe William would mistakenly chase her into the woods, maybe she could get back into the house, maybe she could take her car or his and batter through the drifts on the causeway somehow, maybe maybe maybe . . . Maybe was better than nothing. Maybe was a shot. Sam hoisted her legs over the side of the hot tub and plunged in.

The Rabbit

On my way across the basement I grab something from the worktable because like an idiot I left my trusty box cutter in the Rabbit Hole. It turns out to be one of those double-sided mallets that has rubber on it—I don't know what you use those for, but it'll do nicely for what I have in mind. William is standing in front of his desk, staring at his laptop, while wind and snow howl into the room like somebody blew a hole in a plane. Sam must have run out into the blizzard. His back is to me as I charge across the study and wham him in the head.

But my mother always said I move like an elephant, and apparently that must still be true, William must hear or sense me coming, because just as I swing the mallet he turns and it catches him not where I wanted to, on the base of his skull, but over his left eye. He staggers backward and rebounds against his desk. More bad luck: He doesn't have his glasses on, so I didn't even blind him, just raised a bloody lump.

"You," he says. "She said you were in the house. I should have listened."

And while I'm taking another swing he shoves his desk chair at me. It slams me in the stomach and I make a noise like a seal bark, *Rark!* as he uses it to bulldoze me across the room into the wall and pin me there.

He plucks the mallet from my hand like it's a dandelion. "I don't have time for this now," he says. "Simone must be apprehended. I'll deal with you later," and the last thing I see is the look of stern concentration on his face as he raises the hammer.

CHAPTER 39

THE HOT TUB

U sually when Sam was in the hot tub, she imagined herself as a dumpling in a vat of soup, bobbing gently, skin steaming. Now, as she crouched beneath the lid, weighted down by her and William's sodden clothes, she felt like a rock. The water was lukewarm, as she'd hoped, and she'd pulled the cover back over the tub to the best of her ability, preserving the temperature. Hopefully it would look aligned from the outside. Hopefully the snow would continue to fall and mask the area Sam had brushed off, as well as any tracks she'd left. Hopefully William was searching in her car or the forest or had wandered onto the lake. Or his faulty heart had finally given out from the strain.

Sam floated, suspended in the dark. Feeling was returning to her feet, hands, and face, and it was excruciating, a burning as if she were filled with bees. At least that meant they weren't badly frostbitten. Sam clenched her jaw and breathed through her nose, as quietly as possible. She had no idea how long she'd been in here. She tried to count the seconds, *one Mississippi two Mississippi*, and how long would be long enough? How much time had to pass before it was safe? What was the plan, since she couldn't be sure where William was? Should she try her luck in the woods or—

There was a grinding noise, and with a blast of cold and whirl of snow, the tub cover slid back.

"Well, look at you!" said William. "How clever you are, Simone."

He beamed down at Sam, framed in the white rectangle between lid and tub. His face, surrounded by a fur-lined hood, was red with cold, one of his eyes much smaller than the other beneath a raw bleeding lump. How had he injured it—had he run into a tree branch? No goggles for him after all.

"I'm glad I found you," he said, extending a gloved hand. "You led me a merry chase. Come get warm. I've got your robe ready for you by the fire, and a towel—"

Sam heard herself growl. She thought she might have bared her teeth at him.

"No?" said William. "Simone. Please. This is ludicrous. You'll die out here."

"I'd rather do that!" Sam shouted suddenly. She was shuddering, from cold, adrenaline, rage. "I know what you're going to do to me in there. You did it to them. Didn't you. The dead girls. The writers. You killed them all!"

William just looked down at her, his face sagging, a little jowly. Usually when Sam saw him from this angle, gazing at her from above, he was doing much more pleasant things.

"Why?" Sam said. She was crying. "Why did you? Why did you do it? I know why, so you could take their books. But why, William? Why? Why? Why?"

He laughed, his face split in his old sunshiny grin.

"Oh, Simone," he said. "You've got it all wrong. I *helped* them. Do you think any of those women could have made it on their own? Do you think even one of those novels would have seen a bookstore shelf, let alone the bestseller list? At best they might have self-published. None of them had the talent—not Becky, nor poor sad Kaelynn, nor Cyndi—"

"Don't you even *talk* about Cyndi!" Sam yelled. "Don't you even say her name!"

"—or the Irish one," said William, as if she hadn't spoken, "I forget her name now, or what's-her-face, Medusa. They didn't have the skill. All they had was story. I provided the rest. The words. The power. My reputation. My *name*. Who were they? A bunch of nobodies. Community college instructors. *Adjuncts*. Library aides. Literary primordial soup. I *elevated* them. I plucked them from their quotidian existences and gave them what every writer wants: eternal life, via print. Now come out of there, love. Let's do this gently."

"Fine," said Sam. "Okay. You win." Smiling, William reached down to help her out. Ignoring him, Sam used one hand to drag herself up, the other to heave William's boot, which she'd been gripping underwater, against the side of his face. Soaking wet, it weighed as much as a cinder block.

William fell back and vanished into the white. Sam was struggling to her feet, amazed this had worked, when he reappeared, his hood knocked askew and another bleeding purple welt on one cheek.

"That was unkind, Simone," he said.

He lunged for her, and Sam tried to scramble back under the lid, but in her waterlogged state she was too slow. His hands in their thermal gloves closed around her neck.

"Why, Simone?" he said. His thumbs found the base of her throat, the suprasternal notch, the little bowl he loved to kiss and lick. He began to press. To squeeze.

"You think I didn't know what you were doing in my study? Digging like the untrustworthy little bitch you are. Trying to steal my work. To ruin my good name."

Sam slapped at William's iron grip on her throat. She kicked and thrashed. Somewhere in the back of her mind she couldn't believe this was happening. She'd read that all people who were about to die felt this incredulity—*But I was driving to my sister's house! But I was going to have the good salad for lunch!* But this was William. Silent flowers bloomed before her eyes, white, then black.

One of William's hands slipped, maybe because Sam's neck was wet. Sam heaved up out of the tub, choking in a huge breath. She tried to crawl out and past him. But he grabbed her braid, pulled her back, pushed her down into the water, his hands resuming their deadly work.

"If I let you go," he said, "you'd probably die fairly quickly, but what if you didn't? What if? I can't let you send me back there, Simone. To the mountain. To the mist. To the place I was before I became William Corwyn. The writing, the books, that is how I escaped that terrible place. Pen helped me. By dying she gave me her book, and by her book she gave me life. You know the saying *Give a man a fish and you feed him for a day, teach him to fish, you feed him for a lifetime*? Pen taught me to fish. The other women, they're my catch. And I need them because I have the talent, the words; what I don't have are the What Ifs, the stories. I never did. I can't invent them on my own. Even when we were children, Pen had the ideas and I had the talent. A cruel division, don't you think? Jayne called me a vampire, but that was mean; I'm more a literary diabetic, unable to produce on my own what I need to survive. I've accepted it and found a workaround and given back, and I thought, I hoped and prayed, with you it might be different."

Sam twisted and bucked. William's face was an inch from hers, red and quivering with effort, a thin white line of drool dangling from one side of his mouth. His eyes were like black raisins, his expression neutral, as though he were reading the paper.

"I loved you so much that I stuck with you when you stopped writing our book. So much I gave you another chance after you tried to steal my life for your so-called thriller. So much I even ignored the fact you're a thief. So much I even invited you into my home," he growled. "If only I'd trusted my instincts. If only I hadn't let you back in. If only you could be trusted. I warned you, numerous times. You brought this upon yourself, Simone, my darling . . ."

His voice grew faint. The black flowers had eaten most of Sam's vision. Her hands fell, beating against the bottom of the tub, a final spasmodic jerking. Her right fingers touched something on the slick surface, a long cylindrical object.

"I love you, Simone," William was saying sorrowfully. "But now our story must end—"

With the last of her strength and consciousness, Sam made her fingers close on the object and swung it up and out as hard as she could. William's grip slackened, then dropped, and as Sam struggled to breathe, to force air into her swollen throat, she saw what was sticking in William's: her fountain pen, which must have fallen out of her braid, now lodged in the side of his neck.

CHAPTER 40

INTO THE WOODS

The pen looked so wrong jutting out of William's throat that Sam had a hard time believing it was real. She had more urgent matters to deal with, like trying to suck oxygen through an airway the size of a pinhole, but while she fought for breath, clawing at her own neck, she kept blinking in disbelief at the pen.

William, too, seemed to be having a hard time comprehending recent events. He raised his hand to his throat, which was jetting blood in time with his pulse, and touched the pen. More blood sheeted down his parka, drip-drip-dripped silently into the snow. William glanced at his red hand, and then back at Sam in bewilderment, and somehow this broke Sam's paralysis. She pushed past him, up and out of the tub, and ran.

Or the closest thing to it a person could do in thigh-high snow. Breaking trail was hard work. It was nearly impossible when you could barely breathe, when air sawed in and out of your throat like a serrated knife, when you were dizzy and felt vomity and your head throbbed and your vision was still consumed by black dots that expanded and contracted with your heartbeat, when you had only frozen socks on—at some point, Sam must have kicked off William's other sodden boot. Still she floundered on, her eyes on the woods. She could see it now, so the snow must be getting lighter. She didn't know what she would do when she reached it. All she knew was that she must get there. She must reach the trees.

"Simone."

William sounded different now too. His voice was garbled, had a terrible wheeze like an organ pipe with a hole in it.

"Come back here, Simone."

Sam did not turn. She threw herself forward. Her clothes, soaked in the tub, were already starting to stiffen and seemed to weigh a hundred pounds. Just get to the trees. There would be something there. A branch. A rock. Something—

"You stabbed me, love. You tried to kill me with your fucking pen, you little bitch."

William's terrible new voice sounded closer now. Sam didn't want to look back. It would scare her more. Slow her down. And it didn't matter how close he was. He'd move as quickly as he'd move, and the only thing Sam could do was move herself. She looked. Whipped her head around— her throat screamed—to cast a terrified glance over her shoulder. William was lunging after her, threshing through the snow, two feet behind her. Now a foot. Closing in on her. Was the pen still in his neck? Yes. Was the blood still spouting? No. But pumping down his neck in a river. Sam pressed on.

"I told you we could do this gently," William said. "Now look. Look where we are."

Sam was yanked backward off her feet by the hood of her sweatshirt— *Zoop!* The collar dug into her swollen throat and she tried to scream. She produced only a little whistle. William threw her down in the snow and Sam tried to backpedal, her icy socks scrabbling for purchase that they didn't find. William bent, staggered, fell to one knee, and seized her ankle, pinning Sam in place. His hood had come off and he was bareheaded, the wind sieving through his hair. The mortal mineral stench of blood, wet iron, was overwhelming. "I was clear with you," he was growling, "I was very explicit about what would happen." He dragged Sam toward him with a businesslike I-told-you-so look as she thrashed and silently howled and his blood pattered onto her legs.

Suddenly there was movement behind him, a large shadow running up in the snow, and William turned. The shadow hit him on the head, and William crumpled and fell, mercifully face down. Blood pumped from a new wound on his temple. One of Sam's feet was trapped beneath him, and she wrenched it away with a horrified grunt that lanced her hurt throat, then scrabbled backward, using her hands and heels to propel herself away from William's prone body, sobbing soundlessly and without tears.

The shadow came toward her. "Hey," it said. "It's okay now."

Sam stared up, uncomprehending and terrified. The shadow materialized into a woman who crouched over Sam, hands on knees, her own hair whipping around her face. She was in a ski jacket and pajama bottoms and she, too, was injured, a gash on her forehead, drying blood forming a crust down her cheek. She was breathing hard.

"He won't hurt you anymore," she said.

Sam looked at William, the full length of him in the snow. Blood spread around his head in a dark, uneven halo, steaming. *Is he dead?* she asked, or tried to. Her throat hurt too much, and no sound came out. She put a hand on it.

But the woman seemed to know what Sam was asking. "I think so," she said.

They both crept a little closer. The woman got on her knees next to William. Oh God don't do that be careful—was all Sam had time to think before William's hand shot out. It grabbed the woman's arm. She and Sam both stared at it as William reared up, blood-soaked, eyes bulging with purpose—and Sam grabbed the thing the woman had clocked him with and hit him again, herself. On the top of the skull, where the bone was thinnest. There was a horrid sound like one pool ball hitting another, and he collapsed again, a fresh indentation in his skull that Sam did not want to look at.

Oh my love, she thought.

The woman crawled over to Sam, and they waited. *One Mississippi two Mississippi . . .* Snow filtered silently through the trees at their backs—Sam had almost made it—and onto the lake. This time William remained quiet. He had fallen backward with one knee bent beneath him and the pen still in his neck. Snow landed in his unfocused eyes, one big and one small, and melted there, drew clean tracks in the blood, ran into his ears like tears.

The woman nudged him with her foot. His body rocked. He didn't move.

"I think he's actually dead this time," the woman said.

Sam looked at the object she had dropped in the snow. The award from William's desk, the Mt. Washington Post Fiction Award that had probably belonged rightfully to Pen. William's hand was stretched toward Sam, his long, beautiful fingers that had typed millions of words, held dozens of microphones, cupped her breasts, been inside her, braided her hair. Slid a ring on her own hand. Throttled her neck. Killed the others, in ways Sam would never know.

Sam reached forward and tugged William's hood down over his face. She couldn't bring herself to close his eyelids, which would still be warm, because she knew it would be the last time she would ever touch him. She couldn't think about that. She tried to clear her throat, which hurt like a motherfucker. She turned her head and spat blood in the snow.

"Thank you," she whispered hoarsely to the woman.

"You're welcome," the woman said. She smiled shyly. Even with her overbite, or maybe because of it, her grin was beautiful.

"It's you," Sam rasped. "You're the one who's been following us."

The Rabbit nodded. "Yup," she said. "I'm Emily. I've been trying to keep you safe, all along."

EPILOGUE

Come, children, let us shut up the box and puppets, for our play is
played out.

—William Thackeray, *Vanity Fair*

"Oh, Jake," said Brett, "we could have had such a damned good
time together."

... "Yes," I said. "Isn't it pretty to think so?"

—Ernest Hemingway, *The Sun Also Rises*

The one thing Sam remembered from being in a TV studio as a child
that had not changed in the intervening years was how hot the lights
were. It was like being a speaker times ten, and she had chosen her outfit
accordingly: a sleeveless silk halter dress whose collar the techs could
clip her mic on. It was, of course, red, though this time for a different
reason.

What Sam was not used to and had not encountered in the past
couple of decades since being in her dad's studio, when instead she'd
been on local cable channels or university TV, or, on one occasion,
C-SPAN, was the live audience. Luckily the lights onstage were still
bright enough that it was difficult for Sam to make out any faces, so

she couldn't spot her codependency group. She refused, absolutely refused, to look directly at Drishti. Sam was also not accustomed to being one of two subjects in an interview, as she was now with Emily, who sat in the chair on her right, nor being face-to-face with one of the most famous and beloved faces in America, if not the world, who had chosen Sam's novel as her Book Club Pick and who was, like most TV people, surprisingly smaller in person but with larger facial features, as if she were a Broadway actor with a visage designed to be seen from the back row, or some beautiful demigod.

"Are you ready?" she asked, and Sam said she was. Emily nodded. She wore Doc Martens and an electric purple dress, her hair freshly dyed the same shade. Her new nose stud, a gold rabbit, glinted near one nostril. Aside from her stage makeup, applied in the greenroom, she looked like exactly what she was: a bookseller. She also looked a little petrified. Sam winked at her.

The host patted Sam's knee.

"I cannot *wait* to talk about this book," she said.

A tech held up a sign that said QUIET and the cameraman counted them down. Sam stared at the little red dot on the camera facing her and tried to smile in a natural, nonfrozen way, which was impossible.

The cameraman pointed at the host.

"Helloooooo, book lovers!" the host said. "*Y'all.* Who is as excited as I am for today?" The audience clapped and cheered. "How many of you have been *literally* counting the hours until we could talk about this book?" The host raised her hand and pointed dramatically to herself. "I have been awake since I read it," she said, turning to Sam. "I haven't had a good night's sleep for *weeks*! I'll be sending you my bill for my undereye-bag cream."

"I will happily pay it," said Sam.

"*Thank* you," the host said, and turned back to the camera. "But seriously, though this book is sensational, and I mean that in every sense of the word, it is also deadly serious. Not only does it expose some of the most shocking murders of our time, it focuses on an underlying issue most of us don't talk about, that affects so many of us and our mental health. So let's talk about—"

She held up one of the copies of Sam's book stacked on the end table between them.

"MURDER YOUR DARLINGS," she said. She showcased the hardcover, which featured a fountain pen whose nib was bisected by a jackrabbit, by moving it from side to side, then put it back. "The megahit bestseller of the season, the breakout book of the year, number one on the *New York Times* list since the day it dropped, and rightly so."

She golf-clapped toward Sam, who bowed her head back at the host—it was her recommendation, of course, that had put the book on the list.

"Today," said the host, "we're talking with the author, Sam Vetiver—*and* the woman who saved her life, Emily Brown—"

Somebody in the audience yelled "THE RABBIT, YAAASSSS! WE LOVE YOU!" and there was laughter. Emily smiled down at her boots.

"We *do* love you," said the host, leaning forward to look past Sam to Emily. "The outpouring on social media ever since we announced has been *astronomical*. I hope you feel it."

"I do," Emily said. She nodded vigorously. Her ears were blazing red.

The host picked up the novel again. "And this book! Whoo! People! You practically need oven mitts to hold this, am I right? It has *everything*. Sex. Murder. *Lit*erature. And heartbreak. Because even though it's written as a novel . . . it's a true story."

The studio grew very quiet.

"We *all* knew the major players in this book," said the host. "We read Sam's earlier wonderful novels. And we all knew William Corwyn."

The light beam from the control box at the back of the studio shifted colors, and Sam knew that behind her, on the big screen, there was now the giant projection of William's author photo, his face. She would not look.

"It was *such* a shock to find out about William," said the host. "That we had a serial murderer not only in the very *heart* of the literary community but, for so many of us, next to our beds. And in our cars and on our walks and at the gym, on our earbuds. And in our minds and souls. Because that's what authors and books do, isn't it? They get inside us and they *change* us. So to find out that William's books, which affected so many thousands of lives, were not his but belonged to women he had murdered—"

Somebody shouted something from the audience Sam could not hear. Her heart was thundering in her ears. Sweat rolled down her sides into her Spanx. She exhaled a long silent breath.

"It was *mind-blowing* for all of us who loved his work. Just unbelievable. I remember reading the news story and saying to myself, That can *not* be right. So I can only imagine what it was like for you, Sam."

There was a pause, and Sam realized she was supposed to speak—they had *dead air*! Since William, performance was harder than it used to be. She glanced at the host, who gave her a you-can-do-it nod.

"It was shattering," Sam said.

"*Tell* us," said the host, "what it was like from the inside."

"I was in love," said Sam. She cleared her throat—it had not been quite right ever since the hot tub, her vocal cords roughened with scar tissue. "I was in love with William. How could you not be in love with William? He was the bad boy of literature. And bad boys make good stories." There were appreciative chuckles from the audience, and Sam started to find her rhythm. "But really, it's tough out there for us singletons. Those of you out there who are divorced, or have God forbid lost your person, you know what it's like to be alone, like really alone, or on the apps, scrolling through all the guys with little heads and big fish. All you can think is, is *any*one out there like me?" She felt rather than saw the nodding beyond the lights.

"And William was like you," said the host.

"He was like me," Sam confirmed. "Except for the serial killer part."

The audience murmured. "What's so *astonishing* to me," said the host, "and so frightening, is that you really did not know. That nobody knew—except Emily, and we'll dig into that a little later. But nobody else had a clue, not William's editor, or his agent, or anybody in the industry—including me! I had him on this very show! For his novel, or rather Becky Bowman's novel, *You Never Said Goodbye*. He sat on this very stage where you are right now, Sam! How could *nobody* know?"

Sam shuddered, an involuntary ripple of flesh. "Well, the devil is charming," she said, and there were sounds of recognition from the viewers at this. "And William was *so* charming. He was master level at it. And seduction. And manipulation. And transposing other writers' ideas into his own words."

"*Why?*" said the host. "Why do you think he did it? That's what we all want to know."

"I'm not sure we ever really will," said Sam. "I've spent hundreds of hours thinking about it, not just researching the book but lying awake at night, going over it in my head. From everything I've read, William was a malignant narcissist. He didn't see other people as people but as commodities he needed. He said something like that about the women while he was—toward the end. That they were food. For his books. That he was like a vampire who could write but not come up with his own stories."

"And this is the hallmark of a malignant narcissist."

"One of them. I've interviewed several psychologists who specialize in this disorder and in sociopathy, trying to sync up what they said with what I knew of William personally. It's safe to say he was a sociopath. And one doctor had a theory, which I think is true, that William didn't remember murdering the women. He just skipped right over it in his own mind. William came from a terrible trauma background—he mentioned it only a few times to me, and his family is all gone now, so I couldn't confirm it. But what he did tell me was horrific, and this doctor's theory is that when something was truly traumatic, including when he caused it, William blanked it out."

"Fascinating," said the host. "Truly fascinating. And terrifying. And you never knew. Never knew you were living with a serial murderer."

"No," said Sam. "I knew—or sometimes I thought—things were a little hinky. You could ask my sponsor, who's sitting out there somewhere with my codependency group, hi guys!, and she'd tell you that from the beginning I was questioning my own instincts. But that's part of the problem. As I wrote in the book, I have my own trauma background, so I have a hard time knowing what to believe."

"And that is really the *heart* of the book for me," said the host. "Not the shock of finding out who William Corwyn really was. Or the murders of the writers, may they rest—and by the way, we're offering all their novels reissued in their rightful names as a bundle," and there was applause. The host turned back to Sam. "For me the heart of the book is really the codependency. Talk about that."

"Sure. Technically, it means anyone who's ever concentrated on another person's life instead of their own—"

"—which is every woman here, am I right?" said the host. She made boxer's fists in the air. "I *so* related to this. Putting aside your own perceptions, beliefs, needs, even your identity for another person."

"Yes," said Sam. "I thought I was done with it. I'd done so much work, in therapy and group. I'd left a marriage—to a great guy in recovery, hey, Hank!—to put my own needs first. And then I walked into the biggest wolf den of all."

Her throat ached, and she looked at her hands, ringless now, in her lap.

"I remember thinking," she said, "right before I met William, that I was so lonely I'd give up everything else in my life if only I could meet the right person. My career, my books, everything I'd built, I'd trade it away just like that. And I did. I left it for this shining dream he created, that he dangled in front of me like bait, that maybe we both believed in but that never really existed at all. I abandoned everything to be with him— including my very self. And I'm—" Her voice wavered. She touched her scratchy throat. "Still working to forgive myself for that."

There was applause, and Sam tried to knuckle tears from the corners of her eyes without smearing her makeup. The host handed her a Kleenex.

"Are you cured?" she asked. "Of codependency?"

Sam applied the tissue, using the movement to buy time. There was

something she had told nobody about, not Drishti, not her new therapist, not any of the doctors she'd spoken with about William, not even
Emily. And she never would. It was this: When William had been stran-
gling her in the hot tub, when his hands were around her neck, pulver-
izing her windpipe, crushing her throat, what Sam had seen flash before
her eyes was not her own life but the life they could have had. The one
they'd never have. Of dinners, of walks, of strapping themselves into airplane seats side by side to go to Hawai'i or France or Greece, of reading each other new books, of watching leaves bud and burst and bloom
and wither, of watching each other's hair whiten and thin and their skin
wrinkle and droop, of smelling increasingly like mothballs and menthol,
of growing stooped and achy and sitting together on the red Adirondack
chairs on his lawn and holding hands when they were too old to do more
in bed together but sleep. Talking. Laughing. Ever touching. Keeping
company. And finally floating off into the nighttime sky like lovers, holding each other among the cold stars. What Sam had never told anyone
and never would was what she had seen right at the end, what heaven
would be for her: She was walking along the lake surrounding William's
house, beneath the pine trees, and it was early fall and the sky was blue,
the sun hot, the clouds reflecting in the water. And there was a *crunch
crunch crunching* that turned out to be William, walking over the pine
needles and through the trees to her. As he came into sight, he ducked
under one of the boughs—he had to hold it out of the way because he was
so tall—and he smiled, that sunshine grin that contained his whole heart
in it. *It's you*, he said. And Sam said, *It's you*.

Sam shook her head now. "No," she said. "You're never cured of codependency. Like any other addiction. You just learn how to manage it.
Hopefully, now I'll value and trust myself more. I won't make the same
mistakes in the next relationship."

"Hell yeah!" yelled someone in the audience, and Sam and everyone
else laughed.

"That's my sponsor," said Sam, and the host said, "I hear that. Take
a bow, sponsor," and Drishti jumped up and twerked and everybody

clapped, including Sam, and Drishti gave Sam the I'm-watching-you fork fingers, which Sam returned, then sat back down.

"*Will* you date again?" asked the host, and Sam said, "Hell yeah!" and the viewers laughed. She smiled. "I'm almost ready, I think. So, ladies, send me your sons and uncles and dads and brothers. Nonsociopaths only, please."

A woman wearing a rabbit-ear headband was waving her arms in the audience. The host nodded, and a staffer ran to her with a mic.

"I have a question for Emily," she said, and there were cheers and wolf whistles, signs bobbing in the semidarkness beyond the stage featuring rabbits, WE ♥ U EMILY!, EMILY IS MY SHERO. "Emily, how did you find the courage to do what you did?"

Emily was so red it was visible even beneath the thick pancake makeup. "Thank you," she said, "but it wasn't courage. I just did the right thing."

"You just did the right thing," the host repeated, deadpan. "You just rearranged your life to track a murderer when nobody would believe you, and incurred injuries and financial hardship, and gave up your job, and moved *into his house*, and risked your life to protect another woman you had never met, all because it was *the right thing*."

"Well, yeah," said Emily, grinning, and the audience gave her a standing ovation.

"I've heard you don't think of yourself as a hero," said the host when they settled down.

"I don't," said Emily. "I'm just somebody who knows what it's like to be used. To have some man use her and throw her away. William did that to me, and I thought it was bad, but I didn't know I was one of the lucky ones whose book he didn't want. And once I figured it out, I knew I had to try to save the others."

This time the applause and cheering and stomping went on so long that the host had to pat the air several times. "We could never make as much noise as you deserve, Emily," she said. "You deserve it all."

Emily shrugged, and Sam took her hand. "Yes," she said, "you do."

The host smiled. "And obviously you two are friends now," she said. "I mean, beyond the book. Beyond the time you spent together so Sam could give Emily voice."

"Yes," Sam said, and "Yup," Emily said.

"But Emily, you're a writer as well," said the host, "you went to graduate school with William. You didn't want to write your own part of this book?"

Emily shook her head, her face reddening again. "I'm done."

"You're not going to write anything, ever?"

"Nope," Emily said. "Being a writer's way too dangerous," and everybody laughed.

"Besides," she said, "I'm perfectly happy working in my store."

She grinned shyly at Sam, who smiled back.

"And thank God," said Sam. She squeezed Emily's hand. "We writers, all of us, need booksellers. And readers! What would we do without you? You save our lives."

ACKNOWLEDGMENTS

For all the tea I've spilled about the writing life in this novel, the one thing I haven't addressed is the ACKS & DEDS, i.e., the acknowledgments and dedication. My favorite part, thanking the people who've helped me make this book what it is.

First, my wondrous team at HarperCollins, who've alchemized my manuscript into a book for the third time in a row. Thank you: Edie Astley, for being so prompt and patient. Miranda Ottewell, for being impeccably and ridiculously smart as always. Joe Jasko and Nikki Baldauf, for astonishing attention to detail and catching my numerous errors. Becca Putman, for facilitating the magic moment when I saw my book for the first time. Design team, I worship you, especially Robin Bilardello and Joanne O'Neill for this book's cover, clever beyond my most hopeful dreams. Anna Audia, thank you for getting me on to my favorite place, the road. Heather Drucker, you are *the* world-standard publicist— it's a privilege and delight to work with you.

Sara Nelson, you are my home and North Star, menthol-cool, brilliantly incisive, fiercely loyal. I give thanks every day that you're my genius editor.

Thank you to the crew at Massie McQuilkin & Altman, best literary agency ever.

To Elisabeth Rohm and Kara Feifer of Rohm Feifer Entertainment for taking a chance on this novel when it was still in utero, and to Robin Kall Homonoff, head of books at Rohm Feifer, for matchmaking—and for being the Olympic book champion you are via *Reading with Robin*.

ACKNOWLEDGMENTS

To all the event hosts, influencers, bookstore owners, librarians, and teachers who've invited me to speak: I'd be sitting sadly at home in my Spanx without you, and my books might all be remaindered. Thank you, thank you. I love visiting you.

I especially want to shout-out Susan McBeth of Adventures by the Book; Pamela Klinger-Horn of Literature Lovers' Night Out; Mary Webber O'Malley of *Thoughts from a Page Podcast*, Andrea Peskind-Katz of Great Thoughts, Great Readers: if you are AT ALL interested in books, you should follow this literary goddess quartet.

To my A Mighty Blaze fam, who've introduced authors and new books to readers every week since March 2020: Caroline Leavitt, Mark Cecil, Hank Phillippi Ryan, Ellen Comisar, Margaret Pinard, Karen Bellovich, Hannah Crowley, Kendall Bousquet, Abby Teich, Blazers past and present. Thank you for keeping our flame bright, you luminaries.

If dear friends are stars who you don't see every day but know are there, here's my writer constellation: Chris Castellani—with thanks for introducing me at every launch!; literary Renaissance man Alex George; Jane Green, the fount from whom all good things flow; the General, Pam Jenoff; my dearest soul sister Sarah McCoy; my loveliest creature-by-the-sea Alyson Richman; my Puppet, Julie Hirsch.

So much gratitude to my early readers, who snort-laughed with me and provided encouragement: Kimberly Hensle Lowrance, Kenna Jones-Shanks, Jane Roper (thank you for the Wi-Fi catch!), Tracy Hahn Burkett, Stephanie "Goodie" Devlin, Sharon Wetzel, and Jenn Bowman Ryznar. Special thanks to Josie Almond for the encyclopedia of comments; Whitney Scharer for texting me "It's SO GOOD"; Julie Gerstenblatt for taking the book to the beach; and Mark Cecil for post-midnight real-time reactions.

To the *Sun's Out, Buns Out!* Club, especially its magnificent host, Chuck Garabedian. Trisha Blanchet, Tom Champoux, Edwin Hill, Cat Mazur, Jane Roper—and Hillary Casavant, who came up with the "murder your darlings" explanation idea while we were paddleboarding...to William Island.

ACKNOWLEDGMENTS

Thank to everyone in the Writers' Room, who kept me Zoom company every day and lured me back to the desk when I otherwise might've gone shopping: thriller buddy Chuck Garabedian, Cathy Elcik, Erica Ferencik, Meiera Holz Stern, Hillary Casavant, Kerry Savage.

My pirate crew novel workshop for OVER TWENTY YEARS, stars of Chapter 14 and of my life: Trisha Blanchet, Hillary Casavant, Mark Cecil, Tom Champoux, Jenn DeLeon, Julie Gerstenblatt, Edwin Hill, Sonya Larson, Kimberly Hensle Lowrance, Jenna Paone, Whitney Scharer, Alex Hoopes Sunshine. Life is so much better with all you weirdos.

A handful of people stood by me every day while I wrote this book, in the most important ways. Erin Almond, thank you for the Cathedral, paddleboard, hot tub, and tarot time. Kirsten Liston, Answer Girl, you are better than ChatGPT. Cat Mazur, thank you for dousing and bringing joy everywhere you go. Janna Giacoppo, I rely on our love note podcasts. Tom Champoux, thank you for the hikes and talks.

My dearest Breau, Mark Cecil, you were there at the beginning, listening to me make insane noises on the phone when this novel started falling into place, through the doubt and jubilation, to this moment and beyond. Ever an honor to be on the crusade with you.

Kristy Graves, you let me live in your home to write parts of this book and, even more heroically, READ IT ALOUD all the way from Boston to Florida. I love you more than I can say, girl.

I am blessed with the best everyday pal, my black Lab, Henry Higgins, who makes himself into a little grunting ball on his bed behind my desk while I write, with great patience although he thinks the whole endeavor unbearably boring.

My family, Lesley M. M. Blume, Greg Macek, and Oona Helene Macek; Joey, Kristin, and Robbie Blum. My most wicked and beloved darlings.

My agent, Stéphanie Abou, to whom this book is also dedicated: Nothing in my writing life happens without you. Twenty-three years! You're the best. No, YOU.

To the Rabbits of the world: I see you. And appreciate you.

The readers, the readers, the readers. William says this, and Sam says it, and it cannot be said enough: You are why I write. If anything I've said here, scary or funny or painful or beautiful, stays with you, it's all I can hope for, and my job here is done. Except to say again: Thank you.

JENNA BLUM IS the *New York Times* and #1 internationally bestselling author of the novels *Those Who Save Us, The Stormchasers,* and *The Lost Family*. Readers voted her one of the Top 30 Women Writers on Oprah. com, and she is the cofounder/CEO of the online author interview platform company A Mighty Blaze. Jenna earned her MA in creative writing from Boston University and has taught writing workshops at Grub Street Writers and other institutions for more than twenty years. She interviewed Holocaust survivors for Steven Spielberg's Survivors of the Shoah Visual History Foundation and is a professional public speaker, traveling nationally and internationally. Jenna is based in downtown Boston, where she's the dog mom to her black Lab, Henry Higgins.